CW01239438

Lord of Ruin

BY K. M. ENRIGHT

The Age of Blood

Mistress of Lies
Lord of Ruin

LORD OF RUIN

K. M. Enright

orbit

orbit-books.co.uk

ORBIT

First published in Great Britain in 2025 by Orbit

1 3 5 7 9 10 8 6 4 2

Copyright © 2025 by K. M. Enright

The moral right of the author has been asserted.

All characters and events in this publication, other than those clearly in the public domain, are fictitious and any resemblance to real persons, living or dead, is purely coincidental.

All rights reserved.
No part of this publication may be reproduced, stored in a retrieval system, or transmitted, in any form or by any means, without the prior permission in writing of the publisher, nor be otherwise circulated in any form of binding or cover other than that in which it is published and without a similar condition including this condition being imposed on the subsequent purchaser.

A CIP catalogue record for this book
is available from the British Library.

HB ISBN 978-0-356-52482-5
C format 978-0-356-52481-8

Typeset in Caslon by M Rules
Printed and bound in Great Britain by
Clays Ltd, Elcograf, S.p.A.

Papers used by Orbit are from well-managed forests
and other responsible sources.

MIX
Paper | Supporting
responsible forestry
FSC® C104740

Orbit
An imprint of
Little, Brown Book Group
Carmelite House
50 Victoria Embankment
London EC4Y 0DZ

The authorised representative
in the EEA is
Hachette Ireland
8 Castlecourt Centre
Dublin 15, D15 XTP3, Ireland
(email: info@hbgi.ie)

An Hachette UK Company
www.hachette.co.uk

orbit-books.co.uk

Content Warnings

Gore, body horror, disembowelment, violence, murder, blood magic, animal death (rat), anthropophagy, bloodletting for purposes of magic, discussions of classism and racism.

Explicit sexual content including oral sex, vaginal sex, anal sex, erotic asphyxiation, blood drinking during sex, impact play, knife play, pain play, teratophilia, kink (both negotiated and spontaneous).

There is no transphobia, misgendering, or deadnaming.

To Jo—I literally could not have done this without you

Previously, in Mistress of Lies

In the land of Aeravin, a class of blood mages known as Blood Workers rule the nation. They are led by the enigmatic Eternal King, who has lived for over a millennium, fueled by yearly blood sacrifices to extend his life. Under his guidance, the Blood Workers keep the magicless Unblooded in place as they exploit those beneath them, building lives of decadence and debauchery.

On the eve of spring, Shan LeClaire assassinates her father and takes his place as head of her family. Shan has spent her life building her own base of power, using blood magic and her skills as a budding spymaster. Now she plans to bring her Aeravin to its knees. After witnessing the Eternal King's annual sacrifice, Unblooded Samuel Hutchinson stumbles upon a body that's been murdered by illegal magic and becomes caught up in the investigation. Until now, Samuel has spent his life avoiding the Blood Workers, to hide his own secret magic—whenever he gives a command, the listener must obey.

When Shan's spy brings her the knowledge of Samuel and his gift, she recognizes it from an old rumor and suspects he may be a secret descendant of the King's bloodline. Seduced by Shan's promises of change and hope, Samuel agrees to meet with the King, who confirms their relation and agrees to keep Samuel's magic a secret. But the murders keep happening and all evidence points to a member of the King's Court. Unable to trust even his most loyal of retainers, the

King turns to Shan and Samuel for aid using their unique skills. If they succeed in stopping the murderer, the King promises to reward them handsomely—including helping Samuel master the gift he still fears.

They begin their investigation, and Samuel adjusts to his new life among the Blood Worker ruled high society, even forming a friendship with Shan's magicless brother and something more with the King's second-in-command, Isaac de la Cruz. Shan also reconnects with Isaac, her first love, before he abandoned her to take his place at the King's side. But old wounds are slowly mended, and the three of them start to fall for each other, a delicate courtship budding around the fear and mistrust that Samuel carries around his terrible gift.

As more bodies appear, the clues start to point to Shan's brother, but Shan refuses to believe it and sets out to prove his innocence. Her efforts distract them from the trail of the real culprit until the fear of the murderer moves the Unblooded to mass protest, destabilizing the fragile peace of the nation. The King reveals the secret underpinning the murders—the tie that Shan and Samuel wouldn't have figured out on their own. All the murdered were part of a secret slaving ring, delivering unwanted persons to the King's private Blood Factory, where they were drained of their blood till they died, fueling the ever hungry magical coffers of the Aeravin. And worst of all, Isaac, as the Royal Blood Worker, is the man behind it and likely the next victim.

If the life of the one they have both grown to care about isn't enough, the King gives them an ultimatum: find the murderer within a week, or he will execute Shan's brother and turn Samuel's gift into his personal weapon. Faced with disaster all around her, Shan reveals to Samuel that her ultimate goal is to dethrone the ruthless King and replace him with someone far more human. Someone like Samuel. Though shocked and disturbed by her admissions, Samuel agrees to help her take down the King, but first they must find the killer and save Shan's brother—as long as he's not the murderer.

With no other choice, Shan investigates her brother, soon discovering the secret he has been keeping from her—he is not the murderer, but he is one of the founders of the Unblooded rebellion, and it is his actions that have led to the unrest across the capital. With no other leads, Shan and Samuel turn to protecting Isaac, as an upcoming public event will leave him vulnerable. But the event goes wrong as Isaac reveals the truth of the Blood Factory to a surprised nation, having killed one of the King's own Councillors as a practical demonstration. The truth comes out—the killer was Isaac, working on his own revolution to assuage the guilt of what he had done as the King's right hand.

A riot breaks out, and the King swoops in to declare martial law, establishing a curfew for Unblooded along with a sweeping list of cruel new laws. After Shan and Samuel lament their losses, Isaac kidnaps Samuel and tries to recruit him to his cause, but Samuel refuses. To prove his methods necessary, Isaac uses his newly empowered Blood Working to strip Samuel of the gift he hates, revealing that Samuel has had the ability to use Blood Working all along, it had just been stifled by his gift. Shan finds them and attempts to rescue Samuel. Isaac releases a trap, but after she saves Samuel, Shan puts herself at great risk to pursue Isaac. Using his newly discovered Blood Working, Samuel pursues them, capturing Isaac.

Afterward, Samuel recovers from the toll of using untrained magic, and Shan delivers the news to the King. He rescinds the order of execution on Shan's brother and for what they've done publicly raises Samuel to the Council of Lords and elevates Shan to take Isaac's former spot at his side. Weeks later, Isaac is visited in his cell by Samuel, who uses his position to secure a private conversation. Samuel asks if Isaac still wants to bring down the King and promises him that he will be freed soon enough.

But as Samuel leaves him, Isaac reflects on the way his Blood Working experiments have left him changed, thirsty for something he dare not name.

Chapter One

Shan

The grandfather clock chimed one, startling Shan out of her light doze. It was much later than she intended to work; she had planned to only stay an hour after dinner to finish up the latest inventory, but lost herself as she dug into the ledgers that were her main responsibility. The ever-dwindling supply of blood for the Kingdom of Aeravin, diminishing a bit more each day as they ran through what remained of the supply.

She cursed Isaac de la Cruz under her breath; the Blood Factory he revealed was abhorrent, the slow draining and death of the capital's undesirables to fill the Blood Workers' endless hunger for blood, but so was every other option. He had achieved his goal, he had seen the program ended under the threat of civil unrest, but here she was, left to pick up the pieces of his mess.

It was her greatest duty as Royal Blood Worker, and still, months after her appointment, she found no reasonable solution.

She gently closed her notebook, setting it aside with the ledger for the next day's efforts. It looked so small on the grand desk, a mahogany monstrosity etched with hand-carved details of roses and thorns. It matched the rest of the furniture she had inherited with the office—large, oversized pieces that made her feel small, from the chair that dwarfed her to the shelves that covered the walls to the wide bay window that overlooked the capital and the grand sea beyond.

Some nights, she wished she could fly out that window and never look back, but every time she so much as dared to dream, she remembered the shackles that held her fast and the work she had yet to do.

Work that she was only just learning the importance of, the complexity of balancing a nation wound together in intricacies she never learned, back when she was just a foolish girl dreaming on the burning of hope of change. But she knew better now—knew just how painful the cost of her grand schemes would be. So here she was, Royal Blood Worker, chipping away at the little gains she could achieve.

But there was nothing she could accomplish now, not with ache in her back and the way her eyes threatened to drift closed one more. She needed rest, her soft bed, and the comfort of Samuel's arms if she had any hope of solving any of the great issues left at her doorstep.

Pushing herself up, she carefully brushed the stray locks of hair from her face, taking a moment to refresh her appearance. Despite the hour, there would still be people flitting about the Academy—students cramming for exams, instructors frantically preparing the next lesson, and the nearly invisible servants gliding between them, ensuring that everything ran smoothly. As soon as she stepped out of her office, the sole bit of privacy she had would vanish as the performance began again.

Appearances had always been important, as a LeClaire, as a child with foreign blood. As the Royal Blood Worker following de la Cruz, it had become *everything*, the entire court of Aeravin watching her every movement, waiting to see if she would make the same mistakes he had, if the quality of her blood would be as poor as his.

Yet another mess he had added to her plate, another bitterness left where there had once been the hope for something more. It was uncharitable of her, she knew that, but it was better to be angry at all he had done than to mourn everything she had lost.

That was the lie she kept telling herself, anyway.

Prepared to face the night, she exited her office and stepped out into the top floor. The witch light had been dimmed for the night, casting a warm glow over the couches and low tables throughout the space, places for the enlightened of Aeravin to mingle as they discussed the newest bits of theory and magic. Empty, thankfully, except the door to the Eternal King's Archives. The sole door was cracked open, light spilling out across the marble floor.

Shan's heart sank into her stomach as she realized who was there. There was only one person who could access it on their own, whose blood would allow them to pass through the ward and into the room beyond.

It seemed that the Eternal King had been stirred from his own offices again, as he had many times in the past few months, poring over the knowledge he had spent a millennium collecting as he tried to understand what had been done to Samuel. It was a great puzzle in his eyes, nothing more, a bit of intellectual inquiry that he wanted to solve. Whatever pain Samuel went through did not matter.

Still, she squared her shoulders as she stepped through the ward, the buzz of her own magic sizzling against her skin—no doubt the King knew she lingered, and it would be better for her to go to him. She had learned that lesson the hard way.

The room was large but windowless, bookshelves lining the walls and reaching almost all the way up to the ceiling. A long ladder was braced against the shelves, attached to a railing that allowed one to roll it to the proper stack, climbing through the very ranks of history itself. Each shelf was carefully preserved against the ravages of time by being encased in specially made glass, a collection of journals and books dating back all the way to the founding of Aeravin itself.

Journals full of knowledge that Shan, in her time before serving the King, had not even been able to imagine. There were too many of them to get through in her meager lifetime, not unless she devoted herself solely to this endeavor, but there was a part of her that ached to try.

The Eternal King stood in the middle of the room, the brightness from the witch light casting shadows across his face, as inexorable as ever, a man who never changed or aged. There was a sternness to him that she knew waited just beyond the surface, a promise of unyielding will and cruelty, but she had learned to walk around the edges of it, managing his moods just as she managed everything else.

Still dressed in his court finest, the Eternal King stood with his hands pressed into the wood of the table, a slight frown marring his otherwise flawless features. Before him was one of his old journals, bound in leather and filled with his scribbled handwriting, a journal that he protected even from his own skin with the special gloves he wore to flip through the pages.

"Good evening," the King said, without looking up. "How goes your work?"

Shan still had to fight the urge to lie, the words already hung on the edge of her lips, but she swallowed them down like the bitter fruit they were. "Things are not going as well as I would have liked. We are burning through blood faster than our initial projections called for, even with the increased Blood Taxes and the rationing we established."

Even with the first two collections of the doubled Blood Taxes, two pints from every Unblooded citizen over twelve, she hadn't been able to balance the looming deficit, given just how much of the supply had come from the secret Blood Factory. So, she balanced it as best she could, pulling back in the scant areas that she could find, fat that she had been able to trim from the endless requisitions that came to the Royal Blood Worker's office. Under Isaac, it had been brushed off to aides and secretaries. But in these new conditions, she had to account for every single drop of blood in their coffers, and there was only so much rationing that the nobles would allow.

The entire balance of their nation hung on a tightrope, and with each step Shan feared that she would fall into the abyss.

The King only hummed, turning the page in his journal with a careful hand. "I am sure that you will come up with something. I know you are too clever to let something as minor as this defeat you."

Fear thrummed a heady beat in her veins. Shan still didn't know how she withstood it, the level look the Eternal King sent her way, eyes as hard as emeralds, peeling away all her schemes and lies to get to the heart of her. His faith was a burning potential, almost too much to bear, but she could not flinch away.

"I will," she swore, though she did not yet know the particulars of how she would appease him. She just knew she had no other option, lest she end up like all the others who had crashed and burned. Like her father.

Like Isaac.

The King only smiled, gesturing her forward with a gloved hand. "What do you think of this?"

He stepped aside, allowing her to take his place at the research table, but lingered close enough that she could still feel the warmth of his body, the nearly overwhelming taste of his magic on the air. He had stopped masking around her, when it was just the two of them, no longer even bothering to play at being merely human. Perhaps it was meant as an intimidation tactic, a reminder of just how far above her that he was. Perhaps it was a kind of trust, the only way he could be able to show it.

But it did not matter why. In truth, all it did was make her hungry. What would power like that feel like, in her hands? Who would dare challenge her? Would it let her, for the first time in her life, know what it would be like to be free?

The journal before them was one she had seen before, one of the first he had shown her after her ascension to Royal Blood Worker. In those early weeks, they had spent so many nights in this very room, poring over theories and details as they struggled to understand exactly how the Aberforth Gift had been decoupled from Samuel. It had been entirely fruitless, but here was the Eternal King once more, searching for answers they could not find.

She bit her lip, trying to find what exactly he wanted her to see. It was always like this with him—he never just gave the answer, she had to find it first. And when she succeeded, his praise felt like a buoy on her faltering soul, the only thing keeping her afloat when she felt like she was drowning.

Leaning over the notebook, she scanned the lines, used to the untidy scrawl of the King's handwriting, a slight flaw in his otherwise immaculate persona. The journals were not neat or well-organized, most of the notes a sprawling stream-of-consciousness as the King's mind jumped from other perch to another, interspersed with sketches and notes and the odd equation. It was difficult work, parsing out the information from the chaff, but part of Shan relished it.

Perry worries about the cost, the blood. What we are trying is such an elemental rewriting of his Blood Working, and to do it will require more power than the typical Unblooded will provide, but access to blood is not an issue for me.

Shan blinked slowly, the thought hovering just out of reach, as ephemeral and difficult to catch as mist. She read it again, slower, muttering the words under her breath, as—

"Ah."

"You see it, then," the King said, less a question and more an affirmation. She had passed the test, and the weight of fear slipped from her shoulders.

"I do," Shan said, tilting her face so she could meet his expectant gaze. "Dunn." The last murder, the Councillor of Law that Isaac had so callously used as a demonstration of the Blood Factory's efficient cruelty. That was the piece they hadn't dug into, hadn't known if his death was part of Isaac's experiments or merely a statement that he felt necessary to make.

"De la Cruz is not the first to use Unblooded in this manner," the King said. He stepped between her and the table, carefully gathering his journal as he went to return it to its normal resting place halfway up the wall, where it was shelved chronologically with all his other notes. "Even if he used every Unblooded he murdered to enhance his own ability, it shouldn't have been possible to do what he's done. But Dunn..."

The King slid back down the ladder with a sigh. "Kevan was powerful, and compounding that into his own body? That might be enough."

Shan swallowed hard, ignoring the way she hungered for this knowledge. This bit of magic that no one besides their King was allowed to practice, the very way he had extended his life and his power across generations. "Have you ever done this with a Blood Worker?"

"No," the King admitted, turning back to watch her. He wasn't upset with the question, with the discussion. Sometimes, she wondered if he actually enjoyed it. "I have never needed to, and the consequences of such actions ... well, the price isn't always worth the power."

"The price?" Shan echoed, wondering which of the endless journals here had the answer. If he would show it to her, or if he expected her to find it on her own.

"Mhmm," the King replied as he pulled the ladder to another stack, as he climbed up to it. "It was something I discovered early in my reign, something that I strove to keep hidden. We are already feared enough, and stability in the game of nations is a delicate balance. But I've kept it for centuries, and to think that de la Cruz stumbled upon it entirely by accident ..."

Shan donned a pair of gloves, stepping to his side to receive the tome he handed down. This was a thicker one, an older one, the very binding that held it together starting to fray and fail. "Your Majesty, may I?"

He glanced down at her, imperious as ever, but he nodded.

"Why did you not show this to me until now?"

"Ah, that is a good question, Shan." His smile was cold and sharp as the claws she normally wore on her hands. "Because this knowledge is dangerous, and I did not want to share it with you unless it was necessary."

It was almost crueler in its simplicity than it would have been if he had meant an unkindness. The fact that, despite elevating her to be his right hand, he still did not trust her. Not fully.

She could spend the rest of her life proving herself to him, and it still wouldn't be enough.

"So I followed other paths," the King continued as he climbed back down, "all the way down to the bitter end. But now there is only one thing to do, only one option left. Truths that I hoped had faded entirely to myth, monsters that I hoped the world had forgotten."

Shan dragged her thumb across the spine of the journal, her curiosity peaked. Myths and monsters, false tales of what countless fools had thought of Blood Workers. Perhaps there was some truth to it after all. "Are you saying that vamp—"

"Read it," he repeated, cutting her off before she could even finish the word. "Read that, then tomorrow night we'll see to Isaac."

Shan clenched her hands around the journal as she bit back a sigh. Another night without sleep, then. It was foolish to resent it—she had never wanted the position of Royal Blood Worker, but now that she had it, it was more power, more knowledge, more access than she could have ever dreamed of.

She had been foolish to think that any of her previous schemes or ploys were power. That she, as bright as she was, as capable as she strove to be, could ever hope to bring about real change, that the King would not swat her down, her efforts as insignificant as a gnat's. Her little network, her little ploys, that wasn't power.

This was power—standing next to the Eternal King, his knowledge gifted freely, his experience guiding her to places she had never dreamed to reach.

And now that she had it, she would never let it go.

"As you say, Your Majesty." She clutched the tome to her chest as she bowed before her King, ready to serve.

Chapter Two

Samuel

Samuel's head was pounding and they hadn't even reached midday recess yet. The air in the Royal Council's chambers was stifling without even a window to open, the heat from the various fireplaces in the Parliament House that kept all the other corners of the building comfortably toasty turned this one room into a damned oven.

While Lord Rayne droned on and on about taxes and loans and interest, Samuel fidgeted awkwardly with his cravat, wanting nothing more than to loosen it. But even here, among those he might not be able to call friends but were certainly something more than acquaintances, he knew that it would draw him undue attention. That the stark scars on his throat would still catch everyone's eyes, a reminder of what he had been through. It wasn't just on his throat either—the darkened lines trailed across his body, along all the paths that his veins and arteries travelled, a reminder of what had been done to him.

It had been months and they had not faded in the slightest, the touch of Isaac's magic a memory he would carry on his skin for the rest of his life. A tale of loss and suffering that anyone could read, even if they did not know the full context of what had been taken from him. And, despite the way Tristan had put him on display that night when he had changed both his and Shan's lives, it was not a tale that was anyone else's right to see.

And so, he suffered.

Even if it left him hot and sweltering in his long-sleeved shirt and pants, his hands hidden by soft gloves, the cloth at his collar obscuring the delicate line of his throat. The others had shed their coats, had rolled up their sleeves in a desperate attempt to chase the littlest bit of comfort, stirring an unkind spark of jealousy that lodged itself in the back of Samuel's throat.

"Enough," Belrose said, leaning back in her seat and draping her hand across her eyes. It was strange how different they were, like this, without the weight of expectation and decorum.

When they were grappling with the details of their work during the official recess, nailing down the different motions they would bring forward with the new Season, as they worked together to hash out what was left of their government after the King had stepped in last summer. Sweeping laws that restricted the rights and movements of the many Unblooded citizens of the nation, only now just starting to lift, like that damnable curfew.

Though that was only because enough Blood Workers had been complaining about it, how terribly difficult it was to schedule their employees' and servants' work around the legal regulations, funneled through the offices of the Councillor of Industry. A minutia he never would have even considered, a year past.

It was more than he had expected, back when he had first joined the House of Lords, less than a year ago. It had all seemed so frivolous. And maybe it was, then. There had never been a political shift like this in all of Aeravin's history, not since its very founding.

They were in uncharted waters, and as the least experienced member of the Council, he did not know what the Eternal King had been thinking with this appointment.

"Jenna," Lord Rayne pressed, only for Belrose to shoot him a quieting glare.

"You've made your point quite well, Matthias." She straightened in her seat, hands draped over the edges of the armrests. "We are fucked."

Samuel couldn't help but wince at her blunt language. She wasn't wrong, as far as he could tell. The particulars were beyond him, truthfully, but the basis of it was clear enough.

In addition to a blood shortage, Aeravin was teetering on the brink of financial collapse.

"Then perhaps you should do something," Rayne muttered, looking every bit of his seven decades. "Trade is our only option."

"Not our only option," Lady Holland said, leaning forward. Any spark that she once had burned out over their many meetings, as she made the same argument again and again. But none would side with her, none but Samuel, as what she asked for was so absurd that it was laughed out of hand.

For why would the richest of Aeravin consent to a rise in monetary taxes when they already had to suffer the effects of blood rationing? But that was the joy and frustration of working with Lady Holland—she was always willing to look at issues through the lens of sheer practicality, even when it was uncomfortable.

Especially when it was uncomfortable.

Lady Belrose did not even dignify Lady Holland's comment with a response, her attention firmly on Lord Rayne. "As you are aware," she shot back, "I cannot simply change tariffs on my own. We'd need Royal approval."

Several sets of eyes shot in his direction, a question hanging unasked on the air. It was something that had been happening ever since his appointment. It had been over a century since an Aberforth had been on the Council, and he couldn't blame them for wanting to use him to their advantage. He was uniquely positioned as the only living blood relative of the Eternal King ... in addition to his close ties to the Royal Blood Worker.

Licking dry lips, he turned his attention to Lady Belrose. "If you have a proposal written up, I can ensure that it is brought to his attention."

"Can you truly?" Lady Morse interjected, drumming her fingers on the table. Even here, in the privacy of their secluded meetings, she was as unyielding as stone. A hardened military leader in a land where the military hadn't mattered for centuries. "His Majesty has not responded to any of our other proposals of late."

"I am but the messenger," Samuel replied, spreading his hands wide in a placating gesture. "The King is busy with his studies."

It might have been the truth, as far as Shan had been able to assure him, but that didn't make it any easier to bear. The problems were stark, and the King's ongoing policies were only making things worse. The Blood Taxes had been raised, rationing had been enforced, the curfew had only just been lifted. Outright rebellion had been ceased under the threat of violence, but the unrest continued.

And unless Tristan Aberforth, the Eternal King of Aeravin, could be bothered to get off his arse and do something about it, this fragile peace would shatter under the slightest weight.

"We understand, Samuel," Holland assured him, offering him something of a sympathetic smile. He wasn't sure if any of the other Councillors could truly be called allies, but if there was one, it would be Zelda Holland. "But we are running out of options."

"I know," he said, with more fervor than he intended. "I know." The futility of it all was nearly enough to drive him to madness, but he couldn't bring himself to not try.

Trying was all he had left.

"Very well," Belrose said, with an air of finality. "I'll have the draft on your desk by morning, Aberforth. As for the rest of us, I propose that we take the rest of the day as a recess. We all know we need it."

The rest of the Councillors muttered their agreement, pushing away from the table as they gathered their things. Samuel didn't object—hells, he agreed, even as it felt like they were giving up. Another meeting, another waste of time, and what was there to show for it?

A plan that the King would probably never deign to look at, no matter what pretty promises Samuel made.

Holland crept over to his side as the others made their way out of the room, hovering awkwardly as he collected his notes. "Could I borrow a moment of your time?"

He hesitated for only a second before flashing her a smile, one that he had practiced in the mirror under Shan's careful instruction. It wasn't quite second nature yet, the charming yet untouchable role of Lord Aberforth, heir to the Eternal King, but it was coming easier with each passing day. Rarely did he feel the bile creep up the back of his throat with every lie, nor the flush of shame that marred so many of his early days in this role.

Each day he sunk a little deeper into the lies that he had learned to wear like armor, and he didn't know if he would ever be able to claw his way out again.

"After you," he said, inclining his head towards the door. Holland nodded, accepting with a small smile, and he followed her through the halls of the Parliament House. They walked in comfortable silence—Zelda had never been the type to fill the air with idle prattle, like the rest of the Councillors. When she spoke, it was direct and with purpose, and Samuel was always thankful for that.

Several minutes later, she unlocked the door to her office, and Samuel swept in to take a seat while Zelda instructed her aide to bring them some refreshments. Her office was sparse but not spartan, the most striking feature being the floor-to-ceiling bookshelves that contained tome after tome of information.

Unlike many of the other Blood Workers he had come to know, especially of the nobility, Zelda gave little care to appearance or politicking. Her focus was on the work that she excelled at, managing the many little laws, regulations, and ordinances around industry in Aeravin. Out of all the Councillors, she was the only one who gave a damn about the Unblooded, though not out of any particular care for them. She just understood their value in her many calculations.

But that was something he could work with.

It didn't take long for the girl to return with a fresh pot of tea, Samuel pouring for the both of them as Zelda dismissed the aide. "Well," Zelda said, settling behind her desk and accepting the cup. She placed it carefully on a stack of papers, as there was not an inch of it not covered with something. "We are continuing to get jack shit done."

Samuel didn't bother hiding his smile, truer this time. Though he couldn't trust her motives, he could trust her actions, and that was more than the others. "Your directness is refreshing as always, Lady Holland."

She snorted into her tea. "Don't waste time with bullshit, Aberforth. We need to readjust our strategy. We won't be making any progress at this rate."

He fiddled with his cup. "We do not even know what things will look like, when the House of Lords returns this year."

Zelda's frown was so severe that it changed the entire topography of her face, her normally quiet and mousy appearance turned into something fierce. "I can almost forgive him for what he did at the summer solstice, and I don't even fully disagree with all of his measures. But this..." She steepled her hands in front of her. "We barely had a functioning government as it was."

"While I don't disagree," Samuel said, picking his words with care, "I do not know what you expect me to do about it."

"Honestly, Aberforth? I don't know either." Leaning back in her chair, she let out a defeated sigh. "But you're the only one I trust to actually put forward anything that will benefit Aeravin, not just yourself."

"Lady Belrose is not so bad," Samuel offered, but Zelda scoffed.

"A year ago, I might have agreed with you. But she hasn't been the same since Dunn." The frown was back, exasperation bleeding through each movement. "Nasty way to go, I won't deny that, but Dunn was a piece of shit who barely cared to manage his own affairs, let alone that of his station. You may be bold, but at least you care."

"Thank you." The praise was a welcome one, considering he was only beginning, and looked upon with much distrust. Dunn had left the Guard to run on their own, a machine built on its own corruption, greased by bribes and favors. Samuel was doing his best to undo that, bit by bit, but...

"I have a long road ahead of me."

"That you do," Zelda agreed. "But I think you just might be able to pull it off. Which is more than I could have said for dearly departed Kevan." Leaning forward, she rested her elbows on the table. "Let me be blunt, I want to propose an alliance. I believe our goals are aligned, and we can do more working together than we could do separately."

Samuel considered it for a moment. He knew what Shan would advise. This was a golden opportunity, power was an ineffable thing, and having another Councillor in their pocket would only help them in the long term. The choice was obvious.

It just made him sick to his stomach.

But he smiled gamely. "Why, Lady Holland, that is something I can agree to."

Chapter Three

Isaac

Isaac understood what was happening the moment the Guards—two of them, this time, instead of the regular one—dragged him to the bathing room.

First, it was off his regular schedule, the carefully built structures of his captivity having settled into a strict, rote repetition that was nearly maddening in its consistency. Second, it was a more thorough cleaning than usual, the water scented with rose oil in addition to the simple soap he had gotten used to. His hair, which had grown into a long and tangled mess, was carefully brushed and trimmed. A valet was called in to tend his beard, and the shave was closer and more precise that anything he had received in months. And finally, after all the prepping had been done, his clothes were replaced with new ones, soft and clean, if not fine.

They did not give him a binder—they hadn't given him a binder since he had been imprisoned. But thankfully, the shirt was loose enough to hide the small swell of his breasts, and if he was careful enough, no one should notice.

It was the closest he had felt to being human in a long time, but Isaac knew that such considerations were not for him. No, there was only one reason why the Guards would care that he was clean and decent and somewhat cared for.

The Eternal King was coming to visit.

When they returned him to his cell, the Guards didn't bother to latch him back into the dreadful chair that he was bolted into for most of the day, nor the muzzle that kept him from speaking. It was always one or the other, locked into the chair as the Guard tipped water down his throat; muzzled and manacled as they let him walk circles around the cell to prevent muscle atrophy.

He was weak and tired, thin and drained, as he waited for his death.

But today, they let him roam free as they returned to their posts, back to the brick wall across from the cell as they watched him.

For a second, he wondered if he could do something, anything, to fight them. That maybe, with a bit of his own blood, he could manage it. Overpower the two Blood Workers staring him down, armed with claws and daggers and a long blade on a pike—long enough that they could strike him down through the iron bars if they so chose. Once he had surmounted all that, he would need to make it through the series of wards and all the Guards in between him and freedom.

To attempt it would be insanity, and Isaac let the idea fade before even the tiniest bit of hope could sink its claws into his heart. The words that Samuel had whispered in his ear, near a month ago now, were bad enough. There was no escaping his fate, and despite the bold words he had whispered to the man he betrayed the most, Isaac wasn't sure if he even deserved it anymore. All the despicable things he had done, both for the King and to undermine him, only to fail?

If it had worked, he could have forgiven himself. Justify the terrible costs if it meant that the world was better off. But it hadn't worked, so how was he to live with all the blood on his hands?

The ward above him shivered, splitting and cracking, and Isaac heard the soft rhythm of the King's heartbeat. Steady as a metronome, never faltering. But there was someone else with him, someone whose heart fluttered an unsteady beat. He recognized that sound, he had grown all too familiar with the way it echoed in his own chest. It was a heart driven by fear.

What poor soul was the King bringing into this mess with him?

The footsteps grew louder as his guests descended the stairs, sinking into his own little private piece of hell, Isaac stepping forward to wrap his hands around the bars. The guard on the left twitched, his hand tightening on his weapon, but snapped to attention as the Eternal King rounded the corner with Shan LeClaire on his arm.

She looked just as beautiful as the last time he had seen her, when she had cut down Alessi and ruined the last of his plans. Then, she had been brilliant with fury, incandescent with rage, but now she was every bit the proper Blood Worker. She wore a fashionable gown of deepest red, the bodice pulled tight so that his gaze fell naturally to the heave of her breasts. It tapered to her narrow waistline, accentuated so that he ached to wrap his hands around her, before spilling in waves around her legs to drape across the floor.

And on her hands were silver claws made of shining steel, elegant in their simplicity, but still sharp enough to rend flesh.

Isaac swore his breath caught in his throat as he looked his fill, but she didn't look at him. No, her gaze was cast low and demure in a way that did not feel like an affectation, nearly hiding behind the waves of her hair. She wasn't playing at coy—he recognized the tension in her shoulders and the rapid beat of her heart. Was it disgust? Anger? Disdain? No, it wasn't any of that. It was something altogether worse.

Guilt.

So much guilt that she couldn't bear to look at him, for it was her that saw him captured, imprisoned, and stuck in this interminable limbo as he awaited his death.

And yet, despite all that, he wanted her. His desire for her was written in his very bones, and he would go to his grave craving her touch.

He couldn't let her know how much sway she still had over him. He drummed up the last bits of his anger, the bitterness that he nursed on all those dark, lonely nights in his cell. "You," he spat, his voice rough from disuse, but it still landed true.

Shan flinched away, as if she had been struck.

"My dear boy," the Eternal King said, smooth as ever. As if nothing changed at all, and this was just another one of their many little meetings. There was something coldly cruel about the way that the Eternal King was looking at him, as if trying to find the exact right place to strike. "That is no way to speak to your Royal Blood Worker."

The scream caught in his throat, the shock so sudden that he could barely even breathe. He hadn't thought about what had happened, in the aftermath, only that despite his own efforts, Shan and Samuel still lived. Isaac never even considered that he had doomed Shan to follow his bloodstained path.

This was the cruelest thing the King could have done to punish him, and from the slight pull at the corner of the King's mouth, Isaac knew that the cruelty was the point.

"Shan," he choked, unsure what he could even say. But it worked, she looked at him at last, and there was no love left in her eyes.

"It is Lady LeClaire to you," she said, with a haughty little lilt that he wasn't used to hearing from her. "If you must address me at all."

Isaac pushed away from the bars, blood rushing in his ears as the King dismissed the guards. There was nothing true to glean from this ... this farce. Perhaps she still loved him, perhaps she did not. If this was one of her masks, it was so perfect that he could not tell if it was true or not, a protection around the King or the depths of her own heart.

Either way, it did not matter.

Nothing mattered anymore.

"Why are you here?" Isaac said, staring away from his visitors. The brick wall was the same as it ever was, but it was better than facing the things he feared the most.

"Now, is that any way to talk to your King?"

Isaac bit his tongue to swallow any reactions before they could be loosed into the world. His *King*.

Tristan Aberforth had ceased being his King the moment he took Isaac down into the bowels of the castle, showed him the truth behind Aeravin's blood supply, and forced him to become the monster in the shadows to see it filled.

"Forgive me," Isaac said as he turned to face the King, infusing his words with as much acid as possible. He dipped into a bow, low, held for just a second too long to be sincere. "How may I serve you today?"

"It really is a waste." The King looked him over from head to toe, assessing but pitying. "There was such potential in you, only for you to throw it away. And for what?" He pulled back his lips, not quite a smile. "Because your bleeding heart felt bad?"

Isaac did not bother to respond. The King wasn't interested in his arguments, he knew this from experience. No, he was motivated by hubris alone, hubris and the sheer inability to understand any perspective that wasn't his own. A thousand years of ruling, of power, of immortality, could do that to a person.

"Does it matter?" Isaac asked. "What's done is done."

The King inclined his head, ceding the point. "Fair enough, de la Cruz. I am less interested in your *whys* and far more interested in your *hows*."

Holding out his arm, Shan stepped forward to join him, taking her place beside the King. They made such a pair, the sheer power of their Blood Working rolling off them in waves, overpowering in a way that made his stomach churn and his jaw ache. Shan, as Royal Blood Worker, was more than he could have ever hoped to be, taking to it like it was her birthright.

Perhaps it was. Her father might have failed, once, but her bloodline could be traced all the way back to the founding of Aeravin. She was a born and raised Blood Worker, a Lady who had been moving in society for her whole life. And no matter how hard he tried, how desperately he had sought their approval and how shamelessly he twisted himself to stand among them, it would never have been as effortless as it was for her.

The gap between them had never felt so stark.

"We were hoping," she said, sweet as honey and just as sickly, "that you can answer a few questions for us."

"What questions?" He didn't want to fight, to make this a struggle.

He'd answer their questions if it got them to leave, because he wasn't sure he could survive this much longer.

The door to his cell opened under Shan's touch—of course, the King couldn't be bothered to do it himself—only for the King to step forward with purpose, closing the distance between them with a scant few steps, as he reached out to grab Isaac around the throat.

Shan made a soft huff of surprise, and something inside of Isaac was soothed by the knowledge that she wasn't fully behind the King's actions. But that brief bit of light was smothered by fear as the King pressed harder, nearly lifting Isaac off his feet as he leaned in, the tip of his claw pressing into the rapid beat of his pulse. It wouldn't take much pressure at all to pierce the skin, to bleed before the King and Royal Blood Worker.

For them to taste all that he had gained.

"You took Dunn's blood, didn't you," the King said, as calmly as if they were discussing the weather. "To empower yourself."

He wasn't entirely sure if it was a question, but Isaac croaked out an affirmation anyway. "I did."

"And the process, it is the same as what I do at the annual sacrifice?"

Isaac swallowed hard, hardly able to think. "Please, put me down."

"Fine. If you can be civilized, then I suppose I can be as well." The King dropped him, but the threat was still clear. Behave, or it would be back to treating him like he wasn't even a person at all.

He rubbed the skin where the King's hand had just been, tender and sore. "It was similar, but not exactly the same." The words came slowly at first, like he had to fight himself to even get them out, but as both the King and Shan waited expectantly, it came easier.

As if it was something that he had been waiting to do.

"Pulling power from blood is complex," he said, starting at the beginning even though it wasn't fully necessary. The Eternal King's understanding of Blood Working was so far beyond what Isaac could ever hope to attain, but part of him was still proud of what he had discovered and wanted them both to know it. "What you do annually is focused on the life force—"

"Whereas you don't care to extend your life." The King tilted his head to the side with a frown. "You were only interested in power."

"I had a goal to achieve," Isaac replied, "and that goal did not include living forever."

"No," Shan said, interjecting at last, voicing the thing that they had spent so long dancing around, never brave enough to confront head-on. "You wanted power for a specific purpose. To kill our King."

"I did," Isaac confirmed, just to see how Shan would react. "I do. I used the blood to strengthen my own power, I stripped them of every bit of life they had so that I could—" He cut himself off, clenching his fist at his side.

They all knew what came next.

Shan didn't so much as blink, her expression impassive. Once, he had thought she would agree with the goals of this scheme, if not the particulars to see it done, but now? Now he didn't know at all.

She could have been a stranger.

"And Dunn?" The King circled back in front of him, rustling with a restless energy—he was excited, intrigued, the same as he was when he was picking apart a particularly thorny bit of theory, but now the theory was him.

"What of Dunn?" Isaac asked, resisting the urge to rub his temple.

"Dunn," the King enunciated slowly, "was a Blood Worker. Unlike the others. Unlike the doomed souls that I drain in the Annual Sacrifice."

Isaac blinked slowly. He hadn't stopped to think about that, the difference that Dunn being a Blood Worker would make, not when the statement mattered most of all. Could that have been—

"Yes," he said, idly, as his mind raced forward. The changes in him, subtle and insidious as they were. The way he could almost sense blood, waiting for him just beneath the thin veneer of skin. How he could hear the beat of every heart. The hunger for something he dare not name, aching in the pit of his stomach.

The King caught Isaac's jaw, gently this time, his thumb brushing against the lower lip. The claw was gone—when did he remove it?—and the touch burned. It was too intimate, this touch that the King took as his due, and it took all of Isaac's self-control to not spit in the King's face.

"All this time," the King whispered, "I assumed that you killed Dunn merely for the message, for the shock. But what a glorious fool you are, Isaac." He forced Isaac's mouth open, running his bare finger across the upper teeth, feeling for something. "You're making yourself into the most exquisite monster. It's almost a shame that I have to kill you."

Something in Isaac shattered, and he attempted to snap his teeth down on that invading touch. But the King was too fast, pulling back with a laugh.

"I was right, Shan," he said, turning away from Isaac as if he didn't matter at all. "You have my permission to study him until the time comes for him to die."

Shan didn't answer for a moment, chewing her lip as she considered. "Are you still going to drain him, then? Wouldn't what is happening to him..."

"No," the King said, dismissively. "I am no amateur. I know how to drain the power of the blood without draining the Blood Working itself." He held out his arm. "Now come, Shan, we have much to discuss."

She didn't even look back at him as they showed themselves out, as they locked the cell and disappeared around the corner.

The guards would return momentarily, Isaac knew that, but he did not care. The King was still going kill him after all, but in the meantime...

He pressed his finger against his own teeth, looking for whatever the King had been searching for. There was nothing wrong, nothing out of place, until he pressed against something sharp, flinching back with a hiss at the sudden bite of pain.

Pulling his hand free, he stared at the pinprick blemish, a single drop of blood welling against his skin.

Chapter Four

Samuel

Samuel tangled the bed sheets in his grip, holding on for dear life as Shan rode him with a punishing speed.

She had one hand firmly on his chest, holding him in place as she took her pleasure above him. Her other hand rested at the apex of her thighs, rubbing at her clit as she clenched around him. She was beautiful like this, all her masks and lies stripped away, leaving her as bare and as vulnerable as she ever was, focused on finding the release that she desperately craved. Her cunt was so warm, so slick, and he wanted nothing more than to lose himself in her. But she was the one who had mounted him, who had needed this—reduced to just a body in motion. So, he could give her that.

He would give her the world, if she asked it of him.

Samuel let out a slow breath as he struggled to hang long enough for Shan to find her peak. He released the sheets, moving his hands—one found her waist to help her balance, the other found her left breast, thumbing across her nipple, rough, just like she had shown him. Shan cried out, her eyes drifting closed, as she approached her climax.

"Yeah, love," Samuel rasped out, meeting her thrust for thrust. "Just like that."

Shan threw her head back as she came, sinking down and taking his cock all the way to the hilt. He could watch this for the rest of his life, her entire body flushed, her hair hanging in mad tangles, pressed against the column of her throat by sweat, her lower lip pulled between her teeth as she swallowed her cries.

She slumped against him, gone completely boneless, so Samuel wrapped her in his arms, flipping their positions and pressing her into the bed. Finally, he allowed himself to chase his own completion, Shan spreading her legs and smiling oh so sweetly as Samuel thrust into her. He was so damned close, the bedroom filling with the sound of flesh-on-flesh as he wrapped a hand around her thigh, opening her wider and allowing himself to sink deeper.

It was so good, but he couldn't quite get there—it was missing something, he needed just a little push.

And Shan, blessed Shan, understood, brushing his hair from his eyes and whispering, "Come for me, Samuel."

He pressed his teeth into the meat of her breast as he came, unable to resist the directness of her command, as she gifted him the release that he needed, but only at her behest.

They lay together afterwards, bodies entangled and pressed so close that Samuel wasn't entirely sure where he ended and she began. After the frantic nature of their lovemaking, it was a peace that Samuel needed, the way their pulses calmed and their hearts started to move in sync, the sweat drying on their skin.

Pressing his lips to her forehead, he whispered, "Mind telling me what that was about?"

Shan grumbled, shifting so that she could press her back against his front, nuzzling into him as she hid her face. "It's nothing, really, just work."

Samuel did not stop caressing her side, even as he hid his sigh in the pillow. It had been like this for weeks—Shan slipping off to the King's side, committing whatever nightmares the Crown needed from her, then crawling back to his bed, slipping in his arms and demanding he fuck her through all her doubts and fears.

And he did not mind it, truly, but...

"You can talk to me, you know."

The words hung awkwardly on the air, and Samuel wished he could snatch them back just as soon he said them. Shan stiffened in his grasp, and he could feel her closing him off as she pushed herself into a sitting position, the blankets shifting under her. "You're sweet, Samuel, but really, it's only the normal trivialities."

Shan slid from the bed, reaching for her dressing gown. Somewhere over the past few months, Shan has been steadily moving more and more of her things into the Aberforth townhouse. She had claimed it was simply for convenience's sake, but Samuel knew the truth. That her home was far too empty and lonely since her brother had moved out, and she couldn't face the ghosts that haunted her alone.

It was one of the many secrets that lay unspoken between them, and Samuel had gotten quite good at reading between the lines. It was how he knew that Shan was lying now, as well, and he could push all that he wanted, but she wouldn't relent. She thought she was protecting him from all the horrors that came with being Royal Blood Worker, sparing him the blood on her hands, but she couldn't understand that he did not care about that. All he wanted was to help her, as he had failed to help Isaac.

Which reminded him—

"There is something I'd like to talk about."

Shan looked up from the cigarette she had been lighting, another new habit that started in the last few months. The red tip flickered between her fingers as she took a long drag. "What is it?" There was a hint of exasperation in her voice, as if she knew what he was going to ask.

The argument they had been circling for so long now.

The words caught in his throat, so Samuel shifted to buy himself time, grabbing his sleep pants from where they lay discarded. He had been thinking of a new way to approach it, to couch his arguments in a different framework. To make her understand that whatever they were doing, there was one thing they couldn't let happen, not unless they wanted to become the very thing they feared.

That he feared, at least. He wasn't so sure about Shan, anymore.

"I visited Isaac," he admitted, at last. "A few weeks ago. I toured the dungeons, looked for—"

Shan huffed, loudly, cutting him off. "Samuel, please. Not this again."

"If not now, then when?" Samuel stood and crossed the room to stand in front of her, but Shan still didn't respond. She simply stared off to the side, taking another deep inhale of her cigarette. "If we don't do anything, he will die."

Shan flicked the ash into the tray that contained far too many stubs, the growing proof of her discontent. "He will die regardless. There is nothing we can do to stop that. There is nothing we can do to stop this." She looked up at him, finally, but the spark he was so used to finding there was gone. "You need to accept it."

The finality of her tone was a stark dismissal, and he couldn't help the snarl that followed. "This isn't what we agreed to."

Last year, when the curfew had first been laid, when the Eternal King had set down the laws, he and Shan had come to an agreement. They would do anything they could to stop Isaac in the moment, to keep the nation from crossing the line from civil unrest into civil war.

But the plan had never been to let Isaac actually die, had it?

"Shan, please," Samuel continued, sinking to his knees before her. She didn't respond to his touch, his hands on her knees and his eyes wide. It was a cheap tactic, but he wasn't above begging. "I can't just stand by and do nothing."

For a moment he thought it wouldn't work, but then the edges around her eyes softened. She crushed out her cigarette with an oath, then leaned forward, placing her hands over his. Her thumb rubbed soft circles into his skin, comforting and grounding, but something in Samuel feared that he was being manipulated. That she couldn't stop manipulating those she loved, even if she wanted to.

"I know you care deeply about him," Shan said softly, "as I once did."

"Once?" Samuel echoed, fear choking him before he could say anything more. When had this changed? When had *she* changed? Was it in the quiet but steady way that Shan had been shutting him out over the past months, withdrawing from him bit by bit, the mystique of lies that he had worked so hard to breach slowly building itself back up?

Loving her was like trying to hold smoke—the harder he held on, the more she slipped away.

"Shan," he breathed, "please."

Her hand moved to his face, cupping his cheek, brushing at the wetness that spilled from his eyes. He hadn't even realized he had been crying, but here she was, catching his tears. "Do you trust me?"

Hells, he wanted to, but that certainty fractured a bit more every day. "I am trying to."

Her touch turned rough; the gentleness replaced by something crueler. "If nothing else, trust that I know what I am doing. There are things you do not know, that you cannot know. And some things that a person cannot come back from, no matter how much we wish it so."

Her voice was haunted, her gaze far-away, and Samuel realized where he had seen it before. He had seen the same pain in Isaac, the same loneliness and resignation. Whatever the King was asking her to do, the work as the Royal Blood Worker that she kept, even from him, it was destroying her.

And Samuel didn't know how to save her.

"Please," he said, but she only stood, and Samuel dropped his hands to his lap, clenched his fists where she couldn't see. It wasn't supposed to be like this. They were supposed to be a team—she had promised him that, once.

"I should go," she said, stepping around him. "There is much I need to do." Her hand landed on his shoulder, squeezing tight, and then she was gone, her footsteps echoing on the floor as she entered the en-suite bathroom.

Samuel rubbed his eyes, dashing away the rest of the tears. If she wouldn't help him, then he would have to do it without her.

And there was one other person who might be able to help him.

—✦—

It wasn't difficult to find Antonin LeClaire, even after he moved out of the LeClaire townhouse. In the past months he had divested himself from Shan's home and circle, striking out to make a life free from the machinations of his sister. And despite the tangled web of affection between Samuel and Shan, he understood why Anton needed to do this.

Even if Shan could not.

So, he found Anton at the Fox Den, beside a roulette table with a glass of bourbon in his hand. If Anton was surprised to see him, he did not show it, welcoming Samuel at his side as they gambled the night away, moving from roulette to craps to vingt-et-un. But when the night ended and the carousing was over, Anton slung an arm over Samuel's shoulder and led him back to his flat.

It wasn't the first time that Samuel had been to Anton's new home, but it still struck a pang of jealousy deep in his gut. In design, it wasn't that different from what Isaac had, once, a small set of rooms in a boarding house, perfect for the life of a bachelor who didn't need the full townhome or the entire fleet of servants. It was simple and private and cozy, and Samuel wished that he had the freedom to choose to live like this.

The last time he had been there, though, the flat had still been quite bare—empty of everything that would make it a home, but in the intervening time, Anton had made it his. The furniture was mismatched in style and haphazard in color, but each piece looked like it was chosen for maximum comfort instead of style. There were colorful throw blankets and plush pillows and even a few plants in pots along the windowsill.

Stepping closer, Samuel brushed his fingers against the greenery, recognizing them for what they were—herbs and spices, grown fresh for a single man's needs.

"The food is the thing I miss the most," Anton said, appearing by his side with a small watering can. "From home. This boarding house offers meals to its residences, but I had to learn to cook my own if I wanted anything good."

Samuel couldn't help the laugh. He understood what Anton meant—Shan had retained the Tagalan cook that Anton had hired, and the meals Samuel had at their table were unlike anything typical Aeravinian households had. "You are a chef now?"

"Aspiring, maybe," Anton returned. "But for you own sake, I will stick to offering more basic refreshments. Do you still take tea, Samuel?" Samuel nodded, touched that Anton remembered his aversion to wine and spirits, and Anton clapped him on the shoulder. "Make yourself comfortable, then. I'll be right back."

Samuel sank into the couch, sighing as the strangeness from the night started to slip away. The gambling had been part of it, he knew. It would have been too obvious if he had just showed up and whisked Anton away. It needed to look casual, accidental, nothing so deliberate.

In this, Anton wasn't too terribly different from his sister, always playing the game, and Samuel had learned to follow their lead.

Anton reappeared with a tray, placing it on the low table in front of him. The tea set was also mismatched, the pot covered in soft, hand-painted florals, roses and wisteria and ivy, but the cups came from a different set entirely, a plain white base with a gold rim around the edges.

Such incongruences would have driven Shan mad, Samuel knew, but for him it felt more like home. Before ascending, before he had been taken to the King and elevated to the status normally denied a bastard like him, everything he had owned had been bought second-hand in thrift shops, where function mattered more than aesthetics.

"Thank you," he said, taking the cup. "For this, and for meeting with me as well."

"Well," Anton said, doctoring his own cup with a truly shocking amount of milk and sugar, "it was clear to me that you were not simply looking for a good time. Still not a fan of gambling?"

"Am I that obvious?" Samuel said, with a wince.

"No, not really." Anton winked at him over the edge of his cup. "It's only that I know you so well. Your reputation as Lord Aberforth will remain intact."

Samuel let out a sigh of relief—it was so hard to manage, the mask of Lord Aberforth that he had to wear. To this day, he still didn't know how he managed it, holding the true parts of himself separate from the man he needed to be to succeed in Aeravin's society. It was exhausting, and he felt like with each passing day that there were fewer and fewer people he could be honest with.

Which was why he was here in the first place.

"I need a favor," he began, "and you cannot tell Shan."

That piqued Anton's interest, who set aside his cup and leaned forward. "Oh?"

It was so strange, seeing in him the same mannerisms and habits that Samuel had learned to catalogue in Shan. Despite their feud, the twins were more alike than either cared to admit—both of them were cunning and clever, both of them masters at spinning their reputations to their advantages, and both of them played secret games that would see the future of this nation changed.

If they didn't destroy each other in the process.

In another world, in another life, Samuel would have been happy to call Anton a brother, but in this one, simply being here was a betrayal to the one who held half his heart.

But to not even try would betray the other half.

"It is something that might be difficult for you," Samuel said, after taking a bracing breath. "It's about Isaac de la Cruz."

Anton stilled, his easy grace turned cold, an instant chill of ice stilling his normally expressive features. "What about de la Cruz?"

Samuel wet dry lips. "I am planning to rescue him, and I need help."

"You—" Anton cut himself off with a groan, rubbing at his eyes. "Blood and steel, Samuel, are you mad?"

He had expected this—he had expected worse, honestly. Samuel didn't know the full story behind their animosity, but he knew that there was no love lost between Anton and Isaac. "Shan seems to think so, but ... " Samuel closed his eyes, it was almost too difficult to say. "I can't lose him, Anton. Please."

Anton stood, pacing, hands clamped behind his back. Samuel didn't press him. What he was asking for was beyond difficult. "I don't see how you think I can help," Anton said at last. "If even my sister seems to think it impossible."

"Ah, that's not it." At last they had reached the worst part. Samuel could grovel, he could beg, he could commit himself to whatever was needed. But admitting the fears that he had locked away, so deep that he need not confront them?

That was like carving his own heart out of his chest, but he did it anyway.

"It's not that Shan doesn't believe that he can be saved," Samuel said, each word another twist of the knife. The only explanation that made any sense, as difficult as it was to face. "It is that she doesn't believe that he should be saved. That he is a ..."

He trailed off, but Anton rested a hand on his shoulder, grounding him in the moment before his fears could carry him away. "And you believe differently?"

This was cruel of Anton, to make him say the things that he had been so carefully avoiding for so long. Thinking them was one thing, but putting them out into the world? That was a commitment.

"I don't know if I would have made the same choices Isaac did," Samuel admitted. "But I cannot fault him for taking the only path out that he could find." He clenched his fist in his lap, took a deep breath. "We all speak of making things better in Aeravin, and he was the only one brave enough to take his fight to the Eternal King himself. Shan is wrong, playing the King's game won't change anything."

It would only destroy them, slowly. Like it destroyed Isaac. Like it *was* destroying Shan.

And Samuel could not let that happen. Shan would understand and forgive him eventually.

"I do not know the particulars of your work," Samuel said, looking up at Anton. "Only the broadest strokes, but you are also working towards the betterment of Aeravin, are you not? Wouldn't saving the man who exposed the secrets behind the Blood Workers' excess be a boon? Wouldn't it be enough to save the one the King plans to sacrifice?"

Anton hesitated. "I ... see your point, Samuel, it is just—"

"I know you don't like him," Samuel interjected, and Anton let out a soft laugh, almost hollow.

"You're right, I don't like him," Anton admitted, quietly. "But it is clear that I underestimated him. I never thought he would have the courage to stand up to the King, let alone—"

Groaning, Anton slumped back in his chair. "I can't believe I'm doing this, but fine. We'll find a way to rescue your man, but if you really want to help Aeravin, then help me. Not just Shan."

Samuel couldn't say he hadn't expected something like this. It was exactly what Shan would have done. And, if he was being honest, part of him wanted to. He was living it now, all the faults of the system that Shan wanted so desperately to reform.

And it wouldn't be enough.

Holding out his hand, Samuel invited Anton to shake on it. "I'm in."

Anton accepted with a firm grip, his teeth glinting in a fierce smile. "Welcome to the rebellion, Samuel. We have a lot to do."

Chapter Five

Shan

The front parlor of the LeClaire townhouse was filled with bodies, the heirs to grand house of Aeravin made cozy in Shan's home. The room was strategically filled with chaises and chairs, structured so that little groups could form naturally, but not separated enough that anyone felt excluded. The low tables were set with cakes and biscuits and ever-refilled teapots, handled by the serving girls who had mastered the art of going unseen among their betters. The stage had been set perfectly, and everything ran so smoothly that Shan did not even need to pay it any attention.

It was a riot of colors and silks, each young lord and lady showing off their latest purchases of lace and velvet, the witch light glittering off the claws on their fingers as they held dainty teacups in their hands. The parlor was filled with the soft chittering of laughter and robust conversation, but Shan just wished it was all over. It had been hours, and there was only so much even she could stand.

Her salons had become a booming success after her appointment to Royal Blood Worker, but what had once been a useful twice-monthly opportunity to gather the latest gossip had become nothing more than a waste of time. She hadn't been out as the Sparrow since that dreadful night when she rescued Samuel, and though Bart was doing an admirable job picking up where she had left off, managing the network and their many birds, there was just so much work that needed to be done.

So many arcane secrets to learn, and not for the first time that night, she wished that she was back at the Academy, poring over some ancient text in a barely legible scribble. But here she was, letting the other young nobles of Aeravin pick at her for a change.

"Do you know if the House of Lords will resume this spring?" Miss Grover asked as she reached for a biscuit. "I know the whole thing was terribly done, but I must say my mother has come to enjoy the freedom."

Shan bit the inside of her cheek to keep from saying the uncomfortable truth. Lady Grover enjoyed being free of the House of Lords because she never had a single original thought to contribute to something so unimportant as politics. But such things could not be said, not openly, so Shan merely smiled. "The House of Lords will return this season, the Royal Council has already sent out the information. I'm surprised your mother hasn't mentioned it."

It was a slight dig, an unkind allusion to Lady Grover's laziness, and while Miss Grover sputtered out a response, Lady Amelia Dunn shot her a smile over the rim of her teacup. Shan had no option but to respond in kind. Her hit was seen and acknowledged; the point gone to her.

Forever trading glancing blows, if only to prove who among them was the strongest and cruelest.

Once, Shan thought that was what power was. What a naive fool she had been. She would never make such foolish assumptions again, now that the Eternal King had taken her under his wing and shown her what true power was.

Power was something even more ineffable—it was knowledge and courage and the ability to shift the long game of nations even the slightest bit to the side. Building up in increments so small that most would never even notice it, but when the time came, all one needed was the slightest nudge.

And this was just a complete waste of time.

Amelia shot her a wink, then steered the conversation off into another direction completely, away from the House of Lords and whatever she was plotting for the upcoming session. She had taken up the mantle of Lady Dunn after the untimely death of her father, and despite the proper level of mourning she carefully demonstrated, Shan could tell that she was eager to step into the role.

They were so alike, more so than Shan was comfortable admitting, mirroring each other despite their differences. Both daughters of despicable fathers, both striving to find a place for themselves in this cut-throat world. Shan was a more powerful Blood Worker by far, but Amelia didn't have the stain of a foreigner's blood so visible in her very skin.

They could have been the best of friends, but both of them were too savvy for that. Blood Workers did not have friends, and that was a lesson that Shan learned far too late.

But she forced herself to focus on the salon, smiling at all the right moments and dropping only the most cutting of comments. Thankfully, it was already winding down, and by the top of the hour she had already managed to gracefully steer most of her guests towards the door.

Except the one.

Finally alone, Amelia smiled at her with too many teeth, like they were the oldest of confidantes and not two souls pushed together by the machinations of a man months in the grave.

"It was a lovely get-together," Amelia cooed, and Shan wished that she could just get to the point. "You always throw the best of soirées, despite how much time your new role must take."

Shan offered the expected smile in return, polite and just a little demure. "It is a lot to manage, but I do strive to do my best."

"And we love you for it," Amelia assured her, though they both knew it was a lie.

Once, Shan had been a novelty, a girl of some potential and no great ambition, but since her ascension, everyone was watching and waiting, convinced she would fail like the one that came before her.

And it ruined every plan she had ever made, being thrust from the shadows into the spotlight, but Shan was nothing if not adaptable.

So, when Amelia settled back down in a chair, Shan did not up and demand that she leave, instead taking the seat opposite her like it was the most natural thing in the world.

"About the House of Lords," Amelia began, drumming her fingers on the armrest. "I know that your new position requires much of your attention, so I merely wanted to offer my aid in the upcoming session."

Ah, that was the game then, the issue that many Royal Blood Workers had to balance. Entire alliances had been built around it, allies who stepped in and advocated for the causes the Royal Blood Worker—and the Eternal King—wanted to see championed, all in exchange for the intangible currency of favors. Ideally, this is what Samuel was for, but there was only so much one man could do.

Especially as he continued to back such unpopular policies.

This was something Isaac never had to worry about. No matter how high the King elevated him, he couldn't overcome the commonness of his birth and grace the House of Lords with his presence. Sometimes, she envied him that freedom.

She was *so* tired.

But she beamed at Amelia like it was the most brilliant suggestion, clasping her hand across the tea table, the movement delicate as claws clinked against claws. "Amelia, that is exactly what I need. I was hoping that we could connect like this, so I am quite thankful that you brought it up."

"It is a natural progression," Amelia replied, squeezing Shan's fingers. "After all, given how well your policies aligned with my father's, rest his soul, I knew that I would be foolish not to pick up where he left off."

"He was taken from us too soon," Shan lied, and Amelia dabbed at suddenly wet eyes, both of them performing for each other. If Amelia missed her father, it was only because of his place on the Royal Council and the wealth of information that must have brought to the Dunn family.

Which explained why she was here, cozying up to the Royal Blood Worker. Oh, how the tables had turned in only a few months, but for some reason, it did not give Shan the thrill she expected.

Amelia rose with a smile, dropping into a quick curtsy, an attempt to ply her with kindness that only soured Shan's stomach for how transparent it was. "I will be sure to convene with you at the start of the session, Lady LeClaire."

"And I am looking forward to it," Shan replied. "We can do much together, Lady Dunn."

"So much. Aeravin won't know what hit them. It has been an interesting year," Amelia said, with a cruel little smile that let Shan know exactly how much she supported the King's new laws, "but I am sure we can bring forth new policies that will lead to a better future."

"A better future," Shan echoed, realizing with jolt that it was actually true. Oh, her past self would have railed against this revelation, but she had been fooled by the idealism of youth. The Dunns of the world were right. An entirely new game was opening up to her, and through it she could achieve more than she ever dreamed of.

With her success gained, Amelia dismissed herself with a round of polite words that did not even stick in Shan's mind, leaving her alone in the empty parlor, surrounded by the ghosts of the successes she continued to collect.

This is exactly what she needed, and yet, it still felt empty.

The servants swept in, collecting the leftover treats and the empty cups. Shan nodded at the youngest of them, a quick permission for her to take it back to the kitchens to share among the staff. It was the least she could offer after all the work they put into this event—and all the others.

Rising, she eased out of their way, slipping up the stairs and leaving the commotion behind. Perhaps she just needed a bit of quiet, a reprieve from the scheming as she allowed herself a moment's relaxation. But as she turned into her study, she found Bart sitting at her grand desk, sorting through alarmingly large piles of paper. Doing the work she had left behind.

She closed the door behind her, offering him a smile that was more true than any she had shared that night. "Hello, Hawk."

Bart barely spared her a glance as he continued working through the pile in front of him. "Shan."

Shan, he had said. Not Sparrow. A small distinction, likely one not even meant as a slight, but there was still that cold fissure of pain in her chest. It should not have hurt this bad, this was the decision that she had made, after all. She could have kept going as the Sparrow, if she wanted to. But she had chosen to hand off the bulk of the work to her beloved Hawk while she circled around the edges of it, her attention pulled elsewhere.

And yet . . .

She stepped up to the desk, idly flicking through the discarded notes. It was mostly what she had expected, little bits of gossip about the masters of Aeravin, little sins that wouldn't be of any actual value in the information market. Still—

"Here," she said, pulling a small piece of paper from the pile, a note from one of the many fences in the capital. "The Kellys have replaced some of their jewels with well-made counterfeits. That suggests they are having money problems."

Bart brushed the note aside, instantly dismissive. "That is old news. I've been tracking their expenditures for months, thanks to the bird I got into their home."

"Oh." Shan's hand fell to the side, hanging limp next to her skirt. "I did not realize."

"Well," Bart replied as he finished his sorting. "You have been busy, have you not? Can you burn these for me?"

Shan took the offered stack, cradling them close to her chest as she crossed to room to the hearth. The fire crackled merrily, its warmth welcome on these chill winter nights. Shan knelt down and fed the notes to it, the paper vanishing into smoke and ash between her fingers.

She shouldn't be disappointed, she knew that. She should be proud. Bart was incredibly skilled in this, just as skilled as she was, if she was being honest. Though the network of birds had been her creation, it now flourished without her.

If it wasn't for the blood in her veins and the last name she had never asked for, Bart would have no need of her at all. For that is what she was now—*his* bird, the one who flitted through the courts of Aeravin, collecting shiny little baubles to bring back and lay at his feet.

"About tonight," she began, only to feel Bart's hand land on her shoulder, startling her out of what she had been about to say. When had he snuck up on her? Months ago, that wouldn't have been possible, but here he was, still moving on silent feet while she had let her skills atrophy.

Just another difference that was coming to light, the gulf between them growing wider with each passing day.

Bart noticed her discomfort, giving her shoulder a reassuring squeeze. "It's all right, Shan. I know you haven't been sleeping well lately. Go get some rest, the girls will fill me in later."

Shan bit the inside of her cheek, tempering her anger with the sharp bite of pain. He had gotten it wrong, but why should she have expected different? When she had spent her life learning to hide all the worst bits of her, especially from those she loved the most. She had spent a lifetime walking careful circles around her brother, and now even Bart followed in his footsteps, leaving her behind.

She closed her eyes, took a deep breath, then accepted his hand as he helped her up. "Thank you, Bart, I think I shall retire."

"Of course," he replied, inclining his head towards her. "Goodnight, Shan."

As she approached the door, Shan gave him one last, long look as he got back to work. He was in his element, and she should stop resenting him for that. So, she took that anger, that bitter disappointment, and swallowed it down. She would lock it away with all the other ugly bits of her, never to be seen again.

And she would do the work she was called to do, no longer the Sparrow in the dark, but as Lady LeClaire, Royal Blood Worker, standing in the spotlight for all to see.

Chapter Six

Isaac

It wasn't the unknown heartbeat that got Isaac's attention, but the sudden snuffing of one, extinguished as quickly as a candle being blown out. The sudden lack is what pulled Isaac's attention, his awareness reaching out and snagging on the intruder as their heart didn't even stutter at the quick and casual violence, moving onward to the next Guard. Isaac could track the very path the assailant took, weaving through the floor above and leaving a path of dreadful, sudden silence in their wake.

Ironic, that thanks to the gag in his mouth and the chains he wore, he was not even able to warn his own personal Guards of the imminent danger.

Isaac wasn't sure if he would have bothered with it, if he could have. The Guards had not been overly cruel to him, and he wasn't treated any worse than the others who had earned the Eternal King's wrath. But they were still part of this broken, shattered system, and he had little sympathy for anyone who was simply following orders.

He couldn't help the cruel grin that cut across his face, hidden by the muzzle and twisted by the bit between his teeth, as the assailant crept down the stairs on silent feet. The assailant was tall and thin, dressed in all black, including the mask that covered their face. Most intriguing, though, was the lack of claws on their hands. If this was a Blood Worker, they were not using their magic, instead relying on a pair a wicked-looking daggers in their hands. There was no blood on them—no doubt the assailant had taken the time to clean the knives, if only to stop the telltale drips of blood onto the marble.

From his angle, back to the far wall and facing the bars that kept him in, he had the perfect view of the attack. The assailant moved quickly, closing in before the Guards had even noticed them, driving the blade of their dagger into the throat of the one on the left.

He dropped to his knees, his already arrhythmic heart beating wildly out of control. It wasn't a quick death, and Isaac would have cursed the assailant if he could, as they were moving towards the second Guard while the first still breathed.

Leaving a Blood Worker alive to heal their wounds, no matter how grievous they seemed, was an amateur mistake.

But as the uninjured Guard and the assailant continued to clash, circling around each other as they dodged their respective attacks, Isaac kept his eyes on the first man. He ripped the dagger from his own flesh, a geyser of red that splattered onto the floor as he let the dagger fall from his fingers. But the flesh wouldn't knit, the wound still gaping even as Isaac felt the man reach for his power ...

The scent of the blood itself was tainted, sour, and Isaac breathed the pungent taste of it in through his mouth. Poison.

The assailant was using poison, and Isaac barked a laugh of genuine surprise. There were few poisons that worked well against Blood Workers, and each of them was rare and expensive, but they were dreadfully effective. That Guard was as good as dead.

He turned his attention to the scuffle still happening—while he wasn't looking, the assailant had managed to slice their way across the Guard's arms and chest, a series of thin red lines that shouldn't have bothered the Blood Worker. But the poison worked too well, the blood flowing freely, spilling down the Guard's body in seeping waves of crimson.

Isaac could smell the taint on the blood, sour like fruit gone to rot, but he still ached to lap his tongue through the puddles that stained the marble floor.

The assailant drove the Guard against the cell, rattling the bars. Isaac couldn't see the exact exchange, but with the way the assailant moved their arm and the sudden, jerking motion of the Guard, he had an inkling of what happened.

His suspicions were confirmed a second later, when the Guard's heartbeat spluttered out of control.

Such a wound, a strike to the heart itself, would have been difficult for a skilled Blood Worker to heal, even without the stress of a battle. But with this poison that caused the blood to bleed free and fast?

The Guard was dead before she even hit the ground.

It was just the two of them, then. The assailant stood over the body, chest heaving, as they stared Isaac down.

Were they there to help him or kill him? It didn't really matter, in the end. Isaac knew what the King was saving him for, and he was just spiteful enough to let himself be killed in a way that would inconvenience the Eternal Bastard.

He just wished he had the ability and courage to do it himself.

But he'd take whatever—whoever—this was. Isaac steadied himself by digging his teeth in the leather bit as the stranger fished the keys from the Guard's corpse. They moved with quick efficiency, slipping the key in the lock and easing that great door free and stepping closer. They moved carefully, like they were approaching a rabid dog, and Isaac had to resist the urge to snarl.

Leaning back in his chair as much as he could, Isaac stared down his rescuer, daring them to do something. Anything.

"Now, I know you're an asshole," the stranger said, voice eerily familiar. "But please don't make this difficult."

He knew that voice all too well, but he couldn't imagine what he was doing here. Helping him. He had expected the fool to celebrate the day he died and dance on his grave. But the stranger stepped closer, pulling his mask down to rest around his neck and revealing himself.

Antonin LeClaire, throwing that too-casual smirk of his in Isaac's face, like he hadn't just slaughtered his way through the dungeons to stand before him. "Surprise!"

Isaac couldn't do more than grunt around the muzzle, but Anton offered him some small mercies, stepping forward to carefully remove the damned contraption. Isaac spluttered as the bit pulled free, his mouth aching and dry. He needed water, he knew this, but the twisting in his stomach craved something darker.

Something he couldn't bear to face.

So, he focused his attention on his rescuer, falling back into that old familiar pool of spite. They had never gotten along, but here Anton was, looking down at him with something akin to pity, and Isaac wanted to throw that back in his face.

"Well, if it isn't little Anton," he said, his voice harsh as steel dragged across stone. "I never thought you had it in you to be a killer."

Anton huffed, not even bothering to look insulted. "Sometimes you need to get your hands dirty to get the job done. Something I thought that *you* would understand."

The words hung heavy on the air, the weight of what he had become a miasma that followed him like a shroud. And the most galling part was that Anton was right—Isaac had learned the necessity of staining his soul in order to affect change.

He just didn't know if it was worth it yet.

Clearing his throat, he tried in vain to wet his lips. "Does Shan know?"

"What?" Anton's smile was cold and cruel; there was no trace of that foolish brat who had wormed his way into polite society. This Anton was one he did not know, and Isaac wasn't sure what to do with that. "That I can kill or that I am saving your worthless skin?"

"Both," Isaac croaked.

Anton tilted his head to the side, considering. "No," he said, after a long moment. "She doesn't. But save the rest of this interrogation for when you're safe, all right?"

Isaac nodded, admitting for the second time in short succession that Anton was right—an uncomfortable feeling that he would have to deal with later. Anton was already releasing the cuffs at his wrists and ankles that kept him bound to the chair, and Isaac eased into a standing position, ignoring the tingling feeling of pins and needles as he braced himself against the wall.

"Can you walk?" Anton asked, not unkindly.

Isaac's pride still felt a little bruised, even though he was well within his rights to ask. The Eternal King wanted him to be able to walk to his own death, and so the Guard kept him exercised as best they could. Though he was weaker than he had ever been, he wasn't fully atrophied. "I can."

"Then let's go." Anton pulled the mask back up, stepping towards the door and the growing spill of blood.

The unnatural thirst rose again, clawing its way up Isaac's throat as he eyed the fallen Guards. The metallic smell, copper and salt, filled his nose, and it took everything within him to not cast himself at the corpses and lick the sticky mess dripping from dead flesh.

He dashed across the cell to the table where the water pitcher rested, lifting the whole thing in his hands and drinking straight from the brim. The water was tepid and sour, nothing like the liquid he craved, but he downed it anyway. It eased some of the hunger in him, his throat no longer feeling quite so dry, the ache tempered.

He still craved the blood, but he had enough of a grip on himself to be able to walk past it.

Anton watched him from the doorway, brow furrowed in confusion. Isaac just dragged the back of his hand across wet lips. "Now, we go." He pushed past Anton, crossing past the pool of blood before his resolve snapped, praying that whatever he had unleashed within himself could be controlled.

He was proud of himself when he did not falter.

Anton caught up to him at the foot of the stairs, glancing at Isaac sidelong and pressing a finger to his own lips before taking the stairs two at a time. Isaac hurried after, trying his best to remain silent, even if it was unnecessary.

They turned onto the next floor, the administrative space between the dungeons below and the palace above, but it was as desolate as a graveyard. There were no bodies to be seen—Anton must have hidden them away behind the many doors, but it didn't matter. Isaac could hear the stifling silence, the sounds of life dwindled to the emptiness of death with the aftertaste of blood on the air.

Anton had been methodical and vicious, and Isaac felt his respect for the man growing by the minute.

In silence, he followed Anton through the dungeons, clearly retracing the path he had carved to find him. After this was over, Isaac would question him on where he got his intelligence, for he moved with the certainty of a man who knew his exact path, leading him not to the entrance that led up to the palace above, but to the side entrance where Guards and servants entered to do their duty.

There was still the matter of the blood ward, a shimmering barrier across the door, barely noticeable to the naked eye but zinging across his skin like little sparks of lightning. Before Isaac could question what came next, Anton was holding out his hand, a bracelet dangling from his fingers.

"You really thought of everything," Isaac said, as he slipped it around his wrist. He did not know whose blood it carried, exactly, but it must be attuned to the ward to grant them entry. His suspicion was confirmed as he reached his hand out, the ward splitting around his fingers as the hair on his arm raised.

"Your lack of faith is forever galling," Anton quipped as he pressed through the ward to ease the door open. It was a heavy thing, creeping forward by inches, as he peered out through the crack.

After a long moment, he slipped through, signaling for Isaac to follow. Isaac stepped out into the night, tasting fresh air for the first time in months. It was still Aeravin, the sounds of the city washing over him—the clap of horse hooves on cobblestones, the rattle of the carriages and hackneys as they rolled down the street, the soft sounds of indistinct conversation floating over him. The relief was so powerful that it felt like a punch to the gut, his grip loosening as the door fell from his fingers, closing behind him with a soft *thunk*.

Despite the promise that Samuel had whispered to him, all those weeks ago, he never believed that he would taste freedom again. That he even deserved it. Yet as he stood there, face tilted up towards the night sky and the stars above, he swore that he would never be a prisoner again.

Anton clapped him on the shoulder, a firm grip that steadied him. "Celebrate your freedom when we get away from here."

"Right." He turned to follow Anton, who eased along the side of the prison before ducking down a side alley. "Where are we going?"

"Someplace safe," Anton replied, pulling the mask off and tucking it away in one of the folds of his outfit—gone, like his daggers, hidden by a long winter cloak that help him blend in with the rest of the city. "Almost done."

Isaac followed him to the end of the alleyway, right as a hackney pulled up and came to a stop, blocking the rest of the street. Isaac only got the briefest look at the driver, a serious Black man dressed in the simple clothes of a driver-for-hire, but Isaac could have sworn he was Shan's personal secretary.

Before he could even ask, Anton was pulling him into the carriage. The door clicked shut and then they were off, rolling through the capital before Isaac's ass even hit the bench, leaving the prison and all those months of suffering behind.

Anton grinned, so terribly pleased with himself, as he tossed Isaac a long cloak. "Congratulations, de la Cruz. You're a free man again."

Chapter Seven

Samuel

The Aberforth townhouse was filled with more people than it had held in decades, and Samuel wasn't sure if he was more pleased or exhausted. Rooms that had been unused since the youth of his own father were aired out, a ballroom redone and draped in ivy and an array of summer's night-blooming flowers, the fresh fragrance the price of carefully managed Blood Working, a seemingly unjustifiable luxury in a time of rationing.

But Shan had been right—it was worth it for the mere gossip it would kindle.

The plans for this ball had been in the works for weeks, ever since he and Shan came to the conclusion that a marriage between them was too good an opportunity to pass up. It was easier to play into the expectations around them than waste precious time and energy building up alternative alliances, and a marriage was the perfect cover for all the times they would slip into each other's townhouses.

And it didn't hurt that Samuel was deeply, madly in love with Shan, so much so that he was willing to forgive the way she had to look at everything like a puzzle-box, studying it from all angles until she deemed it advantageous enough. It was only after that she had assured him that her heart was his either way, regardless of the official terms they put to it. But if they were to be engaged, they would do it properly, a show of force to Dameral and the rest of the country.

So, after all the work he had put into this, to ensure that it lived up to the standards expected of his bloodline, Samuel wanted nothing more than to sit back and bask in it. The ball was a resounding success, couples twirling across the dance floor as the soft music of the string quartet floated in the air. Their announcement had been met with cheers and applause, and they had spent the intervening hours accepting the congratulations of everyone and their brother.

And all Samuel wanted was a moment to just breathe.

But that was impossible, because even now, as he stood with a loosely held glass of wine in his hand, his gaze kept drifting to the large grandfather clock. Even at this very moment, Anton should be pulling Isaac from his cell—and there was absolutely nothing he could do to help. His job was to remain here, with Shan, to ensure that no matter what happened, the two of them had a solid alibi.

A warm hand brushed against the small of his back as Shan appeared at his side. She was a vision, dressed in a new dress from Laurens, a beautiful fall of silk in the same color as her Royal Blood Worker robes, lest anyone forget her position. Unlike her robes, however, this featured a low-cut bodice, the intricate embroidery drawing the eye to the delicate rise and fall of her breasts.

"Love," she said, voice pitched soft enough that it would not carry to the rest of the room, "you will make a poor host if you continue to ignore our guests."

"Forgive me," he replied, pressing his lips to her forehead in a gesture that he was used to reserving for moments of privacy. "I merely needed a moment."

The barest hint of sympathy shone in her eyes as she lowered her mask for a moment. "It has been a long night, but we're not through yet."

"I know." He held out his arm, allowed her to steer him back towards the party. She strode with her head held high, easily slipping back into the games of politics that was their lives.

She did not have to worry about Isaac; Samuel had worked hard to keep it that way. Whatever fear the King had put into her heart, Samuel only hoped that when this was over, she would forgive him.

That she would forgive them both.

But that was a question for later, and so he plastered his much-practiced Lord's smile onto his face as she steered them towards Lady Dunn and the rest of that little court. The young lords and ladies of Aeravin's oldest lines, the compatriots that Samuel should have been ingratiating himself with.

Despite the difficulty of working with the Council of Lords, sometimes Samuel was grateful for the excuses it gave him, sparing him from the worst of Shan's soirées.

"My, my, Shan," Lady Dunn said, giving Shan a most winsome smile. "Congratulations are most certainly in order. Lord Aberforth is quite a catch." She tossed Samuel a saucy wink, and he could feel the unstoppable blush creep up his cheeks. "And so modest, too."

Shan laughed, leaning in to chat like they were the dearest of friends, and Samuel squeezed the back of her arm in thanks. There was something about Amelia Dunn that always gave him pause, a kind of cunning craftiness that he recognized in his own fiancée, but without any of the caring he knew hid behind the mask. It was the most interesting study in contrasts, and if Samuel were a cleverer man he would be looking for ways to use this.

As it was, Samuel was content to let Shan handle the thorny bits of their politics, dazzling the court of Aeravin with her winning smiles and her endless cunning. He could play the doting husband, could live with the rumors that she was pulling him around on a leash, nothing more than a pampered pet who existed to please her.

Because, at the end of the day, it wasn't that far from the truth, and he did not care one bit what others thought of it.

His hand drifted across her back, landing on her waist and pulling her closer to him. He could feel the warmth of her skin through the layers of their clothes, and he wanted nothing more than to bury his face in her hair and breathe deep.

But there was a commotion echoing in the hallway, and as Samuel's young footman came hurrying into the ballroom with a panicked expression, he had to step away from Shan with a sigh. "I'll handle this, darling."

Shan gave him a soft peck on the cheek before turning her attention back to Lady Dunn, as well as the young Miss Lynwood and her beloved Miss Rayne, abandoning him to his duties.

The work of a host was never done.

He caught the boy's arm, carefully steering him away from the party and his overly interested guests. Only when they were out of earshot did Samuel speak, his voice low and quiet. "What is it, Frank?"

Despite the perfection of the boy's outfit and appearance—a simple but proper suit, a perfectly tied cravat, his dark hair slicked by from his eyes—Frank had the air of a man just this side of panic. "It's the King, Your Lordship, he is here and demanding a meeting."

Samuel's stomach lurched as the message processed. "The King is *here?*"

"Aye," Frank repeated, his hands twisting around themselves. "I have set him up in your study, but he is demanding to speak with you and Lady LeClaire. Immediately."

"Hells." Samuel glanced towards the grandfather clock again, its hands slipping even further into the night, and he knew what this was. He just hadn't expected it so soon. "Thank you, Frank. I will handle it from here."

"But," the boy sputtered, and Samuel couldn't help the swell of affection. Frank was a good boy, and a better servant than he deserved.

"Everything will be fine," Samuel reassured him, hoping that his smile was comforting enough. "Return to your post." Clapping him once on the shoulder, he turned to scan the crowd for Shan's signature red dress.

She had moved towards the windows with the rest of the group, the night cold and sharp through the panes of glass. Outside, snow had just started to fall—big, thick flakes that stood in sharp contrast to the roses that bloomed fresh on vines creeping up the walls of his ballroom.

Another study in contrasts that he wished he did not have to consider. But as much as he wanted to simply give up, this was the next stage in his game. And he had to face it with courage.

He swooped into the group, sliding his arm around his fiancée's waist. "If I might borrow my beloved for a moment..."

Lady Dunn only smirked at him, giving him a leering look from head to toe. "Far be it from us to impose."

Shan only laughed, giving Dunn a light little smack on the arm with the back of her hand—a teasing gesture, claws turned inward and away. "Behave, Amelia."

"If you think I'm going to give you the same advice," Lady Dunn returned, "you don't know me at all. He is just delectable."

Samuel cleared his throat, loudly, earning a round of laughs from the group. "Thank you, Lady Dunn."

"Ta ta," she cooed, throwing one last smirk his way as he started to pull Shan away.

Leaning in, Shan muttered, "Is something the matter?"

"I don't know," Samuel said, the lie bitter on his tongue. It was better if Shan didn't know yet; let her reactions be true and honest. It would be difficult enough to school his own response. "But the King is here and wishes to meet with us."

Her hand tightened on his arm, the pricks of her claws still noticeable even through the fabric of his suit. "I take it that he is not here to offer his official congratulations?"

Samuel huffed a short laugh. "Knowing him? Unlikely. But he is waiting for us in my study."

Shan only nodded, standing a little bit straighter, a little more confident. Though the Eternal King sought them out, they were in their element—this was their home, and in coming to them, the King had tipped his hand. They had the power, here, which is exactly what Samuel had hoped for.

Was this what it was like for Shan, with all her schemes and plans?

He was starting to understand her a bit better. Little victories like this were intoxicating.

The Eternal King was waiting for them, and he led Shan back through the house proper, up the grand staircase towards the room he had claimed for his own study. They paused on the landing, the music and conversations from below still audible, taking a moment to steady themselves for whatever was to come.

Meeting with the King still felt a bit like going to war, but Samuel only knocked once on the door before throwing it open. He pulled Shan in after him, not giving the King time to respond, and Shan gave him an approving squeeze.

She supported his boldness, and he could only hope that the King would as well.

But the King wasn't even looking at them, did not even seem aware of their presence. He was dressed as impeccably as ever; even with the grand ball that he had sidestepped completely, he still wore one of his many fine suits like armor, a kind of untouchable power that Samuel still did not know how to mimic. Despite the way that they mirrored each other, connected by a tie of blood that spanned more generations than Samuel wished to consider, for every bit of humanity in Samuel the King reflected it back in stone.

And yet, tonight the King exuded an air of frustration and anger so palpable it nearly choked them, even as he stood with his back to the door, peering into Samuel's liquor cabinet, which still existed mostly for appearance's sake. Even with the issue of his gift nullified by Isaac's interventions, Samuel preferred to stay away from the hard liquors.

Navigating this world was difficult enough while sober.

Still, he was thankful that Jacobs insisted on keeping it stocked as the King helped himself to a glass of bourbon, the amber liquid sloshing into a pair of crystal glasses as the King poured with a heavy hand.

It was an unusually aggressive motion from the usually restrained Eternal King, and that brief moment of confidence Samuel felt shattered, souring into the bitter taste of fear.

Perhaps he had been too bold after all.

"Your Majesty?" Shan asked carefully, stepping forward. Something in her had changed, suddenly, like a lever had been thrown. Lady LeClaire was gone, and in her place was the Royal Blood Worker, ready for duty. "What has happened?"

The King did not respond immediately—shockingly, he just passed her the first glass before downing his own. It was strange to think that the King knew their habits and preferences so well.

Shan just held her glass in loose fingers, the tension ratcheting even tighter as the silence dragged on.

Finally, the King dropped his empty glass onto Samuel's desk with a *thud*, his gaze dark and expression grim. There was something just this edge of feral about it, in the way his green eyes glinted like gemstones and his lips pulled into a snarl. "There has been a breakout," he began, voice low with rage. "Somehow, Isaac de la Cruz has escaped, and he left a trail of bodies in his wake."

The glass fell from Shan's hand, shattering into pieces as it hit the floor, the bourbon seeping slowly into the wood. Samuel had never seen Shan so flustered, her mouth forming the shape of words without a single sound being uttered.

The King noticed it as well—this wasn't a reaction that could be faked, and of course he would suspect her first and foremost. She was the schemer.

Samuel was the pawn.

He put his hand at the small of her back, stepping into the conversation with a single word. "How?"

"Now that is the question," the King seethed. Samuel was still getting used to it, the sheer force of the King's power, something he had been unable to pick up on before.

Another gift from the very man they were discussing. It was a thorny mess of emotions, from the bruising betrayal that Samuel had nursed alone on long, lonely nights to the unrelenting relief from being free of the Aberforth Gift. To the uncomfortable realization that after spending a lifetime believing himself to be Unblooded, he was a Blood Worker after all.

So, when the King saw that reflected in the expressions that Samuel had not yet learned to master, he missed the very thing Samuel needed him to. The relief that his plan was working—*had* worked. Now he just had to see it through.

"What do we do?" Shan said, finally shaking her uncertainty.

The King nodded, settling into Samuel's chair and steepling his fingers. This was the way he preferred it, both of them turning to him like he was the master of them all. Yes, they had their roles, but in the end, the King expected them to serve.

Samuel couldn't wait for the day when they needn't grovel any longer.

"I'm sorry to interrupt your engagement ball, truly," the King said, inclining his head with an artfully designed expression of sorrow. It was almost believable, it might have been, if Samuel hadn't been learning the contours of the King's lies, the way he was too perfect, too exact. "I know how much work the both of you put into it. But you needed to know as soon as I did. We must begin work first thing in the morning to rectify this—we cannot let them spin the narrative."

"Naturally," Shan agreed, with a slight sneer. "Those pamphleteers haven't stopped."

The King clenched his fist on the table—a bit of frustration that did not feel entirely affected—and nodded. "Quite. Tomorrow, I need my Councillor of Law to get ahead of this. What happened tonight was a disgrace, and we need to ensure that this does not happen again. If they will not listen to reason, perhaps they will respond to fear."

He did not wait for Samuel's response—there was no need to. Despite the bile that burned the back of his throat, Samuel couldn't contradict him directly. Instead, the King turned to Shan. "And while he sees to that, we will need something else to distract the presses from this. Tell me you have a solution to the problem of the blood supply, Shan. Give me anything to work with."

For his Royal Blood Worker, he would give a moment to respond, an opportunity of agency that Samuel hadn't earned.

He tried to not let the jealousy hurt.

Shan, for her part, merely inclined her head, looking strangely resigned. "I have an idea, Your Majesty. But I need a little time to finalize the details. Can I present the proposal to you tomorrow?"

They waited for a long moment as the King considered, then he nodded. "Very well, LeClaire. I'll have my secretary reach out to yours. Tomorrow, then." Standing, he cast a final look at Samuel. "And the same to you, son, once you've handled things with the Guard."

And with that, he saw himself out, leaving them behind, shaken, like a storm that had swept through their lives and left it uprooted.

Meetings with the King often felt like that.

Turning to Shan, Samuel caught her hands, pressed his lips to the back of them. "Your plan, what is it?"

Shan curled her fingers around his, gentle with her claws on his soft gloves. "Let me finalize it first, Samuel. It's ... complicated." Closing her eyes, she let out a long sigh, a bit of vulnerability that she wouldn't have dared show even a moment before. "Besides, the question of Isaac is far more pressing."

"Ah, about that." He braced himself—deceiving the King, while terrifying, was one thing. Deceiving Shan—he still wasn't sure if that had been the right thing to do. "I have something I need to tell you."

"Oh?" Shan said, infusing the word with so much weight that Samuel felt fear slice right through him.

"It's a long story, but first," he pulled back, "let us finish this party. Then, we shall meet with Isaac."

He waited for her response, expecting anger, but she only raised her hand to her temple and groaned. "Blood and fucking steel, Samuel."

Chapter Eight

Shan

Shan quietly fumed the whole way over to the safe house.

There had not been a moment to discuss things since Samuel dropped the revelation, as he ushered her back to the ballroom to handle the end of the Engagement Ball. It was lucky that it was already so late into the evening and that one of Samuel's servants let it slip that the King had dropped by.

She would have to give that boy a bonus later; that was quite well done. He had allowed them to break up the party with a minimal amount of fuss. Duty called, and if people were to gossip about the Eternal King's private business, all the better.

But still, little over an hour later they were cutting their way across the city, taking advantage of the recently relaxed curfew laws. The streets were not as bustling as they had been before all this had started, but they were not the only souls on the move, scurrying along with their heads dipped low. There was still the bitter scent of fear on the air, but Shan could use that as they crept along the shadows, having traded their fine clothes for something simpler. In this moment, they were not a Lord and Lady of Aeravin, but two anonymous souls in the night.

It was difficult for her to admit, but Shan missed this. The freedom of being the Sparrow, the excitement of learning every dark and depraved secret, the thrill of taking that ill-gained knowledge and solving the greatest puzzles of the kingdom. Being the Royal Blood Worker was its own sort of thrill, but it had never been the path she wanted to walk.

But there was no bringing it back, especially now. With Isaac's escape—rescue—whatever this foolish plan of Samuel's was, any progress they had made in the last few months would be swept away.

Undone in a heartbeat, and for what?

She just hoped that Isaac would be worth it. No matter how she cared for the man—and oh, did she still long for him—one life was not worth the price of an entire nation whose peace hung by the thinnest of threads.

Samuel lifted a hand, and she came to an immediate stop. They had never worked like this before—there had never been a chance to train him in this, to test how he would handle the darker side of her work, but they fell into such an easy and natural rhythm, as if they had been doing this their whole lives.

Samuel was her perfect match in every way, which only made this hurt all the more, a wound deeper than any of her daggers or claws could cut. The way that he had gone against her wishes, had organized it all behind her back?

She didn't know if she should be proud or heartbroken.

Inclining his head ever so slightly, Samuel indicated the building ahead. It was very similar to the last safe house she had found her brother in, if in a completely different neighborhood. One door in and out, a townhouse in the midst of a row of townhouses, the windows covered in dark curtains that were not entirely out of place. As defensible as any such building could be, as anonymous as any other home in the capital.

It had been months since she had spoken with her brother, but she was still so damned proud of him.

Samuel pulled out a key and unlocked the door, stepping into a narrow hallway, lit by the slowly dripping candles above. No witch light here, though she wasn't surprised, with the rationing. The other doors were closed, no doubt hiding away some part of her brother's little rebellion, but she didn't care about that. Not when Samuel was leading her with such surety towards the stairs.

"You and Anton are quite close these days, then?" she said, at last, the bitterness she had been trying so hard to swallow bleeding out. He paused, turning back to look at her with an expression so open, so hurt, that she regretted speaking at all.

The rift between her and Anton was a mess of her own making, and she had drawn Samuel right into the mire with her.

"Come on, Shan. It will be easier to explain this only once." He continued up the stairs, leaving her behind, and she had to hurry to follow, one step behind.

They climbed the stairs, passing even more closed doors hiding secrets that she itched to ferret out, but Samuel kept climbing, story after story, till they emerged into something like a loft on the topmost floor.

It was a well-appointed, if small, flat, filled with simple but sturdy furniture. There was a small kitchenette against the far wall, a set of low couches by the windows that overlooked the street, and a small shelf filled with a collection of second-hand novels. It was simple and homey, made even more so by the sight of her brother sprawled out on the couch, his head resting in Bart's lap.

She took quick stock of their outfits, Bart wearing the uniform of a hackney driver while Anton lounged in the same outfit he would wear while working the network they had created. Comfortable leathers, designed for ease of movement, dark as the shadows through which they slipped.

"Sister," Anton drawled, barely bothering to look at her. It was so lazy, so bored, that she immediately bristled.

"Not tonight," Bart warned, dragging his hand through Anton's hair like he was soothing an angry cat. It had grown long in the past few months, the carefully maintained hairstyle her brother once prided himself on now shaggy and messy. There was a roughness to him that Shan hadn't seen in a long time, a break from the carefully cultivated image he had worked so hard on.

She wasn't sure if it was a sign of freedom or failure, and she hated that she didn't know her own twin well enough to tell the difference anymore, if she had even known him in the first place.

"Bart's right," Samuel said, stepping in before things could get even more awkward. "We're here for Isaac. How did it go?"

Anton flicked his gaze towards Samuel, the tension bleeding out of him with a sigh. "Fine. He was cleaning up in the washroom, but you can probably check in on him."

Shan made a harsh movement towards her brother, but he just shook his head, stopping her. "There'll be time for that later, Shan. See to your man."

Her man.

That's what Isaac was, wasn't he?

Hers.

And Samuel's. Once, they had dreamed of a future with the three of them, together. A united front who could come together to make Aeravin better, stronger, fairer. But Isaac had been playing the game with an entirely different set of rules, even if she hadn't realized at the time. And now, she didn't know where they stood, if they could even begin to repair all the ways that they were broken.

But Samuel had risked everything to save this man that they loved, and blood and steel, she owed them both this much.

She knocked once on the bedroom door before throwing it open.

Isaac was sitting on the bed, head in his hands, before looking up at the intrusion, shock flitting across his expression before he shuttered it into something colder, harsher. It had only been days since she saw him last, in the King's own dungeons, but it was much the same. A flicker of what once had been, before he hid it away, waiting to see if it was safe to share before making the first move.

Just like she did.

Hells, they really were the perfect pair, weren't they?

Samuel, though, let out a wordless cry of pure happiness, crossing the room in three large steps before he plopped onto the bed at Isaac's side. He pressed Isaac against him, his hand caressing Isaac's cheek as he whispered sweet murmurings. Isaac hesitated for only a moment before melting into the embrace, shifting to bury his face in Samuel's shoulder.

And Shan had never felt more like an intruder in her life.

She closed the door behind her, buying them a modicum of privacy from the others in the next room before joining them on the bed. They froze as her weight dipped the mattress, Isaac's dark gaze wary and questioning. But she held out one hand, an offering, and after only the slightest waver of indecision Isaac took it, twining his fingers with hers.

He pulled her into the embrace, and she let herself fall, knowing that she would be caught by the two men she loved the most in the whole damned world.

For a few moments they didn't move at all, tangled together in a mess of limbs and shared breath, the heady sandalwood scent of Samuel's cologne blending with the sharp tang of the cheap soap Isaac had used. It was the closest thing she had known to peace in a long time, and she never wanted it to end.

But it had to, because no matter how much she wanted time to stop, it kept marching on. And their Eternal King had expectations of them.

She was the first to lean back, to dash the tears from her eyes and straighten her spine. "Isaac," she said, firmly. "Samuel. We need to get our story straight."

Isaac huffed a laugh, soft and breathy. "Still the same, aren't you?"

"Someone needs to ensure we keep our heads," Samuel said, running his hand down Shan's arm. "Right?"

"As always," Isaac agreed. He shifted back, adjusting the pillows and leaning against the headboard. He looked so tired, a detail Shan should have noticed sooner. He was thinner than he had been, before his imprisonment, the dark circles under his eyes even more prominent, but despite the way the King and his Guards had treated him, that spark in his eyes still shone.

His ordeal hadn't broken him, and Shan allowed herself to feel the rush of relief at the realization.

"So," Shan began, turning her sharp gaze onto Samuel and watching him wither. "Why don't you fill me in?"

Samuel flushed that pretty shade of pink that she loved so much, but just cleared his throat and began. He laid out the plan that he had concocted with Anton, the way they had arranged it to fall on this night so that the King and all the rest of Dameral would not suspect their involvement. The way Samuel had decided to shield her from it, for her own protection.

She noticed the way he spoke around her fears, the way she had argued to leave Isaac to his fate. Whether it was a kindness to her or a kindness to Isaac, she did not know, but either way, she was thankful.

He was learning so much at her side—the Samuel of a year ago would have never thought to work such a scheme. She should have felt pride at his growth. Instead, she feared that she was ruining him forever.

But Isaac had taken over the storytelling, laying out how he had been rescued, the lengths to which Anton went to rescue him. As good as a liar as he was, even he couldn't hide the disbelief. She looked to Samuel—only he could have managed this.

The things that man could do, if only he had the opportunity.

Still, it was good to have the full story, and Shan rubbed her temples as she considered the mess she had gotten into. "I know you are aware that I am Royal Blood Worker now," she said at last, only for Isaac to look so genuinely pained that she almost lost her train of thought. "It's all right, Isaac. We have been using this to our advantage."

"But," he began, only for her to silence him by placing a finger to her lips.

"Hush," she instructed. "But nothing. I am the Royal Blood Worker, but Samuel is the Councillor of Law. And between our respective positions, we should be able to smooth things over. But you will need to be careful for the time being. And then we'll need to figure out how to get you out of Aeravin."

"Out?" Isaac echoed, his voice low and rough. He stilled like an animal caught in a trap, afraid the wrong move would get him killed. "What do you mean *out*?"

Shan blinked slowly, refusing to let the confusion stop her. "You are now the most wanted fugitive in the country, Isaac. You cannot expect to stay."

He leaned forward, fists tangling in the sheets. "And what? You expect me to run away? Leave the fight to others?"

"What fight?" she asked, enunciating each word with care. "There is nothing more you can do. Samuel and I are working to bring change to Aeravin—change that rescuing you has set back quite significantly, I might add—but we can only do that so long as we remain in our positions."

"Shan," Samuel interjected, but she ignored him, focusing on the look that Isaac was giving her.

The disappointment in those eyes, affection turned sour, trust turned to disbelief.

"Please," she breathed, already prepared to beg. "Understand that I am doing this out of love."

"Love," Isaac scoffed. "Shan, I don't know what this is, but it isn't love. It's control." He shifted, kneeling on the bed so that their faces were so close, breath shared between them in some mockery of intimacy. "And I won't let myself be controlled anymore, even by you, darling."

Anger clawed its way into her, overriding the hurt and shame that she could not let herself feel. But Samuel was already moving, inserting himself between them before the fight could begin.

"Please," Samuel said, with one hand on Shan's shoulder and the other on Isaac's, forcing them apart. "Not tonight. Whatever this is . . . we have time to work it out."

She met Isaac's eyes, inclined her head. Samuel was right—this wasn't the time for it. Isaac was still recovering; he needed time to come to terms with all that he had lost. With enough space, he would understand that this was the only way they could keep him safe.

So, she could agree to a truce for now.

"It's been a long day," she admitted, twisting so that her feet rested on the floor. "And I have much to prepare for tomorrow."

"That is understandable," Isaac said, not unkindly. But there was still a wariness to him, and she knew she wouldn't be able to reach him tonight. She wouldn't be able to reach him for a long while, but she had learned the art of patience, and for him, she could play this game once more.

She leaned back, brushed her lips against his. If nothing else, this would be a reminder that, no matter what, she still cared about him. It would be easier to tear the heart from her own chest than to lose the love she had for Isaac.

She just had to remind him of that.

"Goodnight, Isaac."

Isaac blinked up at her, nodding slowly. "Shan, I . . ." He cut himself off, and Shan wished she knew what he had almost said. "We'll see each other soon?"

"We will," she promised, then looked to Samuel. He only shook his head—he would be staying then. That was fine.

Let them have a moment without her. After all they had been through—all that they had done to each other—they likely needed it. This love had been born in a web of lies and betrayal, but that didn't make it any less true.

She let herself out of the bedroom, blinking away the last of her tears.

Anton and Bart were both looking at her strangely, but Shan couldn't let them see the weakness in her heart. She needed them to see her as strong. She needed to *be* strong.

Else she would crumble before this next stage of her plans even began.

"Bart," she said, her voice clear and commanding. "Let's head home. We have a lot of work to do."

Chapter Nine

Isaac

Isaac watched Shan leave with his heart in his hands, wishing he knew the right combination of words and actions to reach her. But Shan had built herself up so strong and proud that he might as well have been reaching for a statue carved of ice, all his pretty words falling like dust at her feet. No matter how desperately he wished to mend their bridges, there was an entire chasm between them.

He had helped dig it just as much as she had, through actions great and small, and he would regret that for the rest of his life. So, he just stared at the closed door between them, listening wordlessly as she spoke with Anton and Bart, the trio of them disappearing out into the night, leaving him behind again.

Well, at least he wasn't alone. Samuel had remained with him, still nestled close and resting his head on Isaac's shoulder. It was a comfort that Isaac knew he did not deserve, and as much as he wanted it—as much as he wanted so much more—there were too many unresolved hurts that they needed to address first. And just like with Shan, the blame was his to bear. More so, even, because Samuel had never done anything to earn Isaac's cruel side.

He closed his eyes, took a deep steadying breath, then turned to Samuel. "We should talk."

Samuel didn't respond for a moment, just dragged his gloved

fingers against the soft skin along the inside of Isaac's wrist. It was such a strange touch, separated not by claws but a thin layer of cloth, the silken glide raising gooseflesh on his skin. "If you'd like."

It was an opening, an out, and some craven part of Isaac wanted to seize upon it. To bury the pain in the past where it belonged. But he was wise enough to know that there was nothing worse than letting it fester, and he would not lose Samuel to his own cowardice in the same way he was so close to losing Shan.

"I would," Isaac breathed, taking Samuel's hand in his. He ran his thumb along the edge of the glove, slipping it underneath to the warmth of bare flesh. "May I?"

Samuel's hand landed on his, holding it fast. "You don't have to do this, Isaac."

"I do." It hurt him more than he thought it would, but he had to see it for himself. He had to understand what he had done to Samuel if he could ever begin to ask for forgiveness.

Because without that, whatever this was between them had to come to an end.

"Fine," Samuel agreed, at last, pulling away. "But know that I do not blame you. You did what you had to do."

Samuel rose, turning away from the bed as he removed the gloves, laying them on the low wooden dresser that Anton had been kind enough to stock with simple clothes for him. Isaac looked away as he heard Samuel shift, pulling his shirt from his trousers.

Ah, this was how it was going to be, then. Isaac would have to grapple with the full extent of the wounds he left on Samuel's body, the mistakes of his hubris and his desperation to prove himself. The Aberforth Gift was a weight that Samuel should not have had to bear, but it had not been Isaac's decision to make.

The shirt fluttered to the floor as Samuel inched closer to the bed, his bare fingers brushing against Isaac's cheek. "Look at me, love."

Isaac allowed himself to be guided, his gaze caught on the full expanse of bare flesh in front of him. Yes, the after-effects of his Blood Working still lived on, deep, dark scars following the lines of Samuel's veins, each and every artery sketched out on skin pale like ivory. It created a map that Isaac wanted to follow, tracing every line with his tongue, even though he was the villain that had put them there.

He twisted his fingers into the bed sheets to keep from reaching out, but Samuel only smiled down at him, daring Isaac to look his fill. There was a softness to Samuel's body, now, the life and wealth of his found family allowing him to fill out more, and Isaac wanted to explore each and every inch of it. But Samuel's hand drifted to his trousers, slung low across his hips, his thumb brushing against the soft trail of fair hair as his fingers toyed with the button. "There is more to see, if you are interested."

"Samuel." Isaac ground out his name with a growl, but Samuel only smiled, the teasing edge replaced by something softer. The same gentleness and kindness that Isaac had been so desperately smitten with in the first place, treating him with compassion that he did not deserve.

"There is no need for you to restrain yourself," Samuel said, sinking to his knees at the edge of the bed. The shift brought them eye to eye, close enough to touch.

Isaac still held himself back. "I need you to know that I am sorry." The confession spilled from him, a jumble of words and wants with little sense. "I should not have done it in that way, I only meant to—"

He was stopped by the press of Samuel's mouth to his, all his words swallowed as Samuel tangled his hands in his hair. "I know," Samuel whispered back. "I did not want that power, anyway..." He let out a deep sigh of relief. "I am truly glad that it is gone. As for your methods, I forgive you. I will say it as many times as you need to hear it."

The dam that was his self-control crumbled at last, and Isaac pulled Samuel onto the bed with him, spread his thighs so that Samuel could nestle between them. Samuel laughed, catching himself on either side of Isaac, his weight a comforting pressure.

"You're too good to me," Isaac swore, allowing himself to finally feel all that skin, tracing his fingers through the soft, barely perceptible hair along Samuel's chest.

"Somebody has to be," Samuel breathed. "And I am more than willing to be that man."

If there was one thing that Isaac had regretted, all those months in his cell, it was that he had never had a chance to know Samuel like this. Their timing had been poor, the very world in which they had lived and the magic in both their veins conspiring to keep them apart. A handful of stolen kisses and promises never fulfilled, but now they were finally together at last.

Isaac caught Samuel's lips with his, rolling them so that he pressed Samuel back into the mattress. His hand splayed against Samuel's chest, holding him firmly in place, and Isaac could feel the thrum of excitement as Samuel's heartbeat kicked faster. Hells, Samuel was looking up at him through heavy-lidded eyes, the pupils so blown that they were swallowing up nearly all the green, and that dark hunger stirred in him again.

That want he dared not face as Samuel bared his throat to the beast, tempted by the vein that throbbed so prettily, plump and full of blood.

Burying his face in the dip between Samuel's neck and shoulder, Isaac bit down on muscle with blunt teeth. "Can I touch you?" he begged, desperate to trade one hunger for another, even as Samuel squirmed beneath him.

"I think I might die if you don't," Samuel muttered, but kept his hands firmly clenched at his side. Biting his lip, he stared up at Isaac through his eyelashes, looking suddenly unsure. "But ... is there anything I should know? Any way you won't like to be touched? Any things you would not like me to do? Words I should not say?"

"Oh." Isaac rocked back on his heels, giving them both some space as the kindness of Samuel's asks hit him. Truly, he hadn't stopped to think about it—his lovers had been few and far between, and with Shan it had been different. She had been with him when he had begun transitioning, had learned the ways of his body and his pleasure along with him, but Samuel did not have the same base of knowledge.

Still, he was touched by the question, dipping forward to press a gentle kiss on Samuel's brow. "You're sweet, darling, and I appreciate that. I am fairly easy to please, but if you'd like details..."

He shifted off the bed, standing proudly in front of Samuel, the feeling of being so on display sending frissons of desire to his core. Pulling his shirt off, Isaac tossed it to the ground where it landed on top of Samuel's. Anton had been unable to provide him with a binder yet, something that Isaac did not blame him for in the least, so his small breasts hung free, Samuel's eyes latching onto them with an immediacy that made Isaac smirk.

"You can touch me here, if you'd like," Isaac said, raking his fingers through the dark hair his treatments had sprouted across his chest and between his breasts, circling his thumb across his sensitive nipple as a jolt of pleasure shot straight to his rapidly hardening dick. "You can use your hands, your mouth, even your cock. Or, if you'd prefer..."

He trailed his other hand down lower, still teasing his nipples in the meantime, but Samuel's heavy gaze followed the path down until Isaac hooked his thumb in his trousers, taking care to ensure he snagged the edge of his underclothes as well, shoving them down in one motion before he kicked them to the side. Samuel's gaze caught on the heat between Isaac's legs, his tongue peeking out to wet dry lips.

"Or you can touch me here," Isaac continued, spreading his lower lips to let his cock bob free, hard and straining. He could feel it throb, eager for touch, but he restrained himself, savoring the ache as Samuel stared.

Samuel swallowed hard, and when he spoke, his voice was low and rough with want. "And do you like to be penetrated?"

Isaac hummed to himself as he considered. "Not often," he admitted. "I like to be sucked, I like to frot, but..."

"That's okay with me," Samuel said. "But... I think I would be open to you doing that to me, if you are amenable."

"Oh, I most certainly am." The image was burned into his brain just from the suggestion, Samuel splayed open underneath him, taking his strap so sweetly. He knew he couldn't do it this night—his cock wasn't that large, he wouldn't be able to penetrate Samuel like many other men could, but he was nothing if not creative.

And there was so much fun they would have once they had the right toys, so he needed to make getting them a priority.

"We don't have the tools for that now," Isaac purred. "But I'm sure we can think of something."

He prowled forward and Samuel fell back on the bed, almost instinctively, offering up himself as Isaac slid over him, dragging the heel of his hand against the hard length in his trousers. Samuel let out a small whimper at the touch, bucking against the stimulation, and oh, was Isaac going to enjoy this.

He had respected the need Samuel had for taking it slow, for ensuring that his gift was managed or contained, but blood and steel, had Isaac wondered how he would be in bed. If he would be just as needy and desperate as Isaac hoped. There was a delicious tension bubbling under all their interactions, a heady desire that was always at the edge of boiling over.

And Isaac would not be satisfied until he had all that Samuel was willing to give.

Catching Samuel's mouth with his, Isaac pulled the other man into a scorching kiss as he worked Samuel's cock through the scant layers of clothes left between them, using the friction to bring him to full hardness.

"Please," Samuel babbled, his hands scrabbling at Isaac's waist. "Please, please, please."

Isaac couldn't help himself, he laughed low and dark, charmed by the way Samuel was already unraveling under his touch. "Please what, darling? You need to use your words."

Samuel's teeth dug into his lower lip as he blushed, and Isaac was thrilled to see that it spread past his face—his neck and chest turning the same charming shade of pink. "Please," Samuel begged. "Use me."

Isaac's cock twitched. "If you insist."

He ripped the rest of the man's clothing off, leaving them both bare, before lowering his face to lap at Samuel's length. Samuel keened as Isaac's tongue made contact with the silky skin, licking up the underside before suckling so gently at the tip. He leaked into Isaac's mouth, so wet and eager, and it took all of Isaac's self-control to not just mount him right there.

This would work perfectly.

Shifting forward, Isaac spread his legs as he hovered over his lover's waist, positioning Samuel's cock so that it nestled between his own slick folds. Rocking back and forth, he spread his own wetness along Samuel's length, smoothing the glide, before pitching forward to rub his dick against the hardness trapped between them.

It felt so good that Isaac nearly came right there.

But he had waited so long for this, and Samuel's eyes were wet with tears, his hips jerking forward in harsh, minute thrusts, and Isaac would not let this first time be wasted. He would take Samuel like this, bracing his hands on each side of Samuel's head, until they both came.

He continued rocking, his muscles burning as he took care to grind his cock against Samuel's without crushing him. His breath came in harsh gasps, his words caught somewhere in the back of his throat, but he didn't need them. Not when Samuel ran his large hands up his sides until he found Isaac's tits. The touch was warm and shocking, Samuel fondling their weight in his palms before catching the nipples between his nails, giving them a sharp tug.

Isaac groaned as the shock went straight to his cunt, leaking even more slick as their rutting grew rougher, more desperate. Samuel writhed beneath him, more senseless babble falling from his lips as he continued to thrust along the warmth of Isaac's cunt, as Isaac took and took and took, his pleasure coalescing into a sharp ache.

"Please, I'm ... ah ... close," Samuel cried, tossing his head to the side, his neck long and bare and so, so warm.

Snarling, Isaac pressed closer, sinking blunt teeth into the tender flesh off Samuel's throat and sucking hard—a gentler replacement for the violence he still craved. And yet, Samuel tensed as he came, his spend splattering between them as Isaac jerked one last time, feeling his cock tremble and throb as he found his own release.

He collapsed to the side, pressed up against Samuel as he pulled the trembling man into his arms. They laid like that for several long minutes, the sweat and the come cooling on their skin, but Isaac did not care. All he cared about was the steady beat of heart next to him, the contented sigh as Samuel nuzzled into his embrace.

As long as he had Samuel, he could handle whatever came next.

Chapter Ten

Shan

The Parliament House was quiet this early in the morning, but when Shan had scheduled this meeting, she had thought it best to get it out of the way as early as possible, immediately following her meeting with the King. She had presented her plan to him with little fanfare, and he had agreed to it just as easily as she had hoped he would.

With a gleam in his eye that spoke of something deeper than pride, he dismissed her to the Parliament House, tasked with carrying out his will.

She followed the footman through the marble halls, her blood-red robes flowing behind her and the clacking of her heels reverberating in the empty air. Even so early, she knew that she had to make a statement, just in case. Shan could never be caught at anything less than her best, even if she was exhausted from spending the entire night tweaking the details of her plan, going over every word with care and intention.

News of Isaac's escape was still being kept quiet, for the moment, and she understood the King's desire to move quickly. Her proposal was bold, and it would solve so many problems, which is precisely why now was the moment to unveil it. She had been trying for weeks to come up with something else, anything else, to fill the gap.

Aeravin was built on a sea of blood, and there was only so long they could continue to tread water. This proposal would solve all of their issues, but it wouldn't be without its share of detractors. Samuel, especially, would hate it, but she had run out of time. He had forced her hand, whether he realized it or not, and he would have to live with the consequences of that. For Isaac's life, she could bear the weight.

She just prayed that Samuel could as well.

The footman let her into the private chambers of the Royal Council, a room she hadn't been in since that night she had brought her father's blood to be tested. So much had changed since then, the slow game she had thought she had been playing turned into something much more. No longer just a LeClaire, searching for every scrap of information and power that she could get her inferior hands on, but the Royal Blood Worker. Right hand to the King in every way that mattered.

Someone with just as much power and authority as any of the other faces before her, and she greeted them with a fierce smile. All five of them, waiting patiently for her arrival, the same serious and grim faces that she had faced at the start of it all, bar one.

Samuel sat on the left-hand side at the edge of the curved table, gloved hands folded in front of him. He was dressed in one of the many fine suits she had arranged for Laurens to make him, looking as delectable as a treat, even so covered up.

She deliberately averted her gaze from him—the news of their engagement had no doubt spread, but she had earned this position on her own merits, whether she wanted it or not.

"Lady LeClaire," Belrose said, from her seat at the center of the table. She was just finishing out her term as the leader of the Council before it shifted to Lady Holland when the next Season began. It felt almost nostalgic, being back here again, as she began her speech.

"Lady Belrose," Shan returned, inclining her head. "And all the esteemed members of the Royal Council. I am sorry to call you all here so early, but there is a proposal that needs your attention." She laid down her portfolio on table, opening it to pull out several hand-copied pages summarizing her plans. "The full details of the plan will be delivered to your offices this afternoon, but the salient details can be found here."

She started at the end of the table opposite Samuel, as if delaying the inevitable would solve any of her problems. But as she handed the last page to him, she hesitated just long enough for him to scan it, just long enough for his expression to twist into unfiltered disgust.

Unable to bear the weight of his judgement, she turned her attention back to the others, waiting with her hands folded demurely in front of her.

"Well," Belrose said after several long moments of silence, her eyebrows raised so high that they nearly brushed against her hairline. "This is ... bold. But I suppose we should expect that from you, Lady LeClaire."

"I am well aware that it is unorthodox," Shan replied, "but we live in unprecedented times, and sometimes that calls for equally unprecedented measures."

"It would certainly solve our issues," Morse added, drumming her fingers on the table. "And I believe a more accurate adjective for this plan would be *ingenious*."

Shan bit back a smile as a rush of relief coursed through her. Getting the first vote of confidence was always the trickiest part. After that, the rest would fall like dominoes.

To that end, Lady Belrose had managed to school her expression, nodding along with Morse's assessment, and Lord Rayne looked positively gleeful, a more active response than she had expected from the old man. Lady Holland merely looked thoughtful, perhaps a bit unconvinced, but she had expected that from the Councillor of Industry.

It would be the details in the full plan that would eventually convince her, with her head for numbers and her books of data. There was no sentimentality in that woman, and in moments like this, Shan was thankful for it.

Which only left Samuel, who looked positively thunderous—which was an issue, as this plan would fall directly under his purview.

"You cannot be serious," Samuel said, speaking up at last, and

Shan had to control her grimace. She had heard him take up that tone before, that righteous fury that threatened to see the entire world burn. Once, she had hoped to harness it, bend it to her will and use his anger to her own ends. Once, she had wanted nothing more than to light him up and watch him burn.

But never did she expect to see that fury turned on her.

"Oh, come now, Aberforth," Rayne interjected, coming to her rescue, but Samuel silenced him with a glare so regal and imperious that it took Shan's breath away.

What a terrible influence Shan had been on him, taking the sweetest boy she had ever met and turning him into a Blood Worker like the rest of them.

"Let him speak," Shan said, surprising even herself. "As it affects his realm most of all."

Silence fell over the hearing chamber, the kind of heavy quiet that was used when someone was being patronized. She wondered if Samuel was adept enough to recognize it.

Or if he even cared at all.

"Affects my realm," Samuel repeated with a sneer that reminded Shan of the Eternal King. "As if, under this plan, it wouldn't be my hands getting dirty." He crushed the paper in his fist, all of Shan's careful work transcribing it ruined in seconds. "Taking increased Blood Taxes from criminals. It's inhumane."

Shan did not allow herself to so much as blink. This was the response she had anticipated, the reason why she had struggled for so long to find any other viable solution, when this was sitting right there.

Ready to be taken advantage of.

The open disdain still hurt though, a reminder of all the ways he had faith in her, and all the ways she continued to come up short.

"Aberforth, please," Morse groaned, rubbing at her temple. She spoke with the same weariness of a governess dealing with a particularly unruly child—and from the way Samuel bristled, he certainly recognized this. "It is a simple and elegant solution. Even as new as you are to this position, you must recognize how rare these sorts of opportunities are. Besides ..." she paused, her smile turning cruel "... as Councillor of Law, this will give you more opportunity to work with your intended."

Shan glanced away, not sure who she was more worried in disappointing. Samuel, for putting him in this terrible position. Or herself, for fearing that this would look like exactly like it was—the idea that she hadn't risen on her own merit, but only for her ties to one person.

One lost prince, reluctantly returned.

Blood and steel, did she miss being the Sparrow. As the Sparrow, this would have never fallen upon her. She would be working to undermine this decision, not spearhead it. But that was before she was tasked with balancing the many needs of an entire nation upon her shoulders, and she could only hope that after this meeting she would be able to convince Samuel that this was the only option.

He had forced her hand with his ill-timed rescue of Isaac, and he would have to learn to live with the consequences.

"My relationship with Lady LeClaire notwithstanding," Samuel said, his voice as icy as the chill of winter's night, "I still object to this plan, and I will campaign against it when it is brought to the House of Lords."

"When ... oh." Shan took a deep breath. Blood and steel, but was this a mess already, and of course Samuel would make this mistake. "I am sorry that I did not make this clearer, but that will not be happening. The King has already approved this plan—it is not up for debate or vote."

She could feel the support in the room vanish as the rest of the Council studied her with renewed interest. Their ire shifted like the wind, away from Samuel and his naiveté towards Shan and her presumption.

What fools they were. Just moments ago they had been eager for this plan, but with this little breach of protocol, their entire attitude changed.

"As much as we would like to follow typical process, we do not have the luxury of time," Shan continued, infusing her voice with steel. The Eternal King would not allow such questioning, and neither should she. "It will be months before the House even reconvenes, let alone how long it would take to move this through committee. The Blood Coffers are draining fast, and we need to start replenishing them now. Aeravin hangs on a knife's edge, and we must take action before we fall."

The Council had no response to that—they knew the truth of the matter, knew how desperate things could become. With each passing day, the restrictions from the rationing chafed harder, and if there was one thing the Blood Workers of Aeravin did not abide, it was restraint.

"Well," Belrose said, with a small sneer, "it appears that we do not have any choice. Your proposal is accepted, LeClaire, though I will be looking forward to seeing the full detailed plans this afternoon."

"Of course," Shan said, graciously. "They will arrive by midday. If you have any questions, please direct them to my office." Turning, she finally met Samuel's gaze, his eyes hard and glinting. There was no sign of the man she loved in that expression, and she was so terribly proud of him. "And Lord Aberforth? Lady Morse was correct; we should meet ourselves to discuss the particulars. Will three in the afternoon suit?"

Samuel only nodded—a confirmation and a dismissal at once. He was making himself a better Blood Worker and a Lord of Aeravin with each passing day. Shan ignored the tug of desire that pooled deep in her core. There would be opportunities for that later. And if that was how he wanted to play it, she could meet him on his terms.

"This afternoon then," she said, with a smile laced with poison, before executing the most perfect curtsy before the rest of the Royal Council. "I thank you for your time and consideration."

She left with a flourish—if she could not have their respect, she would settle for having the last word. They could squabble among themselves, if they so chose, but there was only one person she answered to.

Being the right hand to the Eternal King did come with some benefits.

—✦—

Samuel was waiting for her in his office, precisely at the appointed time. There was a steaming pot of tea waiting for her, complete with an assortment of small pastries, but Samuel wasn't waiting at the other side of his desk, like all the other times they'd met in recent memory.

No, he stood by the window, gloves and cravat discarded, sleeves rolled up to display his strong forearms, riddled through with the dark imprint of his veins.

Well, there was that, at least. After the King had displayed the scars Isaac had left burned into his skin, Samuel had taken to covering them up as much as possible, except around her. Whatever anger simmered between them was not enough to fully break their bond.

Not yet.

She skirted around the table, ignoring the siren call of tea despite how badly she needed it. Instead, she slid her arms around Samuel's body, rested her head against his shoulder, holding him tight as she felt the tension he carried dissipate bit by incremental bit.

His hand came to cover hers, their fingers twining together before he raised them to his lips, pressed his lips against the metal claws on each of her fingers. Soft and gentle—he was always so gentle with her, like she was something precious. She had done nothing to earn such loving care, and after this morning, she wasn't sure she deserved it at all.

But she swallowed all those fears, tucking them away where they couldn't hurt her, because she had a mess to fix. "Did you have a chance to read the proposal?"

Samuel scoffed, pulling away at last. He put a deliberate amount of space between them, far enough that she couldn't touch him, and she let him, folding her hands behind her back. "It is a ... thorough accounting."

"Thorough," Shan echoed. "Yes, I wanted to close as many loopholes as I could, before we even started this."

Samuel hummed in response. "I see. Well, you succeeded, though it must have taken you quite some time to draft."

She heard the unspoken questions hanging between them, the things he did not even have to say. The *how long have you been planning this* and the *why did you never tell me* and the most damning of them all, the simple *how could you?*

It was the same things she had asked herself night after night, but standing here before Samuel and his foolish, admirable sense of justice, all her excuses felt paltry.

"There are no other solutions," she said, at last, hating the slight quiver in her voice. "I searched and searched for options, but there is *nothing* that would replace the amount of blood they were bringing in, nothing that wouldn't be—"

"That wouldn't be worse?" Samuel finished for her.

Swallowing hard, she nodded. For that was the crux of it. What had existed was a horror that should have never been allowed, but one did not simply harvest that much blood while still standing on the side of righteousness. And she thought that Samuel understood it, too. That there was no way to continue to serve the Eternal King without getting their hands dirty.

She so hated to be wrong.

Samuel groaned, rubbing at his eyes. "What are we doing, Shan? This isn't helping anyone. *We're* not helping anyone."

"But we are." Shan stepped forward, unable to stop herself from reaching for him. "What I said this morning was true, Samuel. If we do not find a way to solve the issue of rationing, then this fragile peace will shatter. And if that happens ..."

If it wasn't the Unblooded, it was the Blood Workers. If it wasn't the merchants, it was the Lords. If it wasn't their Eternal King, then it was everyone else. Aeravin was a fragile web of spider silk, and even the smallest disturbance would send it fluttering away in the wind.

"Please," she said. No. *Begged.* "I cannot do this alone."

Samuel stepped forward immediately, his frustration replaced by pity, and as sour a taste as that left in her mouth, it was better than anger. "Oh, Shan," he muttered against her hair, his large hand warm and tender against the small of her back. "You didn't have to bear this alone. We could have come up with something."

"Could we?" she whispered into the safety of his body. Like this, he couldn't look at her. Like this, she could imagine that he was looking at her with understanding. It also made it easier for her to slip the noose around his neck. "You have done things without my knowledge to protect *me*, haven't you?"

He stilled. "Yes," he said, walking straight into her trap.

"As I did here, for you." She tilted her head, staring at the deep imprint of a bite mark on the pale skin of his throat, one that she had not left there. She pressed a kiss to it, laying claim to the mark Isaac had left on him, and she could feel him shudder at the contact. "Look at us, still fighting to protect each other. Still fighting to protect those we love."

She dared not say his name, even in the privacy of Samuel's office. Some secrets were too risky for the Parliament House, but with the way Samuel's arms clenched against the small of her back, she knew he understood it.

What flawed creatures they were, but she still showed her love in the only way she knew how. Her affection was a deadly poison, wrapped in layers of deceit and artifice, but she would protect those who held her heart.

Even if they didn't recognize her protection for what it was.

"I am sorry it had to be this way," she breathed. "But it needed to be done. And do not fear, I'll help you with the rest of this."

She released him, finally heading towards the teapot, but Samuel looked after her with a strange look on his face. It was only there for a second, before he hid it behind that mask of Lord Aberforth that he worked so hard on perfecting, and pride twisted with the acid in her stomach.

He took his seat at his desk, so stern, the perfect image of an aristocrat. "Let's get to work, then."

Chapter Eleven

Samuel

Shan's new proposal was going to be the death of him, and Samuel hadn't even enacted it yet.

He had spent three days locked away in offices, either his own at the Parliament House or Shan's at the Academy or with the Captain of the Guard at the largest Guard Station in Dameral. The only moments he got to himself were in the blessed silence as the Aberforth carriage took him from one meeting to the next, and the cold, lonely nights he kept deliberately away from Shan, wrapped in his own self-inflicted misery.

Soon, he would face her alone, stripped of the titles and the duties that moved them, but for now—for the sake of his own soul—he couldn't risk it. She would whisper such reasonable arguments in his ear, would talk about practicality and the fragile tightrope of power that they walked, would convince him that a little blood on their hands now would be worth the stability of tomorrow.

But what she had done, the work that she had foisted on him with a pained expression, an untenable weight that dwarfed all the King's little cruelties, was abhorrent. And he could not let himself forget that.

Especially now, facing down the Captain of the Guard. Vaughn Dabney was a fortress of a man, with broad shoulders and a permanently grim expression, like he had just stepped out of a funeral.

He was older than Samuel by decades of hard work, and despite the resources at his disposal, Dabney refused to let the Blood Healers reset his nose, which had been broken at least twice, nor ease the long scar that bisected his cheek. It gave him a fearsome appearance, but Samuel wouldn't let himself be cowed.

Dabney was a relic of the past, ruling the Guard with an iron fist, and he had not taken kindly to Samuel's appointment as Councillor of Law. They had butted heads time and time again, and this new plan was no exception.

"We need to have protections in place," Samuel repeated, for what felt like the hundredth time, "to ensure our prisoners are not mistreated."

Dabney scoffed. "I find your lack of faith in our people disheartening. The Guard of Aeravin is filled with good and honest folk, and I will not accept any insinuations to the contrary."

Biting the inside of his cheek, Samuel held back the tirade that threatened. Either Dabney was a fool or a liar—the Guard cared not about serving the good of their nation. They only cared for the Blood Workers that filled their ranks and paid their wages. Samuel had learned this the hard way, thrust into this position in the aftermath of the Eternal King's sweeping laws. The gleeful way the Guard took to enforcing the strictest curfew, the way they raided innocent people's homes on the slightest suspicions. The cells had never been more packed, and damn it all, Shan.

This plan would work far too well.

But the truth rarely brought success, and so Samuel tried a different route. "Then it wouldn't hurt to have these details codified into law."

"Those details can come later, my lord," Dabney replied, with a usually hard emphasis on the honorific that made it sound like a slur.

Despite the way he wore his title like an ill-fitting coat, Samuel couldn't help the way he bristled. Dabney was not a lord himself, not an honored son of Aeravin. No, Dabney was a Blood Worker of common background, crawling his way up to whatever position of power he could reach and clinging to it with a brutality that made Samuel sick.

Dabney should have known better, should have understood the consequences of what they dealt in.

"These details come now." Samuel slammed his hand on the edge of the table, but Dabney didn't even blink. "Or this project stops here."

Dabney finally lifted his gaze, his eyes hard like flint. "Are you going against the Eternal King, my Lord Councillor? Because based on this—" he tapped the pile of papers before him "—this is happening, whether you like it or not."

The blueprints stretched across the massive desk, gifted to them by the Eternal King himself, pages and pages of information detailing how the previous iteration of the Blood Factory had been run, along with a promise of limitless funds to expedite the process of building their own. Perhaps it was a relief to the King, outsourcing this work to the Guard, freeing him and his Royal Blood Worker for other pursuits. Perhaps he just needed to get it done as quickly as possible. Either way, Dabney was right.

There was no stopping this, no matter how wretched it made Samuel feel.

"If that's how you see it," Samuel ground out, "then perhaps I should leave you to handle the logistics."

"Perhaps you should, lordling." Dabney rose to his full height, a good head taller than Samuel, crossing his arms over his chest so that his breadth suddenly seemed so impressive. "Leave the hard work to the men who can handle it."

Samuel didn't flinch away from the insult, even though he wanted to. Dabney didn't understand—none of them understood. It wasn't the work that he objected to. But there was no way to convince these people that the Unblooded were anything more than walking sources of power, there to exploit as they saw fit.

And damn him as a fool for even trying. There was no chance of reaching him, man to man, so Samuel pulled the only trick he had left. He donned the mask of Lord Aberforth. If he could not convince Dabney to be an ally, then he would not give the man a choice.

There were other gambits in play, and it wouldn't take much to shift his focus.

"You're right," he said, and Dabney narrowed his eyes at the simple acquiescence. "There is little that I can offer with this sort of planning. My expertise is needed elsewhere, crafting new laws, and since you have nothing to add ..."

"Just you wait, Aberforth—"

Samuel cut him off by inclining his head, not quite a bow, but enough of a proper acknowledgment to startle Dabney. It was a trick he'd learned from Shan—showing respect, just a hair of it, dripped in sarcasm, that threw people off their game. Treating them like they weren't even worth his time, as unimpressive and unimportant as an ant beneath his boot.

It worked like a charm every time, especially given his damned title, the blood that tied him to the Eternal King. Dabney might never respect him as a person, but he would respect the title he held and the power of the name he had been gifted.

"I will allow you to get back to your work, Dabney," Samuel said, stepping back from the table, taking a moment to carefully smooth the planes of his suit jacket. "Please have your secretary send daily reports to mine. If I have any need of you, I'll send for you."

He saw himself out before Dabney could get another word in, past the startled guard that waited just outside Dabney's office. His second-in-command always lingered nearby, a shadow that lurked around the edges of their conversations. She was a woman near Samuel's own age, plain and mousy in appearance, but Dabney was grooming her to follow in his footsteps. She eyed him with distrust as he brushed past, and any hopes of a different alliance burst as soon as they bloomed, the woman's name fading on his lips.

Lorraine Strickland would be no ally. There would be no allies here, no matter how desperately he hoped.

He swallowed the disappointment down, strolling through the headquarters of the Guard like he owned the place—which, as Councillor of Law, wasn't far from the truth. Though his work pulled him to the Parliament House more often than not, this was the realm he supposedly ruled, if not for men like Dabney undercutting him at every opportunity.

But he couldn't let his frustration show, not if he wanted to be respected. So, he kept his head held high as he walked through the narrow hallway between rows of offices, where captains and detectives worked their cases. Samuel took a moment to brace himself at the top of the stairs, knowing what waited between him and the way out.

The holding cells and the interrogation rooms, where they held the criminals brought in for processing. Dabney had said the design was ancient, a safety precaution as they stacked Blood Workers both above and below, a deterrent against jailbreak. Once, it seemed safe enough. What Unblooded was foolish enough to stand up to so many Blood Workers?

But in the aftermath of Isaac's escape, a new tension loomed, strung through the building like a held breath right before a battle. Guards paced the hallways in an endless rotation, flashing their steel-tipped claws in warning as the Unblooded crowded towards the backs of their cells. The floor was frigid, the early winter chill seeping in through the brick. There were no fires in the winter or open windows in the summer—a security precaution, Samuel was told—leaving the Unblooded to suffer in whatever conditions the unfeeling weather had for them.

Samuel slipped past them, sinking his teeth into his own tongue to hold back any ill-thought-out words, any lashing of rage that threatened to burn its way up his throat. He did not stop to look upon what he could not change, but he saw it anyway. People who had once been just like him, poor and exhausted, pulled from the streets to be stuffed into cells like cattle, nearly overflowing. With the new restrictions, as vaguely defined as they were, the Guard had every excuse to drag Unblooded back to the Guardhouses, to hold them with little reason besides the casual violence that they could.

And that was *before* Shan's ingenious plan, and now Samuel ignored the way that he had seen the same souls here, day in and day out, waiting for processing and trials that never seemed to come. He understood what it was for, the deliberate halt of progress as Dabney waited for the new Blood Factories to be built, ready to retroactively apply new punishments to the so-called crimes that came before it had ever been dreamt up.

More blood to drain from those who could barely afford it, not with the recently doubled Blood Taxes. Samuel saw its effects all around him, the pallid skin and the exhaustion writ into their very skin. It was unmissable, once one learned to look for it—he saw it here in these hells, in the servants that staffed the Parliament House, even in his own home, his secretary Jacobs moving with a stiffness and a fragility that came out of seemingly nowhere.

It was so obvious to him, but he did not believe any of the other Blood Workers around him even noticed. Not even Shan, for all her talk of helping the Unblooded.

There was nothing that Samuel could do about it. Not here. Not like this, not while Dabney still ruled this roost. No, if he was to make any change, if he was to make any headway at all, it would be through his role in the Parliament.

He gave one last, long look back at the cells, catching the eye of a young woman who glared at him with the most vicious expression. She couldn't have been more than eighteen, dressed in an old dress that was far too thin for this chill, but she held her head high, undaunted by the Blood Workers who sneered as they passed. Samuel didn't know if she recognized him for who he was—the Aberforth pulled from the slums, the greatest traitor to their suffering—or if she was just reacting to the richness of his clothes and the healthy shine to his skin. It did not matter, for even without saying a word, Samuel saw the truth.

She hated him, and she had every right to.

Though he could do nothing to reassure her, he made a solemn vow that he would fix this, one way or another. That he would stop it before the cost grew too high to be unforgivable.

But first, he needed to learn the right way to play the game, and for that, he had a bill to draft.

Chapter Twelve

Isaac

The hunger returned, driving Isaac to consider leaving the safety of the safe house. An endless rumble in the pit of his stomach, dryness in the back of his throat that wouldn't abate. His mouth ached; jaw clenched as he fought the urge to sink his teeth into something. What he hungered for, he knew but dared not name, and whether it was a blessing or a curse, he knew that he couldn't find it here.

But he was used to suffering, so choked it down.

He dressed himself in the simple clothes he found in the closet—plain dark trousers, a white shirt that hung loose around his throat, a binder that thankfully mostly fit, snug enough to compress but not tight enough to hurt. It did not leave him quite as flat as the ones he used to have, especially tailored to him, but he had endured worse.

A lot of people like him had endured far worse.

Still, it left him feeling oddly bare, vulnerable in a way that he had not felt in years. These were a working man's clothes, not the fashion of a Blood Working adept, the plain grey robes the Academy gifted to students who did not have the funds for more. It certainly wasn't the clothes he had worn as the Royal Blood Worker, when he had to find a tailor who would work with him, despite his lack of pedigree.

The man in the mirror looked nothing like the man he had been.

Isaac was thinner, graver, almost sickly, wrapping his arms around himself and feeling just how slight he had become. His skin was paler than it had ever been after months indoors, and his dark hair hung lankly against his scalp. There was the beginning of his beard unevenly filling in—he would have to ask Anton for a shaving kit, the next time he saw the man—but, still, Isaac could hardly recognize himself.

And to think, Samuel had still touched him, in spite of the absolute wreck he'd become. Without knowing the monster he was becoming.

He pulled back his upper lip, staring at the point of his eyeteeth, thankfully no sharper than the last time he had looked. And yet, there was something predatory about him, with that inhuman hunger that just would not fade, a constant ache in the back of his throat.

He needed help, and there was only one person he could even hope to trust with this. And things between them were already so fragile.

The door crashed open, and Isaac jumped away from the mirror, but his heart settled when he heard Anton call out, impatient and brash as always. "De la Cruz? Are you still here?"

"Where else would I be?" Isaac huffed as he entered the main living space, small as it was. "Did you really think me that much of a fool?"

"Do you really want my answer?" Anton grinned at him from where he stood behind the small table, sorting through the bags he had brought. It wasn't a cheerful smile—it never was with him. No, Anton treated every one of their interactions like it was a battle to be won, even after all these years.

"I don't know what Samuel had on you," Isaac continued, ignoring the little slight for what it was, "to get you to agree to this, but it must be something particularly dark."

Anton placed his hand over his chest, miming a harsh blow. "And do you really think so little of me? That I would not do the right thing?"

"Not for my sake," Isaac admitted, and his directness seemed to startle Anton.

"Well, that is not unfair," Anton replied, just as carefully. The sudden shift in terrain seemed to throw the both of them, and neither knew what do with honesty when they were used to carefully designed barbs dipped in poison. But Anton broke the silence first, cursing lowly under his breath as he pulled a bottle of amber liquid from the bags. "This is actually what I came to talk to you about, but I am not getting through it sober."

Isaac huffed a laugh. "Smart thinking." The smile Anton gave him was a little more true, and Isaac felt the tension in his shoulders ease, bit by bit.

"Take a seat, de la Cruz," Anton said as he turned towards the kitchen, "I'll be right over."

Isaac didn't bother responding, already heading towards the small seating area by the window. The drapes were still closed, as they had been the night he arrived, but he took the time to pull them back, wanting to see the world beyond. The street below was so different from the world he had lived in. Here, there were no private carriages or hackneys, no ladies in their fine day dresses or lords with their walking sticks. No, they were just people, heading home in the last fading light before the day's end, with gentle, fat flakes of snow falling only to melt the moment they touched the cobblestones. Cloaks were pulled tight around shoulders as people moved with a strange bit of urgency, a frantic tension that he did not recognize.

Anton appeared beside him, pressing a healthy glass of bourbon into his hand, but his attention was down on the street as well. "Curfew may have been lifted, officially, but people are still nervous."

Isaac's voice came out rough. "Curfew?"

Sending him a sidelong glance, Anton gestured for Isaac to take a seat, and though it was difficult to pull his attention away from the city he had risked so much to save, Isaac did as he was told. "How much do you know about what happened after you were captured?"

"Not much," Isaac admitted. "Shan is Royal Blood Worker now."

"That she is," Anton said, staring directly at Isaac, refusing to let him look away. "And Samuel is the Councillor of Law, taking up the position that you saw vacated."

"Yes, Shan mentioned that as well."

Anton rubbed his temple, looking suddenly exhausted. "Then I take it you don't know about the laws the Eternal Prick saw enacted?"

Isaac took a sip of his drink at last, the bourbon burning down his throat as he braced himself. "I do not."

Leaning in, Anton quickly sketched out the changes to the law that Isaac had missed, all those months in prison. Curfew and doubled Blood Taxes and the universal tightening of control around the Unblooded, the creation of a new bit of law around sedition literature and treason. The growing instability as the blood coffers of Aeravin steadily drained to the point where rationing had been exacted.

Isaac drank his way through the conversation, thankful that the drink was at least good, so that by the time Anton finished, so had he.

"I didn't mean for it to go like that," Isaac said, and whether it was the bourbon or the simple shame that prompted him so, he would never know.

"I know," Anton said, with more kindness than Isaac deserved. He rubbed his hand across the back of his neck, let out a dramatic sigh. "I can't believe I'm saying this, but I misjudged you, Isaac. I thought you were just like the rest of them. Just like ... " He trailed off, and Isaac didn't need to ask whose name went unspoken. Isaac had thought the same thing, in the end.

Brilliant, daring, incomparable Shan—she could bring the world to its knees, if she so dared. But instead, she played the careful game of politics, attempting to change things from within, as if her only enemy was the Eternal King.

What would it take to convince her that some things needed to burn?

"I do not regret my actions," Isaac said, pulling Anton's attention back to him, "but I do regret the consequences of them."

Anton didn't respond, only nudged the bottle of bourbon closer. Isaac took the hint, refilling his glass before he continued on.

"I don't know if Shan ever told you," Isaac began, running his finger along the rim, "that she saw the Blood Factory. The King showed her—how it worked, what we did to people." From the furious glint in Anton's eyes, Isaac had his answer. "Ah, I see not, then."

"That's the thing about my twin," Anton said, with a smile that became more of a grimace. "She has convinced herself that she is the only one who can protect us and has twisted herself into a web of lies to do so."

"Yeah," Isaac replied. The truth was a double-edged blade, and he had cut himself on it for years. "But we still love her anyway."

Anton held out his glass. "To Shan, the best and worst sister I could have asked for."

Isaac clinked his glass against Anton's. "To Shan, love of my life, even though she may kill me yet."

They both drank deeply, and Isaac relaxed, some of the old animosity smoothed over. He might never call Anton a friend, but they both shared in Shan's life, they both had visions of a better Aeravin, and for that much, they could learn to tolerate each other. It was more than Isaac had ever hoped for when they were young.

"So, Shan knew, then?"

"Only towards the end," Isaac said, and it felt good, sharing the truth, even if it was with Anton. "When the last of them had been killed, when there was only Dunn left. It horrified her. For what we did, for what those *suppliers*," he spat out the word like it was acid on his tongue, "did, they needed to die. And I think that deep down, Shan agrees with that."

Anton let out a sigh of relief, and Isaac realized that the man did not know where she landed on it. If her dreaded pragmatism would have overridden her brittle sense of morality. "That is good to know. Sometimes I worry." He rocked back in his seat, studying Isaac again. "All right then. I have an offer for you, de la Cruz."

"An offer?" Isaac echoed, suspicious.

"I know what my sister wants to do with you," Anton continued, as if he hadn't been interrupted. "I know she wants to get you out of Aeravin, for your own good. But you don't want that, do you?"

There was a bitterness there, and Isaac had the sudden feeling that he wasn't the only one to have gotten this particular offer. "I don't. I have unfinished business left in Aeravin."

"Good." Anton pulled something out of his breast pocket, tossed it on the table between them. "Are you familiar with these, then?"

Isaac brushed his fingers against the mess of pamphlets that fell to the table, the headlines and articles different, but the typeset the same. It seemed that the radicals who had upset the King so much continued on, peddling their philosophies and revolutionary schemes.

Isaac wasn't surprised to see that they had carried on, despite the laws the King had enacted. Blood and steel, doing that had probably only helped the revolutionary cause. But for Anton to bring it up with him—

He burst into a laugh as the realization hit him. "You?" he wheezed. "Of course it's bloody you. Hells, this is ridiculous."

Anton leaned back in his seat, looking as satisfied as the cat that caught the canary. "It does feel a bit like a comedy of errors, doesn't it? Shan's schemes, yours." He gestured to the pamphlets again. "Mine."

"All working our own little plans," Isaac added, pouring himself another drink. "Never thinking that there might be others willing to help."

"It is a little mad, no?" Anton crossed his leg over the other, shifted nervously. "But that's why I wanted to speak with you. Shan has made her position clear—" Anton grit his teeth, and Isaac didn't need to pry to know how that had gone.

His foolish Shan, always insisting on doing things her way, no matter how alone it left her.

"—but," Anton continued, and Isaac forced himself to focus, "I think that there could be something here, no?"

"Wait," Isaac interrupted. "You don't mean that you want me to join you?" Anton inclined his head, and Isaac was forced to re-evaluate everything he thought he knew about the man. Every preconceived notion, every bit of disgust he had felt. How much of that boy he knew was real, and how much of it had just been another mask?

He and Anton were more alike than Isaac had ever wished to realize.

"What's your endgame, then?"

Anton spread his hands, spoke as simply as if they were discussing the weather. "This country is built on a flawed foundation, and if we are ever to build something better, we need to start from the ground up." Anton's smile was sharp, looking so much like his sister that it made Isaac's heart ache. "And if that means that the King, the House of Lords, the very laws and rules that bind us have to go too—then that is the price we're willing to pay. You know quite a bit about paying high prices, don't you?"

"I do," Isaac said, pushing to his feet so he could pace. Anton didn't interrupt him, just leaned back and waited, as Isaac worked through this.

As Isaac considered a future where he did not have to fight this fight alone.

"What of Shan?" Isaac asked, at last. Because despite everything, the doubts and the fears and the way their agendas never fully lined up, he wanted nothing more than to remain at her side. And this—this felt like a deeper betrayal than any of the previous wounds they had inflicted upon each other.

They really were a match made in hell, weren't they? Feeding each other's worst parts, love and longing and betrayal all wrapped up together, and Isaac did not know where to even begin untangling it. *If* they even could untangle it.

Perhaps that was Samuel's part in all this, to be the grounding force that kept them together, the light that guided them home in the darkness. The hope that they could have a future together, someday.

"I can't answer for her, but we do have an agreement," Anton said, kindly.

Delicately, like he was on the brink of breaking. Perhaps he was—Isaac ached for things he could not even name, and perhaps he was on the edge of shattering, fracturing into a billion little pieces that could never be put back together.

"What agreement is that?"

"She handles her own plans, and I handle mine," Anton elaborated, pulling his hands apart and holding them off to the side, dangling off the edges of the armrest. "I do not interfere with her and she does not interfere with me. It's ... a kind of mutual respect."

"And poaching me?" Isaac returned. "Where does that fall?"

"Well—" that smile was back, crueler than ever "—you are your own man, are you not?" Anton settled his hands back in his lap with a shrug. "You and I both want something better for this nation—we both want to see those who have fed on the lowest among us punished for their crimes."

Isaac couldn't argue with that, but there was one thing he needed this man, who had been born to privilege but denied the gift of magic, to understand. "This isn't just for the Unblooded, I hope. Oh, yes, they do suffer, greatly, but there are Blood Workers who are being exploited as well. If we are going to risk a revolution, it should be a revolution for all."

Anton didn't respond for a long moment, so long that Isaac feared he had overstepped his bounds. "You're right, of course. For so long we had focused on the Unblooded, but there are others who needed to be freed from the system. People like your late parents, rest their souls."

Cutting him a harsh look, Isaac dared him to continue. But Anton didn't press. Just stood and held out his hand. "Partners, then?"

Isaac looked at the outstretched hand, took it and shook it hard. It was a simple pact, but it felt like the start of something new. Something better. The alliance he had arranged with Alessi had been built out of mutual need and desperation, but this ... this was different.

And to cement that, he squared his shoulders. "I'm with you, Anton, but I still need to talk to Shan—"

"I understand," Anton cut him off. "You don't need to explain that to me." He ran his hand through his hair, let out a harsh breath. "Good luck with that, de la Cruz. You're going to need it. Would you like for me to arrange for something?"

"You'd do that?" Isaac asked. It seemed so easy, too good to be trusted, but Anton just clapped him on the shoulder.

"Trust me, between me and Bart, we can figure it out." He dropped a wink at Isaac's confusion. "What, you think you're the only man to be taken in by a pretty face?"

Oh. Anton and Shan's secretary, then? For some reason that didn't surprise Isaac. He hardly knew Bart, but he couldn't imagine how complicated this was for them.

How complicated it was about to become for *him*.

"Very well, then," Isaac agreed. "I'll take you up on that."

"Good." Anton knocked back the rest of his glass. "I'll leave the bourbon with you, and that parcel over there contains the rest of our literature. You should read through it, then I'll arrange for you to meet the rest of us."

"And the Blood Workers?" Isaac pressed. "You'll help them too?"

Anton did not even hesitate. "I will—but you must know, not all of them will side with us. Even those who would be better off, in the long run."

"I know," Isaac agreed, even though it hurt. "Just like all the Unblooded won't side with you."

Anton only nodded in response, because what else was there to say? There would always be those who chose a system that allowed them a little power over others. It was why he had killed those who turned over their brethren to be drained and killed for a small amount of money. It was why the revolution that they dreamed of would be washed in blood.

And still, he would choose it anyway, because giving up was worse.

Chapter Thirteen

Shan

The Eternal King came to her, finding Shan in her office once more, the bustling sounds of the Academy coming to life around them. Their meetings had become more regular over the past week, no longer related to short sessions among their other duties or poring over journals in the dead of night.

No, now the King joined her first thing in the morning, sitting across from her in the small space set aside for meetings—two plush armchairs of deep green velvet, separated only by a small table wrought of iron, the image of vines and roses spiraling down the legs. Her secretary arrived in perfect silence, delivering them a plate full of pastries and a steaming pot of coffee. With all the late nights she had been running, tea wasn't doing it anymore—and from the way the King eagerly poured his own cup, it seemed that he was working long hours as well.

Sometimes it startled her, these little reminders that despite the fact that he was Eternal, there was some humanity left to him after all.

"Excellent work with your proposal, Shan. The Guard is working day and night to set up their Blood Factories, and it won't be long until we start to see dividends," the King said, leaning back in his seat. He managed to make the simple armchair look like a throne, dressed in his exquisite finery and looking every bit the regal ruler, and Shan felt that old familiar tickle of fear rise in the back of her throat.

The knowledge that, no matter how kindly he appeared in any given moment, he was still a predator, and there was little she could do to stand against him.

"I've been thinking," she said, carefully, always so careful. The questions that swirled in her mind, now that Isaac was free, now that she had a chance to help him. If he would let her. "About what happened with Samuel and de la Cruz. Of course, we have lost our test subject, but academically speaking..."

The words tasted like ash on her tongue, the way she had to speak of him, of them both—like they weren't even people but subjects to be studied. But such was the way of the Eternal King, always moving people like pieces on a chessboard, and even now, he inclined his head towards her, encouraging her to go on.

"We know what he did with Dunn," she pressed on, "and that it had side effects that we don't fully understand. But what he did to Samuel was something different, and I want to know why."

"Knowledge like that is dangerous," the King murmured idly. Not a threat, but a warning.

But Shan had never responded well to such tactics. She pulled her lips back into a smirk. "It is, but you chose me for this role for a reason, did you not? Let me help you, your Majesty."

The King hesitated, a deliberate inhale of breath, before he let out a soft sigh. "Perhaps you are right, Shan. I have held myself apart for so long that I've almost forgotten what it is like to have an ally. A partner. Being Eternal... it changes you, after a while."

His voice was so quiet, threaded through with a slight tremble, and even though Shan knew better, she could still feel herself being pulled into his web, his strings settling around her, ready to be pulled.

She would let herself be led, for a bit. Long enough for him to let his guard down. With one so practiced at manipulation as the Eternal King was, all she could do was wait and hope.

"Perhaps that was my problem with de la Cruz," he continued, glancing to the side—almost shy, almost mournful. "I was so lost in my own world that I missed his treachery completely. Perhaps I could have stopped him, if only I had been paying more attention."

Shan ducked her head, already calculating the next five steps out. Normally, the King responded well to her being bold, but even he would not tolerate her agreeing that he had been wrong. Blame was a delicate business, quick to shift, and fragile as a house of cards. One wrong move, one misplaced word, and the entire castle would come crumbling down.

"You are not the only one who missed the signs," Shan said, "but his mistakes are his own. We cannot accept responsibility for what he became."

It was the best kind of lie—the kind that was mostly true. Mistakes had been made, signs had been missed, but they weren't the ones the King thought they were.

Huffing a small laugh, the King settled back in his chair, looking more relaxed. His hands hung off the edge of the armrest, spread open in a very *what-can-you-do* manner. "Such wisdom from one so young. Truly, I pulled from the LeClaire line too soon."

Now was the time to be brash. She tilted her chin up, did not bank the fire in her eyes. Everything she had, she had in spite of her father, fighting tooth and claw for a place in this society that did not want her twice over. Once, for her foreign blood, twice for the shame that Lord Antonin LeClaire the First had brought to their name.

And still, despite all of that, here she was, sitting before the King as almost an equal. "You did."

A hint of a smile in the twitch of his lips, but he inclined his head to her all the same. "All right, Shan, if that is how you want to play this, then who am I to deny you." Standing, he held out his hand. "Come with me."

Shan took it, letting him pull her to her feet. The force was a little more than she expected, and she stumbled forward, landing flush against his chest as he wrapped his arm around her, steadying her with a hand at the small of her back. He was so warm, so shockingly human, that her voice caught in her throat as he stared down at her.

As he looked at her with something unfathomable in those ancient eyes.

So similar to Samuel, and yet so different. A mirror of the man she loved, but with a darker edge than Samuel would ever hone. A man more appropriate for a villain such as her, whose darkness could match her own.

She pulled back quickly, as if burned, and the Eternal King just let her go. As if nothing untoward had happened at all.

"Please, follow me," he said, with a slight bow, and her heart lodged in her throat, she followed him out of her office, and eventually, the Academy itself.

The King brought her back to the palace, leading her not to his office, where they had met so many times, passing all of the formal meeting rooms and offices and parlors. He took her deeper than Shan had ever gone, through winding hallways of marble and wide, open windows that overlooked the wide expanse of the ocean below, and it was only when they were nearly at their destination that she finally realized where he was taking her. As they passed through the grand doors that opened under the steady hand of two Guards, as the King pressed his bleeding hand against the ward to split it in two, allowing her entrance to a grand suite, larger than an entire floor of her townhouse.

This was where the Eternal King lived—his private chambers opened to her, and Shan had the plummeting fear that she had gotten in too deep.

They walked into a cavernous sitting room, a marble fireplace stretching all the way to the high ceilings above them, a brilliant fire roaring merrily in it. A grand chandelier hung from the ceiling over the heart of the room, a shining collection of crystals that Shan desperately wanted to see at night, resplendent with witch light. Below that was a series of couches, rich velvet the color of blood over dark wood, with low tables scattered around them. A thick rug underlay it all, a woven masterpiece of colors, so lush that Shan wanted to slip off her shoes and sink her toes into it.

The grand windows continued along the far wall, an almost sheer sheet of glass surrounding the archway of doors to the balcony. Shan could almost imagine how it would be in summer, thrown open to the salt air fresh off the sea, regretting that she only knew it now, in the depths of winter. Only for the hungry, greedy part of her soul to remind her that she could continue to have all of this, and more, if she continued to play her cards correctly. And as the Eternal King turned to her, his mouth pulled into the slightest of smiles, she realized that this was his plan all along.

To tempt her with all that she could be, all that she could have, if she only allowed herself to reach for it.

Taking his hand, she allowed him to pull her past all the finery, down a long hallway lined with vibrant paintings—landscapes of the country he had built, rich expanses of rolling hills and valleys that Shan had never had the chance to visit between the coastlines of Aeravin. An entire nation painted out before her in what felt like an endless spread, the art finer than any she ever had the opportunity to see, collected from a life that spanned centuries and showed no signs of ending any time soon.

Once, she had promised Samuel that no one should be Eternal, but facing the potential of everything it could be, oh, did she understand why one would want to be.

The King stopped before another grand door, pushing it open and gesturing Shan forward. His hand slipped from hers as she passed through, emerging into a study and dwarfed even the finest in the Academy. There was a grand desk and reading nook built into a bay window, but she didn't focus on that, turning her attention to the grand tomes and stacks of journals filling the bookshelves.

So, this is where it all was—all the gaps in knowledge, all the missing pieces. Everything he hadn't wanted her, or Isaac, or any of the other Royal Blood Workers who had come before them to know.

"This is ... magnificent," she breathed, not even bothering to hide the awe. She looked to him, a question burning, and he only nodded. Setting her loose like a child in a chocolate shop, and she raced to pull tomes from the shelves, almost at random, just to see what they held. It would take her years to even begin to catalogue it all, but oh, how she wanted to try.

"It's been a long time since I last had someone in here," the King said, quietly. Shan paused in her search, holding her breath as she waited for what came next. "Centuries, even."

She wet dry lips. "So, Isaac—"

"Never got more than what was at the Academy," the King finished for her. "Like so many others before him, since . . ." He sighed, crossing the room to collapse into the seat of the bay window. Slouching into it, looking so exhausted and dejected, Shan was almost able to forget just who she was dealing with.

Until he spoke again.

"It is difficult, being King," he said, the confession spilling from him, "finding people you can trust. People who are not just using this—" he rolled his wrist, gesturing to encompass all that he was, all that he had "—for their own gain. It was a lesson I learned centuries ago, it's a lesson I learned again and again. Your father taught it to me. Isaac taught to it me. And I thought I was being so clever, locking them out. Playing them against each other, but never letting them step out of their roles."

Tilting his head to the side, he considered her with those green eyes, shining like emeralds. He could have been cut from gems himself, the sharpness of his features so precise and just as unmovable. There was a kind of ruthless beauty to him, a perfection that seemed more than human, and Shan hated herself for noticing it.

For wanting it.

"But . . . in doing so, I also have prevented others from reaching their full potential." He crooked his fingers in, and Shan followed, a moon caught in his gravitational pull, unable to pull herself free, forever orienting herself around him. He waited till she stood in front of him, until he could reach up, brush his fingers against her chin. "I was so harsh, before, but that's only because I see such potential in you. You could be so powerful."

Shan swallowed hard, unable to stop the shudder that flowed through her. "I am only trying to live up to your expectations."

"And you are," he replied, his voice soft as silk, even as his touch burned. He was so warm, the fullness of all his power thrumming beneath his skin. If he wanted to, Shan knew he could destroy her utterly, but as he slid his fingers lower, pressing against the erratic beat of her pulse in her throat, he touched her like she was something valuable, more precious than jewels.

"I know what it must have cost you, turning Isaac in," he said, his kindness somehow more terrible than any cruelties he could have thrown at her. "But you proved yourself to me that day, and you have continued to in the months since. So perhaps I can trust you. Do you want it, Shan? Do you want to serve?"

"I am honored to serve," she replied, hating how raw she sounded, but he only smiled.

Leaning back, he released her, and Shan finally felt free. "Good. Then there is much to do. Perhaps I owe de la Cruz after all."

"Oh?"

"Yes," he replied. "Without him, I never would have found your true potential. Without his treachery, we would have never had the opportunity to expand the Blood Factory. And without his inspiration, we would never be doing this."

He gestured to the desk. "Bring me that journal, would you?"

She stepped back, taking it with trembling hands before returning it to him. He flicked through it with the familiarity of one who knew its contents intimately, before turning it back around, showing Shan a series of diagrams sketched in a skilled hand.

Of men—of *once* men—with vicious fangs, twisted by Blood Working into something monstrous. With dark wings, webbed like a bat's, stretching past their shoulders, dwarfing their lean forms. With sharply tipped claws on broken fingers and a vicious snarl on their faces.

"Vampires," she breathed, before looking back to the King, only to find a dark hunger writ across his expression.

"Yes," the King confirmed, leaning in like he was confiding a great secret. "Vampires. This is what Isaac will become if he continues on that path. And now that he is lost to the wind, we must be prepared. We need to study this, to understand it better than he ever could."

"And how would we do that?" Shan asked, already fearing the answer.

"Well, you gave me the solution to that, my dear." He pulled his lips back in a feral grin. "We're already changing so much, so why not this? We will build our own laboratory, we will study all that Blood Working has to offer, push every limit to see where our arcane knowledge can end. It starts with vampires, but it could be so much more.

"And I couldn't do without you."

There was such conviction in his eyes, and Shan felt the trap close around her. He had pulled her strings so perfectly, maneuvered her into a position where she could not say no, no matter how much even her twisted conscious railed against this.

All she could do was incline her head and swear, "As Your Majesty commands."

Chapter Fourteen

Isaac

Isaac never expected to visit the Fox Den again, but as Anton led him towards the building, he had to admit that it made sense. As one of the few gambling hells that accepted both Blood Worker and Unblooded patrons, it was a key part of the capital's nightlife. And, for the more industrious among them, a realm teeming with gossip and information, if one only knew how to look. A perfect haunt for one such as Antonin LeClaire the Second.

He still struggled to wrap his head around it, the role that Anton had played in his sister's schemes, the Eagle to her Sparrow. Not the diminutive bird that waited from the sidelines, but a fierce bird of prey, fluttering his plumage to catch the attention of those around him. And through that all, he had run a secret scheme behind Shan's back, building up this ragtag little rebellion spreading sedition through the streets.

A rebellion that Isaac was going to meet, and—if he proved himself worthy—join.

Anton veered to the side, pulling away from the front entrance where a burly enforcer would be waiting, only letting in the cream of Dameral's crop. It seemed that for those who had neither name nor prestige nor wealth, well—there were other ways in. Isaac shivered in relief, pulling his thick woolen cloak tighter around him, ducking towards the shadows that spread with the early evening's gloom. The witch lights that had for so long illuminated the capital's streets were dimmed, every alternating post left unlit.

An effect of the rationing, no doubt, and despite the eerie pallor it left on the cobblestone streets, Isaac was thankful for it. It made it far easier for Anton and him to slip by, another pair of poor souls heading to or from work, passing under the attention of the bored Guards who patrolled on their horses.

Anton led him down a short flight of stairs, into the basement of the building beneath the grand hotel, a bustling kitchen that served the needs of the gambling hell. Serving girls and boys danced around their unceremonious entrance, clearly used to the comings and goings of strangers. Anton's steps did not falter as he wove through the bustling space, heading for a set of stairs that did not head down into the hell, like Isaac expected, but up. Up and up, into the hotel, a narrow staircase made for the servants, like so many of these establishments had, allowing them to slip into position without any of their betters noticing it. Little more than tools, working to ensure the perfection of their glamorous lives, all while bleeding for the sheer privilege of it.

Something raw and ugly burned in him, the sour taste of bitterness along the back of his tongue. Everything he had worked so hard for, the dreams he once had when he was young and foolish, back when he thought being Royal Blood Worker would solve all his problems, had been built on this. A series of exploitations great and small, so interwoven into society that there was no way to untangle it without destroying it altogether.

They emerged into a small alcove, and even though Isaac had few opportunities to visit the lounge reserved for the most frequent visitors of the Den, the new angle threw him. The long bar to their left looked smaller, a narrow and slim space, and tables and chairs that spread out from it grander, but Anton did not lead him to any of those seats.

No, he was pulled through a large but unobtrusive door into a finely appointed room, one that looked as lush as any of the King's private gathering spaces in the palace. The room was set as a parlor, with large, plush chairs lined with the softest velvet, interspersed with hand-carved tables, places to rest drinks or small plates of food, the limited menu of the Den made more for sopping up the excesses of liquor than for a true meal. A fire—a true fire, no damning hints of red or the shimmering boil of magic that would have marked it as witch light—burbled merrily in the marble fireplace across the room, a grand centerpiece that took up the bulk of the wall.

But there were two people sitting there, waiting for them.

"Isaac," Anton said, nodding first towards the woman, then the man, "this is Maia and Alaric."

Isaac just nodded as he took a seat, meeting the inquisitive stares of the people across from him. The woman he didn't recognize, and he was sure he would have remembered someone as downright gorgeous as her. Her skin was dark and smooth, her braids pulled back tight against her scalp, highlighting a face that could only be described as striking. There was something sharp about her gaze that felt almost familiar—the same fire that he had seen in his own reflection. The look of someone who had fought for everything they had and was still deemed unworthy.

The man was someone he knew, if only in passing. As a Royal Blood Worker with no noble legacy, Isaac had precious little interaction with the House of Lords, but even he had heard of Alaric Rothe. The Unblooded Heir who refused to be denied what should have been his birthright. He cut a towering figure in the halls of Aeravin's oldest Blood Working families, but here, he seemed a little less frightening. Though he was still as large and imposing as ever, there was a relaxed set to his shoulders that made him a little more approachable, a little more human.

"Well," Maia said, with a smirk. "If it isn't Anton's pet Blood Worker."

Isaac didn't rise to the bait—that was his role in all this, after all. This revolution had started in the hands of the Unblooded who needed it most, and Isaac wasn't going to rip it out from under them.

He was a tool to be used, a promise of a future where it did not need to be an *us* versus *them*. "It is a pleasure to meet you."

Maia's lip curled into a smirk, but there was no kindness there. "Well, at least he's polite. Hardly what I expected, given his reputation. What of your other Blood Worker, Anton? He is late."

Isaac tilted his head to the side, wondering at who this *other* Blood Worker would be as Anton pulled out his pocket watch, a quick check of the time. "Easy, friend. Isaac and I are early."

Maia just sighed, leaning toward a serving table where a carafe of coffee waited next to a steaming teapot—a strange choice for a gathering in a place such as this. Isaac was used to the excesses of the Blood Workers, late night politics and strategy hashed out over wine or spirits, but this was a more serious discussion.

The kind of discussion that held the fate of an entire nation in its hands.

Isaac had just grabbed himself a cup when the door opened again, this time revealing a shock of golden hair and the face of one all too familiar—his beloved Samuel. No, not quite. Not *his* Samuel. Isaac took in the finely pressed suit and the coldly blank expression on his face, realizing that the one who stood before him was Samuel Aberforth, heir to the Eternal King, Councillor of Law. A costume as complete as any he wore as Royal Blood Worker, the true man hidden somewhere beneath, safe from prying eyes.

Behind him, though, was someone he did not recognize—an older woman with a stern face, her dark eyes flicking to him with something like disbelief. Though she wore a fine dress that rivaled any Blood Worker's, a silken sheath of emerald that hugged her form, Isaac could feel no trace of magic from her. It was a stark contrast to the man she stood beside, a gaping lack that he should not be able to recognize so easily.

He ran his tongue across his upper teeth, thankful to find no pinprick of pain, no sharp edge to cut himself open with.

Relief swept through him like a wave, only to be squashed as the woman closed the door behind her, blocking it with her body as she continued to stare him down. There was hurt there, the kind of hurt that felt personal—who was she?

And what had he done to her?

"Monique," Anton said, slipping back into his charming persona without so much as a blink. He took her hand in his, pressing a kiss to the back of it, but she was entirely unmoved, brushing Anton off like he was little more than a gnat. "Thank you for allowing us to use this space. Isaac, this is Miss Lovell, the proprietress of the Fox Den and our gracious host."

Isaac bit his tongue. With the force of the glare she pinned him with, there was nothing gracious about this. But Isaac did not dare risk stoking her ire any further—whatever this battle was, he'd have to win it on his own. There was no help to be found from this rebellion, as Maia and Alaric both watched with intense interest, like he was on trial before them.

And perhaps he was. But he kept his attention focused on the one who proved to be the biggest threat. "Madame, it is an honor to meet you."

"Honor," she sneered, before finally turning her attention to Anton. "How could you bring this murderer here? After he killed my girl?"

Oh, that was it, wasn't it? The dealer he had killed, taken from the Fox Den itself. One of the suppliers to the Blood Factory—an easily justifiable action, from his side of things. But he had never known them himself, outside of Dunn, hadn't known their stories or their hopes or dreams. It had been easy for him to do what was necessary, but he never stopped to think what it had been like for those who had known them, who weren't privy to the atrocities they had committed. Those who were just friends and neighbors and family, their loved ones taken away without rhyme or reason.

The reason came out, eventually, as such things often do. But it would have done little to ease the pain they had gone through in the meanwhile, to undo the very real hurt they had suffered.

And Isaac had never once stopped to think about it.

"He is not our enemy," Anton said, simple as that. He poured himself a cup of tea with an almost sickening amount of sugar and cream, then tossed it back in one go like he wished it was something stronger. "You know things are more complicated than that, Monique, and for the sake of our friendship I ask that you hear us out."

Monique looked like she was about to argue, but Anton stopped her with a significant look, the kind that spoke of years of friendship, reading each other without even needing a word.

Isaac once had something similar with Shan, an understanding that went deeper than time, and he had thrown it away when the King had plucked him from obscurity. Seeing it now, in others, reopened the wound he had long thought closed.

Hells, he had made a mess of everything. He had long history of hurting those he cared about until he found himself deep in the heart of Aeravin's atrocities, where he just hurt everyone instead.

"You both are right," Isaac said, "things are more complicated than they would appear, but I still need to explain myself. If you would be willing to give me a chance?"

Monique and Anton shared that look again, and she let out a sigh. "Fine."

"I'm sure that you are already familiar with my actions last year," Isaac began, wrapping his fingers around his cup of coffee, its warmth the only thing grounding him, "and I don't intend to waste your time. My actions were ... they were the only thing I could think of. There are a lot of things about being Royal Blood Worker that were a secret, even to the highest level of the government."

"That is true," Samuel chimed in, coming around to rest his hand on Isaac's shoulder. "I can confirm that the Royal Council had no information on this matter."

"Ah yes, we can't forget the Councillor," Monique sneered. The look she shot Samuel was assessing, like she was trying to figure out a threat, and Isaac had to catch the inhuman growl that reverberated in the back of his throat.

No one looked at his man like that.

But Samuel didn't flinch at all, simply arching an eyebrow as he projected that calm mask that Isaac was beginning to recognize as Lord Aberforth. Not precisely Samuel, not the man he loved, but what he needed to be to survive in this blood-soaked city. It was sad and a little frightening, how easily Samuel adapted, but there was also a fierce sense of pride.

Oh, Isaac would tear the world apart for Samuel, but he didn't need to. His love was strong enough to survive—to thrive—on his own.

"Yes," Samuel said, smoothly, "I am a Royal Councillor, and yes, I am the heir to the Eternal King. Which is exactly why your little group needs me. I can offer insights and information that you cannot get anywhere else."

"And we are just supposed to trust that you are on our side?"

Anton waved a hand, drawing Monique's attention back to him. "Don't forget that I was there when my sister found him. He never wanted any of this. We can trust him, that I am sure of. De la Cruz, though?" His smile was sharp, a challenge thrown at his feet. "He can grovel a bit."

Isaac couldn't help the little sneer that crossed his face—even now, when they were supposed to be allies, Anton couldn't help but needle at him, ever the brat. But, in the back of his mind, he knew the man had a point. Despite his attempts to explain, he still hadn't proved himself.

So grovel he would.

"I regret the consequences of my actions," Isaac said, holding his head high and refusing to flinch. Regret he had in spades, but he was beyond shame now. "I regret that they led the King to enforce new and harsher laws. I regret that I was unable to do anything to mitigate their bite. But I do not regret the souls whose lives I took, nor the power it brought me.

"Each and every one of them sealed their fates with their actions," he all but spat. "They were all part of the wider problem, kidnapping innocent Unblooded and delivering them to be slaughtered. As long as they lived, as long as their secret was kept, Aeravin would never have been free of those who shackled them." He glared at the woman across from him. "I am sorry for the hurt I caused you, but your girl was not innocent."

"Her name was Sarah—"

"And she was keen to betray her fellow Unblooded," Isaac interrupted. "Just because you never saw that side of her doesn't mean it wasn't real. I think everyone here understands just how steeped in lies this entire nation is, but if we cannot confront the uncomfortable truths, then we will never make any progress at all."

His jury had nothing to say to that. Monique had the decency to look somewhat ashamed pushing for this—it was a truth she wasn't ready yet to face, and though Isaac understood her grief, they did not have time to waste. And for Maia, well, it appeared that she agreed with him, a kind of grudging understanding crossing her expression as she offered a smile. Alaric remained as stoic as ever, but he inclined his head in a quick nod—as much of an approval as Isaac suspected he would get from him.

"Well, then," Anton said, smirking at everyone like this had played out exactly as he wanted it too. Maybe it had. Maybe he was more like his sister than any of them had ever realized, and here he was, already dancing to a new master's tune. "Are we agreed?"

"I don't like it," Monique said. "I don't like *him*."

"I'm not asking you to," Isaac replied. He did not need them to like him, he did not expect them to like him. What he wanted was for them to trust him. "But I can be useful."

Isaac stood, pressing his hands into the table, towering over them. He could smell the sudden tang of fear and unease, their hearts beating just a little bit faster. "I am ready to make up for that, if you would allow me to. If you would only give me the chance."

A fissure of tension went around the room, the pungent taste of fear sour in the back of his mouth. But Anton just stood to meet him, holding out his hand. "Welcome to the Resistance, Isaac."

Chapter Fifteen

Samuel

It was, somehow, even worse than Samuel had expected it to be.

If he was being brutally honest with himself, there was a part of him that was impressed with the sheer speed at which this had been accomplished. The top floor of the building had been reconfigured entirely, offices demolished to create what could, charitably, be called a clinic. There were a series of beds along the left-hand wall, ready for their patients, and the many tools of the trade were stacked in shelves along the other. The floor had been covered over with a glaze to help prevent any spilled blood from seeping in, glistening with an unnatural shine. Samuel could feel the buzz of the ward in the back, even if he couldn't see it, the curtain of magic that protected all the blood they drew from their prisoners.

A pair of Blood Healers in their white robes shuffled around the space, laying out needles and tubes on trays before large glass bottles. Thankfully, there were no large vats under the tables, the prisoners would not be drained until they were dead and desiccated, but . . .

It was still a Blood Factory, smaller in scope and size than what Samuel had once seen in the palace dungeons, but no less horrific. This was just the first of several, spread out through the smaller prisons across Dameral, and, eventually, all of Aeravin. The once hidden work of the Eternal King, codified into law, and built across an entire nation.

And still, Samuel felt like he was the only one who cared that it was wrong.

Dabney stood at his side, arms crossed over his barrel chest, looking just as proud as a father watching his child take their first, fumbling steps. "It's been hard getting this sorted so quickly, but I run a tight ship around here, my lord."

He still drawled out the title like an insult, low and sarcastic, but Samuel didn't pay it any mind. Dabney would never understand it, but despite his title and role, he didn't have any more power at the end of the day. He had learned that lesson well.

"You did very well," Samuel said, stepping aside. There was nothing for him to add or critique. Dabney had taken the basics from the King's plans and transformed it into something that would work for this space.

Honestly, Samuel wished it was the King here instead. Tristan would be truly impressed; Tristan would have praise to give.

Samuel just wished it was over already.

"Excellent. The rest of them should be finished by the end of the week. And now ..." Dabney turned, gesturing to Strickland, who nodded sharply before marching down the stairs. "Time for the trial run."

"The what?" Samuel choked, glancing to Dabney.

"The trial," Dabney repeated, slowly, as if talking to a simpleton. "And, after, with your approval, we can begin the real work."

Curling his fingers in, Samuel dug the sides of his claws into his flesh, careful not to split the skin. So that was what this was about, then. Forcing his hand, his approval, because his attempts to make this system any kinder had failed. It felt like a deliberate snub, an unnecessary bit of cruelty, but there was nothing he could do about it.

As the Councillor of Law, this was the role he was destined. There was no winning, only various levels of losing, and sometimes he wished that Shan had never pulled him from the slums.

"Fine." Samuel stood a little straighter, crossed his arms behind his back. He could look the part, he could act the part—it was what was expected of him, as Lord Aberforth. "Begin."

Strickland reappeared, prodding the prisoner in front of her, a middle-aged white man who moved with his head hung low. Samuel couldn't get a good look at his face but chose not to press the issue. What did it matter? The Guard had arrested this man for some crime that had barely hurt anyone. But once Samuel gave the word, every Unblooded prisoner booked through the system would have to give one additional pint of blood to the coffers, on top of what they had to give quarterly for the sheer privilege of living in this country.

Eight pints a year, minimum—then whatever the Guard could reasonably squeeze out of them.

The rage filled him, but Samuel choked it down, trying to swallow it all as he watched the man be guided to the bed with a dispassionate efficiency. The Blood Healer, a stern older woman with grey hair tucked away beneath her cap, arranged the prisoner on the bed while her younger compatriot unrolled a piece of cloth.

Neither of them smiled at the man, neither of them offered kind words or small talk. They positioned him like he was a doll, wrapping the tourniquet around his upper arm. Piercing the vein without a warning, dipping the open end of the tubing into the vial, measuring the blood as it flowed.

It was so casually cruel, and the worst part was the way the prisoner did not even protest. He let it be done without complaint, without ire, without judgement. Aeravin had already taken so much from him and those like him—so what was a little more blood, in the end?

Samuel felt like he was going to be sick, but turning his face felt like a bigger insult. So, he watched it all, witnessed it all, even though the prisoner would never know that he cared.

The prisoner was distinctly pallid by the time the jar was full, but whether that was from the blood drain or just the stress of the draw, Samuel didn't know. The older Blood Healer sealed the jar with a screw-top lid, sealing it from air and water, before carrying it back to the vault, passing through the ward without so much as a blink. Where it would be stored in careful stasis, ready to be transported to the central treasury of Dameral at the end of the week.

And it was done. The needle was pulled from the prisoner's arm, the tools set aside for sanitation and disposal, Strickland helping the man to his feet before escorting him out.

Not a word had been said the entire time.

"Well, then," Dabney said, shattering the silence with his booming voice. "My office?"

Samuel nodded, letting Dabney steer him towards the stairs, eager to leave all of this behind. They trudged down the stairs in silence, slipping through the quiet buzz of the Guard at work, until they reached Dabney's office.

It was a small space for one so important to the functioning of a city, of a nation. It was nothing like the grand spaces where the Councillors and nobles and the Eternal King held their meetings. It was the space of a working man, too small by far—a desk too large for the room, filing cabinets overflowing with papers, and not even the grace of a single window to ease the dankness.

Dabney closed the door behind him, and once again Samuel felt cowed by the man's size and presence. It wasn't just that Dabney was a walking fortress—because he was—but the confidence with which he moved through the world. He had an unwavering sense of righteousness, backed up by long history of laws and institutions, and Samuel had been such a fool to think he could ever make a difference here.

"Is everything to your satisfaction?" Dabney asked, hooking his thumbs into his suspenders as he waited.

Samuel swallowed hard. "I am positive the Eternal King would be proud of your work."

Dabney merely arched an eyebrow, and Samuel realized that it wasn't enough—this wasn't why he was here.

He was here to give the order to begin, to start the harvest in earnest. How much blood could they drain, so quickly, shuffling prisoners through this process with all the efficiency of a brutally oiled machine? He wasn't enough of a fool to dismiss what would happen next, the way that the Guard would crack down on enforcement, seeking any possible avenue to increase the coffers.

It was a system designed to be exploited, just waiting to be corrupted, and Samuel had run out of time to build in safeguards. The Blood Factories were already up and running, and here he was, forced to approve while his bill sat half-drafted on his desk.

He needed help, and there was only one person he could turn to.

So, he ignored the guilt that rolled through him, forcing out the words that Dabney needed him to say. That the King expected him to say.

"You have my authorization to begin," Samuel said, and Dabney flashed him a feral smile.

Lady Holland's office offered something of a balm to Samuel, a place where he could discuss things in direct language and hard numbers. Where he could figure out fiddly bits of wording and legalese without fearing judgement—Zelda might not care for the wellbeing of the Unblooded, exactly, but she cared deeply about ensuring the country ran smoothly for all parties.

And she was much less skilled at manipulating him than Shan was. Around Zelda, he could keep his head, and hells, was that something he needed these days.

Zelda welcomed him in with a quick nod, gesturing for him to take his seat. The pot of tea had already steeped, ready to pour, and Samuel was thankful that he had not faced much traffic during the ride over, even if he did not want to contemplate reasons why he had made such good time. The way that the streets were still mostly empty, even after all this time.

Curfew might have ended, but the Unblooded still feared to go where they weren't wanted or needed. The fear hung over Dameral like a shroud, and Samuel worried that it would take only the smallest of nudges to tip it back over into unrest.

"I've had the time to consider your request," Zelda said, cutting through his anxieties with the sharpness of a scalpel. "It is very thorough, but I have some notes."

The thin stack of papers sat before her; his half-finished bill marked up in her nearly illegible scribble. It was the draft that his secretary had delivered to hers—ridiculous, as their offices were just a couple of minutes' walk from each other.

But that was another facet of life as a noble that Samuel still hadn't got used to, employing people to do work that they could very well do themselves, and still treating them lesser for it. It soured his stomach every time he had to face their scraping bows and insincere groveling, but Lord Aberforth wouldn't flinch at it.

He so hated the role he had to play.

"Thank you," Samuel said as he pulled the papers towards him, squinting to make out what she had written. Most of them were annotations, a running list of historical cases that had done something similar. The Eternal King had been ambitious in appointing him to this role—there was so much he did not know, the formal language of law completely foreign to him, a whole history of precedents and case law that he had tried desperately to follow. What was and was not within his purview, what should go to the House of Lords, what was reserved for the King himself.

He still felt like he was drowning, but little tips like this kept him barely afloat. If only he didn't have to fear what would happen when Zelda called for the favor to be returned.

"You know," Holland said, conversationally. "This is going to earn you a lot of enemies, especially in the House."

Samuel didn't look up. He couldn't, unless he would falter. "I know."

What he was doing wasn't technically out of scope—many Councillors of Law before him had gone forward with similar measures, sidestepping the long and arduous process of running it through the House. Except they had done it to protect the rights and liberties of Blood Workers, not the Unblooded.

They hadn't attempted to codify protections into the law, extending the requirement for warrants to all cases, establishing a new branch of the judiciary to appoint publicly funded attorneys to anyone who couldn't afford to hire one themselves, outlined a stricter set of punishments for Guards who stepped out of line.

Holland hummed thoughtfully. "Are you sure that you do? Your name will protect you from many pitfalls, but it will not save you from the fallout of this."

Tilting his head to the side, Samuel avoided the question. "Is the law faulty?"

"No," Holland said, with a grimace, "but you know damn well that is not the issue." She spoke slowly, enunciating every word as if she were speaking to a child. "Stop pretending that things are that simple, Aberforth."

"If they have objections," Samuel continued, completely ignoring the kindness she was trying to do him, "then they can argue on the merits of the law. Which, thanks to your help, I am confident that I can defend."

Raising a hand to her temple, Holland cursed lowly. "I was a fool to indulge you in this." Samuel bristled, but she continued before he could even speak. "You are not entirely wrong, Samuel, these are very important things to consider given the Royal Blood Worker's new... proposal." She spat the word like the poison that it was.

And Samuel didn't even feel the slightest impulse to defend her. Even Holland could see the danger they faced, the danger that Shan refused to acknowledge. That their Eternal King did not even care to contemplate.

"But," Holland continued, "this isn't about just protecting the workforce so they can keep the rest of Aeravin afloat. This is your bias towards the Unblooded coming through, and there are deeper politics at play—"

Samuel stood, cutting her off. "And I am ready to face them."

Holland stared him down for a long moment, then finally sighed. "I truly hope that you are, Aberforth, because if you are not ..."

"I am," he swore, because there was no other alternative. He would bear the brunt of the hate, if need be, but he would see it done.

Because there was no other way.

Chapter Sixteen

Isaac

Anton had been true to his word, arranging to smuggle Isaac across Dameral to Shan. It had been a smooth operation, exacted without a single mistake. And as much as it galled him, Isaac was forced to admit that he been underestimating Anton for years.

Anton was far cannier than Isaac had ever given him credit for, a brilliant man held back by a system that had dismissed him for the insurmountable fault of being born without Blood Working. But Isaac had spent the last few days poring over the pamphlets that Anton had left him, cursing the way the Aeravin were content to let such a fine political mind go to waste.

And now he was reduced to this, another sulking villain in the night, sneaking Isaac into the LeClaire townhouse through the servants' entrance under cover of night.

"Please show him the rest of the way to my sister," Anton commanded the young woman who appeared at their side, before turning to Isaac. "Come find me when you're done."

"Find you?" Isaac echoed, arching an eyebrow.

"Shan will know," Anton said with a grin, before slipping up the back staircase, the one reserved for serving girls carrying pots of tea, maids with the laundry, and everyone else who strove to ensure that the household was maintained. Never seen or heard, working forever in the background, barely even seen as human.

It was nothing like what he had known, back when his parents had both still lived, before they had worked themselves to death in the service of the great nation they had strived so hard to join. His father, a member of the Guard, killed in action trying to stop a brawl between Blood Workers that had gotten out of hand. His mother, a Blood Healer, who had held his hand through his first treatments, who had given up so much for him to have a chance at a better life as a Blood Worker of Aeravin, wasting away over a broken heart.

Leaving him alone to fight for the future they had once dreamed of.

His life had been nothing like what the LeClaires had, nothing so grand and fine, and though once he had thought this was the kind of life he deserved, he had learned so acutely how poisonous the fruit truly was.

It seemed that Anton had as well, but Shan ...

That was part of what he was here to determine, so Isaac moved quietly behind the girl who did not bother to even give her name, head ducked low as he made his way through the townhouse. He had not been here that often, only a handful of times really. Before, when the late Lord LeClaire had still reigned, Shan had kept him carefully away, a sort of protection, he understood now. After, there had been so little time before it had all fallen apart.

The girl came to an abrupt stop, inclining her head towards a simple door before vanishing with a curtsy. Gone again, another shadow in this grand house.

The door opened easily under his touch, revealing one of the many little entertaining rooms of the house. Shan waited for him inside, perched on the edge of a low couch, gesturing for him to join her. He settled next to her, so close that her skirts brushed against him, a fall of dark silk that spilled like nightfall, even as her body burned so warm. He could feel the steady beat of her heart, could almost scent the teasing traces of her blood.

He swallowed hard, choking down that dark hunger, focusing on the words he needed to say. "I need your help."

"And you shall always have it, Isaac," Shan said, reaching out to hold his hand. It was so strange to hold her hands like this, without his claws, vulnerable and bare. She could slice him open, bleed him out, and he would have so little to defend himself with. "Anton did not tell me what you needed."

"I ... did not know how to explain it to him," Isaac said, simply. "How I would explain it to any Unblooded."

"Ah." Her tone was gentle, her eyes kind. She treated him with so much care and sympathy, even with the rough way they had left things, the last time they had spoken. "So, what the Eternal King was saying wasn't all lies, then."

Isaac closed his eyes, not wanting to see the judgement that was sure to be there. "He did not lie. There are consequences for what I did, Shan. Things that I barely understood, even with the access to the histories."

"Well, then perhaps you should look at this." She vanished for a moment, leaving him the aching vulnerability that he had created for himself, before returning with a small leather-bound journal. She pressed it in his hands, whispering, "Take all the time you need."

Isaac opened the journal, fingering the ribbon as he studied the vampires in all their glory. He pressed his fingertips against the carefully sketched monstrosities, as if he could wipe away the ink through force of will alone. But they remained unmoved and unsmudged, as he was forced to grapple with the magic he had unwittingly unleashed upon his own body.

A future he both feared and hungered for.

"Where did you get these?" Isaac asked, his voice sounding hollow even to his own ears. He traced his fingers against the claws on the page, skin darkened around nails grown thick and cruel. He hadn't worn his claws, the commonplace symbol and tool of Blood Workers, for months now, his hands feeling so empty and vulnerable. Part of him wondered what it would be like, having talons built into his very flesh so that none would ever be able to take them away, ever again.

"His Eternal Majesty," Shan said, drawing out the title with a little sneer, "does have more information that he hid from us. These are my own renditions, poor copies from memory, but . . . they get the point across." Her gaze fell back on the page, on the grotesque wings and the dagger-like fangs. "It frightens me, Isaac."

Isaac tilted his head to the side, startled by the unexpected burst of honesty. "It frightens you? Or *I* frighten you?"

Shan stilled, but the jackrabbit beat of her heart gave her away. She had never looked so much like prey, the creamy expanse of her neck so bare and tempting. It would take nothing to wrap his hand around it, to force her back onto the couch, holding her down as his teeth tore through the thin layer of skin to the veins beneath.

Would she taste sweet on his tongue, a bouquet of fruits and florals, soft as summer wine? Or heady and rich, with a smoky bite like bourbon at midnight? He ached to know, to hold the bright burst of blood on his tongue, but this was Shan.

Beautiful, furious, dangerous Shan—and she had already been hurt enough.

Isaac forced himself to his feet, crossing the room before he acted on the impulse, his back to the wall, fingers pressed against the wallpaper. He wished for the claws to anchor himself, something to hold him fast.

Shan let out a low, shuddering breath as the fear left her, and he hung his head, chasing the tempting images from his mind. "What do we do, Shan?"

She didn't respond, didn't even look at him as she picked up the journal. "Do you hunger, Isaac?"

He did not want to admit it out loud—he had done so well, burying it deep, choking on it in silence. Admitting it felt like a defeat, like giving in. But she had asked him directly, she was risking so much for him.

So, he answered honestly, pulling each word from the bleeding thorns around his throat. "Always. I can ... hear them around me. The hearts, beating." His fingers drummed out the sound on the wall, the steady *buh-dum, buh-dum, buh-dum* that constantly echoed around him, a cacophony building upon itself, louder and louder. "I eat, but it's not the same. No matter how much I consume, I still feel hollow."

He wrapped his arms around himself, pressing into his stomach as he doubled over, the pangs racking through him. "The thirst is the worst, though," he continued, barely even a whisper. Shan tilted towards him, like a penitent at his feet, hanging on his every rasping word. "I thought I knew thirst, but I drink and I drink and I drink, and I'm never satisfied."

Flitting his gaze back to her and that damned bare throat, he couldn't help the growl that escaped him. "There is only one thing I crave, but I don't know what would happen if I had it."

Shan approached him carefully, but he still flinched as she got close. He didn't trust himself around her, and with the careful way she moved, slow and deliberate, he realized that she knew that as well.

She was approaching him like he was a skittish cat, still halfway feral, and he was consumed by the urge to bite.

He did not, turning his head as she closed the last inches between them, her gentle hand resting over his heart, the sharp points of her claws pressing into the tender skin beneath. "I honestly do not know, either," she admitted, and it felt like she was presenting him with a precious jewel, open uncertainty so rare and delicate. "But the King and I, we're planning to find out."

"Find out?" Isaac echoed. "How?"

She tilted her gaze up, looking out from under her eyelashes, so soft and coy. "That is not something you need to worry about, darling. I can handle the King."

She sounded so calm, so sure, her heart not even skipping the smallest of beats. For someone so skilled at lying, it was alarming to know that she took such things as truths. She was a fool, just like he had been.

He cupped her face in his hands, ran his thumbs along her cheeks, felt the hitch in her breath. "Don't underestimate him, Shan. It will only hurt you more in the end."

The softness melted away, replaced by a frown and the glint of her eyes, darkly furious. "Don't underestimate *me*," she hissed. "I am so tired of it."

Isaac didn't know how to respond, how to make her understand. It wasn't her or anything that she lacked. But the Eternal King was so far beyond them, playing with forces they could never hope to understand, moving them like pieces on a chessboard, already five turns ahead.

"Please," he tried, shifting the angle of attack. "Don't get yourself hurt for me, Shan."

"That's your mistake, love," she replied, sweetly. "I'm not doing this for you. I'm doing it for myself. And if it happens to benefit you, all the better. Besides—" she stepped back, placing her own claws against her throat as she tipped her head to the side "—don't you want to know? Aren't you the least bit curious?"

"Shan, don't," Isaac said, even as he couldn't tear his gaze away from the long column of her throat, from the way she dug the tip of her claw into her own skin until it split, the blood welling up bright and red.

"Come have a taste, love."

He could feel his control crumbling as Shan stared him down, the blood slipping to well in the hollow of her collarbone. Her heart beat just a little bit faster, the rhythm echoing in his ears, her chest rising and falling in quick little breaths as the blood flowed over the swell of her breast, seeping into the neckline of her dress.

The air should have been filled with the pungent taste of fear, sour and bitter, but something different hit him. It called to him, rich and fragrant, the taste of her excitement—and arousal. She wanted this just as much as he did, and though her hunger was for a different sort of meal, perhaps they could both be sated.

Stalking forward, he pressed her back against the wall, dipped his head so that his breath skittered across her skin. This close, he could smell the blood—the strange tang of copper making his mouth water. "Are you sure?"

Shan didn't even respond, just pushed herself up on her toes. An offering, and Isaac was too weak to deny her any longer.

He pressed his mouth to the hollow of her throat, lapping at the blood like a cat.

The growl rose in the back of his throat, unbidden, as the flavor hit. As he dragged his mouth lower, nipping at the swell of her breast before moving his way back up, suckling at the wound she had inflicted on herself, sinking blunt teeth into her flesh and drawing more out.

It was like nothing he had ever tasted before, all his attempts at understanding flavor, at categorizing it, fell flat. It wasn't like wine, or bourbon, or marbled cuts of steak or the freshest fruit of spring, soft and ripe. It was hot and viscous, faintly metallic on the tongue, and it burned like fire all the way down.

Wrapping his hands around her waist, he pressed himself flush against her, and for the first time in months he felt whole.

Shan groaned, low in her throat, as her hands roamed his back, tangling in his shirt, her claws cutting through the thin, cheap fabric to get at the skin beneath. He could feel the chill of her claws slipping under the back of his binder, and he eased back long enough to rip the tattered shirt from his shoulders, to pull the binder up and over his head, tossing it to the floor beside them.

He took a deep breath as his lungs fully expanded, his small breasts hanging free. Shan cupped him with careful hands, sharp tips digging into tender flesh as she put her mouth to use, nipping the sensitive tips before soothing them with her tongue.

"Blood and steel," she whispered, nuzzling against the soft hair between his tits, working him with nimble fingers until he whined, "you're still so sensitive. I want you. Now."

Isaac twisted his fingers in her braid, pulled back hard and caught her lips with his. Shan kissed him deeply, uncaring that he fed her back her own blood. "And I need to feel you," he responded, spinning her around and quickly undoing the series of small buttons running down her spine. Her finery loosened around her as he took her apart, layer by layer, unwrapping her like a present as the silks and the petticoats and undergarments landed on the floor around him.

The claws remained on, catching on the band of his trousers, as she removed the rest of his clothes with more care than she had treated his shirt, as she dragged the back of her knuckle against his hard cock, dipping below to trail through the moisture that had gathered between his folds. "You want me too, don't you?"

"I do," he admitted, even his body betrayed him, so open and wanting. He shuddered as she paused, twisted her finger so that the metal brushed his most delicate flesh. One wrong movement and she would slice him open, would spill his blood onto the floor between them, and still his cock twitched with excitement. "Please, Shan."

"Eager boy," she teased, but she carefully removed her hand from him. She sauntered back to the low settee, relaxing back against the curve of its arm, sprawled as luxuriously content as a large cat. Spreading her legs so that they draped over each side, she gestured him forward with a single curl of her finger. "Don't be shy, Isaac, I'm sure that wasn't enough."

She drew the tip of a claw against the smooth skin of her thigh, the blood welling bright and red. And despite the hunger that yearned within him—as endless and deep as the night sky—he wanted nothing more than to shove his face into her dripping cunt.

But patience was a virtue he had learned over many years, so he knelt between her knees. Ran his tongue along the shallow wound, listened as her moans filled the room. He pressed his thumb against the split flesh, pulled the cut a little wider, and watched the arousal drip down her thighs. "You enjoy this?"

Shan shifted, peering up at him through her eyelashes. "And what if I do? Are you not enjoying it as well? Is the taste of my blood on your lips not making you hard?"

He speared her with two fingers, her back bowing as he filled her easily. "You know damn well that it is," he growled, pumping his hand, the room filling with the slick sounds of her desire. "But I am becoming a monster—what is your excuse, darling?"

Baring her teeth in a feral smile, she canted her hips up, chasing her pleasure. "You know me, Isaac. I've always loved a bit of danger."

Oh, the way she still knew how to play him, even after all this time. He lowered himself over her, letting her ride his fingers as he sought the comfort of skin against skin, his teeth returning to the gash on her neck as he dragged yet more blood from her.

As Shan came in a violent shudder, clenching on his fingers.

He felt like he was going to combust, so filled with power that he could barely contain. It was unlike any Blood Working he had ever done, somehow more potent. He had spent years perfecting how to build a bridge, learning how to weave together the strongest wards, how to imbibe blood from a vial to make his own skills stronger.

But this—supping power directly from another Blood Worker—could never compare to any of that. It felt like he was being remade from the inside out, and he knew with startling certainty that he would do anything to feel this way again. Now that he had the taste of blood, it would be harder to resist, the temptation wrapping itself around him like a shroud.

He removed himself from her body like she burned him, ignoring the ache between his own legs and the way she reached out, pleading without even saying a word.

"This was a mistake," he muttered, running his hand through his hair, tugging at it in a vain attempt to bring himself back from the terrible edge of the precipice he stood on. "We shouldn't have done that."

Shan blinked up at him, languid and slow, molasses on a hot summer day. She looked so self-contented, not just the ease that came after a good fuck, but the satisfied look of a schemer who had gotten everything to go exactly to plan. "But Isaac—"

"Why?" he gasped, the shock faded, replaced with something different. Anger coursed through him as he remembered the way she had smiled, pulling his strings. "You wanted this," he said, as realization coursed through him. "You wanted me to feed on you."

"Of course," Shan returned, rolling her head back on the pillow with a grin. "I offered, remember?"

"No," he thundered, charging towards her so roughly that she flinched. "You manipulated me, you made it so I couldn't resist, you wanted to see—" He cut himself off.

He didn't know why he had expected any different. It had never been about helping him. She had wanted to see what would happen, treated him as some little twisted experiment, offered her blood and her body in return.

She had used him, and as the biggest fool of all, he had let her.

"We're done."

His words fell on a cold silence, and Shan only stood on shaky legs. "If you're so sure," she snapped, crossing the room to grab her shift, pulling it on in one swift movement, "then I don't see what difference anything I could say would make. Get dressed and get out."

She gave him one last look, full of heartbreak that seemed too real to be entirely feigned, then stormed from the room, leaving him alone with only his thoughts and the thwarted ache of his own body.

Chapter Seventeen

Isaac

Isaac led Anton to the clinic, weaving through the early morning traffic. Luckily for them, they were able to blend in with the crowd, surrounded by people hurrying through the streets, on their way to jobs and the market and the other inevitabilities of survival. Isaac kept his eyes open for the Guard, but they mostly ignored him and Anton, looking for those who were more prime targets. Arrests had spiked sharply in the past few weeks, the Guard eager to steal as much blood as possible, leaving a taste of fear on the air, seeping into the way people moved—quick and purposeful, eyes focused only on the next step before them.

It hurt Isaac to know that this was all his fault, the unintended consequence of the choices he had made. He had known his little gambits would anger the King, but he had not intended to fail. Did not intend to let others suffer for his hubris, and yet, it happened nevertheless.

He nudged Anton with his elbow, tilted his head towards a ramshackle building. Two stories high, perched at corner intersection. The lower floor had been many sorts of shops over the years, from a grocer to a florist to one particularly ill-planned summer when it sold delicate stationery none around could afford, even if they wished to waste their sparse income on such frivolities. But what mattered was the floor above, the independent clinic run by a Blood Worker who had abandoned the dog-eat-dog power struggles of their kind.

It was one he had been to many a time, when he was younger and more innocent. When he was just another poor scholarship student, before the King had plucked him from all his peers at the Academy and elevated him far beyond the status of his birth. He prayed that she would still remember him, even after all this time. Celeste had a been a balm for this neighborhood, treating illness and injuries for a fraction of what the official clinics charged.

They climbed the narrow staircase, the handrail weak and wobbling under his touch. It looked even more disreputable than he recalled, though if that was the ravages of time or a fault in his memory, Isaac couldn't be sure. But the door opened easily under his touch, the sharp tang of cleaning supplies hitting his nose, and it was like he was transported back in time.

"How do you know of this place?" Anton asked, quietly, as he took in the small room they emerged in. The small counter was unmanned, but the chalkboard behind it instructed them to sit in a messy scrawl. Celeste was likely in one of the back rooms, treating another patient.

Isaac wasn't surprised—she often didn't have help, couldn't afford to pay them with the little income she got off her patients.

He settled in one of the hard chairs, foot tapping impatiently. "It's where I got my first treatments."

Anton plopped into the chair beside him with a curious hum. "Didn't trust the healers at the Academy?"

"It's not that," Isaac replied, as he tried to find the words. Because Anton was right—he could have gone through the official channels. Even with his family's standing, even with the scant money they had, there had still been options.

But this was what his mother had wanted, so he had acquiesced easily. "Celeste, the Blood Healer here, was a dear friend of my mother's. And besides, she was uniquely qualified to help."

She was like him, born to certain expectations only to defy them completely. And though her transition had been in a different direction and thus her own treatments were different, his mother had been insistent that she would at least understand his struggle.

And she had not been wrong.

Anton took the answer with a nod, but he continued his hungry appraisal, his dark eyes taking everything in. "There aren't many clinics like this in Aeravin."

"No," Isaac agreed, friendly as anything. "But there are some. Not all Blood Workers are your enemies."

Anton laughed, low and quiet. "You've been reading the literature, then?"

Isaac lifted a shoulder in a carefree shrug, playing at casual. "A bit," he lied, like he hadn't spent nights poring over them, picking apart each word and argument. And oh, how they were right—Aeravin hadn't been built for the Unblooded, it had been designed to use and exploit them.

But there were so many Blood Workers who were exploited too, even if they willfully turned their eyes from their own oppression. Isaac didn't have the damnedest clue how to reach them, but perhaps if Anton did . . .

Isaac had been such a fool to fall for his act for so long—despite the lack of magic in his veins, Anton was no less talented than his sister, and certainly no less cunning. It was unmissable as he turned that attention back to Isaac, ever calculating.

"So that's why you wanted me here," Anton replied, running his hands through his shaggy mop of hair. "Fine, then, show me what it's like. Educate me."

Isaac grinned, but before he could say more the curtain behind the desk ruffled, an older woman shuffling through. She leaned heavily on a cane, her wrinkled face shining with relief as she made her way towards the door. She nodded at them as she passed, her voice whisper soft and paper thin. "Don't worry, boys, whatever ails you, our Celeste can help."

"Now don't go making promises that I might not be able to keep, Granny," Celeste called as she stepped into the room, her voice booming through the small space. She was a tall woman, though reed-thin, dark of skin and incredibly beautiful. There was a strength to her features that aways reminded Isaac of a hero out of myth—made of something greater than flesh and blood, eternally lovely and wise. But it had been her strength of presence that awed Isaac, moving through the world as if daring it to tell her that she was lesser in any way.

He had tried to be like that, too, as Royal Blood Worker. He never pulled it off.

He stood, unable to hide the honest grin that split his face. "I don't know, I think that you won't have that much trouble with me."

Celeste froze, hand pressed over her heart, as she took him in. Her eyes raked him over from head to toe, no doubt cataloguing everything that looked ill or wrong with him, before she crossed the room and pulled him into a bruising hug.

"My child," she said, so soft in his ear, "I thought I would never see you again. Not after—"

She cut off, and the old woman chortled. "I'll leave you to this, then. See in you in two weeks, Celeste."

"Two weeks," Celeste confirmed, off-handed, still unable to tear her eyes from Isaac.

Still chortling, the old woman saw herself out, and Isaac squared his shoulders. "I know there is a lot to discuss, Celeste, but I did come here for reason. I need—"

"I know, son," she finished for him, stepping back. "Do not worry, I will see to whatever you need. For your mother's sake, may she rest in peace. And who's this?" She nodded towards Anton, who jumped to his feet, holding out a hand.

"A friend of Isaac's," Anton said, as Celeste gave him a firm handshake. "And someone with a business proposition."

Celeste looked at him through narrow eyes, assessing, but Anton did not so much as flinch. Unstoppable force meeting an immovable object.

They would make good partners, if Isaac could pull this off.

"Well, in that case, I'd be happy to have a discussion, but I will need privacy to see my patient." She stepped back through the curtain. "Let's get this over with. Right this way."

Isaac followed after her, Anton quick on his heels. It was just as

Isaac remembered it—the large room behind the entrance, not quite as sterile as many other Blood Workers' clinics. The floor was wooden, not sealed marble, but the large metal table was the same. Celeste kept her tools hung on the far wall, small blades and large saws and tubes and vials, all ready and waiting to be used.

Most of the time, such implements weren't used, but sometimes, when the damage was bad enough, was old enough that the body had healed itself wrong around a trauma it could not mend, such implements were needed.

He wondered if that would be him, one day soon. Blades sinking into his flesh to reveal the corruption that had spread through his body, peeling away skin and muscle to reveal if what lay beneath was still human.

"So," Celeste said, drawing his attention back to the present. "What do you boys want to talk about?"

Isaac settled on the table, pulling himself up and letting his legs dangle off the edge. It made him feel so young, so vulnerable, but it was Celeste. If there was anyone he could trust with this, it was her. "Do you know what happened last summer?"

"With your antics?" She stared him down, acting the part of the stern aunt, there to judge him in his mother's absence. There were new lines around her eyes that she hadn't had all those years ago, and her hair was streaked through with grey in the roots. Like everyone else in this forsaken country, she was running on fumes and exhaustion, and Isaac wondered how much of that was on him. "Yes, I am aware. *Everyone* is aware. What were you thinking, child?"

He swallowed hard, the all-too familiar shame rising in him. "I was thinking that I had made a terrible mistake, and that if my mother could see me, she would be so disappointed if I did nothing at all."

Celeste closed her eyes, let out a long sigh. "Yes," she breathed, looking so pained, "yes, she would have been. But you've always been too ambitious for your own good." She took his hand between hers, gave it a comforting squeeze. "But how are you even alive? Our Eternal King is not that merciful."

"Well, I have some friends in high places." Isaac attempted a smile, only for it to fall flat. "Friends who do not agree with our esteemed ruler's methods. In fact—"

Isaac caught Anton's eye and tilted his head. The floor was his.

"Isaac does himself little credit," Anton said, stepping in. "His methods might have been ... unwise, but his heart was in the right place. Unblooded should not be used as little more than cattle for the Blood Workers' greed."

Celeste nodded. "You're right about that. What's your name?"

"My name is unimportant," Anton said, reaching into his breast pocket to pull out another of those clever pamphlets. "What is important is the name I choose, and the symbol it could become."

She plucked the pamphlet out of his fingers, turned it over in her hand to see the careful type set across the front page. "Ah, I've seen these before." Glancing towards Isaac, she arched a single eyebrow. "Haven't gotten into enough trouble, have you?"

"Please, Tita," he said, pulling out the old honorific, the title his mother had once insisted he use for her. They might not have been related by blood, but she had been his aunt in every way that mattered. "There is so much corruption at the heart of this nation, surely you understand."

Pulling away, she crossed the room, rubbing at her eyes. Anton stepped forward, but Isaac caught him around the wrist, pulling him to a stop.

This was something that Celeste needed to grapple with herself.

"You know, I never had any children of my own," Celeste murmured, "but I've always considered you to be like a son to me. Especially once your parents passed. But that Academy got its hold on you, promised you—"

"Pretty lies and dreams that never turned out the way that I hoped," Isaac finished for her. "I was too ambitious. I *am* too ambitious. And perhaps my first attempt failed, but that doesn't mean I am going to stop."

Now, he had learned to be more cunning. To be careful and slow.

And most of all, now he was no longer alone. He had Samuel, and maybe Shan, and most surprising of all, the man beside him.

He released his grip on Anton's wrist, and the man stalked forward. He was so confident, so in his element, as he stood before Celeste.

"But," Anton said, full of righteousness that took Isaac's breath away, "change cannot come without everyone's involvement. Unblooded and Blood Worker alike. If we are going to take down the Eternal King, there needs to be something to take its place."

"And how do I fit into this grand plan of yours?"

"My friend," Isaac cut in, "is well connected with the Unblooded, and I have learned the ways of Aeravin's grand lords. But the Blood Workers, like you, who are little more than cogs in the great machine of our nation—that is what we need help with."

"You were just like me, once," Celeste said, kindly.

"And we're back to my dratted ambition." Isaac clenched his fist so hard that his nails dug into the meat of his hand. "I rose so high, only to fall again. There is no place for me there anymore, Celeste. You know this. My words will mean nothing to them."

The look she gave him was so soft, so full of pity, that pain cut through him like a knife. But she only nodded. "You're right, of course."

Anton smiled. "We're going to be expanding past literature, doing what we can to help those who need it. Clinics like yours are important, but so few in this nation, and that is not even touching all the other ways the Unblooded suffer."

Celeste cocked a brow, slowly appraising. "And what kind of help would that be, exactly?"

Anton grinned, easy and casual. "Well, that kind of thing that could get us in grave trouble with the Guard, should they catch wind. But, according to the laws of the land—" his smile transformed into a smirk "—it's not illegal for Blood Workers to participate in any of this work."

"Well, *Friend*," Celeste returned, "it seems that you are a clever one, after all. If it means helping those who get hurt, I can do that. It is what I have spent my life doing, after all. And, perhaps, even steer you towards other like-minded individuals."

"In that case." Anton held out his hand, and Celeste grabbed it. "Call me Anton. I hope this is the start of a fruitful partnership."

"Me too, but now—" she leaned back "—get out so I can treat my patient."

Anton held his hands up in surrender. "All right, all right. I'll be in the waiting room, if you need me. Celeste, until next time."

He backed out of the room with a jaunty little salute, earning a small laugh from Celeste. "He seems like even more of a handful than you, Isaac."

Isaac shook his head. "You have no idea."

"I'm sure I will." She crossed the room to grab a small dagger—it wouldn't take much blood to build the bridge between them, but the actual work of manipulating his hormones was an incredibly delicate piece of work. "The usual then?"

Isaac swallowed hard. "Yes, but ... there are other things going on in my blood, Celeste. Things that I do not fully understand, nor would I expect you to. But ... I need this as well."

She placed her hand on his, stopping him. "I understand, Isaac, believe me. I understand how important this is, and I will take care of your transition needs again. But, if there are other things you need, please know you can talk to me about them. I might not know the solutions, but I am a Blood Healer."

"Thank you." Isaac closed his eyes and held out his arm. "But I might not be entirely human anymore."

It was barely a whisper, hanging between them. The word he was too afraid to say, the knowledge he was too terrified to claim. It was there, even though he refused to look at it—the changes that he had wrought, the hunger that wouldn't end. The myths he had discarded as nothing more than nightmares meant to frighten children, coming to nest in his own body. Hatching into something horrid.

Vampire.

The images Shan had shown him still haunted him, somewhere between a dream and nightmare.

Celeste did not judge him, just carrying on with her business. Isaac had been on the receiving end of this particular work more times than he could count, for all the treatments he had undergone since he hit puberty. But this felt different, the motherly touch of Celeste's fingers as she tied a strip of fabric around his upper arm contrasted with the genuine fear at what she would find.

The needle slipped under his skin, so quick and so precise that it barely hurt at all, and they watched his blood pool in the vial, a deep, dark red that almost bordered on black. Celeste pulled in a sharp hiss through her teeth at sight of it, and Isaac ducked his head.

It was worse than he had thought.

Celeste filled only the one, slipping the tourniquet from his flesh as she ran her thumb over the wound, smearing the blood with her thumb before lifting it to her lips. Pausing before it even touched her tongue, Celeste used her other hand to pin his wrist to the table. "Son..."

He didn't even look down at himself. He had felt it happen, too. The puncture, small as it was, closing itself of its own accord, without even a touch of Blood Working. "I didn't do it," he breathed. "Not consciously."

"Unconscious Blood Working," Celeste murmured to herself, before taking in that bit of blood. He still didn't watch her, even as he knew that his blood was odd, but he felt the moment the bridge thrummed to life, binding them together.

Felt her presence brushing against him before recoiling in shock. There were no secrets here, not bound as they were. Isaac forced himself to watch the way her finger pressed hard against her lower lip, marring the frown forming as her brows came together in thought. "Oh, child, what have you done to yourself?"

"Quite a lot, it would seem," Isaac returned, his voice rough in his own throat. "It wasn't so bad, at first, not until—Dunn. He was a Blood Worker, not Unblooded like the rest, and I wasn't able to absorb the power from his blood without absorbing his Blood Working as well." He wrapped his arms around himself, nails digging into his own skin, agitation coursing through him. He could still picture it, the sneer on the Eternal King's face as he was mocked, as he was called an *amateur*. But in the end, compared to one who was Eternal, that was all he could ever hope to be.

And now he was facing the consequences of that. But that was not the most important question. "Can it be stopped?" he whispered, hating how breathless with hope he sounded.

"I ... don't know," Celeste murmured, dropping her head so that she wouldn't have to meet his eyes. "You were right, it is Blood Working beyond anything I have ever seen. I do not know why or how, but it is changing you at some fundamental level."

He heard the question she dared not ask, the curiosity that burned but she was too kind to press. If he did not wish it, she would let it drop, and he was so thankful that she took her oath as a Blood Healer so seriously. Patient care and comfort and privacy, things many others just gave lip service to, were things Celeste never pressed.

But he did not want to hide it from her, perhaps the only person left who might have some sort of understanding.

He breathed the word. "Vampire."

Celeste shrunk back, fear grabbing her. Isaac did not begrudge her in the slightest—had their positions been reversed, he would have responded in much the same way. But she didn't question his pronouncement, didn't deny its possibility, just looked at him with such tenderness and heartbreak that he feared he was going to shatter.

"Please," he whispered, his voice low and begging, "let's just continue with the treatment."

"I'll get to work then," she said, pushing past all the strangeness in his blood and his flesh and focusing only on the thing that he had come here for.

He was so thankful for that.

Chapter Eighteen

Shan

Shan flicked the last of her cigarette out of the window as they rounded the corner, ending the short journey from the Academy to what was known, both affectionately and derisively, as the Blood Treasury. Yet another of her many scheduled inspections had snuck up on her, another exhausting task that she had to see to, the many little obligations of the Royal Blood Worker twisting around her, the chains she would never be able to break.

The carriage jerked to a stop, and Shan pushed herself from her seat, stepping out of the carriage and tilting her head back to look at the squat building rising over her. It was a bit of an anomaly in Aeravin, a city built of tall, thin buildings, pressed tight against each other like the pages in a book as the city struggled to fill every available space. The Treasury only rose three stories, hardly tall at all, but more than made up for it with its width, wide as a city block, a monstrosity of slate and stone, its narrow windows protected by iron bars crossing over them.

It was a relic of times long past, when Aeravin was a freshly founded nation, still shaking off the slick gore of its afterbirth as it established itself as a world power. And so much of that power was housed here, behind an endless series of wards, patrolled by a robust contingent of Guards, where the Blood Workers of Aeravin stored the very source of their magic—the blood they harvested from their own citizens.

How much of a fool was Shan that she had bought into lies for so long? The sheer scope of it should have rendered the whole farce unbelievable, but as one of the privileged few, Shan had never let herself look at it head-on. It had been a kind of self-defense, a way of protecting all the foundations that her world had been built on.

Until Isaac came along and ripped that out from under her, uncaring if she fell to her death.

But she hadn't—she had taken that moment of chaos to prove herself, climbing to previously undreamed of heights in the process. And now, as Royal Blood Worker, this was one of her many domains, perhaps even her most important one. The slowly refilling coffers of blood were more than her duty, it was her greatest success and her most terrible villainy.

And no matter what lay between them now, no matter the disgust that Isaac harbored for her, she would not let herself fail again. Especially now that he had turned away from her a second time.

She held her head high and strolled into the building, her ceremonial robes trailing behind her. The Guards at the door barely even acknowledged her, flicking once to the unmistakable silhouette of her robes, the shimmer of her claws in the morning light. They weren't there to stop people like her, only the Unblooded who couldn't prove that they were there on their master's orders, handling the affairs of those greater than them.

The building opened in a large atrium, taking advantage of the floors above, a vaulted ceiling that grew to a height that made one feel so terribly small. Chandeliers powered by witch light filled the open air, casting an eerie glow that reflected through the glittering crystals. It cast the patrons in a dim red light that felt odd, especially so early in the day, when the sun shone cool and crisp over a winter morning. A grand and stately theater, run with all the ruthless efficiency of business as lines of untitled Blood Workers and well-off servants stood in line to present their writs of requisitions to the tellers, seated behind sheer panes of glass with only a small gap to slip papers through.

She could hear them, even now, arguing fruitlessly for just a pint more blood. Enough to keep the witch light burning so they wouldn't have to turn to candles, to keep their gardens lush and fragrant even as winter crept in, as steady and unyielding as the dawn. All frivolous matters, when institutions like the Academies and Healing Clinics had far greater need. But none of them had ever known true need, and thus, this very reasonable system turned into a form of oppression.

She turned away from the public front of the Treasury, striding towards a small doorway in the back. It, too, was flanked by a pair of Guards, and as they saw her approach, the man on the left pricked the skin of his palm with his own claw, placing the bleeding wound against the faintly shimmering glow, peeling back for her to pass. It was a simple security precaution, the many wards of the Treasury keyed to the rotation of those who guarded it, keeping the wards as simple as possible to prevent them from fraying and buckling.

Shan knew from experience that she could shatter it, if she wanted, but it would take time—time for the tellers to call for backup, time for the Guards on duty to take her down. Such an elegant system, simple in execution and tedious in its logistics. But she couldn't think of a better solution, embracing the way the ward crackled as she stepped through, the burn of it raising the hairs on her arms as she cleared it. The Guard removed his hand, letting it snap back into place.

And without so much as a glance back, she carried on, passing through ward after ward as she descended to the nearly cavernous chambers beneath the Treasury where the majority of Aeravin's blood was stored. The temperature dipped as she went, and Shan pulled her winter robes tighter around her, fingers pressed in the thick wool, unable to stop the shivers and gooseflesh that ran across her body as she tasted the magic in the air.

Storing blood was an easy enough process, once one learned the proper wards to protect it from spoiling. Some Blood Workers kept their supplies in specially crafted bottles, others in large cabinets warded to keep the blood fresh. But at this scale, something more was needed, and Shan took careful steps down into what felt like an icebox.

And there, waiting for her, was the Eternal King, his normal finery hidden by the long cloak that cut across his shoulders, accentuating his breadth, before falling around him like a spill of blood right from the vein. It shimmered in the witch light, a luxurious velvet so soft that Shan had to resist the urge to run her fingers down its length—a presumption that felt as dangerous as sticking her hand into the maw of a hungry wolf.

But as he turned to look at her, those emerald eyes glittering with something unfathomable, he only smiled and beckoned her forward. "Look at what you've done."

He gestured at the vault he stood in front of, and Shan stepped forward, appraising the change with a heady dose of pride. When she had first ascended, the stores had been packed full, the different vaults filled with rows upon rows of blood, every ounce carefully tracked and accounted for, the grand ledgers of Aeravin's supply carefully tallied in the offices above. But with the disruption of the Blood Factory, that balance was shattered as far more blood went out of the Treasury than came into it, even with the increased taxes. It was like trying to refill a well with a teaspoon as the vaults emptied, one by one.

And now, they were starting to refill, recently empty shelves holding fresh bottles. It would be a long while before they were fully filled again, and rationing would need to continue for some time, lest they lose the careful balance upon which they stood, but it was a start.

A victory, however small.

"You did this," the King repeated, his breath warm against her ear, his voice a low rumble that she felt more than heard. His hands landed on her shoulders, squeezing tight, the strength of him evident even through the layers of wool between them. "I should have come to you a long time ago, Shan. I shouldn't have dismissed your potential, not when you have proven to be the most capable Royal Blood Worker. The last one could barely stand to be in the vaults."

The comment, as vague as it was, still cut her to the marrow. Because yes, Isaac would have never accepted this. Could never have accepted this, and that is where he had failed.

The King had been right to trust her, and though there were those who would damn her for taking this path, there was no other option. She had never wanted to create a new Aeravin built on the bones of those who had come before, had feared the vacuum and terror that would naturally follow any sort of revolution.

And what was the cost of a pint of blood when weighted against a life? Well, nothing at all.

It was a terrible calculus, but one that she was used to. Still, she feared that she would never get Isaac to agree with her. That she was losing her careful grip on Samuel, letting his bleeding heart slip through her fingers.

But as she looked upon what she had achieved already, in so little time, she swore that this was only the beginning. That no matter what happened, she would drag Isaac and Samuel kicking and screaming into the future.

"I need to see the ledgers," Shan said, turning to the real reason she had come. As much as she loved rejoicing in her successes, there was always more work to be done.

The King inclined his head, a shallow but imperious nod. "Of course. Shall we retire to an office?"

"We should," Shan agreed.

The King held out his arm, and after only a second's hesitation, she accepted it, taking her place at his side. "And when we are done reviewing the ledgers, there is something I would like to speak with you about. A new educational opportunity for my Royal Blood Worker."

She tilted her head to the side. "Oh?"

The King didn't respond—he only flashed that smile again, the one that was there and gone again as he refused to answer. It wasn't malicious, she realized. The King was teasing her, a bright bit of playfulness that she never expected from him.

The world fractured around her, everything reframing itself in a single, crystalline moment. She wasn't merely his subordinate, but his colleague. This was respect—an easy and open acknowledgment not only of her title, but of *herself*. So different from all the years of barely disguised pity, or outright derision, from the skepticism that came after she had been appointed Royal Blood Worker.

This was new, this was intoxicating, this was everything she had worked so hard for.

And she could get used to it.

Amelia settled in the chair across from Shan, her cheeks still flushed a charming shade of pink from the winter's chill. Her traveling cloak—a luscious piece of velvet, a blue as deep as the night sky and speckled with flurries that gave it an enchanting, starry feeling—was whisked from her shoulders by an Unblooded serving boy. There and gone again, quiet as a mouse and just as unobtrusive.

Well, perhaps not entirely unobtrusive, as Amelia smirked at his fading profile. "You know, I bit my lip, nary a complaint with the new restrictions, but I did resent the curfew. I never realized how crucial they were to our day-to-day life."

Shan simply hummed her agreement, already reaching for her glass of wine. The curfew had done a disservice to the social scene, where restaurants and clubs such as the fine establishment they were in had to shutter their evening services due to lack of staff. "I agree, it was quite a disappointment. But His Majesty was only trying to safeguard his people."

She hadn't recognized it for what it was at the time, too concerned for the safety of her brother. But Isaac had forced the King's hand, taken an already tremulous peace and shattered it with no regards to the consequences. She was just thankful that, despite his recent escape, he had yet to do anything foolish enough to tip them back over the edge into unrest.

Perhaps there was hope of getting him out of Aeravin yet, despite how roughly they had left things. How he had twisted her attempts to help him through the unkindest of lenses, still expecting the very worst of her. But that was neither here nor there, not with Amelia Dunn waiting on her.

"I have ordered us the special," Shan said, placing her glass down and forcing a smile onto her face. "I hope that suits."

"Of course," Amelia returned, "they have the best shellfish in all of Dameral."

It was true, and access to establishments like this was one of the many little perks of being named Royal Blood Worker. All she had to do was say her title and a table would be immediately found for her, no matter how busy they were. And after so long spent cooped up in the Academy, it was refreshing to take meetings like this, over a spread of shared food and wine, almost like they were friends.

Shan banished that ill thought the second it appeared. She had a hard enough time managing Samuel and Isaac, and the last thing she needed was to find more authentic connections to nurture, especially given the woman who sat across from her. Just as poisonous as she was, a deadly nightshade wrapped in a Lady's carefully cultivated elegance.

The serving boy returned, carrying a large tray of oysters, clams, and mussels—the freshest catch of Dameral, cleaned and served raw with a variety of sauces. Lemon and garlic, horseradish and vinegar. A feast for a single person, but with another to share it, an almost reasonable indulgence.

Guilt clawed at her, a brief and sudden flash as the serving boy bowed and vanished. She knew that he would never be able to dine on such fine cuisine, that Unblooded like him served Blood Workers like her without ever knowing what it would be like on the other side. But as Amelia leaned back, sucking a succulent oyster straight from the shell, Shan realized that for all she had suffered—for all the work she would do that would be forever unrecognized and unsung—she deserved these little moments of luxury.

She deserved this and so much more.

Amelia settled back in her seat, dabbing at her mouth with a napkin, the daintiness of the movement a stark contrast to the sharpness of her claws. "People have been talking about you, Shan."

Shan leaned forward, selecting her first morsel with care, as if what Amelia was here to report was of little importance. In truth, it set her stomach twisting, though she dared not show it. "Have they?"

"They have," Amelia confirmed, looking as smug as a cat with cream. "You know that I never doubted you, of course, but some of our peers had ... concerns, given your parentage. Ridiculous, I say! To judge a child on what they had no choice in."

"It is kind of you to think so," Shan returned, even as she thought of Amelia's own father, the late Councillor of Law who held the seat before Samuel. He had said something similar to her once, with a harsh kind of gentle cruelty, reminding her that she would ever be an outsider till she overcame the stains that marked her as other.

The failure of her father, the foreignness of her mother. Being Royal Blood Worker changed none of it; if anything, it made the scrutiny all the worse.

"It's not kind," Amelia said, with more fervor than Shan expected. "It is truth."

Shan looked up, barely able to keep the surprise from spreading across her face. That did not sound like a well-practiced lie, that had the unmistakable ring of honesty. "I ... thank you."

"There is no need to thank me for that." Amelia glanced away, as if the moment had turned a touch too sincere for her as well. "Thank me for smoothing away the ripples your recent policy has made."

"Ah, that." Shan inclined her head. "For that, you do have my genuine thanks. I knew that the implementation would be contentious but ..."

"But we didn't have time to wait," Amelia finished for her, with the smooth confidence of one who had made this argument many times before. "It was a necessity born from unprecedented times."

Shan smirked at her. "Have you considered becoming a speechwriter, Amelia? You're quite good at it."

Amelia laughed, slurping another mussel then discarding the shell into the ever-growing pile. "Alas, if I didn't have my own seat in the House to think about, perhaps it would make a passingly interesting diversion. But..." There came the cunning smile, the Amelia Dunn that Shan knew all too well sliding to the surface. "I am only following your lead."

Only making herself indispensable, like she had promised at that salon all those weeks ago. But Amelia hadn't waited for the new season of the House of Lords to come around, electing herself to seed Shan's interests to those around her. It was still a new dynamic for her, but Shan couldn't lie to herself.

She could get used to this, holding power easily with one hand while pulling the strings with the other. Sure, this opening gambit had been a daring one, had tested the bounds of what she was allowed in her role and the sensibilities of those too delicate to face the harshness of reality. It was something Isaac would have never dared, something few in the long history of Aeravin would have dared.

And Shan was lucky to have someone like Amelia Dunn to help smooth the way.

"You know," Shan said, carefully, weighing each word. It was always a delicate balance, how much to tempt without making any promises she might not be able to keep. But something deep within her stirred her to try, even if she could not make herself look the impulse head-on. "I appreciate all that you have been doing, Amelia, and I want you to know that I always pay my debts."

Amelia demurred with a blush that made her look softer than her plain features should have allowed. It made her look more fetching, Shan had to admit, a little more approachable. "Please, Shan, I am not so underhanded as to use our friendship in such a matter."

"I did not say you were," Shan said, playing into the dance that they both knew they had to perform. Nothing was ever simple, as women of their station, but Shan found that she was unexpectedly honest in this. "I mean it, Amelia."

Amelia stared at her for a long moment, her eyes calculating—sharp like the jagged icicles—before her entire expression shifted. She looked so much younger in that moment, more innocent, and Shan wondered, perhaps, if there was something true here.

The moment was fleeting, as Amelia tossed her hair back with a laugh, the levity washing away the awkwardness. "We do make quite the team, don't we?" Her hand slid across the table, fingers twining with Shan's in a playful squeeze as the sharp steel of their claws rang a delicate tingle.

"We do," Shan agreed. "And Aeravin won't know what hit them."

Chapter Nineteen

Isaac

The hunger wouldn't abate, not since the moment Isaac tasted Shan's blood. It lingered constantly in the back of his mind, a tickling in the back of his throat that he could not ignore, an endless ache deep in the pit of his stomach. It had been days since that disastrous meeting, and no matter what he ate, what he drank, he could not find satisfaction.

And that wasn't even the worst of it. He could handle suffering; he could handle pain. What he couldn't handle was the way he had to hold himself at arm's length from those around him. Like Anton, who perched on a chair halfway across the room from him, dark eyes shining with something that felt like opportunity, as fearless and casual as ever. The pages he had brought for Isaac's review—new pamphlets meant to be shared with Blood Workers like Celeste, those who could potentially be pulled to their side, lay forgotten, something far more intriguing catching the man's attention.

But it didn't matter. Isaac could hear every single beat of Anton's heart, could smell the tang of his sweat on the air, could almost taste the blood that lingered just beneath his skin, just waiting to be taken.

"Something wrong, Isaac?" Anton asked, the question feeling oddly pointed.

"It's hard to explain," Isaac began, inching towards the edge of his seat. It was foolish of him, he knew he was putting Anton at risk, despite the man's cavalier attitude, his self-control hanging on the edge of a knife.

Even that little shift closer brought another surge of hunger as his jaw started aching. Anton tilted his head to the side, curious as ever, unwittingly exposing the line of his throat and Isaac felt the teeth in his mouth shift, fangs plunging down through his gums as they settled into place, sharper and more gruesome than any claws he had ever worn.

Another new change, another thing to fear, but all rationality was lost behind the overwhelming desire to tear into his ally's flesh. A growl caught low in his throat, and Anton flinched back at last, the sheer primal force of fear shattering his carefully maintained persona.

Like some hapless woodland beast, realizing they were well and truly fucked.

Isaac clenched his hands over his mouth, turning from Anton so he couldn't see the fangs he had sprouted. Like he could hide what he had become, if he just turned his face.

The fool that he was, Anton ignored his own safety, coming to stand in front of him. Isaac breathed in heavily through his mouth as Anton wrapped his fingers around his wrist, pulling it to the side, a demand falling from his lips. "Let me see."

"You don't want to," Isaac replied, muffled by his own skin, but Anton just smiled, slow and cruel.

"Oh, but I do. Let me see what we're working with." Isaac still didn't move, and Anton rolled his eyes. "You do not scare me, de la Cruz."

"I should." But he let Anton move his hand, opening his mouth as Anton leaned in and stared into his maw with something like curiosity.

"Fascinating," Anton muttered, finally releasing him and stepping back. The distance wasn't much, but the extra foot or two of space allowed Isaac a small bit of comfort. "Is that what you saw my sister about?"

"You could say that." Isaac raked his hand through his hair, twisting his fingers in the locks until pain skittered across his scalp. Pulling it back, he stared at his own flesh. Was it a trick of the light or did his nails look sharper, more claw-like, ready to rend flesh apart with a simple press of his fingers?

He blinked and it was gone, a figment of his imagination. There was only him and Anton, who still looked at him like he was the one who was hungry.

"I overheard you," the man admitted. "At Celeste's."

Isaac should have felt betrayed, cut deep by the fact that Anton still didn't trust him, not fully. But all he felt was relief, the knowledge that he did not have to carry this burden alone. And though it pained him to admit it, he told Anton the entire truth—the terrors he had unlocked in his own body, the changes that could not be rolled back, the monster that was yet to come and the hunger that was driving him to madness.

The vampire that waited, deep in his skin, for a chance to break free.

"So, what are you doing, then, for your hunger?" Anton asked with a careless shrug, as if it was something simple. And if he could just go and requisition some blood, buy it as casually as bread from the baker.

"Nothing," Isaac snarled, his voice twisting into something low and inhuman, reverberating in a way that would have sent anyone with sense scrambling, "and you damn well know why!"

But Anton was not a man with sense, not when there was something to be gained—and oh, how like his sister he was, the bloody fool.

"Because you're afraid," Anton challenged.

"I—" Isaac cut himself off, because the asshole was right. He was afraid. Afraid of what more blood would do to him, of what he would find in the mirror when it was done. Afraid that this was a path as brutal and dark as the one he had walked at the Eternal King's side but that would leave him even more destroyed. "Shouldn't I be afraid?"

Anton stepped closer. "No, you should not be. The Eternal Bastard should be. The Blood Workers who make our lives living hell should be. Cause you, Isaac, are the very thing we've been looking for."

"You cannot—"

"You said you wanted to help the rebellion, you said you wanted to prove yourself," Anton interrupted, speaking with a fervor that shook Isaac to his core. This was not the fop he had hated for so many years. This was something else entirely—the man lit up from within, burning with a righteousness that was breathtaking to behold. Though he had but an audience of one, Isaac knew that he could bring an entire nation to its knees.

This was a man who could break Aeravin and build it back up again, if only he had the opportunity to. And he was right. Isaac could grant him that opportunity.

All he had to do was feed.

"So," Anton breathed, "is one little kill really so bad?"

Isaac crept along the shadows of Dameral, head ducked low as he wove through the midnight silence. The streets were empty of pedestrians, which should have been odd at this hour, when most would be making their way from whatever revelries they indulged in. Carriages and hacks still rattled by, wheels clattering on cobblestones, carrying the Blood Workers home, leaving behind the Unblooded workers who would spend the next hours cleaning up after their messes.

All of this emptiness could be traced right back to the choices Isaac had made, and the consequences he had never stopped to consider.

He forced himself to not think about it as he slipped deeper into the night, minutes slipping away like grains of sand through his fingers as he crossed the capital, heading to the home of one Miss Arena. A Blood Worker who had been in the King's personal cohort, plucked from the Academy upon graduation nearly a decade ago, crueler than all the rest. Resentful that he—an upstart, a child, a nobody, a foreigner—had been elevated over her. She might not have been a Lady, too far down in the line of inheritance to ever hope to claim a title, but her lineage and her ability to track her heritage back to the founding of the country made her far better than he could ever hope to be.

She had made his life a living hell, undercutting him at every opportunity, whispering harsh little cruelties in his ear as she tried to murder him under the weight of a thousand cuts.

He had always been the monster, only now it was becoming apparent on his skin, in the blood that he needed to quench this endless thirst. But for every bit of his humanity that he shed, he would grow stronger. And with that strength, perhaps he could find atonement.

He just needed to accept it.

Isaac slipped around towards the service entrance at the back, his steps quick and silent. The household had already turned in for the night, the lights dimmed low through the windows, and if he listened carefully enough, he could hear the steady, unbothered beats of hearts at rest. He pressed the tip of his tongue to the air, looking for the too-familiar taste of magic, but there were no wards to be found.

No, Arena was just as much of a fool as the rest of them, believing their power and privilege were enough to keep them safe. It was time that they learned the truth. Safety was an illusion, and Isaac would prove it to them.

From his position, he could see the balcony above him, a good three stories off the ground. Whether it offered entrance to a bedroom or a study did not matter—what he needed first was to get into the townhouse, and as he traced the growth of ivy over the trellis, he realized that was his way in.

It took nothing to press his tongue against his sharpened teeth, the blood flowing immediately into his waiting mouth. It tasted off, but the power still rushed through him—he was stronger, lighter, faster. He was more than human, more powerful than even a Blood Worker, but not quite a vampire.

Something that he did not know how to contemplate.

But he launched himself at the trellis, fingers hooking in the crisscross of the metal, the crisp, dark smell of the ivy filling his nose as the plants bruised under his grip. He climbed quickly, hand over hand as he pulled himself up the side of the building, not giving the trellis even a second to buckle under his weight, vaulting up and over the edge of the balcony in a matter of seconds. He crouched low, his pulse racing in his ears, as his brain caught up with what his body had done.

And he realized the absurdity of his plan, which was only eclipsed by the fact that it had worked.

But there he was, creeping in the shadows on the balcony off Miss Arena's bedroom, slinking towards the glass door, glancing towards the sleeping form on the bed. He could hear the steady beat of her heart—she was deeply asleep, and as she shifted in bed, he could feel the hunger rise, his throat clenching and his mouth watering.

Carefully, quietly, he stepped forward, the glass door sliding easily under his touch, letting him enter the home with ease. It was everything he had expected from one of them—oversized furniture made of dark oak, each piece featuring delicate engraving that must have cost a fortune. The moonlight illuminated the hand-painted wallpaper and the large mirror that was bolted above the dresser, wrapped in a gold frame. Arena lay on sheets of silk, curled up on her side and her golden hair spilling around her, looking strangely peaceful.

A bedroom fit for a princess, and here he was, ready to ruin it. To ruin *her*.

Blood and steel, she really was a fool. A simple ward wouldn't have stopped him, but it would have been enough to wake her, to allow her to fight back or escape. A lock would have offered similar protection. But there was nothing.

Nothing to stop him from wrapping his hand around her mouth, the tips of fingers pressing into her skin, almost like claws. Arena woke with a start, twisting under his grip, a scream trapped against his skin. Her hands flew to scrabble at his wrist, desperately struggling, but he was too strong for that. With the power of the blood he had absorbed, with the changes he had unwittingly wrought upon himself, there was nothing that Arena could do to fight him.

He just pushed her down, pressing her face into the pillow. She whimpered against his palm, her eyes wide as recognition ran through her. But Isaac didn't give her a chance to speak, didn't relax his grip on her. There would be no reasoning, no begging, no chance for her to cry for help. Just the dark satisfaction that she recognized the man who would kill her and that there was absolutely nothing she could do about it.

It seemed almost just, for every little barb she had thrown his way when they moved in the same circles. For the cruelties she had been born to, and then excelled at. For the way she had never, once, been moved to help those she exploited.

Leaning in, he pressed his mouth against the smooth expanse of her throat, almost like a kiss, but he opened his mouth at the last second. His fangs slipped through her flesh, smoother than any cut he had ever made with a claw, and the fresh taste of blood exploded across his tongue.

It rushed through him with all the burn of a good whisky, but instead of muddling his senses, he felt so much sharper. Her very life force flowed into him as he pressed down harder, the force of it causing her very bones to shatter under his grip, but he ignored her whimpers as he drank and drank.

He could see them, in the mirror, the moon illuminating the grisly scene. Him hunching over her like a beast, Arena struggling valiantly, though her attempts grew weaker with each passing moment. The clear and stark movement of his own throat with each swallow, the way her body collapsed a little more with each pull, her vitality drained away, leaving her withered and empty.

It was like watching the Eternal King on the Spring Solstice, except that he had become the monster he had always hated. But with his mouth full of blood and his body singing with the power it gave him, he couldn't bring himself to stop.

Not until he had every drop that Arena could give him, and she lay dead and desecrated on silk sheets.

He wrenched himself away from her corpse, his teeth tearing

through her flesh, leaving a gaping wound. Rocking back on his heels, he wiped the last drops of blood from his lips with the back of his hand.

And felt so wonderfully alive.

Chapter Twenty

Samuel

The murder scene was even more grisly than Samuel had anticipated, even knowing what Isaac was capable of.

Miss Brittney Arena's body lay where it had been found, untouched by servant or Guard. The first to arrive had laid a blood ward around the bed to preserve the scene, slowing decomposition and preventing further cross-contamination. It shimmered in the air, a faint shine that he could only see from the corner of his eye, but Samuel didn't dare cross it. He had enough of a view from where he stood, leaning next to the doorway, arms crossed over his chest as bile burned the back of his mouth.

Arena's eyes stared straight ahead, empty and unblinking, the lower part of her face crushed by some incredible force, the bones snapped and shattered as her jaw hung half off, connected only by the thinnest strands of muscle and sinew. Below that, though, was the bloody mess that was her throat, a red and raw chunk ripped out of it. The teeth marks were not anything resembling human, and even the cruelest of Blood Workers wouldn't leave a mark so feral.

If he didn't know any better, Samuel would have thought it the result of some animal attack, a mauling by a rabid beast. But he knew better—this was the result of what Isaac was becoming, fears that had been whispered in the quiet of the night between them, Blood Working beyond anything he could have imagined. A creature of blood and hunger that had been released to nip at the heels of the King.

Myths come to life in a dark nightmare.

"This is vile," Dabney said, as he pulled the handkerchief from his mouth, looking more flustered than Samuel had ever seen. He was green around the edges, the sour scent of fear leaking from his pores, but Samuel did not care for his reactions.

No, his attention was on someone far more important—the Eternal King himself, standing within the boundaries of the blood ward, his clawed hands clenched into hard fists as fury radiated off of him. "He will rue the day he defiled one of ours."

Samuel didn't respond, he just noted the King's wording in the back of his mind. He had hoped that the King wouldn't assume that it was Isaac, but that had been a fool's gamble.

Who else could it have been?

"Lord Aberforth," the King said, stepping back through the ward. "A word, if you will."

Inclining his head towards the door, Samuel said, "We can use Miss Arena's study." The King nodded, sweeping towards the door, but Samuel turned his attention back to Dabney at last. "Finish up in here, would you? Then meet me when the King and I have concluded our business."

Dabney sneered, a quick and instinctive reaction, before he schooled his expression. Oh, he had to be careful, now that the King was here. "As you say, my lord."

Samuel smiled thinly at him, then ducked out, following in the footsteps of the Eternal King as they walked through the hallways, dodging the many members of the Guard that Dabney had brought along with him. The rage was still roiling off his liege, a cloying mist of power that Samuel could taste on the air—Blood Working simmering just beneath the King's skin, ready to be break free and be used.

Such anger, and all because this time the victim had been a Blood Worker, a daughter of Aeravin. Just last year, when Isaac had done the exact same thing to Unblooded, no one had cared. No one cared a bit until it was Lord Dunn who had fallen.

There was a twisted symmetry here that he didn't want to look at too closely.

Still, he pitied whoever would face the King's wrath this time, thanking every lucky star that it wasn't directed at him. No, as they stepped into the privacy of the study, a cold room filled with dark colors, as empty as the body of its mistress, the King's shoulders slumped as he turned to Samuel. Not anger, but a kind of empty frustration, as they stewed in silence for several long minutes.

It seemed that even the Eternal King needed a moment to pull himself together. But he did at last, rolling his shoulders as he muttered, "Damn it all, this will be a disaster."

"We can keep it under wraps for a few days," Samuel assured him, "long enough for you and the Royal Blood Worker to get ahead of it."

"I appreciate that, son," the King said, leaning against the edge of the desk as he rubbed his temples.

Samuel swallowed his distaste at the King's attempts at kindness. No matter the relation between them, the history of a lineage that spanned centuries connecting them in an unbroken line, the Eternal King didn't get to claim that. Samuel had never known what it was like to have a father, and the way the King treated him was not love—it was manipulation.

And he would not fall for it.

"In the meantime," Samuel continued, "we'll see what we can find. Though, knowing the culprit, I doubt there will be anything of use."

"He's far too clever for his own good," the King admitted, "though, based on the condition of the corpse, his transformation is already well under way. Which means he'll only get sloppier as he goes on, his control fraying."

Swallowing hard, Samuel sensed the opportunity before him and took it. "About that ... is there anything you can tell me? That will help my men find him and keep themselves safe in the process."

The King looked him over with a serious eye, and Samuel knew what he was thinking. Why didn't he just go to Shan about this? Shouldn't she be the one providing him with information? But things between them were more complicated than that, especially where Isaac was involved, and Samuel couldn't trust her to help him. To help Isaac. So, there was only one other person who could, and Samuel had to play his next few moves very carefully.

What a mess they had made.

"It would be helpful to know," Samuel continued, digging himself out of the hole he had made, "what I can share and what I can't. It is such a delicate matter, after all."

"Ah." The King nodded. "A very fair question. I'll draft up something for you to share and have it sent to your office." Stepping forward, he clapped him on the shoulder. "I was right to appoint you to this role. You're doing well, Samuel."

He forced a smile, one that felt false, even to him. He wasn't doing well—he was drowning. "I appreciate that."

"I'll be in touch soon," the King said, stepping past and opening the door. Waiting behind it was Dabney, looking as sour-faced as ever. "And it seems you have more meetings to attend to, Lord Aberforth."

"Send him in," Samuel instructed, and the King barely even stopped to acknowledge Dabney before sauntering back, back to his palace and whatever other duties mattered to one so important as him.

Leaving the door wide open for Dabney to bully his way through, the deference vanishing as quickly as the King's shadow. "Aberforth," he sneered, going so far as to drop the honorific.

Samuel kneaded at a tender spot where the back of his neck met his skull, the early signs of a tension headache rising through him. Hells, the day had hardly started and he was ready for it to be over. "Dabney. Report?"

Dabney crossed his arms across his chest, the movement accentuating the man's breadth. There was something slightly terrifying about a man who was used to getting whatever he wanted—and worse, thought that he had the right to it. "The coroner should be finishing up with the body soon. We've rounded up the servants and are bringing them back for questioning. We can handle the rest from here, my lord."

Samuel only inclined his head—he recognized a dismissal when he saw one, but it wasn't Dabney's place to kick him out. As the Councillor of Law, he had a right to be here, especially considering who the deceased was.

Instead, he focused on the man's words. "Is it really necessary to book the servants? They've had a traumatic enough morning."

Scoffing, Dabney leveled a glare, speaking like he was explaining that the sky was blue to a particularly simple child. "One of them must know something. There is no sign of a break-in, so logically, that means that one of them must have helped the perpetrator."

Samuel bit the inside of his cheek to keep from speaking out. He knew that wasn't true in the slightest—Isaac had no help, not from anyone inside. But he couldn't say that. "It still seems excessive, to lock them up on a simple hunch and no evidence to back it up."

"If they are innocent," Dabney replied with a shrug, "then they'll be released soon enough, only a pint of blood lighter."

Ah, that was it, then. Samuel should have seen it coming—the man probably didn't believe a damned word he was saying. All of it was an excuse to harvest them, to fill the coffers under the Royal Blood Worker's new system.

Dammit, Shan. This was the reason why it was a bad idea, but she was so far removed from the day-to-day application of it that she couldn't even conceive of what it would be like to suffer under the laws she had created. There was nothing he could do about it—he had already tried and failed. So why did it feel like his hands were dripping with blood?

"Don't be cruel to them," Samuel said, with grumble. "Remember that you have no proof of any wrongdoing."

"My lord," Dabney said, mockingly, "trust me to handle my own job. I have only been doing it since you were a boy."

Drawing himself up straighter, Samuel did not let himself be cowed, even though Dabney was right—he did have decades of experience on Samuel, but that experience only blinded him to the cruelty of the system. Maybe once, when he was younger and more innocent, he would have balked at it. But after so long he had become desensitized—no, worse. Dabney saw his work as just, and Samuel realized that there was no reforming this system.

It wasn't broken, like Shan believed. No, it was far worse. It worked exactly as intended, turning men into monsters to be used against their fellow citizens.

Samuel closed his eyes. There was nothing he could do but try, again and again, crashing against this same wall until it broke or he was driven mad, whichever came first.

"I respect your experience," Samuel said at last, with as harsh a glare as he could manage. "But this system is new, and we are all learning it together. So, unless you can convict them with something solid," he practically spat out the next words, dripping with acid, "do not take any of their blood."

The command hung heavy in the air between them as Samuel waited to see if it would be followed. Dabney swallowed hard, the veins in his forehead throbbing, before inclining his head in a jerk. "As you say, my lord. Is that all?"

Stunned, Samuel nodded, dismissing Dabney with a gesture. The older man lurched out of the study, thundering down the hallway to join the rest of the Guard, and Samuel let out a sigh of relief.

He had expected a fight, an argument, hells, even an outright refusal to listen. What he did not expect was Dabney to agree. He should have been feeling ecstatic about it, but something like shame ran through him, stirring cold and vile in his chest.

A familiar kind of darkness that he had not felt in months. That he had hoped he would never feel again.

But no, that was impossible. Dabney had simply grown tired of arguing, had acquiesced only to end the conversation. Like as not, he would simply ignore the command as soon he was gone.

It was nothing to worry about, especially when there was still much to be done. His day was long from over, and he had to get ahead of this before rumors spread.

Chapter Twenty-One

Shan

Shan never expected to return to the site of the original Blood Factory, but given the Eternal King's latest plans, she had to admit that it made a certain amount of sense. Though the work they had once done was outsourced to new locations, this space still existed, a laboratory just waiting to be used. And if, in the course of a couple of short weeks, the King had managed to have it partially re-outfitted to suit their needs, then he was only doing what any enterprising individual would do.

She should really get the name of his contractor for the next time the LeClaire townhouse needed renovations—clearly, they were a miracle worker. The far side of the factory had been redone to include cells, the same sort that had once held Isaac, a person's entire life reduced to a small square of space, to conditions that she couldn't rightly call humane. But before him, Shan would have never once stopped to think about it, would never have been bothered to think of the countless others who had been subjected to those kinds of conditions.

Perhaps Samuel and Isaac were right about her, after all. Perhaps her scope was too limited, perhaps her perspectives too skewed. She could still feel the echo of Isaac's lips on her skin, drawing out the blood she had been so eager to give, without realizing what she was forcing Isaac into. But then she remembered the sketches she had seen of Miss Arena, throat mutilated, face crushed, and anger sparked. No, her way was the only way forward, if they wanted to make it through this alive.

The King crooked his finger forward, drawing her to the only occupied cell and the terrified young girl within it. It seemed that they would be keeping their test subjects close—and Shan didn't know if that was for their own safety, the simple convenience of it, or the stark reality that, King or not, such experiments would be best kept secret.

But in order to best understand how to stop Isaac, they first needed to understand what he was becoming. The mere myths of times long past and theories of what could be would not suffice, not if they wanted to be able to catalogue his weaknesses, to understand the full scope of the threat he was becoming.

And so, if they had to create their own vampire, then they would do it. Shan would do it—and perhaps, through a careful examination and a fair amount of luck that she did not deserve, she would find a way to save Isaac.

The girl sat on the small cot with her knees drawn up to her chest, her manacled hands wrapped around her knees. There was another of those terrifying muzzles around her face, and Shan realized that this was no nameless Unblooded picked from the streets, but a Blood Worker.

Blood and steel. She had expected this, she had planned for this, but there was something terrifying about actually facing it. Her attempts to help Isaac kept backfiring in her face, and that was with someone she knew. Someone she thought she understood. But she had no idea what had brought this stranger to this place, trapped in the King's games. She had no idea whether she had volunteered or whether it was some kind of punishment, but in the end, did it really matter?

"How are we doing this?" she asked, drawing the Eternal King's attention to her. He stood leaning against the metal bars, drumming his claws against it as he was lost in thought.

"Easily," he said, moving forward. The keys already dangled from his fingers, and he eased the lock open with a quick twist of his wrist. "She's already agreed to help us."

Agreed, he said, like it had been a given. But as Shan looked the girl over again, rocking on her cot in terror, she knew that it was not so simple. Their prisoner was out of her mind with fear, and that would never do. Reaching out, she placed her hand on the King's wrist without even thinking. He glanced down at her in surprise, but to her great shock, he merely handed her the keys and stepped aside, letting her take the lead.

Perhaps he had more faith in her than she realized. Or perhaps it was just another test. With him, one could never tell.

Shan glided into the cell on silent feet, perching on the edge of the cot. The girl flinched back, as if struck, but Shan just held her hands out, palms up in supplication, until the trembling stopped.

"I'm going to remove the muzzle now, if that's all right," Shan said, slowly, and the girl nodded. With steady hands, she undid the straps binding it around the girl's head, easing the muzzle free, revealing her face.

Hells, she was so young—barely an adult. Her features were fair and delicate, despite the rough treatment she had received. Her hair, soft gold, weaker than sunlight, hung in limp waves down her back, her thin lips were chapped and cracked. In a different setting, a different world, she would have been lovely, but she just looked so tired and haunted.

Shan didn't press her to speak, just continued on, freeing her from the manacles before fetching her a glass of room temperature water. She passed it to the girl's trembling hands, stroking the hair back from her face as she drank.

"Thank you," the girl said, finally, wiping the back of her hand across her mouth as she looked up at Shan. Her eyes widened as she took in Shan's deep red robes, her mouth popping open in a little "oh" of surprise. Scuttling back, she rose to unsteady feet, dropping into a curtsy with terrible form, tremors running through her. "My lady."

"Please," Shan replied, taking her by the hand and pulling her back into a comfortable stance. "That is not necessary. What is your name, child?"

It felt odd, calling her that, even though Shan knew she couldn't have been more than a handful of years younger than her. But there was something ... innocent about her, something that seemed so terribly inexperienced. Like she hadn't seen the true cruelties of the world she lived in, and it made Shan feel so old.

"Mel," the girl said, only to immediately catch herself. "Melinda."

Shan smiled, warm and sweet. "Mel," she repeated, and some tension eased from the girl's shoulders. "I'm Shan. It's a pleasure to meet you. Now, why don't you tell me a bit about yourself."

The Eternal King continued to watch them as Mel prattled on about her history, how she was a simple Blood Worker of no grand lineage or power, how she was arrested after she was found abusing her position at one of the clinics, draining Unblooded far past what she was supposed to. How she had then taken that blood and drank it down, seeking ways to supplement her own meager abilities.

Shan paid only the most surface of attention, filing away the details she would need for later, as the King's focus weighed as heavily on her. She snuck a quick glance out of the corner of her eye, but he was watching her with approval.

She had slipped into the role so easily, without even needing to discuss it beforehand, acting the kind hand to counterbalance the King's cruel one. And so, Mel opened up to her, the little terror that she was—hungry for information and knowledge and everything Blood Working could give her. Not satisfied with being a mere Blood Worker, but craving the power and privilege that was granted to the Lords and Ladies who ruled above all.

Shan should have known better than to take her at face value. Her youthfulness and air of innocence was nothing more than a deception. No one in Aeravin was innocent, especially if they were a Blood Worker, and Mel's true sin was not that she had erred, but that she had been caught, delivered right into their hands, the perfect tool to be used.

The last bit of Shan's reluctance faded away. Mel was not a woman to be pitied. She had made her mistakes, and now was the time for her to reap the consequences. And if Shan, through her, could learn anything to help Isaac—

Then this was all worth it.

"You were foolish," the King said at last, stepping into the cell. Shan could feel the strength of his aura, slipping past his leash, a carefully applied threat that had Mel inching away. "And for that foolishness, you need to be punished."

Mel ducked her head, sniffling as tears came to her eyes. "I'm sorry, Your Majesty. You're right, it was a mistake."

It was not a masterful gambit. Shan had seen its like many times, the kind of woman who would weaponize her tears against any who dared to criticize her. And because she was a Blood Worker, because of the power that gave her over others in their society, she had been able to get away with it for so long.

But the Eternal King was not so easily moved.

"The laws are the laws, my dear," he said, his voice as hard as steel and just as cutting as the claws they wore. "And as the King, I am honor-bound to enact justice equally and fairly."

Mel sniffled again, but the King only pressed on. "But I can be merciful," he murmured, gentle as a prayer, "if you can find it in your heart to atone."

Mel threw herself at his feet, pressed her forehead to the cool marble floor. "What can I do?"

"You wanted to know what Blood Working could achieve, did you not?" He nudged her with the tip of his boot, pressing into her jaw and tilting it up so that she was forced to meet his eyes. "Dedicate yourself to helping us, and not only will you live, you will know truths about Blood Working that most people have only dreamed of."

"As you command, Your Majesty," Mel replied, her eyes shining with a fervor that frightened Shan.

Shan only watched, absorbed by the way he twisted Mel's desires, pulling her strings so that she looked up at him with a zeal that could not be faked. His power might have been immense, but there was more to him than his simple magic. It was his ability to twist others to his cause, to radicalize those around him, to turn people into believers.

Shan had been so foolish to think she ever had a shot at standing up to him. There was nothing Lost Aberforth and the Sparrow could have done to stop him. Instead, there was only this. Walking hand in hand with the Eternal King and hoping to temper the harshest of his edges.

Even that felt like too much to dream of.

Following the Eternal King and Mel out of the cell, she watched as he shepherded the girl towards the bed, left over from the days of the Blood Factory. It didn't have a mattress or sheets, nothing to give it any kind of comfort, just the sterile shine of the metal and the leather straps to bind its victim.

Mel hesitated for only a moment, naked fear flashing across her face as she realized just what she'd signed up for. But she pushed past it, perching on the edge of the bed and looking up with those overly wide eyes. "What do you need of me?"

"Trust, my child," he replied, "and faith. The restraints are to help you. The magic we are going to practice is not for the faint of heart, and we don't want you to accidentally harm yourself."

Or them—Shan knew he wouldn't tell her that, tell her just how risky this transformation would be. Besides, he didn't want her getting ideas. She had already proved ambitious enough.

Shan stepped forward, knowing that she had gone too long without participating. Taking Mel's hand, she gave it a comforting squeeze, and the girl shot her a grateful smile, one without any artifice. She could feel the King's gratitude as he watched, as she proved herself to be the partner who could handle this sort of work. As Mel placed her trust in Shan, a mistake that she would come to regret, soon enough.

"All right," Mel said, relaxing against the bed as best she could. It was a stiff and uncomfortable thing, but she didn't fight as Shan went around, strapping her in. She was careful to let the restraints have a little give—if the King was right, the transformation would be brutal.

They did not know how many sessions it would take, how much

blood they would need to bring Mel to the threshold Isaac had found and push her past it, but they would do it again and again, until they found the answers they sought or until the girl expired, whichever came first.

Shan perched on the stool to the side of the bed. "You already know what we need you to do. It's the same theory as for the crime you were caught."

Mel tilted her head to the side. "But that is—"

"Not illegal," Shan reassured her. "Not here. What you did was theft, and for that you must be punished. But this ... this is freely given."

The King came to stand beside her as he rolled up his sleeve, tucking it up past the elbow, leaving the scarred skin of his forearm visible. "It will be slightly different, though. You need to not only absorb the vitality and power in my blood, but the magic itself."

Mel could only stare at his skin, where he trailed the tip of his claw against his veins, not quite hard enough to split flesh. Not yet. "Your blood?" she echoed, and Shan recognized the hunger there.

She had seen it in herself, far too many times. In a different world, in one where she had been a little less circumspect and a little more greedy, she could have been the one in Mel's place. And Isaac would have had hers, watching as she fell into the trap that would leave her destroyed.

She wasn't sure if it was a blessing or a curse that her life turned out the way it had, but she would take the seat of power that it offered. She wasn't fool enough to deny it when it was offered on a silver platter.

"Yes," Shan said, brushing the hair from Mel's face, pulling it to the side and binding it with a ribbon that she pulled from her pocket. There was something almost motherly about the way she was tending to the girl, and Mel leaned into the comfort. "We need to study what happens when two sources of Blood Working mingle, and what it does to the human body."

"It will be power unlike any that you have ever known," the King said. "Are you ready?"

Mel's tongue darted out, lapping at dry lips, and they had her right where they wanted her. "I am, Your Majesty."

"Good." He nodded at Shan, and she grabbed the fresh journal, pages blank to record the transformation. She stayed perched on the edge of the stool, pen in place, and he smiled. "Let us begin."

He drew his claw against the skin of his wrist, digging into the veins without so much as a whimper. The blood welled free, bright red and vibrant and so full of power that it made Shan's mouth water. But it wasn't for her. He lowered his arm to Mel's mouth, and she latched on eagerly, the sounds of her sucking and swallowing loud in the quiet of the laboratory.

Shan could already see it affecting her, her pen flying across the page as she chronicled it. Mel's very skin shone golden, her pale eyes grew brighter, turning a shade of blue so intense that it shouldn't have been possible. All the signs of her imprisonment faded away, the stress fading from her as she became absolutely radiant.

After what felt like hours, but couldn't have been more than a minute, the King pulled back, Mel chasing after him like a dog after a bone. But he only placed one clawed finger to her lips as he licked the blood from his own skin.

Seconds later, it was gone, the wound vanished as if it had never been there.

"There, there," he said, even as Mel whined for more. "How are you feeling?"

She bared her teeth, and Shan was startled to see the change—the way her eyeteeth had elongated, looking more like they belonged in the muzzle of some terrible beast. "Ravenous."

Smiling, the King pressed her back against the bed. She went without a fight, but still tracked his movements like a predator. "Good. It has begun. Let's see what kind of monster you'll become, sweet Mel."

Not even turning his head, he spoke to Shan. "Get the muzzle. Just to be on the safe side."

Mel lurched forward, a hiss escaping from her lips. "I agreed to help you!"

The King just looked down at her with disdain. "You agreed to become our test subject, Melinda. And you will be treated as such. Now, stop resisting."

Shan didn't even argue—she just fetched the muzzle. Mel didn't even fight as she slipped the bit between her teeth and wrapped the straps around her head.

There was no fight left in her.

Chapter Twenty-Two

Isaac

Isaac entered first, slipping through the narrow doorway to the even narrower staircase, the chill from the early winter morning seeping into his skin. Anton followed behind, stopping only to check the series of locks that ran along the edge of the door.

In a different time, Isaac might have called him paranoid. But he knew better, knew that they were doing the best they could without the protections that Blood Working offered, having to use cunning where brute force would have sufficed. No wards, no magic—just a well-placed lock and the careful selection of a proper location.

"Here we are," Anton muttered, throwing back his hood with relief. "I almost thought we were caught for sure."

Isaac only nodded. It had been a harrowing trip, even if it was only the distance of a few blocks. But the Guards were out in force after his slaying of Miss Arena, riding through the streets on their horses, darting from street corner to street corner chasing even the slightest bit of suspicious activity. Isaac knew the only reason they had made it through with as little attention as they had was because of the timing. They had slipped into the busy crowds that came right after the fall of night, as Unblooded across the city made their way home after a long day's work, as those with the dreaded evening and night shifts made their way in.

Traveling through Dameral would only get more difficult, but he couldn't bring himself to regret it, not after it tempered the hunger. Oh, he still thirsted, but it was no longer an all-consuming starvation, no longer a feral craving lurking in the back of his mind, forcing him to eye those around him with a predator's gaze, assessing who was and was not a meal waiting to happen.

It was a temporary reprieve; he knew the lust for blood would return again. The myths were clear—this was the new challenge of his life, but for now, he was safe.

And he would use that time wisely.

They emerged into the large underground room, an unfinished basement below one of Aeravin's many bakeries, filled with barrels of flour and sugar and all the many supplies needed to own and operate one of Dameral's finest establishments. This one was run by a talented Unblooded baker who had honed his craft in the King's very kitchens, who had seen the cruelties of the world first-hand. Apparently, Maia had been the one to work her magic, drawing him into this group that was larger than Isaac had ever imagined, individuals coming together to chip in towards a greater whole.

But why they were here, precisely, Isaac did not know. All he knew was that Anton planned to put him to work—and it was better than sitting alone, stewing in his safe house that felt more like a prison with each passing day. Waiting for the hunger to strike again.

Maia stood behind a large table covered in parcels, wearing a comfortable outfit of breeches and a simple shirt, her dark braids pulled together in a bun at the nape of her neck. She looked so confident in her role, comparing the numbers to a thin piece of paper in her hands. A young man stood with her, thin and slight, loading one of each into a parcel.

There was something oddly familiar about him, a nagging feeling that Isaac had seen this boy before somewhere. It wasn't till they stepped closer and the boy looked up that Isaac recognized him. It was months ago in a tavern, the night he had foolishly taken Samuel out to practice his gift. It was the same boy, the same shaggy dark hair and the same gruff manner—only instead of acting as the rallying cry of the rebellion, here he was, quietly doing his work.

Hells, if it wasn't for Samuel and his indomitable good nature, this boy would likely be dead. If Samuel had been just a hair crueler, Isaac would have used him to take the boy, would have delivered him directly to the King as any good Royal Blood Worker would have. It could have led to the disruption of this whole group, and Isaac wouldn't have batted an eye. He would have done whatever it took to protect his own schemes, even if it damned others.

Even if it damned the ones who were truly working for a better nation.

Perhaps Anton hadn't been wrong to not trust him, but Isaac was learning. He just hoped that he hadn't ruined it all in some other small, infinitesimal cruelty that he wouldn't have even noticed before.

"Toby," Maia said, cutting through the silence and the spiral of Isaac's self-doubt. "This is Isaac. Isaac, this is Toby."

The boy nodded at him, a simple greeting, but there was no malice there. He didn't recognize him for who he was—for *what* he was. If he remembered that night at all, Isaac was probably little more than a face in the crowd. He had no clue how close he had come to torture and execution, and Isaac was not sadistic enough to reveal that. Just like he was smart enough to not reveal precisely who he was, not unless it was necessary. It was difficult enough with the proprietress of the Fox Den, and he did not want to pull attention to himself.

This was not about him—he was only here to help.

"Nice to meet you," Toby said, then passed him an empty parcel. "One of each, then stack them over there." He nodded to a large pile, haphazardly stacked together. "We'll deliver them in the morning."

"I can do that," Isaac said, taking the bag and filling it, one object at a time. There was fresh bread, packages of apples, small bags of dried beans. Even some satchels of loose tea—Isaac raised that to his nose and inhaled deep, catching the signature scent of bergamot, sharp and tangy.

"What is this?" he asked, drawing Maia and Anton's attention.

They both looked up at him sharply, whatever conversation they had done and forgotten, but Maia's gaze quickly softened.

"Toby," she said, "why don't you run upstairs and do inventory on today's leftovers."

The boy glanced between them, his welcome expression shuttering as he studied Isaac with new fervor. His ignorance had ruined his casual disguise, but Toby did not press the matter. "As you say, Miss Maia."

The quiet remained until he disappeared up the stairs, then Maia let out a soft sigh. "Many Unblooded lost their jobs, Isaac, when the King lay down his new laws."

"It was partially the curfew," Anton added, filling the picture in. "As the Unblooded couldn't be out past nightfall. Part of it was just Blood Workers looking to punish those they thought weren't appreciative enough, inflicting suffering just because they could."

Maia nodded, her dark eyes flashing with an anger that Isaac understood all too well. "Since the curfew lifted, many have been hired back. But some have not, and even for those who did, they went months without income or hope. So, we work with people across Dameral to provide at least some of the basics. Food and other necessary sundries, occasionally clothes as well, now that winter has come."

Isaac followed her eyes as she glanced upwards towards the bakery that was now closed. "Toby's father is kind enough to let us work out of here, since he has the space. And with all the shipments in and out—the supplies he gets from grocers, the deliveries he makes to restaurants and homes—it's easy enough to hide these parcels among them. Toby makes most of the deliveries, good lad that he is."

Isaac gripped the bag tighter, a sick feeling twisting in his stomach. Of course this had happened, of course the King's response to his actions led to the suffering of so many. People he had not thought once about, reduced to simple abstractions in his calculations. Oh, he had told himself that every kill was for the greater good, that the Blood Factory he had been forced to run was an abomination that could not stand. And while he was not wrong, while all that *was* true, it was easy for him to ignore the consequences he never would face.

"Fuck," he muttered, leaning against the wall as he wrapped his arms around himself, trying to stop the trembling. Anton and Maia didn't say anything, sharing a long look before she stepped forward, placing a hand on his shoulder and giving him a harsh squeeze.

"I'm sorry," he mumbled, not daring to look at her. Not wanting to face another failure.

His whole life had been failure after failure, each and every fleeting bit of success he chased letting someone down. First his parents, then Shan, then the King. Now all of Aeravin itself as he unleashed an avalanche then did nothing to help all those he displaced.

"Isaac," Maia said, his name gentle on her tongue as she gave him a slight shake. "It's okay."

"It's really not," Isaac breathed, but she only shot him a warning glance.

"You tried," Maia continued. "You did the best with what you had. Without you, none of us would have known the depths of the King's crimes. And you not only revealed it, you destroyed it."

"Temporarily," Isaac ground out. The whole of Aeravin knew of Shan's new policy, and the fervor with which the Guard applied it. "I feel like I just made it worse."

"Perhaps," Anton said, kinder this time. "But you've also brought it out into the open, made it something that the King can't hide. And while there is suffering because of it, people now know where to direct their anger. They face injustice in new and palpable ways, in ways they can't ignore."

Isaac clenched his fists, feeling the press of his nails biting into his skin, almost sharp enough to draw blood. He wished they were—wished he could inflict a smaller pain on himself to distract from the gaping ache within. "You mean you can use this, the mess I made."

"I do," Anton said, with a shamelessness that reminded him of Shan. But this was different in some slight way that he couldn't name. The twins were such mirrors for each other, and yet, here Anton stood, ready to risk everything in a way Shan never would.

"Something we agreed on," Maia said, soothing him like a child, "when we first started this, was the knowledge that we cannot achieve the change the country needs by being nice. By playing by the rules and the system that exists. Now, we had planned to take things more slowly, to build up the support we needed over time, but you gave us a galvanizing moment. And we won't waste it.

"Of course, we regret the suffering and—" she nodded to the packages "—we do what we can to mitigate it, but it's a price that needs to be paid."

Isaac exhaled slowly, then forced himself to look at Anton. The ringleader of this, the one who was forcing him to look. "This is why you brought me here, isn't it?"

"Clever boy." Anton smirked, and it was all the confirmation he needed. "Your attack the other night was good, but it's just the start. I know things are going to get worse before they get better—we all know this. But I wanted to be sure you did."

"You think me a coward."

"No, I don't," Anton replied, and from the steady, unchanging beat of his heart, Isaac knew that he was telling the truth. "But I know that you ... care."

The last word came like he was pulling teeth, but Anton looked at him with an appreciation that hadn't been there before. An understanding that they had both denied the other.

What a fool he had been, turning what could have been a brother into a much-hated enemy. What a fool he still was, for only realizing it now. But there was still time to make this right. "It was never going to be one kill, was it?"

Maia flinched away, as well she should. He was glad there was still someone here who balked at death, who recognized it for the horror that it was. But Anton just turned that smirk on him. "No, it's not. We are just beginning."

He leaned in, taking Maia's hand and giving it a comforting squeeze. "Maia is here to keep an eye on us, to make sure that we return as much as we take."

The shape of the rebellion was starting to make sense to him, the full scope sketched out in his mind. Maia, the heart, holding them back from going too far. Anton, steering the ship and making the harsh decisions that someone had to face. Samuel, providing information that only the Councillor of Law would be privy too, and Bart plucking from the network of spies that Shan herself had created. Monique and Toby and this baker who Isaac had never met, proving that many hands make light work.

"And Alaric?"

"Who do you think funds us?" Anton lifted a shoulder with a shrug. "If the Lords of Aeravin do not see him as a suitable heir to his house, then why shouldn't he use the fortune he was gifted to make them see him?"

Isaac nodded, slotting it into place. There was only one missing piece, then. "And me?"

"You, my friend," Anton said, baring his teeth in a grin that chilled Isaac to the core, "are the one who is going to bring this nation tumbling down."

Chapter Twenty-Three

Samuel

Samuel entered the room, feeling oddly like he was walking to his own trial.

For once, they didn't meet in their private Council room, where they hashed out new proposals and debated for hours over precise word choice. No, Belrose had called them to the grand chambers where the House of Lords met, the rows of seats spiraling ever inward to the ground floor where the others waited. It was so empty with just the five of them, quiet as a tomb as he made his way down the stairs, steps echoing towards the high ceiling above.

He swallowed the fissure of anxiety that ran through him as he came to stand before Lady Belrose, dressed in a fine dress of dark silk, her hair cascading past her shoulders in loose waves. The claws on her fingers glittered in the glow of the witch light, shining slivers of silver crossed demurely at the wrist. She looked every bit the Blood Worker—beautiful, refined, and oh so deadly.

Pulling at the cuffs of his shirt, Samuel stood a little straighter. He knew that he cut a similar figure, thanks to all the work Shan and Laurens had put into him, but despite all the preparation, he still felt like little more than a charlatan. Especially next to Lady Belrose.

He glanced around at the others—Lady Morse did not pay him a lick of attention, standing with military strictness with her arms crossed behind her back. Someone had been kind enough to have a chair pulled up for Lord Rayne, which he relaxed into, his cane balanced across his knee, but he paid him no mind either.

Unlike Zelda, who shifted uncomfortably, her eyes looking everywhere but him.

Ah, so that's how it was to be, then. He had been prepared for this, even if he wished it would never happen, but politics had people switching sides left and right, and he was a fool to think that Lady Holland would ever choose loyalty over political expediency. Especially after how their last meeting had gone.

"Thank you all for joining me here today," Belrose said, calling the meeting to order. "I know that it is an unusual gathering spot for us, but I thought it important to remind our members why we are here."

She took a step back, lifting an arm to sweep wide, calling their attention to the very room they stood in. "When we took these positions as part of the Royal Council, we all swore an oath. Our work is important to the functioning of the great nation of Aeravin, but we are advisers and councillors, not tyrants. We serve not only the Eternal King, but the House of Lords as well."

Leveling her steely gaze on Samuel, he felt the snare catch around his ankle. He knew the trap she was going to lay even before she spoke it, and he had blundered right into it.

"Last year, our esteemed ruler came into this very room, this hallowed hall full of history, and levied a new series of laws without warning, ignoring the voice we are supposed to have in the governing of Aeravin." Her lips twisted into a cruel smirk as she stepped closer to Samuel.

She might have been a head shorter than him, but with the power of her Blood Working thrumming in her veins, Samuel couldn't help but feel so small. "It appears that his heir thinks he can do the same thing, so it falls on me to remind him—you might carry his blood, Lord Aberforth, but even you are bound by the same rules as the rest of us."

Samuel tilted his chin up, didn't allow even the slightest hint of his anger bleed through. "Everything I have done was within the parameters of my position."

Belrose met his gaze unwaveringly. "And yet, you wished to put this bill into action without a vote, without even bringing it to the attention of the House."

"Because it does not need approval," Samuel pressed. "This is a refinement of the rules and regulations already in place, of my domain."

"Still—"

"Still, nothing," Samuel pressed on, all the practiced speeches and carefully thought-out arguments running together in his head. "The Guard are my duty and responsibility, and as such, I can determine if they need additional regulations, especially with the new responsibilities that have been added to our plate."

That, too, had been an expansion of responsibilities without a vote, a command come down on high from the King himself, routed through his Royal Blood Worker. There had been no proposal, no vote—it had fallen in his lap like a rotten fruit, leaving him to deal with the mess alone.

And yet, *his* attempts to tame that injustice needed approval.

"All the more reason," Belrose cooed, "for us to take it to a vote. The Royal Blood Worker's proposal, while unorthodox, is in response to a national emergency. We could not afford to let it lie fallow for months more. But this? A little time will hardly affect anything."

It would affect quite a lot, Samuel was not enough of a fool to discount that, but he knew he could never manage to convince Belrose. The shift had already happened, Aeravin's sudden and immense crackdown on the rights of the Unblooded had freed even the most cautious of political creatures to lean into their hate.

Her mind was made up, but there were others he could reach. "A vote, then," he said, turning to the others, even as ice curled in his stomach. Morse looked bored as ever, Rayne was muffling a yawn behind a thin, veined hand, and Holland was still avoiding him like the plague.

There would be no allies here, and as he turned back to Belrose, he realized that she knew it as well.

"Yes," she said, smoothly. "A vote before the entire House, I think. Do not worry, Lord Aberforth, you will have plenty of time to refine your arguments. Perhaps even gather some data to prove that these regulations are necessary at all."

From the tone she took, it was clear that she didn't believe it was in the slightest. None of them did. But he would fight it, tooth and nail. He couldn't live with himself if he did not.

"Very well." He dipped into a low bow, short and perfunctory and not proper at all. A slight snub, but one that couldn't be called out without Belrose being seen as petty. "Is that all?"

Her claws clenched ever so slightly, but she nodded.

Samuel didn't even bother saying goodbye, seeing himself from the room with a quick pace. Footsteps followed after him, but he did not turn to look at his follower till they had emerged from the chamber, her hand reaching out to catch him about the wrist.

It was Lady Holland, looking at him with such pity in her eyes as she pulled him into an empty room. It was one of the many, many meeting rooms in the Parliament House, there for confidential meetings to hash out all the deals that kept a government running. It wasn't aired out—the furniture covered with sheets and the fireplace empty, giving the air a distinct chill. It was uncomfortable and awkward, the two of them staring at each other without a place to sit, but it did give them a modicum of privacy.

For what, Samuel wasn't sure—she had already fed him to the wolves, so why should she care who saw this?

"I tried to warn you, Samuel. The plan was too bold," Zelda said, and there was just a hint of a plea in her tone, like she was trying desperately to reach him, as if he was acting out and needed to be pulled into line.

"Perhaps," he returned, knowing that he dripped acid, "if I had any backup, things might have gone differently." She didn't flinch. She was unrelenting, and normally, Samuel appreciated that about her. Today, though, it just made his stomach churn.

"Picking your battles," she said, like she was imparting great wisdom, "is the most important tool at our discretion."

And she was right—truly she was. But Samuel could not live like this, making these sorts of calculations, throwing entire groups of people into suffering for the mere hope that he could do something about it later.

He was so terribly unsuited to this work, and here he was proving it all over again.

"We can still remedy this," she pressed. "I am willing to tutor you—it's not your fault that you never had the proper training."

"What, like I am a child?" Samuel couldn't control the anger that cut through him. It was one thing to be hated, it was another thing altogether to be patronized. They all thought him to be a fool because of his background, because of his lack of a formal education, because he actually gave a shit about people before their grand calculations.

Her expression shuttered, the attempt at kindness vanishing as Samuel saw the exact moment she decided that he wouldn't be reached. "Really, Aberforth, this is embarrassing."

"Don't," he began, that insidious darkness awakening within him, unfurling like the bloom of a flower, as deadly as nightshade in his veins. But Holland continued on, blissfully unaware of the danger she was courting.

"We live in a precarious time, and I know you're not too stupid to understand *that*," she went on. "And by all that this nation stands for, one of us needs to make sure that you do not undermine what little control the Council has left. So, you will either work with us or I will report your ineptitude to the King himself."

"Enough!" Samuel barked, and that sliver of power in his chest burst forward, slithering through the air on his command as it wrapped itself around Holland. Her hand flew to her neck as she worked her throat, desperately trying to form words that would not come, her dark eyes glittering with the purest, most sudden fear that he had ever seen.

And for one brief moment Samuel looked on with satisfaction, but then sense caught up to him, crashing over him like a wave. He had not intimidated her with this presence, had not scared her into silence—he had controlled it with this gift in his blood that he had been so certain was gone. That he had *convinced* himself was gone, because if it was not, then what was all that suffering for?

But as Lady Holland took one, trembling step backwards, Samuel had to admit the uncomfortable truth. The Aberforth Gift had returned, and now she knew about it. Someone who had already proven herself to be untrustworthy, had turned his half-finished bill over to the rest of the Council, had threatened to bring the King into this—

No, the King could not learn his power had returned.

Holland bolted towards the door, but she did not make it more than two steps before he spoke again, this time deliberately lacing his words with his power. "Stop."

She came to a halt as suddenly as if she had hit an invisible wall, her body locking up so abruptly that it was almost grotesque. Samuel did not give himself a chance to think about it—could not give himself a chance to think about it—so he circled around to stand in front of her, meeting her eyes and refusing to flinch.

"You will not speak about what happened in this room," he commanded, throwing as much force behind it as possible. He saw the moment the Gift hit her, wrapping around her like chains—dark and heavy enough to pull her into the endless depths. "You will tell no one of what I have done, not with your voice, not with your words, not in writing. Am I understood?"

She nodded, trembling as she tried to fold into herself. He had never seen her try to make herself so small, and there was something in him that liked it.

Another dangerous thought. Another fear he couldn't confront right now. He just stepped to the side, gesturing towards the door, and watched as she ran.

Only then did he let the nausea overtake him, his stomach turning as bile burned the back of his throat. What he had done was obscene, but he couldn't pretend it had not happened. He did not know how long his command would hold, and there was only one person he trusted to help him with this.

―✥―

Samuel struggled to find his words, but Isaac wasn't pressing him. He waited patiently, arm slung around Samuel's shoulders as he pulled him close, snuggled up on the couch as they watched the snow fall through the window. It was so ... peaceful, a reprieve from the endless games and mounting stress that had become his life. Samuel wanted to stash it all away like some terrible dragon, each moment another precious jewel to add to his hoard.

But as the skies outside darkened, night creeping in as inexorably as the rise of the moon, Samuel knew he could not put it off any longer. "I fucked up."

Isaac pressed a kiss to the top of his head, quick and fleeting, but it still grounded him. "It's all right, Samuel. We can fix whatever this is."

"I am not so sure about that," Samuel said, his voice low and rough. "I should have come sooner, I should have ... " He blinked quickly, his eyes burning, but Isaac was kind enough to not mention the tears. "Before, with Dabney ... I thought it was a fluke. A coincidence ... "

"It's okay," Isaac began again, but Samuel quieted him a harsh look.

He hadn't even meant to do it. It wasn't him. It was the mask of Lord Aberforth, the sneering condescension that he had practiced for so long in the mirror breaking out, exactly when he didn't want him.

He was changing—or had this always been in him, just waiting for its chance?

"It's not okay," Samuel breathed, and the sudden shock of anger broke, leaving behind only the acrid taste of despair. "My gift is back."

"Oh."

Isaac, to his relief, did not let go of Samuel's hand, but he had the faraway look in his eyes of someone who had the floor ripped out from under him, and Samuel had to reach him before he tipped head first into free fall.

"Isaac," he said, pressing closer, but the man just shook his head, giving his fingers a rough squeeze.

"Is it okay if I touch you?"

Samuel glanced down at their joined hands. "Of course," he exhaled. "But thank you for asking."

Offering a strained smile, Isaac raised Samuel's hand, pulling the glove free and discarding it to the side. Trembling fingers worked his sleeve up, baring him to the night air, and without its soft, silken cover, his scars stood in harsh relief to his pale skin, the deep black lines mapping the pathways of his veins. Isaac dropped his mouth to the tender skin at the inside of Samuel's wrist—an acknowledgment, a reminder, an apology. "I am sorry."

"Oh, Isaac." Samuel moved his other hand, brushing against the line of Isaac's jaw. "I am not mad at you." He swallowed hard, taking the suffering and wearing it like a mantle, thick enough to keep everyone else out, heavy enough to drown in. "I'm telling you because I need to, because I need your help. And ... so you can protect yourself."

Samuel could track the minute emotions that flickered across Isaac's face, the moment when he decided to bypass the first thing to focus on the second. "I've told you before, and I'll tell you again: you do not need to protect me from yourself."

"But—" Samuel tried to pull back, but Isaac held on. Not cruelly, not demanding, but firm and unyielding, and it only took Samuel a moment to melt into it. That subtle edge of control that he sought so unfailingly, the freedom of being able to put himself wholly into someone else's hands.

Here he was, a breath away from breaking down, and Isaac was once again providing him that dizzying relief he so desperately needed.

"You're not the only monster here," Isaac said, his grip easing, and it felt like Samuel could take his first deep breath in days. "And don't you dare deflect. This is something I've chosen for myself, but you never chose this."

"I didn't, but—"

"But nothing." Isaac bared his teeth, the quick glint of a fang enough to punch the air out of Samuel's lungs. "Do you fear me?"

"No!" Samuel said, immediately, sensing the trap but still running headlong into it.

"If you can love me, with all that I am—" Isaac smiled, tightening the noose "—then I should be able to love you in return. If you do not fear me, then I should not have to fear you."

And hells, he was right. Samuel knew that, deep inside, in that pit of darkness that was both him and not him that he dared not face, he was not so different from Isaac. That the same rage and hunger burned in him, a fire so bright and blinding that he feared he would not make it through this unscathed. That it would burn away everything gentle left in his soul and make him into something that truly deserved to be feared.

But as he faced the world he had been thrust into, Samuel knew that it would change him regardless, so he might as well control what he became. "We are not so different, you and I." Isaac stiffened, ready to deny it, but Samuel didn't give him a chance. "Holland knows. About the Aberforth Gift. And she cannot live to tell anyone else."

He felt Isaac's harsh inhale more than heard it, watched as Isaac studied him in a new light.

"Are you sure?"

Samuel nodded. He had thought about it endlessly since he had left the Parliament House. He had commanded her silence, yes, but they had never tested how long a command would hold. It had always been instant things, him telling them to do something and then they would immediately act it out.

And this was not the time to test any hypotheses.

"I am." Samuel didn't close his eyes, as much as he wanted it. It would have been easier if he could, if he could not look at his beloved as he asked this most heinous task of him. "I cannot be the one to do it, but you ... you need more blood anyway."

"Say no more," Isaac breathed, and Samuel accepted the kindness with a relieved exhale. "I will do it."

It embarrassed him, how unashamed he was in this. He should have felt a stronger sense of guilt, but there was only boundless relief. "Thank you."

Chapter Twenty-Four

Isaac

Isaac glanced behind him at the massacre he had made, giving a quick sweep of the study to ensure he hadn't left behind any identifying markers. It was foolish to even try to hide it—there was no one else who could have committed a crime like this. For all that the average Guard wouldn't understand the scene before them, the King would still recognize it immediately.

As would the Royal Blood Worker, but Isaac couldn't think about Shan. She wouldn't understand why it had to be done, what he was doing for Samuel. She would chastise him for the message he was sending, for the fear and terror he unleashed, and for the cruel way that this woman had died.

But some people didn't deserve a kinder end, and Lady Holland deserved far worse than what she got. Even without the risk she posed to Samuel, even without whatever little cruelties she had tossed at his feet, Isaac still relished this kill. None of the Royal Council had been innocent, and though Holland had been politer than most, it had only made her more insidious. With her carefully tracked numbers and her command of the very minutiae of the law, she had managed to position herself as a moderate while doing the worst damage of them all.

And now, she lay dead before him, right where Isaac had slain her, slumped over the desk where he had discarded the corpse. Dark eyes stared unblinking at the ceiling; long hair torn out from its usually severe bun, spread out behind her in a wild tangle. Her once soft skin was shriveled tight against her bones, the column of her throat torn apart by his fangs, leaving it a shredded disarray of meat. All the blood in her body had been sucked dry—desiccated muscle drawn down to the bone, dry and papery where it should have been dripping and succulent.

Lady Holland was an unholy ruin that he had created, the woman he had known gone and replaced by this mockery of human flesh.

But her power, her magic—it flowed into him, feeding the already boundless Blood Working that dwelt inside of him. He could feel it shift something inside of him, burning through the bits of him that were still human, still limited by the mortality he had been born to. But not for long—not if he kept this up. A few more Blood Workers, a few more drainings, and who knew what could stop him?

He stepped towards the window, ready to slip out into the night when a searing pain shot up his spine, turning his legs to jelly as he crashed against the windowsill. He caught himself at the last second, biting back a scream as he felt his bones snap and re-form, his nails growing hard and sharp in their beds, extending past the tip of his fingers.

The pain did not let up, his shoulders shaking as they seized and shuddered, lines of fire splitting flesh as bone and skin surged outward, catching in the snug pull of his binder and the shirt that covered him, then pulling painfully tight against his chest before snapping free with loud rip.

He tangled his claws in the shirt, ripping the tatters free as he gasped, his breasts hanging free as the large protrusions—the fucking *wings*—that had surged from his back reached out behind him, thin structures of bone woven together with the paper-thin membrane of the patagium tender on the air.

Digging his grip into the windowsill, Isaac doubled over, his balance completely undone. The wood splintered under his touch as he sucked in harsh breaths of the frigid night breeze, the sharpness stinging his lungs with each shallow inhale. *Something* in his mouth swelled, choking him as it pressed against the back of his teeth, catching against his fangs.

Blood and steel—*fangs* that now reached down past his lower lips, as if the rest of it hadn't been enough. Even his mouth was rebelling, his jaw distending to fit the new additions, no longer the dainty little nubs that he could hide behind his carefully practiced smile but monstrous things designed to tear and rend. An ache started deep in his stomach, drool slipping past his lips as he imagined sinking into tender flesh, blood squirting into his mouth as he feasted, an intimacy that was terrible and violent.

The ache deepened, a rumble starting in the back of his throat as he wished for another body to rip into. He was so empty, his entire body racked with hunger pangs as he *wanted*. His breath came in pants as his tongue lolled out of his mouth, longer and thicker than it should have been, dripping halfway down his chest and landing with slick plop.

He flicked it up, scenting the air with it, his nose wrinkling at the stale taste of the body behind him, already drained and ruined, not the kind of meal that he needed. No, he needed something living, rich with blood and life, warm under his claws and teeth. His tongue trembled as he imagined sliding through the warm and raw flesh, digging through the viscera and entrails as flavors he never could have imagined burst in his mouth.

But no, that was not what he was here for. He had already fed this night, and despite the feral call of his body, this monstrous new him that he was not yet able to master, he could not give in.

Blood Working may have been changing him, but he was still more than what instinct made him.

He flung himself out the window, wings spreading and catching on the night air as he flew into the night. The winter's chill was bracing on his skin, sharp as ice on his bare chest, the shock of it cutting to the bone. But it was enough to shake him from the haze that hunger had laid over him, the grip of the primordial instinct loosening. Oh, it was still there, an ache in his stomach so great that it felt like it would split in two, but there was enough of him left to seize control of this strange new form.

The wings spread, an instinctive motion that he did not even have to will into action, as they caught the breeze and jerked him up into the sky. There wasn't enough space to gain proper lift-off, and he glided across the narrow street before crashing against the rooftop opposite Holland's townhome with a thud he felt in all of his bones. Gravity gripped him, pulling him down, but his claws provided a surprising amount of leverage in the shingles as he caught himself. Twisting to lie on his stomach, his tongue dragged across the roof, the bitter tang of dirt and soot and hells knew what else assaulting him. But it was enough for him to brace himself, his feet against the lip of the roof and his claws digging gouges into the roof, as he beat his wings.

It was so easy, so natural, to control them—as instinctive as breathing, and with a roar completely devoid of any humanity, Isaac launched himself into the sky with an ache that felt like freedom.

Dameral shrank beneath him, his dark and terrible city looking so small and strange from this angle. It didn't feel so threatening anymore, the horrors washed away under the shadows from a moonless sky. He could look at it for hours, the urge to drift aimlessly calling to him, but he knew that he needed to return to the safe house before he was spotted and everything he had worked so hard for vanished.

So, he closed his eyes and canted himself south, letting the wind take him home.

Isaac didn't quite manage a smooth landing, though it was remarkably less painful than his earlier crash. He hit the roof of the safe house with a thump that echoed through the building below, but he was able to shimmy his way down till he hung from the edge with the tips of his claws. He swung himself in through the window he had thankfully left open earlier that evening, tangling in the thick curtains before thudding to the floor in an awkward mess of limbs and drapes.

Only to look up to find Anton standing over him, holding a sword in his hand. The man looked at him with abject terror on his face, his handsome features twisted into a rictus of horror that hurt more than any wound the Unblooded man could have inflicted.

He was a monster, then, not just in spirit but in actuality.

Still, he threw up his hands, claws spread and palms out, and though his jaw was barely fit to form human words, Isaac slurred around his new tongue, "Wait!"

Anton didn't seem to react, though the blade fell from loose fingers and clattered to the floor. He just stared at Isaac, unblinking and unflinching, before uttering a single word. A word that Isaac had never heard before, but it carried the same rough syllables and intonation of his parents' native language. A language he only knew bits and pieces of, since it would never serve him well in Aeravin.

"Mana—" he attempted to repeat, only to trip over his hells-damned tongue, still heaving past his lips. It darted out towards Anton, and Isaac could taste the sweat on his skin and alluring depths of the blood beneath. It would be so easy to launch himself forward, to shove the man on his back and treat Anton like a banquet laid out just for him.

Isaac dug his claws into his own body, cutting through the fabric of his trousers to the skin beneath. They sank in with such ease, sharp pinpricks that cleared his mind.

Anton was a friend, an ally, not another body to feed upon. Despite the long history of animosity between them, Anton had saved his life, had given him a safe place to hide, had welcomed him—with only a little bit of doubt—into the rebellion that he formed.

Isaac would not repay Anton's kindness with atrocity.

He leaned forward, bent at the waist so that his forehead touched the floor, his nose pressed into the curtains as he took deep, steadying breaths. As he swallowed down every instinct that commanded him to find another, then, if Anton wouldn't suit for a snack.

But he had fed enough for one night, had wandered far enough down this path. This was power, yes, but he wouldn't let it control him. He was still a man, and if he had to fight his own existence to stay that way, he would.

He remained hunched over as the nightmarish appendages receded—wings sinking back into his back with a sickening crunch, jaw snapping back in place as the tongue and fangs withdrew, blunt fingertips pressed against the wounds he had made in his own skin.

As he was—blissfully, finally—mostly mortal again.

But the monster still lingered under his skin. He could feel it waiting, lurking, and it wouldn't take much of anything to call it back to the surface. And, with just a little more power, another Blood Worker or two, he would transform again.

And Isaac didn't know if he would be able to come back from it.

Anton knelt down beside him, his hand brushing through Isaac's hair in a soothing motion. Isaac melted into it, turning his face towards the man, only to realize that he was crying.

Mourning the man he had been, the man he hadn't intended to lose.

"What did you call me?" Isaac managed to ask, his voice low and rasping in his throat. Not a vampire—no, something else. Something different.

Something . . . worse?

Anton didn't hesitate, didn't flinch, and Isaac was thankful for it. It wouldn't be a kindness to hide it from him. "Manananggal."

Isaac tested the word on his lips, shaping over the syllables. He had heard it before, years ago, but it hovered just out of reach, a dream dissipating upon waking. "What does that mean?"

"It's a myth, not too different from Aeravin's vampires," Anton said, rocking back on his heels.

Isaac rolled on his back, still hurting in ways that he didn't have words for, wrapping the curtain across his chest to cover his nudity—blood and steel, he'd need to get another binder. But that was tomorrow's problem.

Today, he had to reckon with whatever truths Anton was able to share with him.

"Tell me more about this myth," Isaac breathed. "Please."

Anton looked away, unable to meet Isaac's eyes, but that was fine. Isaac didn't need to see the pity written in his expression, or the fear that coursed through him. "My mother, before she left, used to tell us myths from her homeland, and I always loved hearing about the monsters, the nightmares, the things in the dark that mothers used to scare their children into behaving."

Anton laughed, softly. "It never worked on me, you know. Perhaps it was because I already lived with a monster in our home, haunting our hallways."

A rush of sympathy ran through him. Despite the antagonism they once shared, Isaac had seen the horrors that the late Lord LeClaire had inflicted on them with the quiet way Shan would withdraw, disappearing for days at a time to handle family affairs before returning to the Academy, drained and exhausted.

At the time, he had cursed her father for it, had done all that he could to help her keep up with her classes. But looking back on it now, he wondered how much of it was the beginnings of her network, the birth of a Sparrow.

Another secret between them.

But this moment was about Anton, and for whatever reason, the man was helping him now. Offering him explanations for horrors it would have been easier to turn away from. "I didn't realize you knew so much of the Tagalan Islands."

"I don't know that much," Anton said, with a derisive little laugh. "Only what I've been able to teach myself with books, the bits and pieces of the language that I am sure I am butchering." Tilting his head to the side, he looked at Isaac for confirmation.

As if he would know. "I don't know much more about the language than you do," Isaac admitted, though it felt a little like plucking at scar tissue, a dull ache that wasn't quite pain. He never blamed his parents for it. At a certain level, he even understood it. They had done it with all the best of intentions, but it still was a loss he could never recover from. "And probably less of the history and myths. My parents never spoke about it around me, they feared it would hamper my success, make me more..."

Saying it out loud was somehow more painful than his monstrous transformation had been, but he needed Anton to understand. "They did not want me isolated more than I already would be."

"Ah." Anton rubbed his eyes. "You don't need to say more. And maybe they were right. You did manage to make it to Royal Blood Worker, after all."

It was Isaac's turn to huff. "For a little while, for what little good it was worth. And now, I'm becoming a monster out of their myths. My parents would be so proud."

He could almost see it, the worried way they would take this news. The way his mother would stare at him, not in fear of what he had become, but in fear of how Aeravin would treat him for it. They had given so much for his future, had sacrificed everything, and this was how he repaid them.

"The manananggal is a monster," Anton confirmed, "that feeds on the blood of the innocent."

"A vampire," Isaac muttered, closing his eyes. "It doesn't seem so different then."

"Yes," Anton admitted, "and no. Both the vampire and the manananggal feed on humans, yes. But there..." He gestured. "The wings, the claws, the tongue—the manananggal feeds on viscera and flesh as well as the blood. And..."

Anton's hand dropped to his stomach, pressed hard against it, like he was trying to keep himself from being sick. "That's not all."

"Oh," Isaac said, in a poor attempt at levity. "It gets worse?"

Anton's grim frown was a terrible thing, and it made Isaac swallow any future quips. "What makes the manananggal unique among the vampiric myths can be found in the name itself. It translates, basically, to *one who separates itself*."

Anton reached out, pulling back the curtain that Isaac shrouded himself in. Drew shockingly warm fingers across Isaac's stomach, pressing through the pelt of dark hair to the skin beneath. "I'm not even sure you noticed it, the tear here, the way your ..." Anton choked out the next word, "*innards* were slipping through."

Acid rose in the back of Isaac's throat as comprehension hit. Anton was right, with all the other things that happened to his body, he hadn't even noticed it, didn't think to look down and check when he was grappling with wings and claws and tongue, driven by a hunger that he did not want to acknowledge. "I did not notice."

"Well," Anton pulled his hand away. "It was the start of it, but you're not fully there yet. The manananggal can split itself in two." He pressed his hands together, fists stacked on top of each other, then pulled them apart. "The legs remain behind, a vulnerability, but the top half flies free, entrails trailing behind it, as it hunts through the night for its food. Strong, near indestructible, as long as it can be rejoined with its bottom half."

Isaac wet his lips, sat up as he thought it through, as the possibilities opened dark and tempting. He shouldn't be considering it, this coolly calculated brand of terror, but the option was too sweet to resist. "We can use this."

Anton flicked his gaze to Isaac, a quick look of pleased surprise, and Isaac wondered if this had been his game all along, if he had been played. It didn't matter, this was excellent, actually, if they were going to find a way to bring the Eternal King and his entire rotten system crashing to the ground.

"I would not have asked it of you," Anton demurred, carefully, and Isaac bit back the knowing smile that threatened.

"I am volunteering," Isaac stressed, because that is what he would have said to Shan, the kind of game he was used to playing, but this time, it would be the Blood Workers that suffered. "If I am going to be a monster, I might as well be a useful one."

Something strange flickered across Anton's expression, there and gone again before Isaac could comment on it. Anton rose to his feet, held out a hand to help pull Isaac up. "There is much to plan then. Strategic strikes we can make."

Isaac nodded. "But I think I'll need a few more shirts and binders."

Anton shrugged, that easy affability back. "I can get you those, as well as some books on Tagalan history, if you would like it."

It was a bit of a distraction at this stage, Isaac knew that, but he couldn't resist the temptation. The gaps in his own history were too painful to ignore, and besides, if there was anything there that could help him master this new gift, he couldn't ignore it. "I'll take whatever you can find."

Anton took him by the hand, gave it a quick squeeze. "Then I'll get them. I've got you, Isaac."

Chapter Twenty-Five

Shan

The salon at Lady Lynwood's had a very somber air, different from every other party that Shan had ever attended. There was no chattering tingle of conversation, no sly glances and coy laughs. The tea service, one that Lady Lynwood prided herself on, had been replaced by a stronger set of spirits, passed around by glum-looking serving girls, refilling glasses of dark red wine or tumblers of whisky.

Because the news was out—Lady Holland was dead, murdered in her own study, throat ripped out like some feral beast had gotten a hold of her. It was cruel and horrifying, and countless theories floated through the room as everyone struggled to make sense of it.

But Shan knew the truth. Even without the missive from the Eternal King that arrived at her desk immediately afterwards, she knew that it could only be one person. The man she hadn't seen since that disastrous night when she manipulated him into sipping her blood, so desperately curious to see what would happen to him.

If he would become the vampire she thought he could be.

Well, she got her answer, and she wasn't sure if she liked it. He had turned into a beast after all, a vampire feasting on the human blood, and she had set him on that path. First Miss Arena, now Lady Holland, and who knew how many more would follow. Why he had chosen Holland, Shan could only guess at, but if she could be dreadfully honest with herself, she didn't want to know.

It didn't matter in the end. Holland was dead, and the King was determined to find Isaac as soon as possible, leaving Shan with such dreadfully limited options.

Miss Lynwood sniffled loudly, her face buried in her lover's shoulder. Even at her own mother's salon, she couldn't manage the right level of decorum. But, perhaps just this once, Shan could cut her some slack.

"I can't believe Lady Holland is . . ." Lynwood cut herself off with a sob, and Miss Rayne just stroked her dark hair, muttering soothing noises.

"We will all mourn her," Sir Morse said as he stepped forward, offering his handkerchief like the chivalrous man he believed himself to be. "The Council will be lesser with her gone."

Miss Lynwood offered a watery smile as she took it. "She was the best of them, you know. Mother always said so."

Shan bit her tongue, even as she admitted to herself that it was true, in a sense. Holland was by no means a good person, and Shan couldn't honestly say that she would miss her, but Holland had been so talented at the game of politics, setting to the work with a zeal that should have brought the other Royal Councillors to shame, if they had any. If she had lived, she would have been a force to be reckoned with. So, in that sense, perhaps she was one of the best, as dubious a title as it would have been.

But it was a distinction without a difference, and Shan had more important things to focus on. Like the conversation that was happening right in front of her.

"Don't worry, darling," Miss Rayne was saying, "we'll find whoever is responsible for this and see them executed."

"I would put money on it being tied to those Unblooded radicals," Sir Morse continued. "It wasn't bad enough that they took Lord Dunn, now they had to take Holland from us. Two of the Royal Council in a year—it simply cannot stand! I don't care how many of them we have to mow through, justice must be served."

Shan took a heady sip of her wine, ignoring the straight up

misinformation that Edward was spewing. The Unblooded radicals had been separate from Isaac's gambits, two terrible plots running parallel to each other, feeding off the chaos that they created. But, of course, that was before Samuel had convinced Anton to help with the rescue of Isaac. Perhaps there was something more here, something that she wasn't privy too.

"Honestly." Amelia leaned in, speaking for the first time in a long while, having waited for the precise moment when she could have the greatest impact. She dropped her voice conspiratorially. "I agree. We should have kept curfew up. The King was right to crack down on them."

"Maybe if we hadn't dropped it," Lynwood sniffed, "she'd still be alive. Oh, this is horrible!"

Guilt churned in Shan's stomach, because on this—they were right. Holland's death had been a horror, at least in the way it had been done. She had read the reports herself, filled with far more gruesome details than the others had access too, sketches drawn in a steady hand detailing each and every wound on the body.

Blood and steel. This was going to be a disaster if she didn't do something to stop it.

"Perhaps," Amelia said, casting a too-casual glance in Shan's direction, "our dear friend here has some tricks up her sleeve. Your solution to the dwindling Blood Supply was ingenious, after all."

Shan recognized it for what it was—a little nudge, priming the others for what should happen if she needed to act outside of the normal chain of command again. It was a time of emergency, after all.

Too bad Amelia didn't already know about the plans the King had put into motion, the vampire that they were creating to combat the horror that Isaac was becoming. Fire to fight fire—and she had to hope that all of Aeravin wouldn't burn in the process.

"Do not worry," Shan said, speaking up and drawing the attention of the others. "I have a meeting with the Eternal King shortly, and I am already working with Lord Aberforth on the issue."

It was only a slight lie. She and Samuel had been avoiding discussing it as much as possible, a kind of truce they had made around Isaac. But if Isaac was going to risk upsetting the fragile peace in Aeravin even more, then they were forcing her hand. The consequences were theirs to reap, and Shan would not let herself feel any guilt at being the hand that dealt them. Her interference would be much kinder than the King's would be, and hells, they should be thankful for her.

Lynwood reached out, grabbing Shan's hands with a harsh squeeze, eyes shining with tears. "Please do. Oh, you are too dear a friend, Shan."

"It is only the right thing to do," Shan demurred, though the open affection in Lynwood's gaze struck her deeply. She hadn't expected it—her rise in their circle had been entirely manufactured, her friendship with them existing on the very conditional status of what Shan had to offer them. But, in this moment of shared grief and loss, there was something honest beneath it all.

Yes. She could use this.

She squeezed Lynwood's hand in return, a perfectly designed smile on her face. "I will, right now in fact. The King is waiting for me."

She stood, ready to take her leave, when Sir Morse caught her by the wrist. "I speak for my grandmother when I say this, Shan, but know that my family and their vassals stand ready to support you and the King, no matter what."

Shan inclined her head, a gracious acceptance already on her lips. Such a promise was a dangerous thing, the implication that one branch of the government was ready to intervene into another's business. The military and the Guard were separate for a reason, but this meant that Morse did not believe Samuel and the Guards were capable of stopping this threat.

That Morse was ready to step in, in a way that had never been seen in all of their history.

This spoke of deep unrest within the noble classes, and Shan had to fix things before their government shattered completely. And to do that, she needed help.

She needed the Eternal King.

Shan found the King deep beneath the palace, in the laboratory that had once been the Blood Factory. The scope of it always took her breath away, a cavernous space that once held so much, stripped away around them in every direction, an echoing emptiness that should have chilled her. Instead, it teemed with untapped potential—they had needed such little space for what they had begun with Mel.

What more could they do, if they were brave enough? If they had no other choice?

She put that from her mind, focusing instead on Mel and His Royal Majesty, who had perched himself on the same metal slab they had been using for their experiments. He had removed his jacket and his vest, sleeves up to his elbows, exposing the taut lines of his forearm and the old scars that crisscrossed them—jagged lines where blades had sliced deep to reveal the blood beneath. Wounds that he could heal, if he so chose, but that he refused to, for reasons Shan did not understand.

Mel draped herself across his lap, luxurious and utterly relaxed, her mouth latched to the inside of his wrist as she suckled. The King ran his hand through her hair, working out the tangles with a gentleness that surprised Shan. He looked up at her with that ever more familiar smile, gesturing her closer, inviting her into this twisted parody of intimacy. Mel startled beneath him, just noticing that they had company, lifting her head in surprise.

Her mouth was a mess, blood smeared across her lips and chin, the bright glint of fangs shining in the light. She looked utterly feral, her blue eyes glazed over with a primal hunger that Shan had only ever seen in beasts, but Mel was content to dive back to the feast offered to her, dragging her tongue across the gnawed mess that was the King's flesh.

"Go on, dear," the King cooed, and Shan had to fight the disorientating realization that he was truly treating her like a pet. Mel mewled into his skin, a pleased rumble that reminded Shan so much of a cat. "I know you're still hungry."

Mel dove back in, opening her maw wide before she drove her teeth into his flesh. The King didn't even flinch, and Shan stepped close enough that she could hear each squelching slurp.

"She's taking to it even better than I hoped she would," the King murmured, uncaring that she was right there in his lap, listening. Or perhaps not. There seemed to be precious little human about her, though, so far, the only physical difference was in those fangs. The sketches the King had shown her revealed the monstrosity yet to come, and Shan itched to know how many more of these little sessions were needed to tip Mel over the edge.

"How often are you feeding her?"

"Daily," the King confirmed. "And she wants more with each passing feeding. It shouldn't be long now."

Shan licked dry lips. "Forgive me, Your Majesty, but is it wise for you to give that much blood?"

His gaze flicked up to hers, emerald eyes softening. "That is kind of you, Shan, but there is no need to worry. My blood is the strongest, and we do not have time to waste."

Ah, there it was—just a hint of frustration. The opening she needed. She flitted to his side, already formulating the story she would spin. "I just came from Lady Lynwood's salon, and young Sir Morse had the most intriguing things to say."

"I am not surprised," the King said, before she could continue, "and I am glad you brought this to me. This is useful, but—ah, a moment." He glanced down at the creature in his lap, making gentle shushing noises as he pulled her off his arm. "Enough for now, Mel."

The girl whined, deep in her throat, chasing after the wound she had made. But the King only raised it to his own lips, licking the blood clean. Shan could feel the burst of magic as the skin knitted together, smooth and unblemished. Despite the way he fed her his very blood, his very power, he allowed no trace of her to remain—unworthy of the temple that was his body with all its flaws.

The King eased her back, his grip firm but not bruising, as he helped Mel to a sitting position. A cloth appeared in his hands, as he wiped her face clean; she had been a messy eater, blood spilling down her chin to her throat, but the King was too meticulous to let a drop of it get away. There was too much power in that blood, and he'd have been a fool to risk even the smallest speck of it.

Mel sat through her cleaning with a surprising amount of restraint, though her eyes did not move from the space just below the King's hand, as if she were just waiting for the chance to press back against his wrist.

She probably was, but the girl was too well trained by now. She would wait for the King's permission, hanging on his every word like a hound.

"Take her back to her cell, will you, Shan?" The King stood, clenching the cloth in his hand, stained a deep maroon. "I need to clean up."

"Of course," Shan said, slipping to Mel's side. "The muzzle?"

"No longer necessary." He glanced back at the girl, his tone taking on just the slightest edge of authority. "Right, Mel?"

The girl slid off the table, lurching into a particularly clumsy attempt at a curtsy. "Of course not, my lord," she slurred, with all the poise of someone who was deep at the bottom of a bottle, and Shan had to wonder just how potent the King's blood was.

"Come along then." Shan pressed her hand into the small of Mel's back, and the girl blearily followed her gentle instructions, humming a tune to herself as she swayed. There was something almost innocent about it, the fear that had once hung over Mel vanished as the changes rolled through her, as the power became more than a promise.

Mel went willingly back into her cell, and Shan wondered just how badly they had broken this girl, and why she felt so little shame over it. Yes, she had been a coward and criminal, used to flashing her tears to get what she wanted, but they were making her into something little more than a pet, ready to hunt and come to heel. They were doing it kindly, gently, but thoroughly—and as Mel looked up at her with that guileless smile, Shan felt a euphoric rush that went straight to her head.

She met the King across the room, where he stood in front of a recently lit incinerator, a smaller scale one than what she had in the basement of her own home. No, this wasn't for bodies, but for the smaller detritus of their work. The fabric he used to wipe away the mess was already inside, shriveling away into dust and ash, but the King wasn't done.

His slim fingers slipped to where his shirt was tucked into his trousers, pulling it free, a tease of pale skin before he ripped it over his head, revealing the long expanse of his back. Shan knew she should turn away, this was too intimate, too personal. It felt like a transgression that she should be punished for, but she could not stop staring.

There were scars there too, twisted and knotted, not as numerous as on his arms, not as deliberate as their Blood Working demanded. No, these scars were wide and vicious things, the remnants of a flogging that had left him marked forever. Why had he not healed them? He had the power, the skill, the opportunity.

"I can feel you staring," the King said, feeding his shirt to the fire. The flames caught, flaring up to catch his profile in the harsh light. He looked so terrible and untouchable, and Shan felt as helpless as a moth drawn to the candle.

"My apologies," Shan said, forcing herself to whirl away as her heart beat unsteadily in her chest. "Please forgive my presumption."

"No, Shan, I am not angry." The King reached out, grabbing her by the shoulder. He wasn't wearing his claws, bare fingers against the warmth of her skin where her dress dipped to reveal smooth flesh. "I know what it looks like. I know what you're thinking—what everyone thinks."

He was close enough that she could feel his breath on her skin, the warmth coming off his body as strong as the incinerator behind them. A scalding embrace that would leave her utterly destroyed, and yet, she longed to melt into it.

"But, I will tell you the truth, Shan," he murmured, his hands trailing down to settle on the curve of her waist, holding her as tight as any binding. "Because I think you will understand. Once, a long time ago, before Aeravin was born, I had to fight for my right to exist as a Blood Worker, in a time when people thought we were monsters for the magic we were born with. And I endured such terrible things, torments that I refuse to let my people ever experience again. So, I wear these marks with pride, Shan, for how far I've come."

His fingers pressed into her skin, hard enough to leave his own marks, even through the fall of her clothes. His strength was unmistakable—and oh, how he bruised so casually, so easily, like she was his to mar.

"I wear them so I never forget what it was like to suffer." He shifted, slightly, his mouth brushing against her ear. "Do you understand me, Shan?"

"I do," she exhaled, the honesty stronger than any balm she had ever known. No, Aeravin hadn't scarred her in the same way that her King had been, but she still carried deep wounds, buried somewhere beneath her skin. Aching pains that would never heal, the suffering of cruelties that had shaped her just as much as they had harmed her.

And, because she was strong enough to bare it, to remember it, she would take every one of the cruelties done to her and allow it to make her stronger. No matter how much it hurt.

She closed her eyes, blurry as tears threatened. "I understand."

"I knew you would, my brilliant girl."

The King let go, and she swayed, just for a moment, before turning back around.

He had already grabbed another shirt, had pulled it on and was setting himself to rights, as if the moment they just shared had never happened at all. "Anyway, about Lady Lynwood's?"

Right. Shan took a deep breath, recounted the brief facts that he needed to know—the tension that threaded through his people, the seeds Amelia had begun to plant, the not-quite-promises that Edward had made. And through it all, the King listened attentively, hanging on her every word. It was so strange, approaching it from this angle, like she was the bird and he was the Sparrow. Their roles were far more complicated than that, though, but old habits die hard.

It was almost a relief, honestly, to be the one not to have to make the decision, waiting on guidance from someone with more experience and knowledge than she could ever hope to have.

"That Morse boy," the King muttered, with no fair amount of derision. "Always putting his foot in his mouth. Still, that insight into Lady Morse's feelings is helpful, considering—" He trailed off, glancing back to the cell where Mel rested, curled up on her cot and deeply asleep. "Well, that is a bridge we can burn when we get to it. For now, Amelia Dunn. Tell me what you think about her."

Shan blinked at the sudden shift in conversation, but she was almost used to it by now. "Clever, driven, helpful."

She hated to admit it, and would never have thought it would be so, even a year ago, but Amelia was proving herself to be a formidable ally. "I'd rather have her on my side than against it. She has an astute understanding of our current political situation, and a willingness to embrace unorthodox solutions."

"Hmm. I had hoped so. She appears to have inherited her father's acumen, let us hope she surpasses him in wisdom." Catching her hand, he brought it to his lips, polite, chaste, formal—but still, it made her blood warm. "Thank you, Shan. It's been a while since I had a Royal Blood Worker who was skilled in both academics and politics. Your input is greatly appreciated."

"Of course," Shan said, dropping instinctively into a deep curtsy. "I aim only to excel."

"And that you do." He pulled her to her feet, smiling indulgently. It was different from the way he looked at Mel—there, she was as beloved pet, a tool to be used. But in this, Shan almost felt like a co-conspirator. Like a trusted counsellor, though she knew that was not true.

He was playing her, as he always did, but what she would give to believe it, if only for a moment.

"For now, I have work to prepare," the King said, stepping away in a clear dismissal. "If only all of my appointees were as diligent as you, but alas, I fear I must step in."

Shan's stomach filled with ice as she processed the words, knowing the target of his ire, if not the particulars. They had both risen at the same time, but she had given terribly little thought to Samuel of late, too caught up in the needs of her own role.

But he was strong enough to handle it, she had to believe that.

Because if he wasn't, then she had failed him—and she couldn't stand to fail another person she cared about.

Chapter Twenty-Six

Isaac

Isaac pulled his shirt back on, his fingers running quickly along the buttons, covering the dark cloth of his binder as Celeste turned away, dumping the small scalpel into the sink as she washed his blood from her hands. He ignored the way that his blood ran dark and slow, even with the aid of water, thick like syrup and just as sticky, clinging to Celeste's fingers as she scrubbed with harsh soap.

It didn't matter, truly, or that is what he tried to tell himself. He was something out of myth, a manananggal, but still mostly human. At least when he wanted to be. And despite the worried looks that Celeste kept shooting him during their appointment, his treatments continued to be successful. Easier, even, as though his body was continuing to change—to adapt—and in his horror, he would not become lost.

Not in the levels of hormones in his blood, somehow growing more stable, or the changes he had he wrought in himself to create a body he could be at home in. The shape of his face, subtly carved into something more masculine, the cut of his muscles and the breadth of his shoulders, the hair that spread across his body—down his chest and stomach, thickening on his arms and legs. It was alignment, it was euphoria, but this was something more.

He was a beast of fear and hunger, of claws and fangs. He was shedding all the polite trappings that society had forced upon him, leaving him with only the truest, rawest bits of himself on display for all to see.

It was more than a transition, it was a transformation, unlocking something within him that he never even knew to want. He should fear this, he understood that. But whatever the endgame was here, whatever he would be once it was complete—he was still *him*. Even more so than before, and the peace and joy that ran through him was like nothing he had ever felt before.

Even if others couldn't quite understand it.

Celeste slammed a towel down on the counter, the white fabric stained dark with the remains of his blood. It wouldn't come clean, no matter what she tried. Meaning there was only one option—it would have to be burned. "Anything you feel like telling me about, Isaac?"

He ignored the way she asked the question, low and sugar sweet, the same tone she had employed when he was young and had been caught in some minor failure. Plying on his better nature to make him fess up, because he used to be good and kind.

He wasn't good and kind anymore, thoroughly ruined by what Aeravin had made of him. "You don't want to know, trust me."

She huffed, crossing her arms over her generous chest, leveling a glare that would have made his mother proud. "You don't get to make that decision for me, young man."

It was a fair point, and an echo of what he had told someone else recently. When Samuel had tried to hold him at arm's distance, protecting him from that gift that lurked in his veins—the one he had never been afraid of, anyway. Perhaps this was his problem, perhaps he shouldn't be acting this way.

Perhaps he needed to learn to trust.

"I was wrong," he admitted. "I am not a vampire, I'm something else."

Celeste didn't push him, coming to his side and laying her hand on his. A comforting squeeze that emboldened him to continue. "I'm not a vampire, I'm a manananggal."

He saw the confusion on her face, the way her jaw moved as she tested the word on her tongue. "It's a creature from the Tagalan Islands," he began, filling her in on what Anton had shared, on what the books of mythology had confirmed. How he had killed and fed, how each drop of blood made him stronger, made him more of what he was become.

How he wasn't going to stop.

And through it all Celeste watched with her hand on her throat, her discomfort plain on her face. She didn't understand—he should have known better. She was still good in a way he was not. "I thought you wanted to find a way to reverse it."

It was a fair question, but it still sat oddly in his chest. "I was afraid, I think. But I'm not anymore. I am doing what I need to do to see this through."

Her gaze softened; the intensity of her judgement replaced with something like sadness. "And what about you, Isaac? When it's over, are you going to be okay?"

"It doesn't matter," he said, not realizing how true it was till he voiced it. It wasn't something that bothered him. He had already committed to this path, and it was too late to turn from it now.

"Isaac," Celeste began, but he shook his head.

"I am not a child anymore—"

"You most certainly are not," Celeste tried to cut in, but Isaac barreled on.

"—and I appreciate your concern, I truly do." He tilted his chin up, unafraid. "But this is something we can use, Celeste, and I'm willing to pay whatever price I need to pay."

"Oh, son." She blinked rapidly, tears sliding down her cheeks. "This is not the future any of us wanted for you. We just wanted you to be happy."

Isaac stilled. That was what this was about then—it wasn't about him being a monster, not precisely. It was about something more ephemeral than that. The love of a parent for a child, the kind that wished they could protect him from all suffering and strife. It touched an old scar, deep within, the promises his parents had made on the hope of a better future.

A hope that never came to life, not truly.

"I know," he admitted, then stepped forward and let her pull him into a hug. She was tall, still, able to rest her chin on the top of his head as he buried his face in her shoulder. Feeling all of twelve years old again, when he had first whispered the truth of himself out loud, too nervous to claim it loudly. She had held him then as she did now, her arms warm and tight, smelling faintly of the sterile tang of antiseptic, and it felt like he let some of the weight off his back, just for a moment.

"I didn't want this either," he murmured. He was so, so tired, and he wished he could just lay down his arms. "But I cannot live with myself if I turned away from it now."

She squeezed tight, one final time, and then let go. "I understand," she replied, wiping away the tears with the back of her hand. "Even if I don't like it."

"If it makes you feel better," he said, "I don't like it either."

Her laugh was watery, but true. "It does, you know. But fine." She squared her shoulders, took his face in her hands and pressed a kiss to his forehead. "My Isaac, a fierce manananggal."

He squeezed his eyes shut to fight the tears, but they were not bitter things. No, this was relief, threatening to knock his feet out from under him. Despite all he had done and all that he was, the closest thing he had to a mother still loved him.

Still stood by him—would stand by him till the end.

The moment was ruined when the door to the clinic banged open, loud enough to be heard even in here in the back. Celeste moved quickly, placing herself before him in the doorway, as if she could protect him by bodily putting herself between him and whoever had broken in.

But it was no threat. Isaac recognized it instantly, the cologne that Anton favored and the fear that had his heart pounding a frenetic beat.

Celeste recognized him a moment later as he pushed through the curtain, her posture easing, but her tone still testy. "You shouldn't be back here while I'm with a patient, young man."

Anton barely even blinked. "People have been hurt, Celeste. We need help. We can pay—"

She cut him off by turning away. "Keep your money, boy. Just let me grab my bag."

To spare them the troubles of avoiding the Guard and their uncomfortable questions, Anton decided to hire a hackney. Isaac glanced out the window as they rattled through the city, wheels on cobblestone.

They were already approaching the Fox Den, the crowds growing thicker as the early winter night crept in, heading towards their gambling hells and restaurants and theaters. Something like shame twisted in Isaac's stomach, sour and bitter. Not even a year ago and he would have been one of them, playing their games with a false smile while stewing bitterly in his heart. The world he lived in now was far more dangerous—and far less comfortable—but there was something freeing about it as well. He no longer had to hide the anger he felt, the schemes that he planned. He had allies, even if they weren't the ones he had expected.

Anton, leaning back against the far seat, eyes closed as if he could relax into a light nap. Celeste beside him, her expression far more grim than he had ever seen, her big leather bag balanced in her lap, carrying all the tools she might need: scalpels and knives, bandages and antiseptic. And beneath all that, wrapped in thick bundles of cloth, were two large glass bottles of blood, just in case.

He could still sense it, even through all the layers—not quite a siren's call like blood fresh from the body, but still alluring.

He worked his jaw, thankful that the hackney came to a stop at last. He was the first out, holding the door open so that Celeste could follow. Anton flicked the driver a tip before turning on his heel. He led them into the Den without another word, and Isaac bit back the strange feeling of déjà vu. It hadn't been that long since he had last been here, swearing allegiance to a rebellion he once had been tasked with destroying. It felt like a lifetime ago, though, and he ducked around the bustling workers as Anton took them to the same back staircase.

The scent of iron hit him, copper on the back of his tongue, and Isaac deliberately let himself fall back as they emerged into the lounge again, seeing the people scattered about the chairs and lounges, all of them beaten and bloody.

Celeste was already moving forward, cataloguing the patients as she mentally triaged them, and Anton was off to the side with Monique, whispering furtively, nailing down the logistics of the risk they had taken. The High Rollers lounge was to be closed for so-called renovations for the near future, if they could persuade Celeste or some other Blood Healers to help them as they moved the injured and ill through.

It was important work, what they did, but it left him miserably alone, both a boon and a curse. There was no one here to see him struggle, but there was also no one here to help him. Not as the hunger twisted within him, a feral beast aching to burst free of its cage.

His eyes flitted from person to person, landing on a woman not ten feet from him, the wound to her head still seeping red, matting her dark hair to her skull. To the man sitting across from her, his arms scratched like he had been dragged across the cobblestones, flecks of gravel embedded in raw flesh that Isaac longed to lick clean.

He could feel his mouth start to ache, eyeteeth throbbing as they grew into something sharper. It would be so easy to move forward, to rend and tear into those that Anton had brought them here to help—

He shouldn't have come; he realized that now.

Ducking behind the bar, Isaac sank down to the floor, holding his head in his hands as he struggled, desperately, to get a hold of himself. Nails thickened, sharpened, not quite claws but strong enough to hurt as he dug them into his sides, leaving a mottled trail of bruises as a testament to his own fragile self-control.

A body settled next to him, the familiar scent of woodsmoke and brandy giving away his visitor without him even needing to open his eyes. "Can I help you, Anton?"

Anton huffed. "Just checking on you. This is a ... peculiar resting spot."

Anton spoke around his affliction, a kindness to him or the practical necessity of not revealing there was a monster among them. Regardless of the intention behind it, Isaac would take the out. "What happened here?"

Anton gave him a long, considering look, but he allowed the dodge to happen. "There was an altercation at one of the warehouses. The Guard had a tip that it was a distributor of our pamphlets, so they needed to do a search."

Isaac swallowed hard. "And the workers ... they resisted?"

Anton shook his head, a single, tired word falling from his lips. "No."

There was no more elaboration needed, no explanations to give. Isaac was smart enough to figure it out on his own. Either the Guard wanted to provoke them into fighting back, an excuse to arrest them and harvest more pints of blood, or they just wanted the Unblooded to suffer for the pure cruelty of it. Either way, it resulted in them being battered, left with no one to help them—or at least, no one to help them if he hadn't thought to bring Celeste into the fold. One good thing he could claim in this lifetime of poor decisions and heartache.

There was still so much blood on his hands, but perhaps he could wipe some of the stain away.

"Did the Guard find them?" Isaac asked, if only to distract himself. "The pamphlets, I mean."

"No," Anton said, leaning his head back against the bar with a *thunk*. "We got lucky—they shipped out yesterday. If they had been one day sooner ... "

Isaac swallowed hard. If this was how the Guard acted when they found nothing, he could not imagine what would happen if they did find proof of treason. "What will you do now?"

"I don't know," Anton said, honestly. "We haven't had the chance to meet about it yet, not with ... " He gestured towards the room behind him, and Isaac nodded.

That was fair. Everything was quickly crumbling around them, the danger creeping ever closer. Tomorrow's problem. Today was about healing and recuperation.

"I'm sorry I can't help more." Isaac was decent enough with Blood Healing, most Blood Workers knew the very basics. Someone like Celeste would be needed for the more complex injuries but scrapes and cuts and bruises—he should have been able to handle that.

But with the hunger flittering at the edge of his consciousness, Isaac knew that he would be more of a risk than a boon.

"It's all right. Do you want to get out of here?"

It was the wise choice, as much as he loathed leaving this much work to Celeste. "I probably should."

"Well." Anton hopped to his feet, holding out his hand. Isaac took it, accepting the help. "Let's go."

They hadn't even made it to the staircase before they were stopped. "Wait."

Isaac paused, looking back at the Matron standing in the doorway, blocking the view to the make-shift clinic behind her, only just out of its infancy and already covered in gore. Monique hesitated, an inhale of struggle, before she grit out, "I wanted to apologize."

Anton huffed a small laugh of surprise, but Isaac ignored him. "For what?"

"For my doubts ... before." Monique squared her shoulders. "Perhaps you were right, perhaps it's not just Unblooded versus Blood Workers. Celeste seems—"

"*Is*," Isaac interrupted. "Celeste *is* a good soul, and we are all lucky she agreed to help. But there are more Blood Workers like her, if you would be willing to accept their aid." And Blood Workers like him, as well. On their side but a wolf, not an angel.

He just needed to find them.

Monique tipped her head, the point given to him. "You are right, of course. This is ... bigger than what it used to be."

"It is," Anton agreed, "but if we are going to make a better Aeravin, it should be a better Aeravin for all." He met Isaac's eyes, directing his words directly at him. "I was wrong. We all were wrong."

"Yes," Monique echoed. "And I cannot deny the ... effectiveness of our newest ally."

Again, the truth obfuscated, the details kept to only those who needed it. Perhaps he wasn't as free as he thought himself to be, but it was still more than he had before, when it had just been him and Alessi.

And, if he was being honest with himself, he wasn't sure if Alessi had ever cared for anything deeper than her own hurt and anguish. If she cared about the people that would be hurt, or the work that they had so foolishly neglected, in their plans to undermine the King.

This was still enough for him—the monster in the shadow, known but never acknowledged. He could do little else, not with what he had made of himself, so he would hunt in the darkness until it was time to face the King himself.

He would do it, and he would learn to be content.

"I appreciate it, Monique." Stepping forward, he caught her hand, bowed before her like she was as fine a Lady as any he had known in the King's Court. "And for all that you are doing, I thank you as well."

"Aww, isn't this cute," Anton drawled. "Friends at last."

The seriousness of the moment faded with his quip, laughter breaking out between them.

"Fine, be off," Monique said, shooing them away. "I'll see Celeste home when her work is done, you have my word."

"Good," Isaac said, glancing past her one last time, where Celeste hovered by a young boy, no more than eighteen, soothing his worry as easy as she fixed his broken leg. Using the magic that had so often been used to harm the Unblooded for their benefit.

It was enough to give him hope for a future.

Chapter Twenty-Seven

Samuel

Samuel wasn't ready for this meeting. It was their first gathering since the murder of Lady Holland, their work put to a pause as they grappled with the loss that rocked their little world. None of them were safe, not while Isaac lived, and Samuel had to admit that there was some insidious part of him that relished watching them squirm. They had been kept comfortable for too long, and it was time they had felt even a drop of the fear and stress that the Unblooded lived with on the daily.

But his fellow Councillors were not what worried him, no, it was their esteemed guest. No amount of preparation or steeling himself could ease the fear that came with the King letting himself into the Parliament House. That was a wound that went deep, and it was not just his to bear. He could feel the tension that radiated off his fellow Councillors, thick as the morning fog that rolled off the sea.

Lady Belrose looked particularly discomforted, her eyes pinned to the table in front of her, hands clenched in tight fists, the curl of her claws an almost protective shell. He almost felt bad for her—what other disruptions could the King throw their way while it was still her turn to lead the Council?

What would happen now that the one meant to follow after her had been killed?

The King was here to answer that question, his expression as cold and stern as ever. Samuel's gaze quickly flickered over him. His outfit was as fine and proper as ever, his bearing that of a man who had never been questioned, but Samuel did not care about that. He was used to performance of power by now—what did catch his eye was the way the door had been left cracked open behind him, the flash of color beyond it.

Their new Councillor, waiting to join them as soon as they were introduced.

"I appreciate you gathering so quickly," the King said by way of introduction. "I know this was very last minute."

"Quite," Lady Morse agreed. She was the only one sitting without an ounce of fear to her. "But this Council needs its full strength in this trying time, so I, for one, appreciate the speed with which you made this appointment."

Belrose stirred, spurred by the barb hidden in Morse's words. "I agree, Your Majesty. I am eager to meet our new fellow."

Even now, still jockeying to save face, currying whatever little favor they could. Disgust unfurled in Samuel, as delicate as the first bloom of spring. He could tamp it down if he wanted, but he was so tired of seeing the best in people. It only led to disappointment, again and again.

The King tilted his head forward, an acknowledgment. But they had to at least pay lip service to the one they had lost, even if this wasn't a public affair, wasn't a funeral or a memorial.

Perhaps Samuel was being unkind. They had known her all her life, not the scant months that he had. They had considered her a friend and a colleague, not another Blood Worker who had tried to twist him round and round until he had no choice but to follow her lead.

"I mourn the loss of Lady Holland. She was taken from us too soon," the King said, casting his eyes low, the exact right amount of sorrowful. "Her brilliance and her diligence were unmatched, and if she had the chance to flourish, she would have done Aeravin proud."

"To Zelda," Belrose said, raising her teacup. It wasn't quite the formal toast, but with the thickness to her voice and the shine to her eyes, Samuel could tell that it was genuine.

He mirrored the others, even though he was the reason Isaac had targeted her at all.

"As much as I would like to give her the honor she is due," the King said, pulling the conversation back on track, "we do not have time to waste. The threat to Aeravin is only growing, and if he thinks he can target one of my Councillors without reprisal, he will learn his lesson soon enough."

It was a slip, a crack in the impeccable facade that the King had maintained for so long. Samuel could feel the questions building—the different pieces of information the Council had painting a kaleidoscope of pictures, none of them complete. They knew more than the average Blood Worker, knew that Isaac had escaped custody, but none outside the Guard knew the truth of what he was becoming.

Would even dare to dream that something as dangerous as the vampire existed.

Samuel was certain the King wanted to keep it that way as long as possible, if only to keep chaos from spreading. This momentary fluster, this slight mistake, felt like a victory. They were getting to him, and it was only a matter of time.

The King had carried on, not allowing the others to press for information he would not deign to share, and Samuel refocused just in time to hear the announcement.

"—our new Councillor of Industry, Lady Amelia Dunn."

The rest of the council burst into applause as Samuel's ears started to ring, the sheer shock of it nearly forcing him out of his chair to contest this, as if it would make any difference. He only maintained his seat by sheer force of will, wrapping his hands around the armrest and pressing so tightly he didn't know what would snap first—the wood or his bones.

How could it be *her*?

The door finally opened, Amelia stepping through with that eternally smug look on her face. Gliding to the King's side, she stood there like she belonged, hand on her hip, her exquisitely tailored dress shimmering like gold under the witch light, her dark hair pinned over her shoulder where it spilled down in waves. Hells, she could have stepped right out of a ballroom, or perhaps a bakery, a layered cake that was all sweetness and fluff.

Samuel knew that he shouldn't fall for that trick, Shan had told him enough that he knew the apple hadn't fallen far from the tree. She was, in every way that mattered, her father's daughter, and though the Council positions were not hereditary and she would assume a different field entirely, here she stood, taking all that power right back. Looking over each of them in turn as she waited for their congratulations, like her place on this Council had been a forgone conclusion.

Samuel had been a fool to think it wouldn't be.

The others had stood, coming to swarm around her like bees to their queen, and Samuel slowly allowed himself to stand as he watched the power in the room start to shift. It would take time for the new alliances to form, but if there was one thing Amelia Dunn was good at, it was making herself the beating heart of the room. She was already wrapping Lady Belrose around her littlest finger; he could see it in the way that Belrose leaned in with a smile. Lord Rayne seemed agreeable enough, but that was just his usual state, the years weighing on him so heavily that he could rarely be moved to fits of passion in either direction. Lady Morse was the most hesitant, but even he could see the tension ease out of her shoulders the longer that Amelia talked, quickly proving herself to be of the right politics and temperament—not a problem, not like him. It was a masterful dance, every correct step made to the beat only they could hear.

She was so much like Shan, only without the challenge of having to overcome all of Aeravin's preconceived notions and old hates.

Shan would be livid to hear this.

The King had idled over to his side, falling back from the center of attention as he studied the reactions of the rest of the Council. Much like Samuel—an approving nod thrown his way—and the sudden harmony he found with his ancestor tripping him up more than any dissonance could have.

"She'll do well," the King said, lowly, a private conversation just for them. "I had my concerns, as untested as she is, but my Royal Blood Worker alleviated them."

The world came to a crashing standstill around him, his senses narrowing just to the man beside him. "I beg your pardon?"

"She was right, of course," the King went on, as unbothered as ever, even as he was digging this knife deeper into Samuel's gut. "Our Shan has a wonderful intuition for these matters; it's part of what makes her such an incomparable Royal Blood Worker."

"Indeed," Samuel agreed, because it was expected of him. Because, as damning as this was, it was correct. Shan was a master of the chessboard, directing all the pawns. Once, Samuel believed that Shan would play the game to destroy their enemies, but this ... he had no explanation for. Amelia Dunn was not an ally or a minion to be controlled, so why had she done this?

The King clasped him on the shoulder, a friendly gesture, though the press of his claws felt more like a warning, than anything. "I need to return to my work, son. But I trust you will do your utmost to make her feel welcome."

Samuel swallowed down the bitterness that burned in the back of his throat. "I will."

"Good." He let go, stepping to the center of the room again. "Alas, my duties call me elsewhere. Dunn ... " He paused, and she dropped into the most precise curtsy Samuel had ever seen. "I look forward to seeing how you serve Aeravin."

"You will not be disappointed," she said, with all the solemnity of a vow.

The King smiled, chilling as ever, then swept from the room, leaving the rest of them standing there in his wake.

"Well," Samuel said, because if nothing else, he would keep his word, "how about we get you acclimatized, Amelia?"

She turned to him, grinning with too many teeth. "Yes, let's."

That night, Samuel entered his bedchambers to find Shan already there, wrapped in a negligee so sheer that he could see clear through it to the skin beneath, to the fall of her breasts and the tease of her nipples, pebbling against the lace. She lay on the chaise lounge by the fire, legs kicked out and bare, smooth and ready to be touched. The light cast her in a luminous glow, tinting her skin a warm gold and pulling out all the rich shadows of her hair, hanging loose and free and wild around her shoulders.

She was a pretty picture of temptation, and he shifted as he felt his cock stir to life, pressing against the fall of his trousers as he came to half-hardness. It took nothing to rile him up, just being near her got his blood surging and his flesh aching, like his body was trying to make up for all the lonely nights. Now that he had her, he wanted her every day, multiple times a day, breaking her composure and all her careful masks with pleasure.

It was only in those moments, when she was wrecked by climax and struggling to put herself back together, that he found the truth of her. The only moments when that fearful little voice in the back of his head didn't whisper uncomfortable accusations, that she was using him just as much as she used everyone else.

It proved that even without the Aberforth Gift, he was not entirely without defenses. And it was addictive, knowing that he could break this proud woman if he needed to, stopping her clever mind and her endless schemes with his hands, his mouth, his cock.

But this was not the night for that, and he quickly adjusted himself, hoping to hide his body's reaction to her. They had things they needed to talk about, and besides, she had come to him not for seduction but comfort—he could see it in her expression, the exhaustion that she didn't even bother to hide. A half-smoked cigarette hung loose from her fingers, the bitter acrid smell harsh in his nose as he crossed the room to drop a gentle, chaste kiss to the top of her head.

"Rough day?" he asked, and she just turned towards him, chasing his affection like a cat, and the tenderness struck like a dagger to the heart. The knowledge this was another part of her that only he got to see—him, and perhaps Isaac.

If they could ever mend the old hurts that hung between them.

Still, it was a reminder to the dark voice in his heart that Shan was honest with him, that she was more than her schemes, looking up at him with such aching tenderness that he felt bad for even considering that she could still be lying to him.

Perhaps this was the sign he was looking for. Samuel's heart was heavy with fear and exhaustion, and it was clear that Shan's was too.

Perhaps together they could find a way out of this trap, before it destroyed them both.

"It's been a tough few months," Shan admitted, "and I am so tired."

"Me too." He held out a hand, and Shan looked at it for a long moment before tossing the rest of her cigarette into the fire and letting Samuel pull her into his embrace. She was warm against his body, soft and supple, pressed against all the parts where he was hard, and he buried his face in her hair, breathing deep of the scent of roses. "We should talk."

"Oh, is that all you want to do?" she whispered back, and he could hear the smirk in her voice as she pressed her hip against his hard length.

The pressure of it, the tease of the friction that he ached for, had a low hiss escaping his throat. But he pulled away, before he lost himself in her body again. "I mean it, Shan."

Shan pouted, an unserious expression that took Samuel by surprise, but she relented. "At least let me pour a glass of wine."

"Of course," Samuel said, falling back to perch on the edge of the bed, digging gloved fingers against the sheets as he willed his body to relent.

Shan ignored him, drifting over to a pitcher that had been left out, likely at her request, pouring a glass of deep red before taking a long sip. "I don't know what there is to talk about. This is just our lives now. We can only take it one day at a time."

He looked her over, taking in the slump to her shoulders, the lazy way the glass hung from limp fingers. This wasn't artifice, even he could see that. No, it was worse. Somewhere along the way, Shan had given up hope. This distance between them, the way she had been carefully corralling him back to his appointed role as Lord Aberforth, it wasn't that she had lost her way. She just didn't see another way out.

How had Samuel missed that? He had failed her, in some quiet and infinitesimal way.

But he could still fix it.

"I'm not so sure I agree," he said, drawing her attention back to him. Her gaze was as sharp as the claws she so often wore, but Samuel did not let himself be hurt. He just lifted one arm, offering her the spot next to him.

And, like a street cat, Shan tiptoed forward, careful and wary, before sinking onto the bed with delicate grace. The tension lingered for a moment, and he pulled his glove off with his teeth, tossing it aside before he reached around her, bare hand pressed against the smoothness of her curves, warm through her thin shift, as he gripped her tight.

Holding her firm, grounding himself, and maybe her too, by the way her strain faded bit by bit until she relaxed against him.

"Talk to me, Samuel."

Samuel considered his options, but he was too tired to play the game. So he said it outright. "Why didn't you warn me about Dunn?"

Shan took a careful sip of her wine. "What about her?"

"That the King was going to appoint her to the Council," Samuel said, just shy of snapping, the anger in him lashing out. "That she would take Holland's place on your recommendation."

"Ah." Shan stared straight ahead, sipping at her wine, looking so damn exhausted that he didn't know what to do. He just trailed off, unsure how to continue, how to explain the bone-deep hurt of this little betrayal, especially as Shan continued to look . . . well, not bored, exactly.

Exasperated.

"I did not think it would matter," Shan said, tipping her head back, eyes fluttering closed as she swallowed, struggling to find the right words. The calculation was back, and he stared at the soft flutter of her pulse in her throat, wondering if he could shake her by sinking his teeth into the tender skin, worrying it till he pulled a moan from her lips.

Until he broke the carefully constructed artifice she wore like a second skin.

Why did it always go this way, their attempts to connect glancing off each other like swords parrying in a duel? Every time he thought they got closer, she'd feint away, slipping through his fingers like water.

"It matters," Samuel pressed. "Because you put another snake in the pit, a snake that *I* have to deal with."

"She's not a snake," Shan said, with just a bit of frustration. "I understand that you do not like her, but she is a known quantity, someone that we can work with. She's not a fool, she bends to reason."

"She is just like her father!"

"Amelia is nothing like her father," Shan snapped. "You need to trust me. There is so much that you do not know."

And so much that she did. Shan didn't need to remind him of that, not explicitly. Didn't need to dig her fingers into the tender wound that still festered, the constant shame that reminded him that no matter how hard he tried, he would never truly belong.

That no matter how hard he tried, how much he learned, he would always be behind.

"You won't always be able to guide me, Shan," he said at last, even though it wasn't quite what he wanted to say. It was more diplomatic, more careful, and hells, he had really become one of them, hadn't he? Not smart enough, not skilled enough, to succeed on his own. But twisted enough that he was no longer the person he used to be, that he was no longer sure if he could call himself a good man.

Not that it mattered, anymore.

Still, Shan inclined her head, acknowledging his point. A small victory, even if it tasted bitter. "You are right, Samuel, but that certainty will come with time. Besides ..." She flashed him a grin, one that he was nearly certain was sincere. "You know I don't mind helping you."

Leaning in, she pressed a soft kiss to his forehead, and Samuel knew that this was the moment to press. To bear his soul and fears before her, the aching raw beat of his heart as he whispered that it wasn't failure that he feared, but the dark path that she was leading him down.

That her help was even more terrifying than her neglect.

But Shan was nuzzling his cheek now, stepping into the space between his open thighs, her body warm and oh so close. It wouldn't take anything at all to place his hands on the soft curve of her waist, to pull her forward so that she straddled his lap and pressed against his aching cock—to lose his worry in the warm heat beneath her thighs and the raw physicality of a hard fuck.

Perhaps they were more alike than he had realized. Perhaps every time he had thought he was breaking down her walls, she had been manipulating him. Distracting him with the rough stroke of her hand or the slick wetness of her mouth until he spilled, exhausted, and forgot whatever it was that he had been worrying about.

"Why don't you just relax for a bit," Shan breathed against his ear, hand on his shoulder to push him back against the silk sheets. But he found that he was not so easily moved, anger twisting in his stomach as something dark and forbidding stirred in his chest.

"Enough," he snapped, as something slipped past his lips, a wisp of magic that shouldn't exist. A gift that he had not told her had returned.

But it was there, hanging between them like a dark miasma on the night air, as the force of his command hit her hard, forcing her to flinch away, to stumble back. Her hand flew to her chest as she struggled to even breathe, realization hitting a split second behind Samuel.

He dared not even breathe as she stared at him, her eyes dark and wide. He had never seen this expression on her face before, this almost primal fear coursing through her as she shivered. As she struggled to fight as the command sank its teeth into her, a power that even she could not escape.

He wished he was wearing his claws so he could tear into his own chest, pull this gift out of him with nothing more than sheer will. But he wasn't wearing his claws. He didn't have the skill or the knowledge to even understand what was happening.

"Samuel," Shan breathed at last, the power releasing her, but he shot to his feet before the question could be voiced. As if, by simply avoiding speaking of it, he could deny that it had ever happened.

"I," he stammered, incoherent and uncaring of it, as he stumbled around the corner of the bed. "I need to … " He didn't know what, just that he couldn't be here.

That he couldn't be around her, or anyone, not now that this was back.

"Samuel—" Shan reached for him, but he darted back, not daring to let himself be caught, not daring to let her touch him. Not knowing what he would do if she did.

He fled into the night, leaving her behind.

Chapter Twenty-Eight

Shan

The Guards let Shan into the King's personal wing, the grand doors closing behind with an ominous thud. Chills ran down the length of her spine as she heard the doors lock—she understood that it was standard protocol, that the King's safety would always come first. It wasn't a threat or a punishment.

But that didn't do anything to calm the anxiety that spiked, sharp and jagged like glass, with the unsettling knowledge that she was trapped. She ignored the warnings, the instinctual primal sense of self-preservation, holding her head high as she moved forward, looking for the one who invited her.

The King wasn't in the grand living space, the low couches and settees looking pristine and untouched. She moved down the hallway, past a series of closed doors and fine art, heading towards his study—the private study closed off from the rest of Dameral, a sacred space that she still wasn't sure how she had gained access to.

But she still remembered that hazy afternoon, leaning close to him, feeling the warmth of his power washing over her as he showed her ancient sketches in his own hand, detailing myths and monsters come to life. Now, she knew it all to be true, not simply possibility but reality, but that glimmering afternoon felt like it had been the start of something new.

She still wasn't sure if it was something she should fear. But it was her life, whether she wanted it or not. Fixing a cruel little smile on her face, she entered the study, coming to a sudden stop as she took in the sight in front of her.

A version of the man that was far less precise, far less put together, than the liege she was used to serving, another facet of himself that he was revealing one by one, as steady as the passing of the days. He didn't even look up from his work, standing over the desk as he stared down at the papers sprawled in front of him. He was dressed in only trousers and a simple shirt, his frame lean and lithe in the early light. His face was unshaven, the beginnings of a beard calling attention to the strong line of his jaw, and his hair rested loose and tousled, not slicked back and precise against his scalp.

His sleeves were rolled up to his elbows, exposing forearms that were hard and lean, crisscrossed with harsh scars, unmistakable but not as harsh as the other wounds he carried. Shan recognized it for what it was—a reminder of where he had started, and how far he had come. Of everything that he had given for his country, for people like him, for magic that was feared across the world. And there was a part of her, dark and vengeful, that respected him for it.

She raised her gaze to find him staring at her, lips twisted into a small smirk as he looked at her looking at him. Something ineffable hung in the air, heady and undefinable, and Shan couldn't help the fissure of hunger that curled through her.

A betrayal in miniature, a wrongness that should leave her shamed, but the vicious and greedy thing that she was, all she could feel was an endless craving.

"Good morning, Shan," the King drawled, voice dark and slow like syrup, still carrying some of the rasp of morning. "Thank you for joining me."

"Of course, Your Majesty," she replied, dropping into a proper curtsy, only for him to laugh softly.

"Please, I think we're far beyond such things." The warmth of his words dripped down her spine, burning like the drip of hot wax down a candle. "You can call me Tristan, at least when we are alone like this."

"I . . ." Shan hesitated, thrown for once by the invitation. Despite the way her role as Royal Blood Worker had drawn her deeper into his circle, had her spending hours upon hours with the man. But it had always been professional, strict boundaries around the roles they played, a carefully constructed dance where Shan knew every step.

This was not that. This was a dissolution of all those carefully constructed rules, and Shan was standing on the edge of free fall. And the King just tilted his head, daring her to jump, making her believe that he wouldn't let her crash against the jagged rocks below.

No, he'd catch her—he would lift her to new heights. Allow her to fulfill her darkest potential, without once judging her for it.

It was a sweet dream, a tempting manipulation. For that's what it had to be. The Eternal King did not do anything without calculation, allowed nothing if it wouldn't benefit him. He would twist her into something as dark as the vampire they created, but if she had the courage to chase such power, wouldn't it be worth it?

But if she went that route, she would—forever and for always—lose Samuel, the best and most righteous man she had ever known. Shatter the thin trust that bound her and Isaac, confirming every doubt he had about her. If she gave into this slow, delicate seduction the King wove around her, soft as silk and just as luxurious, she would be shattering what was left of her heart.

So, she swallowed her ambition like the bitter fruit it was, poisonous and sour on her tongue.

"As you say, Tristan," she murmured, thrilling her words with just a hint of breathlessness, meeting calculation with calculation. She could play these games, could lead him to believe she was falling. He might be Eternal, but she would not let herself be beat.

Not at the games she had been playing and perfecting since she was old enough to take her first steps.

"Excellent." He clasped his hands together. "Let me call for some tea and then we can get started."

He gestured towards the little alcove where they had sat last time, and Shan drifted towards the chair, her hand landing on its back as she stared out the window. It had started to snow since she had arrived at the palace, the thick flakes falling slow and fat. She had never seen a true snowfall, not with the Dameral's location on the coast. Just little squalls like this, soft flurries dancing through the skies before they hit dirty cobblestones or the harsh waves of the sea, vanishing as they touched down.

Maybe when this was all over, when a semblance of peace was found, she and Samuel could travel. Visit the Aberforths' estate in the country, far from the capital. Experience what a true winter was like, maybe even find a few days of peace.

The King reappeared at her side, holding out a steaming cup of tea, already doused with just a splash of cream to smooth the bitterness. Exactly as she liked it.

When had the King picked up little things like that? What else had he noticed about her, and how much of it was her many masks, and how much of it was the truth of her? Raw, uncertain, and anguished.

"Penny for your thoughts?" the King asked.

She was so tired of the constant manipulations, of second-guessing every action and intention. So perhaps that was why the truth fell so easily from her lips as she reached for the cup, wrapping her fingers around its warmth. "I'm thinking about a holiday."

The King laughed, low and slow, offering a half-smile that looked far more natural than any other expression he had ever worn around her. There was something about it that reminded her of Samuel, of the way he looked when he was fully at ease, untroubled around the few people he trusted.

If she relaxed her eyes, she could almost see it, almost pretend that she was with a different man entirely.

"It has been a trying time, hasn't it?" He slouched against the wall, arms crossed over his chest as his rested against the dark wooden panels. "Perhaps when this is all over, I can spare my Royal Blood Worker for a bit. Perhaps I can spare myself some of this drama."

The wistfulness in his voice took her by surprise. "It gets to you too?"

He rolled his eyes, and the gesture made him look so human, not a king at all. "Of course it does. It's something that few people even attempt to understand, the weight of a crown. Do you think I relish it? The pain we have to cause to keep everyone safe? The cruelty of enforcing justice, fair to all?"

"I had thought," Shan said, carefully, still driven to speak the truth even if she couched it in pretty words, "that you had not thought of it at all. You have always seemed so far beyond it."

He huffed, both disappointed and tired, but not angry. A little impressed, if anything. Just like the first time he had brought her into his confidence, when a little bit of careless honesty earned that first spark of approval. "I suppose that is fair. Over time, the mask I wear has felt less and less like a mask. I can't even recall the last time I took it off. But you know what that is like, don't you?"

Swallowing hard, she glanced away, watching the snowflakes fall. "I'm sure I don't understand what you're implying, Your Majesty."

"Tristan," he repeated, insistent.

Her voice sounded strange to her own ears, the familiarity of it heady and rich, like wine on her tongue. "Tristan," she acknowledged, glancing back just in time to see that half-smile again.

"And I think you know exactly what I mean," the King continued. "I think you know exactly what it means to wear all different kinds of masks, to control what people think of you at all times. The power that comes with it, the freedom. My dear Lady LeClaire, my clever little Sparrow ..." he paused, nearly rasping the next words, "my incomparable Shan."

His praise cut her, soft and sharp as a blade that left her flayed open, her beating heart exposed before him. "I have only done what I needed to to survive."

"And you've done more than that, my girl," the King said, reaching out to take the cup from her shaking hands, the tea spilling over the edges as he placed it on the table, as he returned to cup her cheek.

When had she started trembling, and why was the King holding her so tenderly? His fingers, tips calloused from knives and claws and things far worse than that, were gentle on her skin as he tipped her chin up, as he pulled her with a look that was so searching that it made her flush. "You've thrived."

She had, hadn't she? Shan tried not to think about it too much, the lingering pain of all that she had to leave behind when she stepped into the role of Royal Blood Worker. But just as she had when she first donned the mask of the Sparrow, just as she had when she debuted as Lady LeClaire, she put the past behind and strove to make the most out of it.

She was adaptable, shifting her plans and schemes with every new bit of information gained. Others—her brother, Isaac, even Samuel, sometimes—saw her as mercurial and spineless, driven by fear and the terrible desire to succeed. But she was just doing the best she could with the hand that was dealt her, and she was so tired of being treated like a failure for refusing to accept defeat.

And as the King looked upon her, with understanding and pride and something surprisingly like affection, Shan felt the burning force of absolution wash over her, leaving her clean and reborn.

"Perhaps you are right."

His smirk was back, but he released her, and the sudden loss of his touch left her unmoored. "There is something I wish your opinion on, as my Royal Blood Worker."

"Of course." She sank into the seat as he settled across from her, finally taking her neglected cup of tea back, letting the taste of roses soft and floral sit gently in her mouth. The warmth spread through her, her shoulders relaxing with the savored rush of caffeine.

The King just watched her, sprawling in his seat, legs kicked out in front of him. Another mask removed, another layer shed, and Shan ached to know how much of it was real, and how much of it was what he thought she needed to see.

Blood and steel, he was right about her after all—and worse, they were the same. Whatever their souls were made of, they were both made of the same sort of cunning and hunger. Not just cruelty, but craft, and the willingness to sink into darkness if it gave them the advantages they sought. The price of a soul was nothing compared to the power they could wield.

And that scared her more than Shan was willing to admit, even to herself.

"Your work with Mel has been invaluable," the King began, and Shan felt the shiver of fear twist in her gut. "It's been . . . so long since I had a partner who was brave enough to look unflinchingly into the possibilities Blood Working has to offer. I've spent lifetimes holding us back, Shan."

In that moment, there was something unfathomably ancient and sad about him, a depth of sorrow that despite all the little vulnerabilities he showed her, she would never be able to understand. Not as long as she was simply mortal, not as long as she was slated to die at a fraction of what he would experience.

What a terribly lonely life he lived.

But she couldn't focus on that. Not when there was a part of her that wondered what it would be like, living alongside him for an eternity, dreaming of how much more she could achieve if she just had time. Besides, there was something more pressing—a reversal of what he had told her only a few months ago. A shift that could upend her entire life and her role as the Royal Blood Worker. "Are you reconsidering your stance, then?"

"I am," he admitted, "though not as drastically as you might fear. This level of Blood Working is still fraught with dangerous possibilities, and I surmise that opening it to anyone who was interested would lead only to chaos. But . . . in the right hands, under the watchful eye of the right people, there is much we can do to protect the Crown and the nation."

Shan couldn't even let herself contemplate the future he was implying, settling for simply asking, "How so?"

"We start with what Mel has taught us," the King said, with a smile that was all teeth. "The potential we've unlocked in her, the powerful creature she has become, will be a template for a new kind of Guard. An elite Guard, who will be able to handle whatever foolishness these Unblooded rebels throw at us, as well as act as a larger deterrent. Together, we will make Aeravin more than a nation, but a fortress for our kind."

She could picture it perfectly, the world that he would create. Aeravin existed in such a fragile place, accepting the exiled Blood Workers from across the world while being demonized for it at the same time.

Like her mother had been, once. Feared for a power she had never asked for, shipped across the world to be the bride of a man she had never met, only to flee back to her homeland as soon as she could. Once, Shan had dreamed of following her, of learning the places and the people and the culture that she had come from, but she knew better now. For the magic in her veins and the many atrocities she had been part of, she would never be welcomed there.

It was bad enough being a LeClaire, being a Blood Worker, but being the right hand to the Eternal King? There was nowhere she could ever go, no place where she could flee from her crimes, and she had been a fool to even suggest it to Isaac. This was their home, their only hope, and perhaps he had been right. They had to fight for it, using whatever tools they had, and there was nothing she wouldn't do to make it better.

If only she could get him to understand that.

Still, there was the question of logistics. "If this new elite force is to be part of the Guard—" she began, only for the King to cut her off.

"Yes, I know," he said, with a sigh. "Samuel will be a problem. But I am already working on that." He hesitated, clearly debating with himself before huffing out a sigh. "I know that this is awkward, given your attachment to him. Which has only grown more ... "

Tilting his head to the side, Shan knew the question he wasn't quite crass enough to ask. "I told you that I could handle him," she said, twisting her affection for her fiancé into something the Eternal King could understand, "didn't I? This seemed to be the most expedient solution."

Open relief flickered across his expression, and he inclined his head to her, a King acknowledging an equal. "And you've done a wonderful job so far. I will handle most of this, but if you would just give him a nudge?"

"You don't even need to ask," Shan replied, because she would. Because that was all that she did these days, corralling Samuel and his fool-heart. Assuaging the endless worries he brought to her feet—and hiding the secrets he had brought to her.

The Aberforth Gift was back, Samuel was terrified, and she was so, so tired.

"I'm glad to hear that." The King relaxed into his seat. "I think this will be the start of something wonderful, Shan. And I do not think I could have done it without you."

"Your Majesty," she started to demur, but the King cut her off.

"I mean it, Shan. You rose to the occasion in ways that I could only have dreamed of." He glanced off to the side, shamed and contrite. "I saw the cracks in de la Cruz early on, it's why I never considered anything like this with him. But you, Shan—I was wrong to doubt you, and with a Royal Blood Worker like you at my side, there is nothing we can't achieve."

He looked at her like she was the answer to a question she hadn't realized he had been asking, and Shan felt sick to her stomach, acid churning through all the lies and fears she had swallowed.

But she couldn't let him see that. This was everything she had fought so long for, everything she had ever wanted. She would be the King's Royal Blood Worker, and with that power, wrestle her world back to where she wanted it. It might not be what she had envisioned once, when she was young and more foolish, but it was better than any of her childish dreams.

This was real.

Though it was a bitter victory, she held the poisoned chalice to her lips and drank deeply.

Standing, she held out her hand to the King. "I believe we have some logistics to figure out."

Grinning, he took her hand, rising to stand beside her, almost close enough to share breath. It was too much, too intimate, but Shan couldn't bring herself to pull away. Not when he looked at her like she was most marvelous thing in the world.

"Together, then."

"Together," she breathed, the word as binding as an oath.

At his side, she would bring Aeravin to its glorious future, even if she had to drag the ones she loved kicking and screaming into it. Even if she had to coat herself in blood and horror to do so.

But so long as the King held her in his favor, there was nothing she couldn't achieve.

Shan watched the King watching their creation, perched on a stool and staring into the cell that contained Mel. Or, more precisely, the thing that once was Mel.

She hissed at them from her perch, having managed to scuttle up the corner towards the ceiling, hanging from crooked fingers that tipped into terrible claws. Her feet had shattered, splitting and elongating into talons that hooked around the bars, bracing her weight as her wings fluttered behind her, offering a bit of balance. The wings were webbed and dark like a bat's but twisted and half formed, hanging above a curved spine that sent the girl lurching forward, hardly able to hold herself upright.

But none of it compared to what had happened to the poor thing's face, when they could glimpse it through the matted fall of her hair. Her eyeteeth had become fangs that hung over her lower lip, her tongue flicking between them as she scented the air with it. Her pupils had vanished into pools of darkness, wide and unblinking, and Shan wondered if she could even see anymore. With the way Mel tilted her head, following each and every movement Shan made, she doubted it even mattered. Many creatures relied on senses more acute than human sight, and Shan felt awfully exposed.

"I wonder if her wings can carry her weight," the King said, idly drumming his fingers on the notebook perched on his knee. "It doesn't seem possible, but she did manage to get up there."

Shan swallowed past the dryness of her throat, pleased that her voice betrayed none of her fear. "We cannot tell without releasing her to a wider pasture, and that seems unwise."

"Quite unwise," the King agreed, "but perhaps with the proper precautions..." Trailing off, he started scribbling in the notebook, leaving Shan to watch with a growing sense of disquiet.

This vampire had once been a Blood Worker, a person just like them, but now she was a feral creature with no signs of intelligence or humanity. And the King was just sitting there, chatting like they hadn't done something so profane that they could never find forgiveness.

This was what she had wanted, wasn't it? Everything she had struggled so long for, gathering scraps of knowledge to build herself leverage that could threaten a kingdom. She had killed for it, she had thrown away her life's work for it, she had lost her brother for it. She had twisted Isaac round her fingers to simply study a fraction of what they had done to this girl and potentially lost him in the process.

So why was she so afraid? Here she was with the most powerful man in the world, his most trusted adviser, balking at the first bit of unpleasantness.

No, she was stronger than that. She circled back, grabbing the small cage from under the table. The rat within squeaked plaintively, but she steeled her heart. It was just a stray beast, nabbed from the back alleys of Dameral, plump and overfed from the refuse that it had dug into. This wasn't a cruelty—it was merely pest control.

Shan still lied, even to herself. "Ready when you are."

The King hummed, turning a page and setting his pen in place. "On you, Shan."

The rat squealed again, seeming to sense that its end was coming soon, its cries escalating to shrieks with each step closer. It seemed that someone at least had the sense to fear the monster that they had created.

Shan slashed her palm open with her claw, pressing the bleeding wound to the ward around the cell—a recent safety measure, put in place after Mel had tried to reach through and bite the Eternal King during one of her fits of hunger. It kept her secure, but from the way her nostrils flared, Shan was certain that she could smell the blood on the air.

It didn't matter. Shan opened a small hole in the ward, and before she could second-guess herself, she upended the carrier, sending the rat scrambling through the hole before it landed hard on the marble floor inside the cell. Pulling back, Shan let the ward seal as the rat twisted to its feet, back arched as it hopped back towards the edge of the cell only to hit the blood ward. There was no way out, and Shan forced herself to watch.

Mel's tongue flicked out, a low growl reverberating deep in her chest, a rumble unlike anything that Shan had ever heard before. For a long moment Shan thought nothing was going to happen. Hoped that nothing was going to happen. But then Mel launched herself off her corner, her strong legs pushing off the bars as she soared across the cell.

She caught the rat in one clawed hand, its frantic struggles unable to best the beast as Mel closed her fist. The crunch of its spine echoed through the room as the pest fell limp, but it was still alive. Shan could see the sheer terror in its eyes as Mel sank her fangs into the soft pouch of its belly, tearing through fur and fat to the viscera beneath. A messy affair as Mel drank the creature dry, damaging flesh and muscle in her artless quest for blood.

Bile rose in the back of Shan's throat, acidic and harsh, but she did not say a word, the scratch of the King's pen barely audible over the slurps and gnashing from the cage.

"Fascinating," the King said at last, setting his notebook aside before moving closer to the cage. "I did not expect her hunger to be so ... all-consuming."

"It surprised me as well," Shan said, her voice soft and dull, even to her own ears.

But the King didn't seem to notice, eagerly watching as Mel stripped the carcass clean, her tongue rooting through the rat's corpse, dragging out organs dripping in blood. She ground them in her mouth with an excitement that twisted Shan's stomach, squeezing out every drop of blood before discarding the pulped flesh back onto the floor.

He turned back to the girl, watching as she finished her feast, looking at the creature like it was some prized hound. But as her primal hunger was sated, Mel's body started to shift again, the monstrous transformation receding back, the vampire fading away.

"Excellent," the King breathed, wrapping his fingers around the bars as he leaned in to watch more closely. And Shan, despite the way acid churned in her stomach, leaned in as well.

There was something grotesque about the process, Mel's body twisting and jerking in convulsions as she scrabbled against the marble floor. The claws retracted back into her nail beds, the blunt tips of her fingers emerging as her back cracked, the curve straightening and the wings shrinking into nubs as Mel howled in pain. Her cries echoed off the walls, sending shivers down Shan's spine as she watched the girl sob quietly, awareness slowly coming back to her eyes.

Mel pressed one hand—one small, fragile, human hand—against the remains of the rat, before glancing up at the King. "What have you done to me?"

"Why," the King replied with a smile so cold that he could have been carved from ice, "we've perfected you."

The girl just blinked, and Shan watched as her entire world restructured around her. Everything the young Blood Worker had believed, all her faith in the world and magic and her endless Eternal King crystallizing into something new. She had wanted power, had thrilled in it as she supped blood from the vein, and now had been born into something completely new.

Mel looked up at them with a pout. "I want another."

It earned a laugh from the King, an indulgent smile as he assured

Mel that she would get her fill, but dread still curled dark in Shan's heart as she was unable to deny what they had done any longer.

"It is something more than Blood Working now," Shan whispered. "She's ... she's a vampire."

The King glanced at Shan, not contesting her assessment, head tilted to the side. His eyes were burning with curiosity, glinting like emeralds in the light. "Yes, she is," the King breathed, his voice as soft as caress, "and I simply must know everything. Don't you feel the same, Shan?"

Hells help her, but she did. What they had done to Mel was a blasphemous thing, but there was a part of her, deep down, that was curious. That wanted to push Blood Working to new heights, that wanted to dissect Mel like the marvel that she was, that wanted to see if this experience could be replicated.

But ...

The King seemed to sense her hesitation. He turned his back on Mel and the remains of her meal, the full weight of his attention nearly overwhelming Shan. She shuddered as he stepped closer, brushing the hair away from her face, trailing the back of his fingers against her cheek. His touch was like a brand, burning his dominion onto her, but his words were kind. "Do not be afraid of it, Shan. You are so much more than any of the other fools in my court, and nothing you want could ever disgust me."

Shan closed her eyes as the King's hand drifted further, sliding down her back to pull her close. Blood and steel, she knew that this was wrong. That was a betrayal in ways she did not even have words for. This went beyond her designs to merely play the part the King wanted of her, this was an intimacy that she could never give him. But he held her close like even her darkest parts were things to be cherished, and he was right about one thing.

Never once had he flinched away from the darkness within her, never once had he judged her for it. For all that she tried to deny it, they were cut from the same cloth, and he could understand in ways that Isaac never could.

That Samuel never could.

"I do want it," she whispered, and she swore that she could feel the ghost of his lips on her.

But it was only him leaning into whisper, "There's my girl."

Chapter Twenty-Nine

Samuel

Ice cut through Samuel as the carriage pulled to a stop, Dabney pushing his way forward so that he was the first to stand in front of the Fox Den. Samuel slowly followed, his heart still in his throat, where it had been lodged ever since Dabney had appeared in his office with a smirk, inviting him out on a matter of business. It was "an important task that the Councillor of Law should oversee" and a "trifling matter." It had felt like a trap, but one Samuel could not avoid.

He had been right.

The door to the gambling den had already been kicked open, a pair of Guards in their black robes standing on each side of it, their claws tight around the long spears in each hand. Samuel had the uncanny feeling that he was looking at an open wound, the flashing lights from within illuminating an empty skeleton stripped of life.

Where were the workers, the patrons, everyone who made this establishment a living, breathing part of Dameral?

"Why are we here?" he croaked, and Dabney glanced back, that all too proud smirk a taunt that Samuel wanted to rip right off his face.

"You'll see, my lord," Dabney said, already stepping towards the door.

The inside was even worse that he had imagined. The bar to the side had been completely ransacked, glass and liquor spilling out to the floor in a crystalline nightmare. The counter where patrons exchanged money for tips was completely upended, and a long line of workers huddled against the far wall, hands bound before them, gags shoved into their mouths to keep them from speaking. Shuddering and crying, they flinched away as he and Dabney passed, and something in Samuel cracked.

They had every reason to be afraid—not just of the man he was with but of himself. He was Samuel Aberforth, the Councillor of Law, and there was no mercy to be found in his role. He was just as much a tool of their destruction as the rest of this damned nation, and no amount of lying to himself would change that fact.

Dabney paused at the balcony, looking over the edge to the gambling floor below. Or, what remained of it. The destruction of the lobby was nothing compared to the ransacking below, the tables themselves shattered under the blows of Blood Workers who had amplified their strength. A pointless display of power, meant to scare and intimidate. The staff did not appear to have fought back at all, corralled into a corner where a grim-faced woman methodically chained them up one by one, and still, her compatriots tore apart the Den.

What were they looking for?

Dabney just looked down with glee, a proud parent watching his children. "We finally caught a break, Aberforth. Our investigations might not have brought us to the leaders, but we found one of their little distribution centers. And that's not even the worst of it."

Swallowing hard, Samuel forced himself to ask the question. "Oh?"

"It'll be easier to show you," Dabney said. "Couldn't believe it myself, but here we are."

He sauntered down the stairs, as casual as if they were strolling in a park, unminding of the violence around them. A Guard yanked open the door to a storeroom, dragging a girl out of the shadows with far more force than necessary. He threw her to the ground, her head slamming with a sickening crack as the skin above her eye split, blood seeping out, bright and stark against the marble.

Dabney just stepped around her, not even bothering to give her so much as a look.

Samuel swallowed down the bile, the acid scorching his throat as he burned the image into his brain. He would not forget this. He could not forget this. It would cling to him like a haunting, ephemeral and damning.

They left the chaos of the main floor behind, slipping into the long staircase that Anton had introduced him to all those ages ago, making their way up to the High Roller's lounge. Dabney was quiet the entire way, not giving Samuel a hint of what was to come. The tension wrapped tighter and tighter around him, so thick that he felt like he would choke on it—and then the door was thrown open to something he did not recognize at all.

This wasn't the same lounge he had known; the tables and chairs were all pushed to the side, replaced with pallets where sick and injured people lay cowering.

"This," Dabney said with fervor, "is the worst part. Whatever traitor it is wasn't here when our raid started, but they have a Blood Worker helping them. A healer, if you can believe it." He spat on the floor, narrowly missing the head of the closest person.

Samuel couldn't tell if Dabney had been aiming to hit or not.

"This way, Aberforth."

Samuel meekly followed, feeling nothing more than a dog with his tail between his legs, scurrying after his master. What more could Dabney have to show him? How could this evening get any worse?

Dabney shoved his way through a heavy door, leading them to the very room Samuel had been in, hells, was it only weeks ago? When Isaac had been introduced to the rebellion, when Samuel had met the other leaders.

It felt like a lifetime.

Inside was the Matron, her fine dress torn and stained with what was unmistakably blood. Hers or someone else's, Samuel wasn't sure, but though she was bound to the chair her mouth was uncovered.

Oh, this was an interrogation, and Samuel was expected to be part of it. Terror struck through him before rationality caught up—there were only two living people who knew that the Aberforth Gift had returned, and neither were the type to reveal that truth to the King, let alone Dabney.

No, he was not here for that; he was part of this interrogation in name only, not dragged here to be helpful, but as a test. Dabney was pulling him deeper and deeper in the mire that was the Guard of Aeravin, looking to see when his new Councillor would break. And despite the terrible atrocities he was forced to witness again and again, he would not break. He could not afford to, his position was too valuable.

He knew that he wouldn't last forever, but that one day he would find that line he could not cross. But as he met Monique Lovell's eyes, as she gave the tiniest, barely perceptible shake of her head, he knew it wouldn't be this day.

This day he would look an almost friend in the eye and watch as she fell.

The Guard behind Monique grabbed her by the hair, twisted her locks around his fist as he yanked her head back so that she looked directly up at Dabney. "You," she spat, venomous as a viper, and Samuel had to bite back a smile.

Good. Make them fight for it.

"Now, now," Dabney said, indulgently, clapping his hands together. "There is no need to be uncivilized, Miss Lovell."

"No need?" she sneered, refusing to take the out she was given, even if it would have made things more pleasant for her. She would not acquiesce in advance—she would not acquiesce at all, if she could avoid it.

Oh, what a loss this would be, for there was no way for him to save her by himself.

"Well, if you want to be that way." Dabney stepped forward, backhanding her across the face, the blunt side of his claws leaving burning red marks across the side of her face.

As Monique spat blood, a mad cackle catching in her throat,

Samuel recognized that it had only been a warning. One that Monique ignored. "Gotta try harder than that, swine."

"Really ..." Dabney shook his head, heaving a chair over and sinking into it. "These Unblooded don't know what's good for them, do they?"

Maybe he was supposed to take part in this, play the rough hand to Dabney's reasonable one. But he wouldn't be pulled into that game. Taking his pocket watch out, he flipped it open with a sigh, pulling all the nonchalance he had seen in the King and weaving it around himself like armor. "Do I really need to be here, Dabney?"

A vein in the man's forehead started to tremble, the only sign of his annoyance, before he swung his gaze back to Monique. "See, you're wasting our valuable Councillor's time," he continued, trying to spin this into something he could use. "Why don't you tell us the name of the Blood Healer who helped you?"

"Why should I?" Monique hissed as the Guard behind her tugged again, nearly strong enough to rip the hair from her head. "You haven't made that illegal ... yet."

"No," Dabney conceded, with great effort. "It is not. So, if that is your worry, you need not fear. We only want to chat with your friend."

"You must think me a simpleton if you think I believe that. You're not getting a name from me."

Dabney frowned, grabbing her round the face, digging his claws into her flesh, scarlet just barely starting to well. "You're a defiant one, aren't you?"

Monique said nothing, gave not an inch, and Dabney sighed. "Fine. If that is how you want to play it." He shoved her back. "Guards, bring her back to headquarters, we'll get the answers we need out of her eventually."

The Guard finally let go of Monique's hair, giving a sharp salute. They watched in silence as he freed her from her bindings, then marched her towards the door.

"Oh, and one last thing," Dabney said, that cold grin of his back.

"Take all her employees as well. They might be able to shed some light on this."

"No!" Monique twisted in the Guard's hand, trying to turn herself back around. "You can't do that! They don't know anything!"

"My dear Miss Lovell," Dabney drawled, hooking his thumbs in his pockets. "You had the chance to handle this civilly, but you chose not to. Don't start crying now."

She stared at him, slack jawed, and Samuel's heart hurt just to watch it. But she didn't choose rage—she just picked herself back up, squared her shoulders and walked out, even though she was walking to her own destruction.

Samuel would never forget her.

"Well, that was anticlimactic," Dabney grumbled, retrieving a cloth from his pocket to clean the blood from his claws. "I had hoped that with a little assistance she would have cracked."

Samuel squared his shoulders, making sure the mask of Lord Aberforth was securely attached before speaking. "I have better things to be doing with my time, and you know it. Besides, aren't you always boasting about the skill of your Guards? I'm sure they'll handle it in no time."

Dabney looked him over from head to toe, assessing. "That is right, Lord Aberforth."

There was an almost grudging respect there, as if he'd expected Samuel to cry or whine or kick his feet like a child. Samuel couldn't lie to himself—he wished he could do all that, but it wouldn't get him anywhere. No, if he wanted to do something about Dabney, he would need to get his hands dirty himself.

Perhaps . . .

No, that was a thought for another time. "Is there anything else you need me for?"

"No," Dabney muttered. "As you can see, our people have things in hand."

What an absurd statement. This hadn't been a fight, it was a beatdown, and every soul in this building knew it.

"Quite." He slipped his pocket watch away. "What will happen to this place?"

"Well, we have no use for a gambling den, but perhaps we can repurpose it," Dabney said, that excitement creeping back. "I think this space would make a great Blood Factory, don't you? Perhaps Miss Lovell will be our most favored guest."

"What is that supposed to mean?"

"Oh, just that she will be getting a punishment that fits the crime." He only continued after Samuel gestured for him to, a quiet command to get on with it. "She's going to suffer for a long time, drained again and again, until she has absolutely nothing left to give."

Dabney's smile had turned absolutely feral, his thin lips pulled back to show all his teeth, a hunger for blood that belied the potential that lay at the heart of Blood Working.

He would have made a most terrifying vampire.

"I see." Samuel turned away to hide the pallor that came over him. There was nothing he could do to stop this. He had to get out of here, send word to the rebellion of what had happened, protect that Blood Healer they were working with.

He had to find a way to contain the threat that was Dabney, permanently.

And, perhaps most pressingly, talk to the one person who might be able to help Monique, if she dared be brave enough to do anything about it.

"I'm taking the carriage," he announced as he stepped past Dabney, not caring that it inconvenienced the man. "I expect a full written report on my desk by the morning."

"As my lord commands," Dabney replied, with only the barest bit of sarcasm, but Samuel did not bother with it.

He needed to get to the Academy.

Samuel cut through the top floor of the Academy with purpose, striding past the tables and low couches, the places where Blood Workers could meet and work together. But Shan wasn't there—no, she was in her office, behind a closed door, shut out from reality in a cocoon of her own making.

He knocked twice, only to hear her tired voice call out, "Enter."

The door eased open under his touch, not the slightest creak of the hinges, and Shan didn't even look up from her work, scribbling furiously in one of her many notebooks. Long strands of hair hung loose around her face, having slipped from the tight bun, giving her a slightly bedraggled look, only made worse by the dark circles under her eyes.

She reminded him so much of Isaac, not even a year ago, when he had been in the same role. The exhaustion was writ into her very marrow, and Samuel wanted to pull her away, tucked under some blankets where the world couldn't touch her. But Shan never responded well to concern or care, and it broke his tender heart into countless aching fragments.

If she wouldn't respond to care, perhaps she would respond to logic. He closed the door behind him, clearing his throat to get her attention before her name fell from his lips.

Shan sat up straighter, pen going still in her fingers, as she looked up in shock. A flash of guilt crossed her expression, like she hadn't expected him to find her here. Like she didn't *want* him here. "Samuel. I didn't expect—"

He cut her off, unable to bear the rejection, however small, however well intended. She was always trying to protect him but couldn't see how much it hurt.

"It's a pressing matter," he said, barreling over till she quieted. "And one that you need to be aware of, Lady LeClaire."

"Of course." She gestured for him to sit, wrapping herself in the airs of her official title and station. They were not meeting as lovers, but as political allies—as the Royal Blood Worker and the Councillor of Law. Their true selves were hidden behind layers of deceit, and though she wasn't even five feet away from him, close enough for him to reach out and grab her, if he wanted, Samuel had never felt so alone.

"After a raid earlier this evening, the Guard have brought in a new prisoner accused of sedition. Due to the serious nature of her crimes, she has been isolated in prison, where she will be drained, again and again, until her body gives out." He kept his eyes on her expression, the way exasperation had crept it. What was it to her? Another small tale of suffering, another little tragedy, inconsequential in the grander scheme of things.

He could see the thoughts that flashed across her dark eyes, could almost hear her voice in the back of his head, warning him that the price of progress never came for free.

"Her name," Samuel pressed on with a little snarl, the anger bubbling to the surface—hot and ephemeral, steam slipping through his fingers, "is Monique Lovell, also known as the proprietress of the Fox Den. Which has been raided, nationalized, and set to become another Blood Factory."

The irritated look faded into something softer, pain and disappointment flicking across her expression before she locked it down. If he hadn't known her as well as he did, he wouldn't have noticed it at all, and even if he had, he would have dismissed it with the simple way she responded.

"How unfortunate."

"Unfortunate?" he repeated, unable to hide how the anger became a roiling blaze in his chest, a wave of darkness that crept upwards from the deepest pits of himself, nails ripping through the thin gossamer of self-control, urging him to give into his wrath. The temptation of his power sat thick and heavy on his tongue, truly back and aching to be used. But he had already let it slip on Shan once, so he swallowed it back down, even if it choked him.

It was fine, though. The single word he had uttered had been enough, the shame of it cutting through her more brutally than any rage ever could have.

"Unfortunate," Shan repeated. "Because there is nothing we can do about it. Sedition, you said?"

"Caught spreading seditious literature, if you must know." They shared a long, significant look, not daring to speak more plainly, even within the privacy of her office. They both knew what it meant—she had been helping Anton, and for that kindness, she was facing a sentence that even Samuel couldn't predict. "As well as the unforgivable crime of helping those hurt by the Guard.

"None of the Unblooded caught under this new ... clause," Samuel spat, hesitating to even call it a law when it wasn't one, technically. Just a line in the King's decrees that had been enacted last year, with none of the proper procedures in place, "have had a trial yet. Have any plans for a trial. They are just sitting in cells, rotting, and after everything Lovell has done for you, this is how you repay her?"

"She didn't do it for me," Shan said, leaning back in her chair. She crossed her arms over her chest, the claws glittering in the witch light, and Samuel clenched gloved fingers in his lap, feeling the harsh gap between them like a gulf he couldn't cross. "She did it for the Sparrow."

"And you're not the Sparrow?"

"No," Shan said, with an empty kind of bitterness that hit him like the crash of water, cooling his flames to embers. She did not rage, did not fight, just accepted it like a part of her had been ripped from her chest.

And maybe it had been, because how could one be the Royal Blood Worker and the Sparrow at the same time? They were two forces working in contradiction to each other, and not even Shan was skilled enough in self-deception to hold them apart.

Reaching across the table, he held his hand palm up in offering, and Shan inched forward, resting her clawed-tipped hand in his, clenching it so tightly that he could feel his bones creak. But he took it without complaint, because she was not doing nearly as well as she pretended to be.

And he had come here to pull her out of the abyss, not to cast to the darkness below.

"The Matron was an ally, Shan," he said, softly, "perhaps even a friend. And though you might not be the Sparrow any longer, you still owe her."

"Samuel," she huffed, with a bitter little laugh. "Still thinking that people in our position have friends."

"You can, if you choose to." He pulled his hand away, settled back in his chair as he let her process. "You don't have to give into the system just because it's all that exists."

"And what other option is there?" Shan tilted her head to the side, assessing. "We cannot simply will something better into being."

No, they couldn't. They would have to fight for it, destroy what already existed to keep the rot from spreading further. To build something new and better from the ashes. But he could tell that Shan did not want to hear that, could not hear that.

Her entire being was caught up in the world she strove to create, and who was he to rip that all away from her? No, this was a decision she had to come to on her own, and all he could do was put her on the path.

So, he didn't fight it. Pushing to his feet, Samuel looked down at her with pity and the desperate taste of hope. "Regardless of the state of the world, I thought you ought to know what happened to her. If you do decide to speak to her, I'm sure it can be arranged. You are, after all, the Royal Blood Worker, and she is a lowly seditionist."

"It wouldn't be out of my domain," Shan admitted, and that was as much of an offering as he could hope to get from her. An admission that she would, at least, consider it.

"Precisely." He bent at the waist, a proper bow, the kind that was wholly unnecessary. They were alone, and he was her fiancé, but the bite of formality was enough to make his point. She was wrong—he had learned and could turn the politest movement into a barb meant to bruise.

Shan inclined her head, conceding the point, though it felt like a hollow victory. "I shall see you soon, darling?"

"Soon," he agreed, then slipped out of the office and back into the Academy proper. The weight lifted from his shoulders as he left her behind, even as his chest tightened in pain.

Seeing his beloved should not feel like a battle, but he had made a promise. He would pull Shan back to their side, even if it was the last thing he did.

He couldn't leave her, not after everything she had done for him.

Chapter Thirty

Isaac

Given the nature of the recent raid and the tension that mounted on the streets, Isaac had graciously offered his little safe harbor as a meeting point. There would be no more sneaking to the Fox Den, no hidden back-room strategies, no help for those who needed it, no more slipping pamphlets through and into the hands of the workers, distributing them ever outward like the ever-expanding ripples in a pond. In one night, all of that had been taken from them.

All that and more.

Isaac crumpled the letter that Samuel had sent them, full of explanations and warnings. The threat to Celeste, the horrid fate awaiting Monique, the casual cruelty of the Guard's widespread arrests, just because they could. The only warning he could give, caught up in his position as a Councillor, but it was still enough to get them started.

He brought over a pot of tea and a carafe of coffee for Maia and Alaric, who had cozied up on the chaise lounge, leaning into each other as they whispered. Isaac did not interrupt them, he could tell that it wasn't planning, it was comfort between two old friends when the cracks in their foundation were starting to show. He placed the refreshments in front of them, Maia sending him a grateful look before he ducked back.

Still an outsider, despite it all.

The clock ticked past midnight, and Isaac stared out the window, wondering when Anton would return. He had gone to find Celeste, to move her to another one of their safe houses, just in case Monique broke under the weight of what the Guard would do to her. Torture, Isaac was sure, even if they wouldn't call it that. They would dress it up in trappings of justice and fairness, prices paid for crimes committed.

If she did break, he wouldn't blame her. He was just thankful that they were able to save Celeste first.

The downstairs door whooshed open, a soft sound that Isaac knew the others didn't register. But he heard it anyway, as well as the rapid beat of Anton's heart as he climbed the stairs. It wasn't fear, no, that had a slightly different beat—this was something more. It was fury, pure and unalloyed.

This was going to be a long night.

"She's safe," Anton said, bypassing introductions completely. "At least for now."

The wires around Isaac's heart unwrapped, relief hitting him like a crashing wave that nearly took him to his knees. If anything had happened to her because of him, he wasn't sure if he would be able to forgive himself.

"That's good," he breathed, and Anton gave him a little nod. A moment of solidarity, understanding burning between them as strong as any bridge built of magic—no, stronger. This wasn't magic, but something they had built themselves, true and powerful.

Perhaps he wasn't as much of an outsider as he feared.

Anton shrugged out of his cloak and scarf, gloves discarded as he shed the trappings of winter. From there, he made a direct line for the carafe, filling his cup with so much cream and sugar that Isaac wasn't sure it could technically be called coffee anymore.

Alaric wrinkled his nose in clear distaste, and Anton just threw him a rude hand gesture. "Fuck off, I'm tired."

"We all are," Maia said, her hand landing on Alaric's thigh as she leaned forward. "But we need to plan."

Slumping into the couch, Anton let out a small sigh, digging his nails into the cheap lining, plucking at worn threads listlessly. "I know, I just need—"

"A moment to breathe?" Alaric offered.

"Yeah, that."

Isaac looked around the room as the silence grew thick, taking in their tired and defeated faces. The very air tasted of despair, a cloying weight that threatened to drag them under, and that primal beast within him thrashed at its cage, sensing vulnerable quarry. It would be so easy, they wouldn't even fight back ...

Isaac shot to his feet, using the movement to hide the way he flinched away from himself. All the eyes in the room turned to him, waiting for an explanation, but Isaac had no explanation for it, no lies to couch the too uncomfortable truth. Instead, he reached for the first thing he could think of, the only way forward from this mess. What he needed to do—what *they* needed to do.

"We need to take this to the King."

Alaric arched an eyebrow, and for a moment Isaac nearly forgot that he was Unblooded. There was an imperious kind of nobility in his demeanor, despite the lack of power in his blood. Perhaps it was the only way he could move in a world that would see him disinherited for an accident of birth, but it still chilled Isaac to the core.

It reminded him so much of Shan.

"It was always going to come to this," Isaac breathed, facing the truth he had tried to run from, time and again. The only way out was to finish what he had started, and he was not a man to leave something uncompleted. "There was no version of this where it could have gone any other way."

The silence broke with a sigh. "Hate to say it, but he's right." Anton leaned forward, pouring himself a second cup with the determination of a man who would do whatever he needed to get through this night. "The Eternal Bastard wants to escalate this, well, let's meet him blow for blow. Let's give him a war."

"We're not ready," Alaric began, cowardice seeping through, and Isaac couldn't help the laugh.

He so hated being right.

"We'll never be ready," Isaac breathed, "but we can do things to level the playing field. Listen, if we let the King control this—and he will, trust me—we will always be on the back foot."

If they let that happen, they would never win, and he didn't have to say that part out loud. He could see them all coming to the same conclusion.

Alaric turned to Maia, searching for backup, but she was already shaking her head. "People are already getting hurt, Alaric, people are already dying. Good people, innocent people. And it won't stop. No, we need to do more."

It wasn't the response he was hoping for, and he turned to Anton, who shot him down with a steely gaze. "You knew this was coming."

"I thought we had more time," Alaric pleaded, but Isaac stepped up, the truth like a burning coal on this tongue.

"I took that from you." He spat it out like it was acid, but he wouldn't deny his part in this. The only way forward was to own it. "It was my actions, my killings, my destruction of the very institution that props up this nation of blood that spurred the King into action." Everyone in this room knew it, but there was a difference between knowing and acknowledging, between recognition and adjustment. And if they did not adjust, they were doomed.

What a fool he had been, driven by a rage and a guilt that, if it had been left unchecked, would have destroyed the nation he was trying to save. He wanted Aeravin to burn, but he did not care about those who would die in the process—the very same Unblooded that he had wanted to save. And now here he was, ready to become whatever he needed to be so that he could save them.

"I started this," he admitted, "but if we are not careful, the King will end this. The raid on the Fox Den was not just strategic, it was designed to hurt. He couldn't get to you, so he'll hunt down everyone who ever gave you aid. The King will rain down misery and destruction, because this despair, this hesitation, this fear—this is exactly what he wants."

Alaric slammed his fist down on the armrest, that fissure of frustration cracking into something dangerous. Even with his position in society so fragile, even with his place in the leadership of this ragtag group, Alaric was not a man who took kindly to being countered.

But Isaac's sympathy could only go so far, and he would press on Alaric's weak points until he snapped. "If you're not brave enough to do what is necessary, then why the fuck are you even—"

"Enough," Anton said, not loudly, but firmly, cutting through the tension with all the efficiency of a blade. "Fighting among ourselves does not help. Isaac, you have made your point. Alaric, I understand, I really do, but we need to plan our next moves."

Alaric grumbled but leaned back in the chair with a sigh. Oh, he was still pissed, Isaac could taste that on the air, but he allowed the conversation to move on.

"We cannot fight the King or the Guard head-on," Isaac continued, deliberately more composed than before. "To do so would be suicide, even with the handful of Blood Workers we will be able to recruit to our cause. What we need are careful, tactical strikes. Disrupt their ability to use magic, to communicate, to lead."

"Like you did with that Holland bitch?" Alaric asked, flinging Isaac's cruelty back in his own face. It didn't work; Holland had deserved every ounce of pain she had suffered for the way she had treated Samuel. "Heard it was a brutal affair."

"Just so," Isaac admitted, then looked to Anton. They hadn't told the others, yet, just what he was becoming, even though he was sure they had questions. A man did not kill in the way that he did, and it was only a matter of time before the truth came out, one way or the other. He just hoped it would be on his own terms.

Anton inclined his head, permission granted.

"And that is not all," Isaac continued, even as fear wove around his heart, clenching like vines, piercing like thorns. This was the real risk—the truth that could have him damned, the truth he had dared not share, up until this point. It was just Samuel and Shan, Anton and Celeste, those carefully selected few who needed to know.

He prayed that they would be smart enough to understand its value, if nothing else. Even if they could never fully understand the thin line between man and beast that was the heart of what he was becoming.

"Taking the blood of the Unblooded criminals made my Blood Working stronger," Isaac admitted, with no small amount of pride. "But Kevan Dunn's blood, that awakened something else, Blood Working unlike that has been seen for centuries. From a less civilized age, before our magic had been given structure and order, back when the legends of vampires still hung over the head of every Blood Worker.

"So, where I have failed before," Isaac said, standing and pressing his hands into the table, towering over them. He could smell the sudden tang of fear and unease, their hearts beating just a little bit faster. "I am ready to make up for that, if you would allow me to. If you would be brave enough to use me."

He pulled his lips back, baring the sharp fangs that had grown from his eyeteeth, letting them see just a hint of the hunger that lay beneath. "It seems that the legends were not completely correct—I am not a vampire, but a manananggal out of our own people's legends. Anton can confirm."

The man nodded, but said nothing more—this was Isaac's show, Isaac's pitch, and he wasn't done. "I am getting stronger with each Blood Worker I slay, and perhaps one day soon, I'll be strong enough to fight the King himself. But first, I suggest we cut the ground out from under their feet. If we are to declare war, I suggest I finish what I started and destroy the Blood Treasury and every last drop of their reserves."

"This is very risky for you, Isaac." Anton rested his forearms on his knees, leaning in with a furrowed brow and open concern in his eyes. "I'm not sure I am comfortable with that."

That he hadn't expected. "Don't worry, the risk to me will be minimal."

"But—"

"You're the one who told me about the myths," Isaac interrupted, the near invulnerability that came with being a manananggal. "So, let's see how much truth there is to them."

Anton was about to argue again, but Maia reached over, laying her hand on his wrist. "He's right and you know that. This is the best option for all of us." She fixed him with a steady stare, dark eyes glinting. "And he knows what he is doing, right?"

Isaac inclined his head to her. She had such nerve, and one day, when things were a little less tumultuous, he would love to be her friend. "I am."

"Good," Alaric chimed in, as if that settled matters. "If we plan to do this, I need to liquidate as many of my assets as possible. Once ..." Alaric hesitated, the word stuck on his tongue "... *war* breaks out, it will get more difficult to ensure that my funding goes unnoticed."

"A fair point, and something to consider with our timelines," Anton agreed, and even Isaac had no grounds to argue that. As much of a calculating coward that Alaric had proven himself to be, Isaac knew that the Rothe estate was providing so much of the money that they needed, and things were only going to get worse.

"Then it's time to start arming folks," Maia said, with a glint in her eyes that worried Isaac.

"This isn't a war you can win on strength alone," Isaac cautioned.

"We know that," Anton said, waving a dismissive hand. "This is a war that will be fought in the shadows, pecking away at their power with strategic strikes until we get to the King himself."

"Precisely," Maia said, turning her hard gaze on Isaac. "But we cannot be complacent. Folks will need to be able to defend themselves, even with you on the loose."

Doing most of the work, Isaac was coming to realize, but that was something he could live with. He had made himself a monster, so they might as well use it.

"All right," Isaac agreed. There was little an Unblooded could do against a Blood Worker in any kind of fair fight, but there were options. "Long-range weapons and fast-acting poisons are your best bet—even if it isn't strong enough to take down a Blood Worker on its own, it might give you time to escape."

"Expensive though," Alaric cautioned. "Probably hard to get."

"Some more than others," Isaac admitted. "Though Anton would know that as well." The man flashed him a cocky grin, and it soothed some of his fears. "It's still the best option, unless we gain a lot more Blood Workers to our side."

"Maybe that's something you should be working on," Anton offered.

"Not me," Isaac said, with no amount of heartbreak. He knew what he was, toxic to both sides, claimed by neither Unblooded nor Blood Worker. This is where Shan would have been helpful, but that was the one person they couldn't fully trust, no matter how much it hurt. "Maybe Celeste?"

"I'll ask her." Anton clapped his hands together, looking reinvigorated. "It sounds like we have the beginnings of a plan, and a goal in mind. How long will you need?"

Alaric and Maia shared a long look, an entire conversation passing without a single word spoken.

"As much as you can give us," Alaric said, at the same time Maia said, "Six weeks."

Six weeks felt too long, but Isaac quelled the anxious thrum of his own heart. These things took time, and in the meantime, he could find more targets. He just needed some direction—some guidance from the person who did have his finger on the pulse of the elite of Aeravin.

Samuel would know how to use him, and as the others fell into a discussion of minutiae that he would only be tangentially helpful too, Isaac steeled himself.

A weapon waiting for a hand to wield it.

Chapter Thirty-One

Shan

Shan strode through the narrow hallways, her head held high and her robes fluttering behind her. The cells to either side were filled with the unmistakable scent of unwashed bodies, prisoners kept in the darkness beneath Dameral's largest Guard station, waiting for the next available court date. They were packed several to a cell, hardly bothering to look at which Blood Worker moved past them.

What difference would it make, when the Guard had been through again and again, an endless rotation that signified nothing.

Perhaps Samuel had been right about the conditions they were keeping the Unblooded in. Perhaps her solution had left a gap open for the Guard to exploit. Perhaps there was something—anything—she could be doing. Hells knew that Samuel had tried and failed.

But she was balanced on the thin blade of a knife, and the slightest step out of place would bring all her plans to a screeching halt. There was no way she could risk that, so she took the despair and guilt in her heart and buried it away. This was just another thing on her list, a problem she would solve, when the time was right.

The list was growing so long, worse with each passing day, but she wouldn't think of it now. Not when she had come here for a very specific reason.

She reached the stairs at the end of the hallway, dipping even deeper into the earth. The ward, yet another layer of protection, rippled around her, responding to the ring the Warden had given her. It was heavy on her thumb, glittering like a row of rubies, but it wasn't gemstones embedded in the band of gold. It was a series of droplets, blood from specific Blood Workers, a pass key that granted her access to the deepest dungeons.

Where they kept the worst of all criminals, and for whatever reason, that included Monique Lovell.

Shan didn't question it, not openly. The Royal Blood Worker wouldn't. She was here to press the prisoner for information, an implicit understanding that had the Warden grinning slyly as she ignored the shame that rose, thick and burning like bile, in the back of her throat.

The bottom-most floor had the low tang of musk and sweat, a smell that was almost rancid. The air had a cool, slick feeling to it, the walls dripping with condensation, fat droplets of water budding on freezing stone. It was worse than the Blood Treasury—that was controlled, that had a purpose. This was intentional cruelty, done to make the prisoners suffer, and Shan deliberately turned her face from it.

The cells here were different from the ones before. Above, they had been separated by iron bars, open to the hallway. They allowed the prisoners to speak to each other, a brief bit of connection in an otherwise hellish experience. This floor was worse, the cells being entire rooms walled off from the rest of the space.

Utter solitude, a creeping kind of insanity, a suffering that Shan knew she would never fully understand.

Monique—the Matron—was in the furthest cell, and Shan pulled her key ring from where it hung on her belt, the large lock clicking free under her hand. She didn't allow herself to hesitate, entering the room and closing the door behind her.

The Matron was sitting on the small cot, hardly fit for its purpose, lacking a mattress or cushions. Her back was pressed against the stone wall, legs tucked up to her chest, face pressed into her knees. Gone was the precise and dignified woman that Shan had known for years, replaced by someone so raw and disheveled that Shan hardly recognized her. Her hair hung in loose, tangled knots down her back, her skin sallow. The fine, prim dresses that she wore around the Fox Den had been replaced by a coarse shift of grey—even from across the room Shan saw how rough the fabric was. It must chafe against the skin, another little indignity to be suffered.

Monique glanced up as the door clicked closed, recognition flashing through her eyes, followed by a quick succession of disbelief, fury, and resignation. A woman who had been recognized that she had been played, and worst yet, that there was nothing she could do about it.

Shan didn't interrupt her processing, knowing that nothing she could say would make it any easier. She had built herself up on a web of lies, and as more strands got snipped beneath her, Shan feared there would be nothing left to keep her from falling into the darkness.

"I should have known," Monique said, her voice low and rasping. Dry, no doubt, the simple necessity of water another method of control and punishment. "Your resources were too great, your age too young." She closed her eyes. "Anton—and the Aberforth. Fuck, Sparrow. You were so eager to throw it all away for power, weren't you?"

It was an understandable assumption. If the positions were reversed, Shan would have thought something similar. But it still hurt, the understanding that no matter what she came to achieve, she would be looked upon with distrust and fear, and worst of all, she had brought it on herself.

She reached for that serenity that always served her so well, especially when she felt so raw, wrapping it around herself like a veil of protection, so desperately needed.

"Monique," she began, only to be cut off by the woman's hiss.

"Don't. You haven't earned my first name." Her face was twisted into a sneer so extreme, so daring, that Shan choked on her words. "You're not my friend."

"I ... understand, Miss Lovell." A bit of the strain eased away, but Miss Lovell wasn't relaxed, probably wouldn't be relaxed around Shan again.

"Hmm, at least you still have your manners." The older woman leaned her head against the stone wall. "But why are you here? Did the Royal Blood Worker herself feel the need to come and gloat?"

"It's not that," Shan attempted, the explanation hanging on her lips, if only the Matron would let her.

"Then what is it?" Miss Lovell bared her teeth in a snarl. "I'm not telling you anything, if you think you have leverage against me. I know you have your own networks, Sparrow." She spat the name, and it cut like a blade straight to Shan's heart. "I'm sure you can find what you need, if you look hard enough."

"Stop!" Shan snapped, the last bit of her control shattering. "I came here to apologize. This was never supposed to happen to you!"

The confession hung between them, as stark and startling as a scream, but Miss Lovell only cackled. Her laugh was wild and unrestrained, her entire body trembling from the force of it, and Shan could only watch on in shock.

"You're sorry?" Miss Lovell repeated. "You're fucking sorry? You are really a fool, my lady, if you did not see this coming."

Shan clenched her jaw, refusing to take the bait, but the Matron wasn't done.

"I don't know what kind of games you're caught up in, Sparrow, but there are consequences to your actions." She rose to her feet, standing on unsteady legs, though if that was the fury or the effects of what the Guard had done to her, Shan couldn't be sure. "And it's never you who will have to pay them."

She had heard this all before, knew it in her bones. But to confront it was a different matter entirely, and unlike her brother, there was no way she could save the Matron. There was nothing she could do but apologize, but what good were words at this point?

She had nothing else to offer.

"I'm sorry," she tried again, only for Miss Lovell to cross the room and slam her fist into the wall beside Shan's head. Frail as she was, she still towered over Shan, the pure weight of her anger a palpable force—and though it wasn't enough to intimidate Shan, it did shame her.

"Your apology means nothing, Sparrow," Miss Lovell whispered, her voice as soft and smooth as silk. "You came here to assuage your own guilt, but you won't be getting forgiveness from me."

"I understand," Shan breathed, and Miss Lovell pushed away, stalking to the other side of the room, only a scant few feet away. She crossed her arms across her chest, managing to summon her dignity—a glimmer of the proud, strong woman she was.

That she would be, till the very end.

"If you do have any affection in your heart for me," Miss Lovell said, "if any of your schemes were true, please leave and never return. Whatever happens, I do not wish to see your face again."

It was cruel, and there was a finality to it, a sense of judgement as unyielding and unerring as justice. In the eyes of Miss Lovell, there would be no possibility of atonement. And, in all honesty, Shan agreed with her. She had been a fool to think she could have it both ways, and it was time for her to commit.

All she could do was hope that this debasement would be worth that. That—no matter the price that she had to pay or the people she had to lose—it would all be worth it. That losing her brother, losing Isaac, would be worth it. She had done it once, she could do it again.

Did she even have a heart left to break?

She didn't dare speak again, slipping through the door without so much as a glance back. As she locked the door, it felt like she was condemning Miss Lovell to her death, locking her away where she would never be seen again.

It was the truth after all. They planned to hold her down here till the world forgot about her, draining her blood again and again.

Shan pressed her forehead against the cool metal, eyes prickling with the tears she dared not shed.

—⊢—

Creeping up the stairs towards the small flat that had become Isaac's home and safe house, Shan's heart beat an unsteady rhythm in her chest. She knew she shouldn't be here: it was an imposition, a risk, a violation. Even having taken the needed precautions—having stopped at home to change into her old Sparrow's clothes, having wandered the streets of Dameral to lose any potential tails—it still felt like endangerment. If she was the one who brought Isaac back to the King's attention, she would never forgive herself.

But she couldn't keep lying to herself, couldn't keep living in this contradiction between her heart and her head, so she had to see him. After weeks of tension and silence it was time—for all they went through and all they had done to each other, she wouldn't just vanish without a word. She would give him her goodbyes and her love, a pained farewell as they let go of all they could have been, in a better world.

But, from the low, choked out moans from the next room, she wasn't the only one who had come to Isaac.

She recognized the sounds, had chased them herself on many nights, the signs that Samuel was nearly at the peak of his pleasure. Pressing forward, she eased the door open to see them tangled together, naked and flushed, Samuel spilling over Isaac's hand, his entire body trembling from the force of his release.

As for Isaac, he looked at her as she stood in the doorway, little more than a voyeur. The thrill of getting caught had her body warming, the all-too-familiar ache budding in her lower abdomen, her cunt getting slick from just watching. Isaac smirked at her, his expression smug and knowing, and Shan realized that he had known she was here. His vampiric senses had picked up on her arrival, and he had taken advantage of it to stage this little scene just for her.

He didn't say anything though, continuing to pump Samuel's red, deflating cock, pushing him past the point of pleasure into harsh oversensitivity. His hand was carefully curled around Samuel's length to protect him from the stark brutality of his talon-like claws, darker and sharper than any jewelry Shan had ever worn.

"It seems we have a visitor," Isaac said, his voice calm and steady. In control. Dominant. "A little spy. What do you say, darling? Should we punish her for bad behavior?"

Samuel gave a little moan of approval, too blissed out to form words. But he held out his hand, shifting towards her. Making an offering of himself, the soft lines of his body shining in the candlelight, sweat-slicked and handsome.

Swallowing hard, she jerked her head in a quick motion. Hells, this was wrong. She had come here to end things with Isaac, to cut this off before they hurt themselves even worse. "I didn't come here for this."

"That doesn't mean you don't need it," Isaac replied, gently. "Come on, Shan, let me take care of you, one last time."

She swallowed hard—so he knew it too, knew that whatever they could have had would never survive this world they inherited and the choices they made. That no matter what came next, nobody would win.

So why, then, shouldn't she take this offering? Why shouldn't they say goodbye just like this, a memory to hold onto for the long years to come?

She took one step forward, then another, as tentative as a hare under the watchful eyes of a predator, until she stood at the edge of the bed. Trembling with want. Isaac rose up on his knees, pressing his lips to hers, coaxing her open as he tangled his claws in her hair. The kiss was equal parts bitter and sweet—as tender and as painful as a goodbye.

She could taste Samuel on his tongue, the bitter musk lingering in Isaac's mouth. Both of her men together, and blood and steel was she thankful that she got this even once. For just a few minutes, she would know what she could have had, and though it would hurt when the dawn came, it still gave her just a sliver of solace.

"All right," she breathed, and as consent was given, Isaac pulled her down onto the bed. She landed between them, Samuel moving as they covered her. Their hands roamed all over her body, stripping her bit by bit, tossing her clothes aside until she was as bare as they were.

They nipped their way across her body, the tempting tease of Isaac's fangs pressing into the tender ache of her breasts, scraping over her nipples, never quite hard enough to break skin. Samuel's blunt fingers dipped into her cunt, spreading her open until she keened, his thumb brushing roughly against the sensitive bundle of nerves.

Only to stop when she got close to her release, denying her the pleasure she so desperately needed, slipping away from her slick core and leaving her so painfully empty.

She reached out, trying to grab Samuel but ending up with fistfuls of both of them, her voice a growl in her throat. "Who taught you to do that?"

Samuel laughed, dipping to press a soft kiss to the inside of her thigh. "I have a good teacher."

"He is a good student," Isaac confirmed, catching her wrists and pinning them above her head with a single hand, his grip strong and bruising. The position had her back arching into the stretch, leaving her dreadfully, wonderfully exposed.

Vulnerable in a way that she rarely let herself enjoy, the amount of trust it required too great. But with Isaac, with Samuel, she could find freedom in the lack of control, a release that she tried to deny that she needed. But Isaac knew her too well, knew exactly what to give her, holding her delicate heart in his hands.

"Spread your legs, Shan," Isaac commanded, his voice low in her ear. She spread her legs automatically, even though she wanted nothing more than to snap them closed again, to chase what little friction she could find. But Samuel pushed his hand into her hip, holding down, while looking to Isaac for instruction.

Isaac pulled Samuel closer, using his free hand to split Samuel's lower lip open. Shan watched as he lured Samuel into an open-mouthed kiss, the low buzz of magic sizzling over both of them until Samuel jerked back like he had been stung.

"Hells."

Shan glanced down to see that Samuel's erection had returned, hard as steel, flushed a deep red as precum leaked from the tip. If she had been more aware, she would have laughed at the audacity of it, the quick burst of Blood Healing leaving Samuel ready to fuck. But as it was, she could only think of one thing, her clit throbbing in time with the unsteady beat of her heart.

"Please," she gasped, though it burned her to ask so openly, to beg. She wanted him inside her, wanted to be filled completely until he spilled, filling her to the brim.

Isaac pressed a gentle kiss to her forehead, purring, "Well since you asked so nicely. Samuel—make our beloved come."

Samuel moved instantly, following Isaac's demand without question as he crawled over Shan, slotting between her spread legs. Her hands found his arms, tense under her fingers, as he slid between her folds, so hard and hot against her most tender flesh.

To her side, she heard the slick sounds of fingers against wetness, turning her head to find Isaac with his hand between his legs, using his own arousal to rut his cock between two fingers. He watched the two of them, his gaze dark and intense, as if they were there only for his own titillation. A private show for him to enjoy as he sought his own release.

The casual ownership of it had her clit throbbing, and she wanted to reach out, to slip her hand into him and force him to be just as broken as she was. But Samuel chose that moment to spear her open on his cock, his thick length sinking into her in a slow, steady motion.

A whine caught in the back of her throat as Samuel bottomed out, rocking into her with little ruts that could barely be called thrusts. Isaac huffed his displeasure, abandoning his cock to tangle his hand in Samuel's hair, pulling it back with a harsh tug that had Samuel moaning.

"I told you to make her come," Isaac snarled, and Shan could feel the way Samuel's cock twitched in the tight sheath of her cunt, the way he enjoyed the cruel way Isaac spoke to him. "Now fuck her properly or I'll have to do it myself."

"Yes, sir," Samuel gasped, before Isaac shoved his face down into Shan's chest. He latched on to her nipple without complaint, the sharp sting of his teeth lighting a pleasure that ran right to her core. He laved his attention on her before Isaac moved him to the other breast, the cool air of the room stinging against her damp flesh.

"Better," Isaac purred, his hand sliding down Samuel's back. She couldn't see it, but she could feel it when Samuel jerked forward, the way he pressed those claws into the meat of their lover's ass. "But you can do more."

Bracing himself on his arms, Samuel pushed himself up so that he could fuck into her with hard, steady thrusts, each surge forward slamming his pelvis against the tender bud of nerves, racketing her pleasure higher and higher.

She was so full, clenching on every centimeter of his length inside of her, Isaac directing Samuel like he was little more than a tool to please her. Samuel might have been their lover, might have been the sweet balance that kept their relationship from falling apart, but in this moment he was nothing more than the cock Isaac wore in a harness around his hips.

Samuel bit his lip, worrying it so hard that a fresh burst of blood appeared, red and thick, dripping down on her chest, staining her skin in crimson. He was so pleased to be used in such a demeaning manner, his entire body flushed as he continued to pound into her, trembling as he approached his peak. "I—I'm close—"

Isaac slid behind him, dragging a too long tongue in the sensitive place where his shoulder met his neck. She could see the tip of it, almost insectoid in nature, made for sucking his victims dry. But Samuel just shuddered at the contact, his rhythm faltering.

"If you come first," Isaac warned, words slurring around the press of his tongue and the creak of his jaw distending, "not only will you have disappointed Shan, but I'll have to punish you."

And because she was cruel, because even now, with the men she loved more than anything in the world above her, pleasuring her like she was a goddess, she still had to seize a little bit of control. She clenched around Samuel, pulling him in deeper until he broke, spilling inside of her with a hot rush that almost—*almost*—was enough to push her over the edge. But despite the steady kick of blood to her clit and the soft squelch of Samuel softening inside of her, her release escaped her.

She threw her head back on the pillow with a whine of frustration.

"Pathetic," Isaac said, ripping Samuel back.

There was a shuffle of movement, and she forced herself up on her elbows to watch as Isaac shoved Samuel off the edge of the bed, positioning him to rest with his back against the frame, standing over him. His own cunt pressed against Samuel's plush lips, Isaac groaning as he fucked Samuel's mouth like he owned it. The soft sounds of sucking and licking filled the room, but Shan didn't have a moment to enjoy the sight of it as Isaac grabbed her by the ankle, manhandling her into place as his monstrous tongue unfurled.

As the tip of it—thick and wet—dipped into her hole and swirled around, savoring her juices and Samuel's spend like it was blood, worrying it like a wound and sucking it clean.

Her hand slammed on her clit, rubbing harsh circles around it as Isaac plundered her, forcing more of his tongue into her than she could stand, lapping at the sensitive point just inside her warmth, pushing her to finally come around him.

He hummed as she gushed around him, not letting her come down from her high. His hand slipped over hers, pressing into her aching clit as he forced her towards another peak, too powerful and too tremulous, and she shattered completely, tears streaming from her eyes as she whimpered.

Then, only then, did he release her, his heavy tongue sliding out of her and leaving her blissfully empty, the kind of aching satisfaction that she hadn't realized she needed settling over her.

She lay there catching her breath as Isaac continued to rock against Samuel's face. He was so handsome like this, brow furrowed in concentration as he sought his pleasure. Sweat beaded on his skin, dripped between his breasts and down the trail of hair that crawled down his stomach towards his mound. His tits rocked with each thrust, the harsh buds drawn tight and dark, and Shan couldn't help herself. She forced herself forward, using what little energy she had left to drape herself over him as she tweaked his nipples between her fingers, hard and rough, just the way he liked.

He licked up her neck, sinking his fangs into her as he finally came.

They stood like that for a long minute, tangled together and dripping, before Isaac took a step back, the more inhuman elements of his form fading. He eased Shan back onto the bed before disappearing into the washroom, returning with a pair of damp washcloths.

She laid there, her wild heartbeat steadying as Isaac cleaned Samuel up, whispering soft words of kindness and affection before helping him into the bed next to Shan. She snuggled into Samuel, his arms going tight around her, before she started at the cold press of a wet cloth between her legs.

"Easy," Isaac said pressing a gentle kiss to her hip. "Let me take care of you too."

Shan considered resisting, just for the hell of it, but Samuel was so warm against her, and the bed was so, so soft. She let Isaac clean her, wiping way the mess they had made, and when he had returned with a couple of glasses, she quietly drank her water with Samuel.

It was nice, being taken care of in this way. Loved and pampered, pleasured and adored. And as Isaac slipped into the bed behind her, leaving her pressed between two warm bodies, she realized that she could very easily get used to this. No. *Addicted* to it. To the comfort and safety of these men, who loved her unconditionally, who offered themselves so freely, body and soul.

Isaac's hand slipped over her waist, pressing flat against the softness of her stomach. There wasn't heat in his touch, and lust didn't flutter back to life in her core. Instead, it was something far worse. The warmth that spread through her was the easy affection that she had never dreamed that she would find, burningly jealous of her brother and every happy, innocent face she passed in the street.

And here it was, offered to her on a silver platter. All she had to do was admit that Samuel had been right, that there was a limit to what she should do in the King's name. All she had to do was admit that Isaac had a point, that the risks of the war he threatened to cast Aeravin into was worth the future that they could build.

All she had to do was give up all the power she had worked so hard for and start again.

But she remembered what had driven her to Isaac this very night, the damnation she earned from those she had let down. The distrust and hate that she had earned from the Matron, from all those who she claimed she was helping.

There was no place for her in the world that Isaac wanted to build.

Samuel had already drifted off, pressed warm against her back, peaceful in the innocence that she wished she had done a better job of protecting. Isaac, though, was looking down at her, and they didn't need any words. No explanations, no excuses.

They both knew she would be gone in the morning, slipping away like a thief in the night, never to return.

"Sleep, darling," Isaac said, pressing his lips to her forehead. "Let me hold you, just a little longer."

She pressed into him, though she knew it would only make things harder. But she did it anyway, just because he had asked.

She could give him that much.

Chapter Thirty-Two

Samuel

It was still a strange thing to Samuel, having the Eternal King visiting in his own home. He poured the Eternal King a glass of fine whisky, then poured a second for himself, because appearances still mattered, even if he would hardly touch it.

"Thank you, Samuel," the King said, taking his glass and drinking deeply. He was settled in the large plush chair in front of the fireplace, his dark suit a stark contrast against the lush, verdant green of the velvet. The King leaned towards the blistering warmth as they fought the harsh freeze that had settled over Dameral with the frigid breeze off the sea. Even here, in the heart of comfort, the chill seeped in through stone, lingering at the windows and the edges of the house, fought back by sheer will.

Still, it was an indulgence that Samuel never expected to have, back when he saved his coal and logs for only the coldest nights of the year. But here he was, sharing a warming drink with his liege in front of a roaring fire.

In another life, in a world where he had been taken in by his family, a world where the Mad Aberforth wasn't Mad, perhaps this would be a regular occurrence. A fixture in a life of comfort and privilege that molded him into a true Lord, not this pretender play-acting at being more than he could ever be.

It would never feel natural, and Samuel didn't know if he should feel grateful that his soul still hadn't faltered, or fear that the endless exhaustion of a lifetime of lies would pull him to his downfall. But he played the part well, perching in the chair across from the King. "So, how can I help you today, Tristan?"

The name still felt odd on his lips, a too-personal touch that Samuel couldn't help but feel was some sort of trap. A way to lull him into too friendly complacency, to pull on his good-hearted nature until he wasn't even realizing he was being manipulated.

The King arched a brow, his mouth pulling to a too-calculated smile. "I cannot visit my only remaining relative simply for the pleasure of it?"

"You could," Samuel agreed, taking care to sound as affable as ever, "but you are also a very busy man."

The King hummed in response, holding his glass out in a mocking toast. "Astute as always, Samuel. I did come for a purpose."

Samuel steeled himself for whatever was coming next, what task the King would lay at his feet, what horrible evisceration the King would place upon him this time.

"I came to apologize."

Samuel did not expect that—an apology from the Eternal King himself was beyond even his most wild dreams, especially so freely and casually given. He took a deep sip of the whisky, the burn of it shocking through him like a bolt of lightning to his spine. This had to be a trick, even if Samuel couldn't fathom the specifics. "I'm sorry?"

The King breathed out a soft laugh. "That's my line, Samuel."

"I . . ." Samuel spluttered for a moment before he found his footing, clearing his throat as he forced his thoughts into a neat and orderly row. "I meant that I don't understand. What do you have to apologize for?"

"A lot, if I am being honest." He downed the rest of the drink, staring into the empty glass before setting it aside. "I have seen how well you've been handling things these past couple of weeks. The Guard is beginning to flourish under you in a way it never had under Dunn."

The King said the former Councillor's name with a sigh, a kind of regret that Samuel didn't think Dunn had earned. "He was a good man, and a good Councillor, but more focused on the politics of the House than on minding his own roost. In a kinder time, he would have been remembered as fine steward of Dameral, but he was the wrong choice for a time of chaos. You, however..."

Samuel took another sip of his drink before getting up to refill the King's glass. Even with all the training he had with Shan, even with every scrap of refinement he had learned to wear, he did not trust his expression in this moment. He didn't trust himself to not give away every terrible doubt on his face.

"I am not doing anything special," Samuel said, speaking directly into the liquor cabinet. "In fact, I thought I was doing poorly."

The King hummed, thoughtful. "I'll admit that some of your early proposals for the House were ... unpolished, but I must accept my part in that. I threw you into a rip tide without even bothering to see if you could swim, and that was ill-done of me."

Samuel bit the inside of his cheek so hard that blood bloomed across his teeth, stirring the power that slept deep in his chest. Blood Working and his insidious, dark gift twining together into a longing so intense that it threatened to tear him apart from the inside. But he didn't dare risk it now, this secret that he had to keep, lies wrapped within lies until he didn't know where he stood anymore. "You did what you had to."

"No more, no less," the King replied, with chagrin. He stood, swift and silent as a serpent, slithering to take his place next to Samuel. "I should have taken you under my wing sooner, especially as Shan had to focus on being Royal Blood Worker. She is a masterful being, a once-in-a-lifetime kind of mind, but even she can only handle so much."

"Shan is brilliant," Samuel replied, with an ache deep in his heart. That much he could agree to openly. "She's done so much to help me."

"She has, and we are both very lucky to have her. But that doesn't make my point any less true." The King clapped him on the shoulder, reached past to grab his freshly filled glass. "I should have had stepped in sooner, we could have avoided so much strife. But I am here now—and we have much to plan for."

"Plan for?" Samuel echoed. Not trusting that he wouldn't make any foolish decisions, Samuel left his half-finished drink behind, turning to follow the King as he stood in front of the fire, one arm behind his back and the glass hanging from a loose grip. He was as still and precise as a statue, as the burn of natural fire, untainted by the eerie glow of witch light, cast him in stark lines, so grim and forbidding. The mask of kindness dropped for a singular heartbeat, revealing the truth of the man before him.

Ancient. Untouchable. Unknowable.

And despite the gentle way the King had been treating him, Samuel felt like nothing more than a pawn on his board—a tool to be used, again and again, as long as he was proving useful.

"I have need of the Aberforth estate," the King began, drawing Samuel's attention back to the present, "for some business with the Royal Blood Worker. I have already written ahead for all the particulars to be handled, but I think that you should come with us."

The question fell from his lips before Samuel had even realized he decided to ask it, little more than a snarl. "What do you and Shan need it for?"

It wasn't the right question to ask, hells, it wasn't even a question, it was an accusation. Another secret that Shan had kept from him, coming back to roost. The sting of it had prodded the darkness in him, like a snake uncurling from its slumber, ready to strike.

The King didn't so much as blink, as if he had expected this little outburst. No, there was a small smile curving the corner of his mouth. He was pleased by this, the cruelty in Samuel making a return.

But Samuel was too angry to feel shame over it, even as realization cut through him. This is what the King had been hoping for. He wanted to mold Samuel into something darker, something more like the Blood Worker and Lord he could have been, in a different life.

Perhaps it wouldn't be too difficult to play into it. What was another mask, at the end of the day? He might never be as skilled as his beloved Shan, but he could try to do her proud.

"It's ... a complicated matter," the King explained easily, "and it would be more effective to show you. Suffice it to say that the fruits of this labor will greatly affect your position, Councillor."

The next step in the plan, the noose twisting tighter. Samuel huffed, a deliberate affectation that pleased the King. A small calibration to the persona of Lord Aberforth. "As you command. I will join you in the countryside and see what you have to offer."

"Good." The King clapped him on the shoulder, squeezing hard. "We'll travel out at the end of the week. Clear your schedule and pack for winter—we might even see a true snowfall."

"That would be delightful," Samuel said, torn between an almost childlike wonder at the thought of a winter wonderland and the pure animal fear of being trapped with the King for an interminable amount of time. But what choice did he have?

Besides, he had a job to do, and if Shan wasn't able to reach out to him—or to Isaac, if their little tryst the previous night had proven anything, her disappearing before they had woken, leaving behind only the bitter aftertaste of being used again—perhaps he could use this. If she couldn't bridge the gap, he would do it for her. Before he lost her to whatever machinations the King was planning.

And if a little solstice trip to the Aberforth estate was what he needed, then he would embrace it.

Samuel found Isaac with Anton and Bart, huddled together in one of the small meeting rooms in the safe house. Paper was spread out across the table, a plan being formed in three separate hands, scribbled notes that would eventually collate into something grander. A revolution born in whispers and shadows, but it felt incomplete. Empty without Shan there, parceling out her little bits of brilliance.

Isaac was the first to notice him, a soft smile on his face as he waved

Samuel in. Anton looked up at the motion, barking out, "You're late, Aberforth."

He wasn't angry, not truly, but there was a question there. "I apologize. I had an unexpected visitor." Taking a seat, he launched into a quick explanation of the King's visit, including the information that he would be traveling to the Aberforths' country estate for an indeterminate amount of time.

Isaac didn't interrupt him, but his brow furrowed with concern. Samuel reached for Isaac's hand under the table, giving it a reassuring squeeze. But this wasn't about him, not now.

Turning his attention to Bart, Samuel asked, "Do you have any idea what she's been working on with the King?"

His smile was rueful as he leaned back with a sigh. "If she hasn't told any of you, what makes you think I would know?" He rubbed at the back of his neck, looking suddenly exhausted. "Since her appointment as Royal Blood Worker, she's been pulling back from her work as the Sparrow, and from . . . me."

Anton shifted on his stool, sliding closer so that he could pull Bart against him, a kind of casual comfort. "It's nothing personal," Anton said. "You just know how she is, especially since . . ." He trailed off, but he cut a sharp glance to Isaac.

"I know," Isaac muttered, with the bitterness of someone who had had this conversation many times. Who still blamed himself for the actions he had taken so long ago.

Samuel may not have been around when Isaac had broken Shan's heart for the first time, a relative newcomer to this tangled web of love and heartbreak that Shan had woven around herself, but he still knew that nothing was as simple as it seemed.

That the true reason for all their suffering, on every scale from small to large, was the ruler they were working so hard to unseat.

"It's not your fault," Samuel said, cutting through the tension with the harshness of a blade. "We are all what this damned nation has made of us. Same with Shan. And if retreating into herself is the only way she can survive this, then who are we to judge?"

"It isn't about judging," Anton chimed in, looking strangely pained, "and that was ill-done of me, Isaac."

"Perhaps," Isaac admitted, rubbing his hand across his chin, catching at the stubble. "But it wasn't unearned." Sighing, he turned to Samuel. "None of us are judging her, but what Shan's doing ... it won't work. Trust me, I've been there."

"Then what do we do?" Samuel asked, almost fearing the answer. It felt like time was running out, this plotting coming to a head, and if they couldn't bring Shan into it ...

He didn't want to think about that, even if it made him a coward.

"Perhaps this trip to the countryside will do us some good," Bart said.

"Even with the King there?"

Bart's expression sharpened, not quite a smile, but cunningly victorious nonetheless. "She needs to face the truth of the King head-on, and whatever he is plotting, if it requires the Aberforth estate, it must be something truly terrible."

"Or dangerous," Isaac offered, "if he doesn't want to risk whatever it is in the capital." He drummed his fingers on the table, clearly weighing his options.

"Out with it, then," Anton muttered, as they slipped back into their usual bickering. "If you have something to share with the group."

It was kinder now, Samuel noticed, not quite as cruel and biting as it used to be. When he first pulled Anton into this rescue, he had feared that the two of them would tear each other to pieces. But instead, they had become something almost like friends. Some new understanding had been reached between them, and Samuel was so glad to see it.

"Ah, fuck off, LeClaire," Isaac returned, with a flash of a grin. "But fine, if you insist. Before you broke me out, the King had offered me up to her as a test subject. Exploring the limits of Blood Working, in much the same way that I have been."

Samuel cursed as the implications hit him. "You don't think he's—"

"Not to himself," Isaac quickly clarified, sensing the shape of

Samuel's sudden fear. "But another Blood Worker, one that Shan has been working with. Making his own vampire."

"Fuck," Anton muttered, his face gone pale. "It was one thing when we thought you gave us the upper hand, but—"

"But nothing," Samuel said, with a conviction that surprised even himself. "We will know nothing until the trip is finished, but Bart was right. It is an opportunity, if only for this."

"He's right," Isaac added. "This changes nothing. If anything, it means that we need to accelerate our plans. Six weeks was too long."

Bart leaned back, pensive. "And is that something you're ready for?"

Samuel glanced between them, unsure what he was getting at. Feeling like he was missing some vital piece of information. But Isaac only inclined his head. "In time. I'll need a bit more blood, another—"

"Blood Worker?" Samuel offered, his mind already swimming with possibilities, names of those who were cruel, who were a threat to this war they were preparing to wage. Human beings with entire lives in front of them, but that Samuel would gladly see taken out.

Hells, when had he become so callous? Measuring out the worth of a life, painting targets on the backs of people who thought him, if not a friend, then at least a kindly acquaintance. It was bad enough when he did it to Holland, but that was to correct a mistake, to save his own skin.

Once was a mistake. Twice was a pattern. This was premeditated, and he knew there was no coming back from this.

They were all monsters here, and Samuel knew that he had to stop fighting it. There was no other way to achieve their goals, and it was childish to keep pretending. This is what Dameral had made him, and if they were to succeed, he needed to be honest with himself.

No matter how much it hurt to admit.

"At least," Isaac admitted. "Maybe more."

"Well, then what are we waiting for?" Samuel's throat was dry, but he forced himself to speak away. "Let's teach them a lesson. Send a message. Destabilize the Guard completely."

"And you know where to start?" Anton asked.

"I do. I can give you everything you need." Isaac furrowed his brow, and Samuel could tell what was coming. An out of some kind. But he wouldn't let himself be swayed. "Vaughn Dabney, Captain of the Guard."

Understanding shot through the room, as sudden and shocking as lightning. Isaac's lips curved into a smirk. "As my love commands."

Chapter Thirty-Three

Isaac

Isaac waited until night had fully set over Dameral, the bustle of the evening giving way to the utter silence that only came in the dark hours between midnight and dawn. Despite the newness of his transformations, there was a primal instinct deep inside, a predator ready to slip loose. He could feel the ache in his bones, the way his body wanted to shift and change. To tear through this damned city, striking down all the parasites who thrived on blood and power, leaving a trail of viscera in his wake. It was no more than they deserved.

But he held himself tight, slipping through the dark streets as nothing more than a man in the shadows. There would be time for terror soon enough, but for now, discretion was key. First, he had to find his target without drawing undue attention to himself. After, though ...

Then he could have his fun.

Dabney didn't live in one of the grand townhouses, like his previous victims did, but on the third floor of a fine building of flats—he had done well enough for himself to be able to rent out an entire level of the building for his own comfort. He lived alone, married to the job that he had dedicated so many years of his life to, and for that Isaac was thankful. There was no spouse or children to work around.

That was a line that Isaac wasn't sure he would be able to cross—after all, he had been that child once upon a time. Hell, Isaac once would have admired a man like Dabney, would have thought they were kindred spirits. He was a Blood Worker but not a noble, a man who had risen on the merits of his cruelty and cleverness. He had learned the truth, though, all too harshly. They were separated by too many things to count, from the color of their skin to the very fabric of their souls. If Dabney and the other Blood Workers like him couldn't even be convinced to accept Unblooded as people, then Isaac wanted nothing from them.

In the new world they were building, there would be no place for people like that, not if they hoped to have any sort of equality.

But Isaac wasn't there to explore the foolish mistakes of his past. He had a home to invade and a man to murder. He circled around the back, slipping through the narrow gaps between the buildings. Like the grand homes of Aeravin, most housing units of this caliber had a secondary entrance for staff and repairmen, a way to keep the riff-raff away from the tenants, and Isaac was more than willing to take advantage of that.

The door was locked, but it didn't take much for him to crush it, summoning the strength of his transformation, letting it eke out in small waves. The crack of his fingers shattering and shifting, his nails sharpening into vicious claws. The ache in his mouth as his fangs descended, canine teeth sharpening and elongating.

He stopped it there, as difficult it was, like trying to hold back the tide with his bare hands, slipping through his fingers as the bones of his body shifted beneath his shirt, his abdomen burning with the pain of something he did not even understand.

But Isaac swallowed it down, creeping through the door and up the servants' staircase, his footsteps light and silent as he moved towards Dabney's flat. There were no wards to protect it—whether Dabney was unskilled at making them or just plain arrogant, Isaac didn't know or care. But it did make this easier. He dismantled the knob and lock the same way that he did the previous one, the metal scrunching and twisting under his grip with a screech before snapping off. The sound of it echoed in his ears, loud and startling, but there was nothing Isaac could do about it.

Isaac threw himself into the apartment, the door closing quickly behind him. He didn't have a chance to give the flat more than a cursory glance, the furniture fine and well made, the walls hung with custom art, the rug under his boot a lush and intricate weave that must have cost a fortune to be imported.

Dabney enjoyed the fruits of his ill-gained work, and it just stoked the fires of rage burning in Isaac's chest even hotter.

His target stumbled into sight, perching at the edge of a hallway that led into the main living space, looking as disheveled and disoriented as if he had just rolled out of bed, a dagger held in one hand. But even caught off guard like this, Dabney was a beast of a man, his thick shoulders taking up the entire door frame, barrel-chested and broad. He was like a warrior out of storybooks, strength written in the thick press of muscle on a sturdy frame.

Isaac had to bite back the worry that budded, the primal fear that came with facing a man so much larger than himself. Because this was not to be a simple bare-knuckled brawl. Isaac had grown so much, no longer just a Blood Worker, but a monster. A manananggal. And with the power of his fangs and claws and other gifts his experiments had wrought, he could break Dabney long before Dabney could break him.

He bared his fangs in the shine of moonlight, his tongue rolling out and scenting the air. There was a fine meal in front of him, waiting to be devoured.

"Blood and steel," Dabney gasped, staggering back. "What in the hells are you?"

"Do you not recognize me, Dabney?" Isaac asked, the words distorted by the length of his proboscis-like tongue. "I remember you. What did you love to call me? Ah, right. An upstart."

Dabney shivered, mouth dropping open in recognition, but he raised his blade, taking a defiant pose. The dagger was a thin, narrow bit of protection that would not help him in the slightest. "De la Cruz," he spat, dripping venom.

Isaac shifted his footing, not enough to be seen as an outright challenge, but enough that he was ready to launch himself forward at a second's notice. "So, you do remember me?"

"Such as you are," Dabney returned, with an attempt at a sneer that bled out into sickening fright. "The rumors are true—you have made yourself into a monster to match what you are on the inside."

Isaac laughed, a harsh and guttural noise that didn't even sound human. "You haven't seen the half of it."

Releasing the hold he had on himself, Isaac let his body rip itself apart. The wings grew from his shoulders, a great tear of flesh and bone that cast them in deeper shadows, blocking out the light from the window. But despite that, he could still see every minute expression that crossed Dabney's face as terror overtook him in stages.

First, his eyes widened, the whites of them round and clear, as the pure, primitive awareness of being prey hit him. Second, the dagger fell from limp fingers, clattering on the ground, his only hope of protection gone. Third, the bitter, pungent smell of urine filled the room, darkening his sleep pants.

Isaac bared his fangs and launched himself forward, roaring as a new agony took him over. As he closed the distance between himself and Dabney, his feet remained where they were, rooted to the ground. His torso stretched, his flesh pulling and constricting, like dough rolled out across too much space before it *tore*. This wasn't some small gash, wasn't a small spill of guts and intestines hanging loose.

No, this was more drastic, his entire upper body splitting from his lower half with a burst of pain that nearly threatened to pull him under.

But as he landed on Dabney, claws sinking into skin and drawing blood to the surface, Isaac's hunger sparked to life. The kind of hunger that he couldn't even begin to quantify, all-consuming that it was, taking over every sense and blanking out his mind.

The force of impact toppled Dabney onto the floor, Isaac following him down, a disembodied torso hanging off the terrified Blood Worker. The rest of him had been left across the room, and Isaac could feel the slick slide of his insides against Dabney's legs as the man tried to shove a thigh up into the twisting mass of him in a desperate grapple for leverage. But there was none to be found, and Isaac slid his way down Dabney's body, as delicate and deliberate as a lover, before he sank his teeth into the man.

Dabney shrieked as Isaac ripped his head back, leaving an open, sopping mess of meat and blood where his stomach should be. Trashing against his attacker, Dabney struck uselessly at Isaac, his fists little more than an annoyance as he pounded at Isaac's shoulders.

Isaac held him in place, pressed one overly large hand against the man's large waist, claws curled delicately around it as he pinned Dabney to the floor, the bone compressing with a satisfying crunch. His tongue pressed against the wound he had torn in Dabney's body, the flavor of such powerful blood explosive in his mouth as he lapped at it.

As he needed *more*.

He delved deeper, his tongue almost prehensile as it slithered deeper into Dabney's body, burrowing through the muscle and fat to the soft viscera beneath. He drank it in, quite literally, the blood and small chunks of meat sucked up into his mouth. Each little sip poured down his throat, more intoxicating that the finest whisky, more nourishing than any meal that he had ever known.

Dabney whimpered and sobbed underneath him, too taken by fear and pain to even bother fighting back as Isaac rooted around in his body, wrapped his tongue around organs, squeezing them till they burst—the sweetest juice that he had ever known as he drank the Blood Worker dry.

Each little burst of flavor on his tongue made him stronger, the magic that he had carried in his veins compounding, an exponential growth that he did not even know how to calculate. And despite the way his own innards slid along the floor, blood smeared on the hardwood planks, he had never felt more invincible.

Soon enough, Dabney slumped back, the last of his life draining away as Isaac pulled the wound into a gash, the pulverized remains of his insides swirled around into a soup resting in a bowl of human meat. Dipping his head forward, his mouth to the rim, Isaac fed upon it like a frenzied beast, unsure of when he would find his next meal.

He fed until it was done, till all that was left was a gaping hole in the center of Dabney's corpse. The body pulled apart, the cavity destroyed and emptied, the pain writ into Dabney's expression as his eyes stared up at the ceiling, never to move again.

It was finished, and so he pushed himself up on his elbows. His stomach was so bloated with blood that he had to crawl back to where he had left the other half of his body, his wings fluttering helplessly on his back, doing little more than providing balance. His claws left deep gouges in the carpet, the fluids spilling down his chest and out his gaping hole of a body staining it a deep russet, the color of blood dead and dying.

But he didn't care about that. He had never intended to leave behind a clean scene, the crime clear for all to see. It was a shocking scene of horror, one that even the Guard would not be able to explain.

And his third goal was completed.

He had the power he needed to gather, that only a Blood Worker was able to provide, his full transformation to a manananggal complete at last. He had slain Dabney, Captain of the Guard, and the chaos that followed would only help their cause.

But this—this torn and mutilated corpse—was the final victory. The terror such a murder would spark, spreading through Aeravin like a wildfire. It was a message; one he knew the Eternal King would understand.

There would be no peace in Aeravin so long as Isaac lived. He had made himself into the kind of monster perfect for taking down Blood Workers, an evolution of everything they had hoped to be, and there was nothing on this earth that could stop him.

He reached his lower half, his legs kneeling on the ground and the torn, open part of his body sitting there, waiting to be rejoined.

Circling around behind himself, he flapped his wings, getting enough air for him to launch himself up and over.

The two ends of himself reached for each other, like the pull of a magnet, and his body fused itself back together with much less trauma than the way it had torn itself apart. The monstrous bits of him vanished as his body re-formed—the wings folded into his back, the claws faded away, leaving behind simple, human fingers. The tongue receded along with the fangs, his jaw snapping back into place.

And he was left wonderfully, terribly, hopelessly human once again.

He staggered to his feet, not even bothering to look behind him and the carnage he had wrought. He moved towards the door, snatching the long winter cloak that hung on a simple wooden peg, tossing it around his shoulders to cover the mess he had made of himself.

And with that, he snuck back out into the night, disappearing back into the shadows from whence he came. All while trying to ignore the dreadful truth—that even as vicious and cruel as Isaac had been, there was a part of him that had enjoyed it.

That was already looking forward to his next kill.

Chapter Thirty-Four

Shan

Shan had prepped for weeks for this gala, an unfortunate necessity of her position. It wasn't enough that she had to oversee the Academies, had to keep the Eternal King's schedule, had to aid him with his most complex and harrowing Blood Working—as Royal Blood Worker, she was also expected to be the living heart of Dameral's High Society.

And though she had barely had the time to even sleep in the past few weeks, Shan had ensured that this little gathering to celebrate the Solstice went exactly to plan. A bright light of hope on the longest, darkest night of the year.

It was a tradition, and she had outdone herself indeed, turning the ballroom in the Royal Palace into a scene of winter wonder, with wreaths of pine and holly hanging fresh and fragrant, strategically placed evergreen trees brought in from the countryside, draped in ribbons and tinsel. There were stations with mulled wine and ginger-spiced biscuits, tumblers of finely aged whisky and jam-filled tarts. Shan had even hired the pre-eminent quartet of Aeravin to fill the space with the soft sounds of music, jolly and joyful.

It was a little triumph, only to have it be ruined at the last minute. Only for *Isaac* to have ruined it.

Despite the time of celebration, all the guests floated through the ballroom under a muted haze, whispering about the body that had been found early this morning, dismembered and brutalized. It was a vile and gruesome affair, left there to be discovered. Almost like he intended to make a point, and blood and steel, had he succeeded.

The time of splendor was ruined by the low buzz of panic, soft whispers of harsh conversation buzzing under the music. The dance floor was near empty, only two couples twirling together, a pathetic showing for such a large ballroom.

Shan considered taking to the floor herself, as perhaps seeing the host dance would spur some of the others into action. But she glanced across the floor to find Samuel surrounded by a gaggle of Blood Workers, each and every one of them thinking that they would be the one to get a new piece of information out of him.

As if she had trained him that poorly, as if he'd break that easily. No, he might still have the sweetest, bleeding heart that she had ever known, but he wasn't a fool. He was more capable than any of them realized, and she was so damned proud of him.

Samuel caught her gaze and lifted one shoulder in a quick shrug—an apology, brief as it was. He wouldn't be able to free himself from the mob that dogged his every step, and Shan understood that.

She understood it all too well.

Turning, she sauntered over to one of the long tables along the wall, grabbing a small crystal glass and filling it with the fragrant mulled wine. The spices tickled her nose and she lifted and inhaled deeply, only to freeze as she felt a potent aura of power wash over her. She was intimately familiar with it by now, the way it slid across her skin, burned the back of her throat, threatened to overpower her.

The Eternal King was here.

"What a splendid soirée you've put together, my dear Lady LeClaire," he breathed, his voice low in her ear. "It's a shame everyone else is not taking advantage of it."

Shan turned, dropping into a precise half-curtsy, her mug of warm wine held just so in one hand. "Your Majesty, I did not expect you to be here."

"Rise," he commanded, holding out a hand to her. As she took it, her claws brushing against his, she was struck with the most intense feeling of déjà vu. Another celebration that she had orchestrated, another party that the Eternal King had shown up to, not so long ago. It felt like decades, though it hadn't even been a year, but Shan had grown so much in such a short time. And now, she didn't flinch, matching the King's appreciative gaze as they both looked each other over.

Her dress was exquisite, a custom creation from Laurens in the same deep color of her official state robes, blood spilled upon the snow. But its style was nothing like the prim cut of the robes, instead hugging her figure tightly. Lace braided up and down her arms, a nearly sheer fabric that hugged her chest and corset, showing her décolletage to her best advantage, all while leaving her breasts only the slightest bit obscured, like a present waiting to be unwrapped.

It was an effective style, Shan noted, as the King's eyes lingered there for a heartbeat too long to be proper before sliding down to her skirts. Even those were scandalous—instead of billowing around her legs, the silk hung tight like a sheath, drawing attention to the swell of her hips before it split along one side, allowing her freedom of movement while showing a scandalous amount of skin with each step.

And for him—his suit was, as always, perfection. Dark and fitted exquisitely to his form, the careful designs of Aeravin roses stitched into the waistcoat, winter white and just as intricate as the unique structure of each individual snowflake. He carried himself with the sublime confidence of a man who always got everything he ever wanted, and Shan couldn't hide the swell of jealousy that flowed through her.

Oh, what she would give to move like that through the world, unafraid and bold. And as he took the glass from her hand, discarding it on the table before linking arms with her, she realized that she could be that way too, if she let herself. Hanging off the King's arm as he led her towards the now empty dance floor, she could be whatever she dared to be, because in the end, he had chosen her—and for all the flaws and terrors and little cruelties of her esteemed liege, there was power in it.

And she wasn't afraid to seize it, not anymore.

"I hope Samuel doesn't mind," the King murmured as he swept her up against him as the music shifted to something low, sultry. "But as he is occupied, I thought it would be appropriate for me to stand in for him. It is the least I can do, as family."

Shan flicked her gaze towards Samuel, who offered her a simple smile and a dip of his head. Not quite permission—because even though they were engaged, they didn't need the other's consent for things as simple and trifling as a dance. Still, there was a deeper understanding, an acknowledgment of the fact that what the Eternal King asked for, the Eternal King got.

She couldn't have turned the King down, even if she wanted to. But as all eyes turned to her, an inhaled breath as the music shifted and the dance began, Shan knew that she didn't want to be anywhere else but here.

It was exactly what she needed to turn the party around, and she moved into the dance with practiced precision, letting the King lead her as she followed a heartbeat behind.

It was different from her dances with Samuel, it was easier than her dances with Samuel, who even after all his practice still needed a strong guiding hand. But the Eternal King was a master in this, as he could be in so many things while being Eternal, countless years of routine engraved into his very soul. And as unfairly cruel as it was to Samuel, it was a relief to just be able to shut off her mind and dance. To let her body lead her, without needing guidance or thought.

Oh, how wondrous it was to simply feel, if only for a moment.

They twirled around the dance floor, just a hair's breadth too intimate to be entirely proper, but not quite enough to be scandalous. He led her with a strong hand, his presence washing over her like the heady burn of liquor.

The King was, as ever, a master of control, holding her just so, but she knew that there would be titters about this come morning. The

Eternal King, come down from his lofty towers, attending one of the many socials that he had historically ignored. Pulling his Royal Blood Worker from the sidelines and into the first dance he had done in ... well, centuries. But he held her firm, unmindful of the low hiss of muttered conversation around them.

This close, Shan feared that she could drown in the run-off of his power—that he could overwhelm her with little more than the light touch of his hand against the curve of her waist, with a slight dip of his head, the soft exhale of breath against her skin, as he whispered, "Ignore them all, Shan."

His words were a caress, pitched deep and soft just for her, and Shan couldn't help the shiver that ran down her spine. "They are jealous of you," he continued, his claws flexing against her before relaxing.

A brief fluttering of anger, true and unfiltered? Or another one of his many little manipulations? Shan would never know, but in the end, she supposed it didn't matter. His motivations were unimportant, because he was right.

"They underestimated you," he continued whispering in her ear, each passing word as soothing as a balm, pressing mortar into the cracks that she feared were starting to show, the long, slow eroding of the very foundation she had built her life on. "They thought they were above you, they let their judgement against your fool of a father and their prejudice against your mother prevent them from seeing all that you have to offer."

He pulled her closer as the song swung into its final movement, the low thrum of the strings reverberating in her very bones. Her hands clenched on his shoulders as he swung her around the dance floor, feeling as light as a feather in the safe comfort of his embrace. She could feel the heat of him, the awe-inspiring fount of power that swam beneath his veins, both a threat and a promise, and drunk on the potential of it, Shan wanted to run her fingers through the flames, even though she knew that it would only burn her.

The song came to an end, the sudden silence ringing in her ears as they broke apart. An ache unlike anything she had ever known settled over her, a loss so stark that she feared she would never recover as they bowed to each other. But he didn't let her go, not yet, catching her fingers as their claws brushed, steel against steel.

"I will never make that mistake," he swore, a solemn vow, as he bent low and pressed his mouth to the back of her hand. "I have always seen you, Shan, and I will assure your rise to glory, even if it's over the broken bodies of those who never would allow you to ascend."

When everything felt like it was one second from falling apart, here he had come, with enough confidence to bolster her. With a promise that he would never let her down, and, blood and steel, could she get addicted to this. She was standing on a precipice, and it would take nothing to follow the King over the edge, knowing that the fall would feel like flying—free and wondrous.

But Samuel stepped into her field of vision, holding out a pristinely gloved hand. "May I cut in?"

"Of course," the King said, with an affable smile. "Thank you for allowing me to dance with your extraordinary fiancée."

The two of them bantered back and forth, friendly as anything, but Shan could only hear the rush of blood in her ears and feel the bitter taste of shame in the back of her throat. Because here was Samuel, her beloved Samuel, good and kind and everything she struggled to be in the world, pulling her back from the brink without even realizing it.

She was weaker than even she had realized if the King was able to pull her strings so easily. If she wasn't even noticing it anymore.

Samuel's hand found her as the next song began, the floor filling with more couples after the King's display, and Shan forced a brilliant smile onto her face as he led her into the next dance.

Brow furrowing, Samuel didn't question the obvious falsehood of her cheer, but Shan knew that she was skating on thin ice, and it wouldn't be long before a single slight misstep would send her crashing to the frigid depths below.

The King didn't depart from the soirée after their dance, though he did not honor any of the other attendees by sharing the floor with them. Instead, he glided from group to group, sharing soft conversations with his fellow Blood Workers. Shan couldn't catch most of what he said, even if she was constantly aware of his movements, hovering at the edge of her awareness.

More approachable—more human—than she had ever known him.

And Shan wasn't the only one who noticed the stark change. Even hours later, as the party drifted through and past the midnight hour, the eyes on her were dark and appraising. Re-evaluating just who their new Royal Blood Worker was, and just how much influence she could exert.

This was a gift—Shan wasn't fool enough to dismiss it, as subtly given as it was. A single dance a currency more powerful than anything money could buy. The Eternal King continuing to lift her up, even when she thought she had nowhere higher to go.

The sound of glass shattering cut through the ballroom, along with the vilest string of curses she had ever heard in her life. The music came to sudden stop, as did all the ambient conversation, and Shan whipped around to find the source of the noise.

Sir Morse stood in front of Samuel, his face red and trembling with barely checked fury. The remains of his glass of mulled wine lay in pieces at their feet, delicate shards of crystal in a pool of deep red. Deeper than blood, and her magic didn't catch the low faint hum of power that indicated that either of them had been harmed in the tantrum. Though it looked that if she didn't step in soon, there was the very real possibility that it could change in a heartbeat.

Edward Morse had always been prone to violent solutions, and with the sneer he was sending Samuel's way, puffing up his chest to loom over her man, Shan feared that this might finally be his breaking point. The end of the tether she had hoped to keep Morse on, the reality of what Isaac was doing shattering the fragile state of peace that she had worked so hard for.

"You are a useless joke of a Councillor," Edward hissed, jabbing the tip of his claw against Samuel's chest. "How many of us have to die before you do the fucking job you were chosen for!"

Samuel, for his part didn't even flinch, his expression one of pure disdain, his gloved hands in his pockets as he refused to be bullied. And despite the vitriol that Morse continued to spew, spitting the name of the brutalized dead in Samuel's face—Brittney Arena, Zelda Holland, Vaughn Dabney—as if any of this had been his fault. He did not have it in him, his heart too good for such cruelties.

No, she knew where the blame lay, and as much as it hurt her to admit it, as much as she hoped that she could reach Isaac, as much as she had hoped to stop this before it got too far, she had realized with aching clarity that this road would only lead to disaster.

If Morse got his way, there would be war, bloodshed on the scale that her fool of a brother couldn't even comprehend, and Isaac was only adding fuel to the fire.

But that was a matter for another day. For now, she couldn't let this continue. As the hostess of the event, as the Royal Blood Worker, she was honor-bound to step in. As Samuel's fiancée, she was ready to smack his name right out of Morse's mouth.

Shan stepped away from the group she had been conversing with, Amelia giving her hand a squeeze of support before letting go, stepping a little harder than normal so that heels echoed on the marble floor. Sir Morse turned to face her as she arrived at their side, her hand pressing against the small of Samuel's back in a clear show of support, and Morse cut himself off mid-sentence, his anger clearly at war with his common sense as he remembered where he was and who was watching this altercation he had started.

If it wasn't bad enough that the eyes of the entire ton were on him, the Eternal King was mere feet away, his silence powerful and ominous as the seconds ticked on.

As the tension grew more pressing.

Tilting her head to the side, Shan furrowed her brow, concern dripping from each word, cloying and sweet. "You were saying, Edward?"

A bead of sweat peaked on his brow, rolling down his face as he stammered. "It's just ... just that I ... "

Samuel tilted his chin up, so regal, so casually unaffected that Shan had to swallow down a cry of pride. "Your concerns have been noted, Sir Morse, but suffice it to say that the Guard are investigating matters and any updates will come through official channels."

"Unless," the King said, speaking up for the first time, his low voice cutting like a knife, "you have some concerns about the way my nation is run."

Morse jerked away, turning to the King with a deep bow. "I would never insinuate—"

"Please." The King crossed his arms across his chest, and in that moment the resemblance between him and Samuel was uncanny. "You've gone a far step beyond insinuating, young man. Your grandmother would be so disappointed in your behavior. It is a shame that you inherited none of her wisdom or patience."

Morse flinched at the words, at the way the King threw his relationship to the much beloved Councillor of Military Affairs back in his face. A pointed reminder that they all knew exactly why he was this way, the boots he feared that he would never be able to fill, the legacy he wanted to live up to.

Even if it meant cementing it in blood and violence.

But Shan was nothing if not a politician, so she slipped around the side, resting a friendly hand on Morse's shoulder. "Clearly this was a case of the wine going to your head, wasn't it, Edward?"

He tensed under her touch but didn't brush her off, knowing that she was the only thing that stood between him and complete humiliation. Jaw clenched, Edward nodded jerkily. "The mulled wine was too delicious, my lady. I fear I overindulged."

"I cannot blame you," Shan replied, with a trilling little laugh. "It is a tense time, and we are all a little wound up." She summoned a serving girl with a flick of her wrist, a pale young thing who Shan would be sure to give a bonus to, when the party was done. "Prepare a pot of tea for Sir Morse, would you? Actually, have the kitchens send up a round of it to end the night."

The girl curtsied. "Of course, my lady."

Shan smiled back at Edward as the serving girl hurried away. "Perhaps some of the cake will help you sober up, Edward."

"Yes, of course," he mumbled, looking very much like he had been run over by a carriage. He inclined his head to the others, muttering a quick, "My lord, Your Majesty," before ambling off towards the much picked over dessert bar.

The musicians resumed their playing without even having to be told, and Shan was quite pleased at their professionalism, as conversations restarted in fits and bursts around them.

"Well done," the King said, stepping closer and closing the ring, a little huddle of privacy as everyone else politely turned away. "The both of you. I'm proud of how you handled him."

"Naturally," Shan said, twining her arm with Samuel's, a united couple standing together. He relaxed a little bit, some of the carefully constructed disdain fading with a sigh. "We couldn't let such crass sentiment pass unchallenged."

"Quite," the King agreed, then rubbed as his temples. "It was illuminating, however. There is much work to do, and I'll need the both of you. Soon."

"We are at your service," Shan said, in the same breath that Samuel muttered, "Obviously."

The King didn't call out Samuel's little flub, rubbing at his temple with a sigh. "Good. Good. Shan, I trust that you can see this soirée to the end. There are a couple of last-minute matters I need to see to."

He didn't come out and say it outright, but Shan knew what he referred to. Their latest test with Mel, out somewhere beyond the borders of Dameral. Now all the more pressing, given the unease that Morse had illustrated this very night.

Morse might not realize it, but they were doing far more work behind the scenes than he could even conceive of. Things even the esteemed Councillor of Law did not know of.

She only offered a demure smile. "I can. Samuel, will you make the rounds with me?"

He caught her fingers, raised her hand to his lips, pressing a small kiss to it—chaste and quick, but the relief in his eyes was clear. The thanks that she was sure would come later. "I am, as always, yours to command."

The King huffed a little laugh, clearly amused by them, but he slapped Samuel on the shoulder before leaving. "Look for my letters."

With that he was gone, slipping away from the party without so much as a look at Morse or any of the others.

"Well," Samuel said, with a little groan. "Back to work?"

Shan lifted a shoulder in a quick shrug. There was always more work to do, and it was only sheer luck that this night hadn't gone worse. But she didn't argue, leading him back around the ballroom once more.

Chapter Thirty-Five

Shan

Shan took a long drag on the cigarette, the harsh tang of the nicotine doing little to soothe her nerves. She shouldn't have been surprised. Nothing seemed to help these days, her entire body filled with a creeping sort of dread that left her wound tight, ready to snap at the smallest of things.

She stared at the burning tip, the paper turning to ash in her fingers, before she flung it out of the window. It disappeared behind her as the carriage rolled on, the harsh sound of the horses' hooves and clattering of the wheels echoing around her. The shadow of Dameral slipped away through the window as they left the capital behind, vanishing the longer they travelled out to the country—to a world beyond anything she had known.

She had grown up in the city, had built her entire life and power in its shadow. The wider world of Aeravin was beyond her experience, an intriguing and terrifying mystery, despite the handful of birds she had scattered across the various Academies.

That she *once* had scattered across the Academies, before duties as Royal Blood Worker had consumed her life, causing her network to slip through her fingers. It was in Bart's hands now, but in a better time, she would be using this opportunity to grow her network. Instead, she sat in this carriage for hours as the day slipped closer to evening and they approached the Aberforth country estate.

The King had need of her. Mel had need of her, chained as she was in the seat across from her, arms shackled in front of her, chains hanging between her ankles, mouth held fast with a muzzle. The bridge between them still burned strong, Shan having eased the girl into a restful slumber for the ride.

But though Mel didn't—couldn't—fight her, Shan could still feel the corruption oozing off her, a taint that tasted foul in the back of her mouth, like blood gone sour and thick. That filled her nose with the scent of something monstrous, the unpleasant aroma of fur in the rain. Oh, the girl looked human enough for the moment, but connected as they were, there was nothing she could do to hide the inhumanity that lurked beneath.

The inhumanity that Shan, however indirectly, had helped create, standing by the King's side as he fed Mel his blood time and again, pushing her to see just how far they could go.

Leaning her head against the edge of the window, Shan regretted tossing her cigarette away. She regretted not having something stronger—regretted not *being* stronger and ending up in this position in the first place.

But what choice did she have?

The road curved away from the ocean, leaving the ocean behind as they moved inward. The roads were shockingly empty, only the rare merchant's caravan passing by. Dameral got most of its trade by sea, but once travel between the capital and the rest of the nation had been a flourishing business.

Another casualty of the last year, then. Another change that had swept across her nation.

She leaned back in her seat with a sigh as they approached their destination, the large gate towering over them, the likeness of roses and thorns woven in dark metal bridging a high stone wall. The gatekeeper appeared, a slim figure in Aberforth livery, a spot of blood red against the darkness of the metal, winding the gate open for the carriage to pass through.

Shan couldn't help herself, she leaned closer to the window as the carriage moved on, turning to see the grand house appear before her. It truly was an estate, the home set far back with a wide stretch of manicured lawn between the wall and the house, the long path between disappearing under the steady hooves of the horses. Rose bushes bloomed their heady fragrance, stretching off to the side in neat rows, and the sudden assault of smells made her dizzy.

But she looked past it all to the building beyond, larger than anything she had ever seen aside from the palace, a grand structure of stone and marble three stories high. But its true magnificence was in its breadth. Shan couldn't even see the whole of it from her carriage window, entire wings kept from view, and even with all her knowledge and all her history, she couldn't begin to imagine owning such a space.

Even though, one day, it would be hers by right. The ring on her finger felt so heavy, the sparkling ruby a weight that threatened to pull her under. She tucked her hand off to the side, ignoring the promise it represented, and her loyalty to one of the men she loved.

He would never forgive her for this.

The carriage came to a stop at last, and Shan took a deep breath as the coachman stepped down, coming around to open the door for her—even here, in the middle of nowhere, far from the bustle of her home, propriety and manners still reigned. She was the Royal Blood Worker and must be treated as her station demanded.

She was so exhausted, but she schooled her expression into its usual calm mask before accepting the coachman's hand, stepping down onto the cobblestone path.

How odd, seeing such things so far from the city, but this estate had stood proud and tall for centuries. No doubt the Aberforths who came before had spent an obscene amount of money to bring every little luxury to themselves. Shan wondered if she would be like that, given enough time. Wealth like this was seductive, and after years of managing her family's investments with a careful hand, what would it be like to simply indulge?

But she didn't have the opportunity to think about it, dwarfed as she was by the grand structure. It loomed over her, a colossal beast of stone and brick in a style that felt timeless, a piece of history that still lived on. Grand windows flanked the massive wooden doors, easily twice as tall as she was, and she craned her neck to follow the rows of windows all the way to the end of the home, curtains drawn back to capitalize on the late afternoon sunshine, only to turn and repeat it for the other side.

Shan had never felt so small.

The doors opened before she could say a word, before she could even think about Mel and how to bring her inside. Shan drew herself up to her full height, folding her hands in front of her as the King stepped out, Samuel a half-step behind him.

Fear sank its claws deep in her gut, a sudden shock of shame washing as her voice caught in her throat. The King had said nothing of Samuel, and yet here he was, looking down at her with carefully arched eyebrow. The regal mask of Lord Aberforth firmly in place, only a flicker of doubt in his eyes before it was smoothed away.

"Beloved," he said, stepping around the King, coming down the stairs to take her hands. He pulled her in for a kiss, a quick tease against the lips, a bit of sweet affection between a man and his fiancée.

Shan didn't know if it was real or just part of his act—she had trained him too well. In some grand, terrible way, she had ruined him.

And any ire she earned this day would be deserved.

"Hello, love," she said, as he stepped back. "I did not know you'd be here to today."

"Well, His Majesty said it was time for me to see the full breadth of the Aberforth estate," Samuel said, smoothly. "And he was right. This trip has been illuminating."

Blood and steel, he hadn't even seen Mel yet. What secrets had the King revealed to him? Shan had tried—truly, honestly tried—to keep him safe, protect him from the darkest parts of her work.

But the King just stepped forward with that mean little smirk of his, and Shan wondered what cruel lesson he was imparting this time.

"I'm sure that Shan would love a tour, but first, we need to see to our other guest."

There was no more hiding it, then.

Shan turned towards the carriage, focusing on the bridge that burned in the back of her mind. She ran her fingers through the magic, pulling on it like strings on a harp, waking the girl from her slumber. Mel's magic still felt strange, even after all these hours connected, like Shan had dipped her hand into a still river, covered in moss and algae, catching on her skin like slime. Despite the oddness of the magic, it was still so easy to manipulate Mel, but Shan didn't know if that was her own skill or if Mel had simply stopped fighting.

The girl lurched out of the carriage, taking slow shuffling steps as Shan played her like a puppet. The chains around Mel's ankles jangling as she moved into place in front of the King, her arms still bound in front of her and her head hung low. If Mel noticed Samuel, she made no sign of it—she made no signs of noticing anything at all.

Despite the monster that Shan knew lurked deep within, there was nothing left inside the girl to struggle or rage. She was an empty vessel for the magic the King had stoked within her, and Shan was nothing more than her jailer.

Samuel's mask didn't falter as he took in the poor creature, but he did turn away a shade too quickly, as if unable to look at it head-on.

The King reached out, taking Mel's hand as the other dragged a claw against her inner wrist, the skin splitting easily. She didn't even flinch as the blood dribbled out, dark as ink, viscous and slow. Raising her arm, the King dragged his tongue against it, lapping it like a cat.

Shan could feel the instant the King's magic brushed hers, the overwhelming aura of power that lurked within him. If Mel's magic was like a dark, fetid pool, the King's magic was a boundless wildfire held by the thinnest of strings. Its warmth and glow were a seductive beacon, luring her in, but it would take nothing at all to set it free, leaving nothing but ashes in its wake.

Glancing at Shan, the King offered a chilling smile. Though they weren't directly connected, their magics were still close enough to brush. He knew that she could feel his power, that it would only take a tiny bit of effort for him to taste her fear and awe. "I have it from here, Shan. I plan to run some tests with her before our experiment in the morning."

She severed the connection immediately, the bridge disintegrating into nothingness as it all faded away.

With a simple flick of the wrist, the King dismissed both Shan and Samuel. And some terrible, cowardly part of Shan was grateful—the ride over had been tense and stifling, and she appreciated the opportunity to freshen up before the horrors began.

And, as Samuel carefully took her arm, her claw-tipped fingers digging into the silk of his suit, the time to salvage what she could of her fiancé's faith in her.

Samuel let her into the estate without a word, pulling her through the foyer, their footsteps clipping on the hard marble, echoing up to the ceiling far above their heads. The grand staircase directly ahead curved upwards towards the next floor before bending back around again, a tiered series of landings looking down at the entryway. A chandelier fueled by witch light hung above their heads, the eerie red glow refracted through all the crystals, sending slim beams of light dancing around them.

Hallways split off to each side, no doubt to sitting rooms and ballrooms and dining rooms, the estate large enough to host all of Dameral's elite, if the need called for it. But Samuel didn't lead her down those paths, guiding her towards the staircase, following in the footsteps of servants she hadn't even noticed, carrying the luggage that they must have pulled from the carriage while she was distracted.

She tried to blame it on Mel, on the magic, on the King, but she knew that Samuel's appearance had thrown her off her game. And if she was going to make it through the rest of the trip unscathed, she needed to focus.

Samuel led her up the staircase and to the third level, whisking her away to more private areas of the estate. Like the King's personal chambers, the Aberforth country home was filled with art, pieces of priceless history hung upon the walls, landscapes highlighting the beauty and breadth of Aeravin's natural scenery, grand tapestries that depicted the rise of the nation and the life of the Eternal King, cold and imposing sculptures of people who could only have been Aberforths.

It wasn't a home, it was a museum and mausoleum, a tribute to those long gone. It was a fitting estate for the Aberforths, and not even a year ago Shan would have called it a microcosm of what was wrong with the Eternal King. But that was before she learned the price of power, and the inevitability of one who dared to be Eternal.

"This is for you, Shan," he said, leading her into what was clearly the chambers for the Lady of the estate, but there was no affection in his voice. Just a weariness that even he could not hide as he dismissed the servants.

Shan detached herself from him, drifting through the room. It was larger than even she had expected, done in soft colors—light pinks and peaches and creams. There was a balcony off to the side, and she was sure it had the most charming view of their lands, but the bulk of the room was taken up by a large canopy bed that could easily sleep five. But it was meant for her and her alone, judging by the interior door just off to the side, a style that was centuries old, when partners had slept in separate chambers.

It hadn't been the standard practice in generations, but this home was older than modern traditions, and as they were not yet married, it would do nicely. Intimate, should they decide on it, but still appropriate for a woman of her standing.

Shan hated it—Samuel should be at her side, but there was every opportunity for him to slip away, locking the door behind him. A physical barrier just as strong as this growing void between them.

He stood so close; it would take nothing to reach out and touch him. But he held himself apart, arms crossed over his chest, his expression grave and forbidding. Colder than she had ever seen him, and she knew, deep in her heart, that she was the reason for all the changes.

"So," she said, finally breaking the silence. "You're here."

"I am," Samuel said, not relaxing an inch. "And *you* didn't come alone."

Shan pressed her hand against her head, trying to stop the throbbing headache that was threatening to break loose. "I'm too tired for games, Samuel, please just tell me what he told you."

Her plea worked, the harsh edges fading from him with a sigh. But he still didn't approach her. "Not much, truthfully. Just that you were doing work that was *important to the stability of Aeravin*, whatever that means. I just didn't expect to see . . ."

He trailed off, and Shan swallowed past the dryness in her throat. "It was determined best to keep her sedated, for the safety of herself and others."

Samuel just arched an eyebrow, so imperious. So regal. "And that poor girl was a threat to the Royal Blood Worker? She could barely lift her head!"

"You haven't seen what she is capable of," Shan replied, the memory of the monster's viciousness burned into the back of her mind. "What we've made her. I hoped you'd never have to see it."

"You won't get your wish." Samuel tilted his chin up, stubborn as always. "The King already requested that I be there tomorrow, in my official capacity as Councillor of Law."

Shan sank onto the edge of the bed, the plush sheets soft under her fingers as she struggled to ground herself. So, this was the King's aim, then. Shock Samuel into compliance or break him completely. Force him to stare directly into the darkness and see what remained.

And she had laid the groundwork, hadn't she? It had been a slow and careful transformation, taking the kind man she had found and carving away all his soft and gentle bits until all that remained was Lord Aberforth. She had wrapped him around her finger, bound him to her in every possible way, dismissing all of his very valid concerns with sweet words and physical distractions.

All this time she had thought it was the Eternal King who was the monster, but she was just as capable of cruelty and viciousness as he was. She could no longer hide behind the lies she wove around herself.

She just hoped that when Samuel saw the truth, he wouldn't flinch away from her. Her brother had already left her, she had already ended things with Isaac. If she lost Samuel as well—

She didn't know what she would become.

But cruel as she was, cunning as she was, she still couldn't put that weight on him. Not so boldly. Instead, she tapped the bed beside her. "Can you hold me, just for a moment?"

Samuel didn't move, just looked down at her with suspicion. "There are things that I need to do."

The fracture in her heart grew wider, and Shan knew she was on the verge of total collapse. But when she spoke, her voice was clear. Empty. "I understand. I will see you later, then."

Samuel inclined his head, then strode from the room, leaving her alone with her thoughts.

She dug the tips of her claws into her flesh, using the sharp bite of pain to drive away the tears before they fell.

Chapter Thirty-Six

Samuel

Samuel stood on the edge of the lawn, snow crunching under his boots and flurries swirling in his face. In the summer, Samuel was told, it would be a grand courtyard lined with rose bushes and other greenery, a perfect spot for outdoor galas under the light of the sun. Now, it was little more than a field, the small bumps of the bushes reduced to ridges under the snowfall.

The cold was like nothing he had ever felt, somehow both sharper and deeper than the frigid nights of Dameral. Here, nearly a full day's hard travel from the seaside, winter bit with a harsh grip, reaching down to his very bones with a chill he hadn't be able to shake. He wore a thick wool coat, bundled with a scarf and a knitted cap pulled down over his ears, thick leather gloves stiff around the fingers bundled in his pockets.

It barely helped.

Still, he patrolled the perimeter with his King, forming a giant square between the wings of the house. There were small lanterns of brass and glass placed every several feet, the soft burn of witch light protected from the elements in the soft morning light. The King paced to each one, squatting down to drip one drop of blood into the waiting fire of each through a small funnel in the top. Power burst out from contact, reaching for the next link in the chain, the ward in progress.

"It's less reliable," the King said as they moved to the next lantern, "than more permanent wards. You saw that little piece of ingenuity in the palace libraries, correct?"

"Yes, I did," Samuel breathed, closing his eyes as the King attended to the next link. Those meetings with Isaac, the electric touch of magic washing over Samuel's skin, the brush of Isaac's voice against his ear. Hells, Samuel missed those days, when things were simpler. When he still had hope for a better future.

"Well," the King continued, leading him on, "while I am proud of that, the shifting of the earth beneath our feet is not conducive to maintaining the strong barrier of a ward, and this—" He stopped to fill the last of the line before turning to finish the circuit. "This does have its advantages, though."

"It's portable," Samuel said, the first thing that came to mind. On a different day, he would have appreciated the lesson, but with the weight of the last few weeks on his soul, all he wanted was for this to be over. "Adaptable."

The King hummed in response. "Exactly. Once all this nonsense is handled, we'll finish your education. You have such potential, Samuel, especially now."

The King rarely alluded to it, and never discussed it outright, the way that Isaac had ripped Samuel's gift from him, had taken the very thing the King had seen as most valuable. It was a bitter thought, the darkness that stirred in his chest, that wondered if he would have been better off if Isaac had never cured him. If it would have been easier to be a weapon of personal vengeance than a tool of the systemic oppression.

If he could have learned to live with blood on his hands, if it was the right person's blood.

But it didn't matter, not with the way things had turned out. Not with his power creeping back into his body, an infection of ivy weaving itself up around him until he feared he would suffocate. But the King couldn't know about that, another secret. He was getting nearly as good as Shan was, deflecting away from anything too dangerous with a simple shift in conversation. "Might I ask what we need this protection for?"

The King didn't respond, finishing with a final drop of blood as the ward flashed to life, a nearly invisible shimmer in the snow. Samuel couldn't quite see it, but he could feel the hum on the air, taste the magic on the back of his tongue. Then the King reached out, pulling one of the lanterns out of place, and the whole thing shattered.

"There, we're set, all we need are the pieces." The King gave him that too cunning smile, bright white teeth flashing in the thin light of morning. "And why, this is a demonstration—a test—that my esteemed Councillor of Law should see."

He grit his teeth, muttering a low curse. "I had considered inviting Dabney as well, as it would have greatly affected his work. But de la Cruz took that decision out of my hands. Clever bastard."

Samuel didn't disagree with the assessment but figured it wouldn't be helpful to voice it, especially as the decision to target Dabney had been his own. "What will you be demonstrating?"

"Oh, it won't be me doing the demonstration."

And suddenly Samuel understood. It wasn't the King or even the Royal Blood Worker, it wasn't a display of power. It was something they had created, and he would bet everything he owned that the poor girl Shan brought the previous night would be involved. That the girl was a vampire.

Hells, Shan. What had she gotten herself into?

The King pulled out a pocket watch, checking the time just as the doors to the estate opened, two of the King's personal guard marching out yet another prisoner, someone that Samuel didn't recognize.

He wasn't dressed for the weather, wearing thin trousers and a threadbare jacket, wasn't prepared for the cold bite of winter. He blinked in the uncomfortable burn of sun against the snow, unable to even lift a hand to shield his eyes. He was young, thirty at most, like so many of Aeravin's condemned—pasty and thin and looking so under cared for that Samuel felt sick to his stomach.

Had the King claimed him from one of the many jails across the country, or did he have his own private collection to choose from, test subjects that he could pull from on a whim? Shouldn't something like that be one of the secrets that Samuel was privy to, as the King's heir or as his Councillor of Law?

Or did none of it matter, because what was Samuel but one of the Eternal King's many puppets?

The Guards unchained the man, shoving him into the courtyard. The King had returned the lantern to its place before the prisoner had even hit the snow. It was pointless—Samuel had seen that kind of hopelessness before. He wouldn't have run. Not that there was anywhere for him to run to.

The King didn't so much as look at the prisoner. "Tell the Royal Blood Worker it is time."

"As you say, Your Majesty."

Samuel watched them trek through the soft fall of snow, disappearing back into the estate. Samuel turned his attention to the prisoner, shivering in the cold. The man had his arms wrapped around his middle, head tucked in as he tried to fold in on himself, as if he could keep his body heat trapped. It wouldn't help for long, and though Samuel did not know the King's plan, he couldn't help but think this little added cruelty was a bonus.

Samuel forced out a question. "What's your name, sir?"

The man looked up at him, dark eyes wide and mouth set in a thin line. Samuel thought he wasn't going to respond—what difference did it make, anyway? But the man chanced a glance at the Eternal King, then swallowed hard. "Matt. I'm Matthew."

"Matthew," Samuel echoed. It wasn't much, but he could at least remember this man. The absolute bare minimum, and still more than the King would offer.

The door to the estate opened once again, and this time it was Shan, fresh-faced and toasty. She was draped in a cloak the same hue as her official robes of office, the hood up to protect her face. It was a thick velvet, lined with what appeared to be real fur, and Samuel hadn't realized she'd even had this outfit commissioned.

It wasn't like they had even had snowfall like this in Dameral, and for what little business they had outside of the capital, it was a gross indulgence. A sliver of his old hate rose in him, disgusted by the casual and wasteful displays of wealth.

He couldn't swallow it down, not completely. So, he took the ember and held it close, a cage around his too tender heart, before it got him into trouble once again.

Behind Shan came the girl from the previous day. Unlike Matthew, she looked hale and hearty—strong and well cared for—except for the listlessness to her movements, the blankness of her eyes, as she followed mutely behind Shan. She wore only a loose linen dress, her bare feet leaving indents in the snow. But she didn't seem bothered by the freeze.

She didn't seem bothered by anything at all.

It was only then that Samuel thought to look for it, the low buzz of Blood Working on the air. Shan was doing something to the girl, keeping her calm and complacent, even if he didn't have the skill or knowledge to understand *how*.

Shan came to a stop beside him, ignoring the questioning look he gave her, her brow furrowed as the girl moved towards the edge of the ward, Shan acting the puppeteer. The King deigned to assist, snatching a lantern back just long enough for the girl to step through, before placing it back.

Locking them both inside.

Matthew looked from the girl to the King and back again, confusion clear on his face, confusion that was mirrored in Samuel. But neither King nor Royal Blood Worker would show their hand in advance, so Samuel ignored the burning curiosity and the sick fear that swirled in him, a disorienting mix that left him unmoored.

Shan broke the bridge, the magic snapping away as the girl blinked, slowly, awareness creeping back into her eyes. She spun in a circle, her golden hair shining as the flurries swirled around her, a picture of ethereal innocence, a maiden in a snow-globe, turning her face up to the sky like she hadn't seen freedom in months.

"Where..." she asked, her voice low in her throat, like the rasp of early morning, compounded by suffering that Samuel couldn't even comprehend. "Am I?"

"Thank you for joining us, Mel," the King said, his rich baritone cutting through the frigid air. "You've been brought to the Aberforth country estate, where you will demonstrate the skills you have gained under our tutelage."

Mel didn't respond, just licked her lips, her pale tongue flicking out, almost as if she was scenting the air.

And hells, Samuel had seen that motion before, on Isaac.

He reached out, gloved fingers brushing against Shan's, and she cast him a look so tentative and fearful that he hardly recognized her. That brief bite of shame was somehow worse than any defiance that she could have thrown his way, because she knew that he would never approve of what she had done, and suddenly, every little deflection, every half-muttered denial, was pulled into sharp focus.

He dropped her hand like it burned him, but Shan just stepped towards the ward, all signs of her vulnerability gone. "It's simple, Mel. You are to demonstrate your power and abilities to Lord Aberforth, the Councillor of Law."

"Think of it as a proof of concept," the King added, not to the girl but to Samuel, that cruel little smirk testing his patience. "If de la Cruz is going to sow chaos, then we will meet him on the battleground he chose."

Bile rose in his throat—this was far worse than any of them had anticipated. But this is why he remained, why he hadn't thrown off the yoke that the Eternal King had set upon his shoulders. And since they couldn't trust Shan to risk the slow-seeded plans that she kept close to her chest, this was why Samuel needed to be here. It would be worth it for the intelligence he gained—and for that alone, he would watch this scene unfold.

"Mel," the King said, turning those hard eyes back on the girl. "I am sure you are hungry. So, hunt."

"Wait, what?" Matthew asked, staggering back as Mel turned to face him, swift as a snake striking, her entire pose going still as her body *rippled*. "What the fuck?"

"Run, my boy," the King said. "Run if you can."

A sadistic taunt, if Samuel had ever heard one, because there was nowhere for Matthew to run, trapped within the ward with the girl who was no longer a girl. Whose humanity broke and shattered, great dark wings springing from her back, spine hunching over her bones re-formed. Hands and feet twisted, sharp claws sprouting from soft nail beds, talons to rip and tear. Her jaw lengthened, fangs pressing past her lips, her nose shriveled up small like a bat's, head tilted to the side as she listened. As she tracked the shuffling, whimpering cries of Matthew as he scrambled back.

A shriek pierced the air, shrill and sharp, the very sound of it activating some primitive instinct to flee.

Samuel remained rooted where he was, safe behind the wards made by the Eternal King himself, but he had never known a horror as acute or all-encompassing as he did in that moment. Mel was no longer a girl at all, but a fierce predator out of nightmares, built by Blood Working and hells knew whose blood.

A vampire, come to life.

The details of her transformation were different than Isaac's—a shared history before they split along a divergent evolutionary path. There was some reason for it, something fiddly and academic that was far beyond Samuel's understanding, but he knew what Isaac had become. And feral as it was, like a creature out of a mythological horror, if Anton had been correct, Isaac still had a spark of humanity left to him. His hunger was immense, but his intellect still drove him.

But Mel lacked that, little more than a beast as she went after Matthew, wings flapping and launching her up in the air. They spread wide, catching the breeze, lifting her into the sky as she screeched again, and Samuel recognized what it was.

A cry of joy, of freedom, before Mel twisted in the air, swooping down to make a pass at the man the King had decided would be her breakfast.

Her talons brushed against his chest, a hair's breadth from slicing him open, but the momentum of it enough to send Matthew teetering backwards, tripping over a rose bush and tumbling through the snow, flecks of white sticking to his thin coat as he struggled to regain his footing. Mel just circled back around, gliding in from behind, slamming her feet into Matthew's back so that he fell face-forward.

Blood and steel, Mel was playing with him, toying with her food like it was some sort of game, reveling in his fear. Taking shallow sweeps at him, slicing his skin so that blood welled to the surface, spilling bright red upon the blinding snow.

Samuel chanced a glance at those next to him, but Shan remained as serene as ever, the shadows of her hood hiding the details of her expression. But the King was positively brimming with energy, with pride, as he watched Mel corral Matthew back and forth, a hound chasing a fox.

"She's magnificent, isn't she?" The King tilted his head back, looking upon her with awe. "Shan can tell you more about the theory behind the Blood Working, but the actual process took less than you would think. We can build up a full squad of these Guards in a matter of months."

"Guards?" Samuel echoed, the fear taking shape into something he didn't dare look at head-on.

"Elite Guards," the King confirmed, decisively. It wasn't an offer, but a demand—a new policy that the King was happy to put in place without a vote. Because what Samuel thought, what the Royal Council thought, what anyone with any sense of decency thought did not matter. The King saw a very real threat on the horizon, and so he had built the perfect countermeasure, fighting fire with fire.

Hells, what were they going to do about this?

Mel finally grew tired of her games, driving him closer to where they were standing before landing hard on Matthew's chest. There was the sickening crunch of bone snapping. Matthew sobbed as he tried to pull out from under her, but the creature grabbed him by the hair, slamming his head into the ground hard. Blood pooled underneath it, and Mel leaned forward, lapping it up, looking up at the King like a well-trained dog.

Samuel had been wrong—she wasn't a full beast. She knew exactly what she was doing, turning this hunt into a show for the King's benefit.

For *his* benefit.

Mel tore into Matthew with a viciousness that stunned Samuel, blood splattering up onto the ward, where it hit with a loud sizzle before burning away. Samuel wished it hadn't, wished the spray of blood had acted like a curtain, but he had an uninterrupted view of Mel feeding.

No, feeding wasn't the right word. She *feasted* on Matthew, her teeth slicing through the column of his throat, shredding it to thin layers of meat as she drank him dry. The light left his eyes as the trauma of what was done to him overwhelmed his body, but something as simple as death didn't stop the meal.

She moved from his neck to his wrist, from the wrist to the large artery in his thigh, biting straight through his pants and burying her face between his legs. Swapping from side to side, nuzzling against the cooling flesh, until she drank every last drop. Leaving him a dry and ruined husk, but far more whole than the bodies that Isaac had left. Not unlike what the King did, yearly, in front of a crowd of cheering citizens.

It was the natural evolution of everything Aeravin stood for, and as Mel settled back on her haunches, face turned up to them, covered in blood and gore, slick fluids dripping down her chin, Samuel saw the violent future that awaited them in the endless hunger of the beast.

It was too much for Samuel—he turned away, staggered to the edge of the patio, and vomited over the edge.

The bile was bitter, the smell of his own sick filling his nose as he fell to his knees. But a soft hand landed on the small of his back, rubbing soft circles. "I'm sorry," Shan whispered in his ear, and Samuel didn't know what for.

For her hand in this, for the way he found out, for the fear that hung between them—the uncertainty of whether or not he could ever forgive her. She looked at him, just a second away from pleading, but Samuel turned away.

He couldn't handle this, not right now.

"Why don't you take our Councillor inside, Lady LeClaire," the King said, flatly. "Get him something to settle that weak stomach of his. I'll handle Mel."

Samuel winced, knowing that he had failed the King's test, dashed the King's hopes yet again with his weakness. No matter how hard he tried, no matter how perfect his Lord Aberforth mask became, he would still falter at the worst of it. He would never be able to harden his heart enough to be the Blood Worker his ancestor wanted him to be, and as Shan led him back into the Aberforth's grand country house, he prayed that this wouldn't be the last time he failed the King.

He just needed to make it through the rest of this trip, needed to make it back to the capital to warn Isaac and Anton what was coming.

If he could do that much, then this all would have been worth it.

But as Shan pressed the tips of her claws against his back, steering him towards warmth and comfort, he realized that he was in far more trouble than he first thought.

Because if Shan had been willing to do this, just how far would she go to keep the King's favor?

—✦—

Samuel was still so cold, the chill having seeped into his bones despite the roaring fire that Shan had placed him by, the couch turned to face it and the heat rolling off it. The entire sitting room was designed to be effortlessly cozy, draped in deep earthen colors, the warmth of the world at rest. The rug under their feet thick and soft, the kind that Samuel wanted to sink his bare toes into, and the curtains across the windows held back the relentless creep of winter, a shield of deep green velvet, colored like the vibrant forests that Samuel never had the chance to see. She had stripped him of his coat and gloves and scarf, bundling him tight in a soft woolen blanket, but Samuel still felt the grip of ice around his heart, and he feared that it would never melt.

Shan pressed a steaming cup of tea into his hands, holding it there for a moment longer than necessary, the weight of her claws against his bare fingers a surprisingly comforting squeeze. They remained like that, the tea warming his fingers and the soft scent of rose hips floral and fragrant between them.

She hadn't said a word since she had ushered him inside, treating him like he was made of the thinnest, most fragile of glass—ready to shatter under the slightest pressure. But now, next to each other, close enough to touch, Shan finally turned her dark eyes to him, pain and regret written across her very expression.

For once, wearing her emotions openly, not hiding them away behind layers she was too afraid to shed.

"Samuel, I—" she began, only for the door to the sitting room to burst open, the King standing there, looking regal as always. He, too, had shed his coat and gloves, but his cheeks were still ruddy from the bite of the cold, looking so much more human and alive than Samuel had ever seen.

Shan's expression shuttered immediately, and Samuel knew that whatever moment of honesty they could have had was lost forever.

"Ah, tea," the King said, stepping forward to pour himself some. "What a lovely idea, thank you, Shan."

Samuel only then noticed that there were three cups with the pot. This had been Shan's intention all along, waiting for the King to join them. How much of her life had been spent revolving around him, the star around which her entire life and plans had orbited?

He had been so, so foolish to expect her to break free of the King's gravitational pull.

The King settled into the armchair across from them, leg crossed over his knee, cup balanced perfectly in his hands. "That was an illuminating demonstration, don't you think?"

The question was aimed at him, Samuel was sure of that, but Shan inclined her head, putting herself in the line of fire to protect him. "Mel's control has grown significantly."

"I am aware," the King replied, smug as a cat who had gotten into the bowl of cream. "But I was speaking to my Councillor."

Samuel swallowed against the renewed burn of bile in the back of his throat, clutching his cup even more tightly. "It was. I cannot deny the Guards of... that caliber would be quite impressive."

"Impressive indeed." The King smirked, a flash of sharp teeth that seemed almost primal. "Given your reaction, I was worried that you would find it too... grotesque."

Samuel steeled himself. It was clear that he had failed the first test, but he couldn't falter here. He had to make it through this, just a little longer. "I will not lie and say that I was not... disturbed by seeing the..."

"That is understandable," Shan said, placing her hand on his thigh, a small show of solidarity that, despite the tension between them, was still much appreciated. "I found our early experiments with Mel just as disturbing, and I have far more experience in Blood Working than you do."

The King didn't respond, tapping the tip of his claw against his cup as he thought. "Shan raises a good point. You've grown so much in the past few months, Samuel, that sometimes it's easy to forget that you were not born among us."

"I still have a lot to learn," Samuel said, the closest thing to agreement that he could manage.

"You do," the King said, "and the honesty of your reaction to Mel's gifts is a helpful bit of data." The feral smile was back, his eyes hard and glinting like jewels. "If even my most esteemed Councillor of Law was this overcome, the fools who are disrupting the peace of my nation will not be able to handle it."

Placing his empty cup to the side, the King leaned back in the armchair, as grand as if he was on a throne and they were just penitents at his feet. Judgement was awaiting them, and Samuel clenched his hands at his side, breath caught in his throat as he waited.

"But," the King said at last, having drawn out the moment like he had delighted in the fear and uncertainty, "here you are, ready to accept the unfortunate necessity of what comes next."

Samuel released his breath—it felt like a stay of execution. But it wasn't grace that the King was offering. No, this would be the rest of his life, should he choose not to fight it.

This could not be what Shan wanted with her plans and schemes. Once, she had sworn that she would take the Eternal King down by any means necessary, but here she was, not only listening but making these atrocities possible.

The King continued, "I did not want to have to do this. Once the power of Blood Working is shown to the world, there will be no stepping back. It's a new age for Aeravin, one that Isaac de la Cruz has ushered in with his foolhardy schemes."

Oh, yes, Isaac had started this all, but Samuel wouldn't let his work be tossed aside. Isaac had started it, Shan had enabled it, but Samuel would be the one to end it.

Even if it was the last thing he did.

Chapter Thirty-Seven

Shan

The discussions with the King lasted all day, the shape and details of his plans coming to life as Shan transcribed them furiously in her small journal. Later, when she returned to the capital, she'd have her secretary copy it out to send to Samuel's office, go over it with her to translate her scribbled shorthand into something legible.

Not that it would matter much in the end. Despite his role, Samuel had barely been able to get a word in edgewise, and it had become increasingly clear as the hours dragged on that the King cared little for Samuel's input. Her, he treated like an ally, actively seeking her advice as they sketched out a plan for how this elite Guard would be created.

While Samuel just sat there and stewed, his untouched tea going cold in its cup.

The conversation carried past dinner and well into the night before the King dismissed them. Shan, his clever little assistant, would stay here in the countryside with him, running more tests on Mel, seeing how far her skills extended. By the time they were done, Shan was sure there would be a pile of bodies left to burn, all sacrificed to the altar of knowledge. The price that the King would gladly pay for stability in Aeravin. And Shan would pay that price with him. Though she had never signed up to be Royal Blood Worker, she knew that she couldn't flinch away from this. Not unless she wanted to end up like Isaac.

Blood and steel, *Isaac*. What hells had he brought down upon them? And why did it have to fall on her to clean it all up?

There was a storm coming, and she just hoped that she could get them all through this alive. But that was a problem for the morning, now there was something more important to focus on.

Samuel had slipped away from them as soon as possible, locking himself in his room to rest for the evening. And while she didn't blame him in the slightest, she needed to speak to him. Though she was thankful that the King had determined that Samuel's part in this was done, she couldn't let him slip away when there was so much unsaid between them.

She knocked twice on the door that separated their bedchambers, the sharp rap echoing in the tense silence.

"Come in, Shan."

The door opened easily under her touch—unlocked, then, though that surprised her. With the chilly way he had been treating her all day, and after the brief but violent glimpse he got into her private dealings with the King, she wouldn't have blamed him if he had locked her out.

If he never let her in, ever again.

Stepping through the doorway, her breath caught in her throat as she took in the room. The master's chamber was as indulgent as the rest of the house, even grander than the spouse's chamber where she had spent the last night. A large four-poster bed took up the heart of the room, covered in silk sheets and plush pillows. The walls were covered in detailed wallpaper that looked surprisingly modern, Shan had seen the same shades of blue in fine houses across Dameral.

The King must have had it redone, then. A gift to his heir, though Samuel would spend little time outside of the capital. She ignored the finery—the well-made furniture, solid and aged, but cared for in a way that made Shan think they must be heirlooms. Fine paintings hung on the wall, faces she did not recognize but all having the same shocking blond hair, the same glittering green eyes.

She didn't care about the Aberforths that came before, she didn't care about the Eternal King and his endless schemes. In that moment, all she cared about was Samuel.

He was sprawled in an armchair that he had dragged close to the fire, as if he was desperate to be as close to the warmth as possible, his jacket discarded and his cravat pulled loose. He had lost his gloves in the past hour, rolling up his sleeves to show the bare length of his forearms, the dark lines of his scars still as stark as the day he received them.

Shan crept closer, flinching as real flames crackled, untouched by Blood Working. The log crackled merrily, filling the room with a soft, smoky scent that felt surprisingly comforting.

Samuel didn't even look up at her, raising a glass to his lips, the glint of amber catching her attention.

"You're drinking." It wasn't a question, and Samuel huffed, his only response to down the rest of it. "I didn't realize you drank."

He leaned forward, placing the glass on the mantle. "Things change."

"That they do." She twisted the ring on her finger, a restless tic that she shouldn't indulge, lest it became a habit, a tell that would give her away. But she shouldn't have to worry about that, not with Samuel.

Habits were a hard thing to break, even now.

"I thought we should talk."

Samuel leaned back in his chair, chin tilted towards her, looking up at her with that unwavering, righteous sense of judgement. Even though she was the one standing, she still felt so small in front of him, like he was the King she once thought she could make him. But that was before she knew the steel at his heart, unflinching and uncompromising, and before she had fallen so terribly in love with him.

He was the purest, most good-hearted man she had known, and she wanted nothing more than to fall at his feet. To rip out every little doubt that had wormed its way into her chest, to find the exact right sequence of words to explain that she had no choice.

That *they* had no choice, not if they wanted to survive in this court of blood.

But she remained upright, because if it was to be the end of everything they had, she would face it with her head held high.

Samuel rolled his hand at the wrist, a motion she had seen the King make so many times—telling her to carry on.

"I should have told you sooner," she said, starting at the beginning. An admission of fault, such as it was. "Helped prepare you for this."

"Prepare me," Samuel echoed, and Shan winced at how empty his voice sounded. "Why didn't you?"

It was a simple question, and one Shan wished she had a good answer for. The lies were already sitting on the tip of her tongue, but she swallowed them down like acid, burning herself from the inside out. "To protect you."

"Of course." He ran his hand over his eyes, and Shan felt her stomach clench in fear. "Always looking out for me, aren't you? Always making sure I don't get too distressed, or see something too painful, or get my hands too dirty. Distracting me every time I tried to push for answers. I don't know why I expected anything different."

"Samuel—" She reached out, but he stood abruptly, stepping to the side so that she couldn't touch him, catching the edge of the chair instead.

"Don't touch me!" he snapped, and Shan flinched back at the harshness of his words, the sliver of darkness that hung between them. The gift that they had both hoped was gone, slinking around her, shackles waiting to lock closed. Not that he needed to use his gift. If he did not want her to touch him, she wouldn't.

It still hurt, all the same.

She gripped the chair tighter, uncaring that her claws sliced through the soft velvet, forest green against metallic silver. Gouges that would not easily be fixed, a wound that would scar forever. "I didn't mean to hurt you."

He finally smiled, though it was something soft and broken. "You never do, not really. Just like you never meant to hurt your brother. Never meant to hurt Isaac."

"Don't—" Shan hissed, as though she expected the King to saunter into the room, to catch them in something terribly close to treason. "Don't mention him."

"We are safe here, Shan," Samuel countered. "Unless there is another reason you don't want to talk about him."

"I—" She cut herself off, rather than fumble for the words she did not have. Samuel gave her the time she needed, as she pulled each syllable out piece by piece, the words catching in her throat like shards of glass.

"I love him," she whispered, a confession that she did not know would cost her so much. "But I cannot let him destroy this country. Samuel, you must understand that everything he does, every escalation he takes, the King will match him. And do so much worse in retaliation."

Warm hands landed on her shoulders, the touch of bare skin on hers searing. But Samuel didn't pull her close, didn't give her the opportunity to lose her worry and her cares in the simple release of their bodies. The way she had done with him so many times now, because it was easier that way. To use her body to say the things she was unable to vocalize, but oh, how he had misunderstood her.

She had never meant it to be a slight.

He just steered her into the seat, kneeling in front of her to hold her hand—chaste, gentle, kind. Forcing her to look him in the eye as he pressed her to continue speaking, to mine her every pain, excavating it like a precious gem to be measured and polished.

"I know you're frightened, Shan," Samuel said, thumbs slipping under the chains of her claws, holding her fast. "I am too. But that doesn't mean that you have to play by the King's rules."

Blood and steel, how she wished it could be that simple. "If we don't, then there will be war."

"And sometimes," Samuel returned, shattering her already

fragile heart, "that is a price we're willing to pay, because this is not sustainable."

"Samuel—"

"Once, you told me that you wanted someone else on the throne."

Why was he bringing this up? Solely to force her to confront plans that seemed so childishly idealistic in hindsight? He wasn't that cruel. "You didn't want it."

"And I still don't. I still don't think that anyone should have a throne at all." He leaned in, his words a whisper, an offering of his most fervent hopes and his wildest dreams. "And we can change that, Shan. All you have to do is stand with us."

"Us?" The single word burned on her lips as realization came crashing through her, all their conversations and decisions of the past few months reframed as she understood the breadth of the tapestry before her. "It was more than saving him. You've been on his side this entire time."

Samuel didn't so much as blink. "I do not understand how this could be a surprise. I gave so many signs."

He had, but she had refused to see them, as if by turning her face from it their problems would disappear. She had refused to see it because she couldn't bear the fact that the one good thing in her life wasn't good at all.

"You," she all but gasped, the pain of it so intense that she thought it might tear her in two, "you were supposed to be on my side."

"Shan," he chastised, like she was a child acting out, like he was so tired of her excuses and deflections. "This isn't about sides. It's never been about sides, and you know that. It's about what is *right*."

"And Isaac killing his way through the Blood Workers of Aeravin," Shan snarled, "that is *right*?"

"Yes," Samuel replied with that stone-cold certainty of his. "Because each and every one of them is an active participant in the King's plans. They live off the stolen blood, they built a society that keeps the Unblooded in their place, in the mud beneath their boots."

Each new point felt like a nail hammered into the coffin, another slap to the face. But Samuel was far from done. "None of them are innocent, Shan, and though I never expected you to fully understand the horrors of the world that you were born to, I had hope that you were serious about the claims that you wanted to change Aeravin for the better."

"I do—"

"You don't," Samuel interrupted her, "not really. You wanted your brother safe. You wanted me safe. You want those Unblooded you care for to be protected, but you don't care about the *Unblooded*."

Shan ripped her hands out of his, covered her face as she felt the tears start to threaten. Because—he wasn't wrong. It was a truth she kept hidden for so long, even from herself. She had wrapped it in trappings of love, in the goodness she longed to believe she was capable of, but Samuel was right.

Everything she had done had been first for Anton, and Anton alone. And everything since then—that had been for power. A single taste of it and she had fallen, desperate to cling to whatever shreds of authority and domination she could seize.

"I tried."

"I know," Samuel said, with such tenderness that it felt like a bruise, "but after today, after seeing what you and the King have done, I cannot continue to be part of this. So please, come with me."

She didn't understand. "Come with you?"

"Back to Dameral, back to Isaac." He was a breath away from begging, and Shan felt like she might be sick. "Stand with us, help us break this system before it breaks you."

She wanted to, she wanted it with all her heart, to slip into the carriage with him at first light and leave it all behind. But it wasn't that simple. "You know the King asked me to stay."

"He did, but we can find an excuse."

A helpless laugh bubbled up her throat. Oh, that sweet, sweet idealism. "We cannot—*I* cannot." He was asking too much of her. Everything she had fought so long for, every long-earned victory and every painful sacrifice that she had made. "I have to stay."

Samuel swallowed hard, licked his lips. "That's all right, then. It's better, actually. You can find out more about what he's—"

"Samuel, please," she ground out, because he didn't understand. Still, she was thankful that he stopped immediately, that he still respected her enough for this. "I did not mean just for this trip." The silence between them grew, tense as a wire about to snap. "I know I cannot make you understand, but this is the only option we have. If you care about . . . us, you will find a way to make Isaac stop. For all of our sakes."

Samuel's eyes glistened, unshed tears turning their bright tone into emeralds. "I cannot do that."

"Well, it looks like we have reached an impasse." Shan glanced up at him through her eyelashes, unable to bring herself to look at him directly.

"We have." Stepping away at last, Samuel leaned against the mantle, his back to her. "I trust you will not go and tell the King first thing in the morning."

She hated that he even had to ask, but even as much as it smarted, she couldn't blame him. "I will not. But . . ." It took everything in her to force out the next question. "What about us?"

Samuel glanced back, the fire gilding him in a golden glow that stole her breath away. "I honestly don't know."

Shan unhooked the clasp keeping her claws in place, the chains slacking as she unwound them. Fingers free, she used her other hand to pull the ring off, heavy in her hand as she deposited it on the mantle, inches from Samuel. "Hold onto this then."

"Shan—"

"You can give it back to me," she continued, "when you've decided for sure. And if . . . if not, I understand."

He turned, reaching out for her, but she slipped past, dodging his attempts as she made a direct line for the door, putting an entire wall between them.

She didn't lock the door behind her.

Collapsing onto her bed, silent tears streaming down her face, she waited for him to knock, to burst into the room, to crawl under the covers and hold her till the shaking stopped. She waited and waited, but he never came, the night slipping away to the early light of dawn, the pressure in her chest growing tighter with each passing moment.

So, it was decided.

They were over.

Chapter Thirty-Eight

Isaac

Isaac stood looking out the window, his heart breaking as he listened to Samuel's tale. How he had waited only until night had fallen before he had stolen across Dameral, slinking into the safe house like a cat in the shadows. There, he had found Isaac, spilling everything he had seen, from the King's experiments to his plans for the Guard and then, finally, Shan.

Brilliant, bold, foolish Shan. He had hoped that it wouldn't come to this, but—damn it all.

"What do we do?"

"We launch our attack as soon as possible," Isaac said, with a shrug. "We can't give the King the time to create more *elite* soldiers."

"That's not what I meant."

Isaac turned back to Samuel, who sat on the chaise, shoulders tucked in like he was trying to make himself as small as possible. He looked like he had been through hell, his face unshaven, light stubble budding across his jaw, hair pulled back in a half-hearted attempt at a bun. But Isaac ignored all that, his gaze dropping to the silver ring in Samuel's hands, the ruby like a drop of blood, worrying it endlessly.

He had seen that ring on Shan's hand, had known that the bond between her and Samuel had grown stronger during his time in prison. And though they couldn't openly claim Isaac, not with the

King and half of the country wanting his head on a platter, he had been supportive of them. Happy for them.

He sank down next to Samuel on the couch, putting his arm around his shoulder and pulling him close. Samuel melted into the embrace, always so eager for affection, and Isaac's heart broke a little more.

Damn it, Shan. He understood the tension between them. That was something they had been navigating for years. Clashing and fighting and pushing and loving, and if the stakes weren't as high as they were, he wouldn't have had it any other way.

He could forgive Shan for her transgressions against him—they had hurt each other so many times over. But breaking Samuel's heart? Sweet, precious Samuel, who deserved none of the cruelty that they had brought into his life.

That was unforgivable.

"I never wanted you to have to pick a side," he said, placing a kiss to the top of Samuel's head.

"I had to," Samuel replied, though his words were muffled against Isaac's chest. "I couldn't ... live with myself otherwise."

"You're too good for this," Isaac begun, only to be cut off as Samuel tilted his head up, pinning him with a single look, stealing whatever kind platitudes he had right out of his mouth.

Samuel roughly pushed himself upwards, swinging his legs over to straddle Isaac's lap, placing his hands on the couch over his shoulders. Pinning him in place as his eyes flashed with a rage so bright, so strong, that Isaac wanted to drown in it.

"Don't. I'm not the good man you think I am," Samuel hissed, and something dark and dangerous slipped out with his words. A power that Isaac remembered all too well, creeping into his body, stealing his very will away. A power that Isaac had failed to take from him, now come back to the surface.

It was a reversal of their usual dynamic, but Isaac couldn't help the shiver that ran down his spine as he placed his hands on Samuel's waist. It wouldn't take anything to crush it between his fingers, to let the ache in his fingers expand into claws, tearing through his flesh to all the sweet viscera beneath.

Samuel was right. They had both changed in some fundamental way, the men they used to be washed away in the blood they had shed. Goodness had been left behind long ago, and now they were flawed creatures who would do anything to save this foolish home of theirs.

No matter who they lost along the way.

"No, you're not a good man," Isaac agreed. "But you're perfect, nonetheless."

He wasn't sure which one of them moved first, which one of them closed the distance, but Samuel's mouth was on his, his hands tangled in his curls, pulling him back as he held him in place. Kissing him with a ferocity that Isaac never knew Samuel could possess, rough and sloppy. Samuel didn't even grant him a moment's relief, and that wouldn't do at all.

If Samuel wanted him so badly, then that is what he would get.

Isaac caught Samuel by the throat, holding him up with his preternatural strength, pressing back so that he cut off the other man's breath. Samuel trembled in his grip, completely helpless. It was obscene, holding his lover like this, but Isaac spared a quick glance down to see his lover's cock was hard, tenting his trousers as he choked, lovely pale skin turning red as he scrabbled uselessly at Isaac's hand.

"What do you need from me?" Isaac breathed, relaxing his hold enough for Samuel to gasp for air.

"Your worst," Samuel spat. "Give me your worst. Hurt me until I . . . until I don't feel bad anymore."

Oh, Samuel.

He had seen this need in him long ago, the way he had craved this debasement, this surrender. His entire life, Samuel had known nothing but the cage of his remarkable self-control, a good man struggling against the wickedness that lay within. And he was so, so tired of fighting.

They may have lost Shan, but they still had this—they still had each other. And he would give Samuel whatever he needed, because there was no one else who could.

"I'll give you what you ask for," Isaac promised, sealing it with a delicate kiss. "But promise me that you'll tell me to stop when you need it. Pick a word so that I'll know."

Samuel licked his lips, hesitant, but then he whispered, "Eternal."

The thing he feared the most, the monster he feared that he could one day become. It was macabre, but Isaac understood it.

"All right then." He let go, and Samuel crashed to his knees before him, landing with a thud. "Crawl to the bed."

Samuel hurried to obey, his head ducked low as he moved through the flat. Isaac stalked after him, a test of his own determination. Samuel wanted him at his worst, but needed him at his best, and for this, he would sublimate his own needs, his own hungers.

"Undress," Isaac commanded, as Samuel came to a stop at the foot of the bed, "but do not touch yourself."

Samuel hurried to obey, but Isaac stepped right past him, stripping as he headed for the dresser where he hid his little gift: a glass phallus, harness, and bottle of lubrication that he had foolishly gone out to purchase. It had been an unreasonable risk, at the time, but now Isaac felt justified—he had the tools to give Samuel exactly what he needed.

It took him a couple of minutes to pull the harness on, adjusting the way it hung over his hips and settling the glass phallus in place. Blood and steel, he had missed this in a way he never could fully articulate. Though he had learned to be comfortable in his body, had welcomed the changes that his treatments had brought him and learned all the ways to bring himself pleasure, there was something about a strap that made him feel complete.

Hanging heavy between his legs, a part of him that he didn't always feel like he was missing, but was still a puzzle piece sliding into place. He dropped the phallus, gripping the edge of the dresser with both hands as he sucked in a harsh breath through clenched teeth. Denial was its own form of pleasure, and he would not let himself fall over the edge too soon.

Turning back to Samuel, he saw that the other man understood the lesson as well, having stripped himself naked and kneeling at the foot of the bed, back straight and head bowed. He was so handsome like this, chest heaving with each breath as his skin flushed so pretty, excitement painted across his skin in shades of pale red. His cock hung heavy between his legs, reaching towards his stomach as his flushed tip dripped with anticipation, twitching as Isaac stepped closer.

"Good boy," Isaac purred, running his fingers through Samuel's hair, knocking it loose from its bun so he could tangle it in his hand. Pulling gently, he tilted Samuel's head back so that he could look into his eyes, the pupils blown so wide that they nearly swallowed the green. "Needy little thing."

Samuel panted, arching into his grip, and Isaac dragged him up. "Hands and knees on the bed." He watched as Samuel got into position, the curve of his ass and the heavy weight of his sack, balls tight as his erection bobbed, leaking a single drop onto the rough sheets.

Isaac stepped into place behind him, dropping the vial on to the mattress before manhandling him into place, spreading his knees then pressing against Samuel's back as he lowered him into position, face pillowed on his arms and ass in the air.

Drawing a hand back, Isaac delivered an open palm smack against the meat of Samuel's arse, the clap of skin against skin filling the room as Samuel groaned. "Hells," he swore, but still he pressed himself back, asking for another.

Well, if he was that eager for it—

Isaac spanked him again, this time on the opposite side, before starting a rough series of smacks, alternating sides until the skin was a rosy red, warm under his touch, and Samuel was sobbing the sheets, a mess of tears and moans.

Smirking, Isaac stopped, dragging the tips of his fingers against the inflamed skin, the nails sharpening just enough to bite. One day, he would take his claws to his beloved, carving him open and healing him again, and Samuel would enjoy it, the way pain and pleasure curled together in an unrelenting spiral. But for tonight, Isaac could tell that Samuel was far too close, and when he came, he would come with Isaac inside him.

Samuel bucked back against him, babbling nonsense, but he grabbed his waist, holding him in place. "Easy now, let me prepare you."

Clenching the sheets, Samuel stopped trying to fight back, going lax under Isaac's hands. "I'll be good. I promise."

"I know you will." Reaching over, he grabbed the bottle that had nearly rolled to the edge of the bed, willing the budding claws away, concentrating till there was nothing but blunt human fingertips.

His much-needed control, hanging by a thread.

He drizzled the contents between Samuel's cheeks, rubbing his thumb against the tight ring of muscle before slipping in. "Relax, if you can," he said, as his fingertip slipped in. "It'll make this easier."

Samuel let out a whine, but mustered his incredible self-control, laying there panting as Isaac carefully eased one finger in, getting him gradually used to the intrusion before adding another, stopping only to add more of the slick liquid before he began to scissor him open.

"Look at you," Isaac said, as he twisted his fingers to find that sweet spot that had Samuel wailing, "begging for my cock like a whore."

"Please, please, please," Samuel babbled, as Isaac added a third finger. "I'm ready, I promise, just—"

Isaac pulled his hand out, leaving Samuel whimpering with the sudden emptiness. It wasn't as thorough of a prepping as Isaac would have liked, ideally, but Samuel wanted this to hurt a bit.

"Impatient slut," Isaac said, as he lined up the tip of the glass phallus with Samuel's loosened hole. "You want it so badly, then fine." He pressed in with no warning, sinking inch by inch until he bottomed out.

Samuel buried his face into the sheets as Isaac held himself still, letting Samuel get used to the weight of a cock inside him. But Samuel didn't want that, shifting as he tried to fuck himself on Isaac's strap, startling a genuine laugh out of the man.

"You'll really spread your legs for anyone, won't you?" Isaac asked, giving in to Samuel's demand as he rocked his hips in gentle waves, in and out, slow and steady. Not quite the rough fucking that Samuel was clearly desperate for, but a slow tease, driving Samuel mad. "You don't care who uses you so long as you get fucked, so cock hungry that you let a beast like me ruin you."

"Isaac," Samuel snarled, even as he pressed back into Isaac's motions, meeting him thrust for thrust. "Don't talk about yourself like that."

A tendril of magic slithered up his back, the old familiar chill of Samuel's gift worming his way into his chest. It was a weak attempt, one that Samuel likely hadn't even meant. All that practice they had done had paid off, letting him shrug it off without too much discomfort.

"Are you sure," he asked, slowing down as Samuel turned to glance over his shoulder. "I have no illusions of what I am, and I thought you wanted the worst of me."

"I do." Samuel sighed. "But you're not a monster. You're a ... marvel."

"Samuel," Isaac breathed, lips pressed to Samuel's shoulder, fangs he did not ask for slipping out and grazing the skin. They weren't quite sharp enough to draw blood, but the press of them left stark red lines on Samuel's body. His delicate skin, so easy to blush, easy to bruise, easy to wound. "I don't want to hurt you."

"But I want you to," Samuel gasped out, and, blood and steel, was that the wrong thing to say.

Pulling out roughly, Isaac flipped Samuel around, slamming his back onto the bed and knocking his breath out of his lungs. He reached over Samuel's head, grabbing a pillow to slide under the small of his back.

"I told you that I don't care about my comfort," Samuel grumbled out, and Isaac bit back a smile.

He wanted to be hurt, but Isaac cared about him too much to do this the wrong way. He doubted Samuel was in the right headspace to hear that, so he lowered his voice to a low rumble, growling out, "It's not about your comfort, but mine. Making the angle easier for this."

He ran his hand along the still slick strap, drawing Samuel's attention to it. It wasn't a lie, not exactly—both parts of it were true, and Samuel accepted the pillow under his spine without any more fuss. It didn't take much more to wrestle him into position, pulled to the edge of the bed, his legs spread wide, his hole still open and loose, and his lovely, thick cock untouched and leaking onto his stomach.

Samuel was such a pretty picture, debauched and nearly ruined, and Isaac felt his pulse kick between his legs, his dick throbbing in time with his own heartbeat. Samuel was looking up at him with such need that Isaac put all thoughts of his own control aside as he sank the strap back into Samuel in one, smooth, fast motion.

Samuel keened as the strap stretched him, his body yielding to invasion as Isaac pounded. The pressure of the harness against Isaac's swollen length was nearly enough to make him see stars, but he grit his teeth against the onslaught of pleasure, determined to make sure that Samuel came first.

He grabbed Samuel's cock, the sudden touch on his length causing him to buck and writhe. Isaac didn't relent, continuing to fuck Samuel as he jacked him off, the dual-fronted attack causing Samuel's back to arch as he spilled between them, his seed hot and thick, spurting in ribbons up his chest.

"Fuck," Isaac groaned, sinking the strap all the way in, even as Samuel squirmed with oversensitivity. He couldn't bring himself to care, though, as he fell forward, burying his face in the space between Samuel's neck and shoulder, fangs suddenly descending and slicing through flesh.

Blood flowed across his tongue at the same moment his release hit, power rushing through him in a coil of pleasure that was unlike anything he had ever known, curling in his gut as his transformation rolled over him, bones snapping and reforming, claws shredding into the bed as his wings tore through his back.

With the last dregs of his self-control, he ripped his head back with a howl before he could harm Samuel further, his cock pulsing as his cunt clenched, an exquisite agony that left him trembling.

And Samuel looked up at him like he was something beautiful, soft fingers coming up to trace at the hideous maw that his face had become—dagger-like teeth in a distended jaw, his proboscis-like tongue pressing into the holes he had made. Samuel only moaned at the intrusion, his spent cock twitching in vain attempt to get hard once more.

A depravity that Isaac could never understand, even as he wanted to take Samuel again and again, until they were nothing more than shuddering beasts, fully spent and shattered.

"You," Samuel breathed, "will never scare me." He dragged his thumb against Isaac's lower lip, pressed it against a fang until a single drop spilled. "No matter what happens, I will aways love you."

Isaac leaned in, pressed his forehead against Samuel's, not bothering to hide the tears that fell from his eyes. They were truly made for each other, and no matter what happened next, as long as Samuel never abandoned him, Isaac knew that he could face it.

Isaac was the first to the meeting room, a strong aroma of coffee overwhelming the pot of tea he had brought down from his room moments before, just for the others. They probably wouldn't touch the coffee, claiming it was too strong and too bitter, but that was fine. He didn't want to admit that tea did nothing for him anymore, the once delicious blends tasting like nothingness on his tongue, the caffeine too weak to have any effect on his mind or mood. His body was evolving in ways that frightened him, food and drink like dust in his mouth, only the strongest flavors and most potent drinks having any effect.

He drank deeply from his mug, grateful that he at least had this left, even if he wasn't sure how much longer it would last.

Anton and the others bustled into the room as Isaac filled his second cup, though the mood dropped significantly when they saw the look on Isaac's face. He didn't bother trying to school his expression into something softer—he was angry, and he wasn't afraid to show it.

Anton shed his coat, setting in on his usual stool. "Is Samuel still here?"

"He's resting," Isaac replied, glancing up at the ceiling. They had stayed up nearly all night fucking and plotting, whispering their ideas and plans in-between desperate rounds of sex as they burned themselves into each other. A stronger consummation and binding than any official claiming or ceremony could be. But Samuel was so exhausted by the end of it that Isaac figured he'd let the man rest—sleep was yet another thing his body needed less and less of.

"Far enough," Maia said, with a shudder. "I cannot imagine spending as much time with the Eternal Bastard as he does."

Alaric inclined his head in agreement, already pouring the tea for the others. "He's a surprisingly good sort, for an Aberforth."

Isaac didn't point out Samuel wasn't an Aberforth, not truly, not in any way that mattered. Or that just weeks ago they had been just as suspicious of him. It was a fragile sort of trust, one that still felt so tenuous, a candle that could be snuffed out with the slightest misstep.

But he would take that sliver of trust they had extended him and solidify it, laying out the information that Samuel had brought to him, the threat that this Mel posed, and the plans the King had for more of her kind.

"We need to act fast," he finished, looking over the rest of them. "I propose we launch the attack on the Blood Treasury as soon as possible, if only to keep the King from making more vampires."

"We'll need a little time," Maia said, "just to warn as many as we can, keep them off the streets in the immediate aftermath."

Isaac inclined his head to her. She was right—they needed to do whatever they could to prevent collateral damage. It was something he would not have thought of, before, but he was glad that there was someone to rein in his most dramatic impulses. "How long?"

"A day or two should suffice," Maia said. "But I'll need to work quick."

Isaac swallowed hard. "The day after tomorrow, then?"

Anton grinned, getting to his feet. "The day after tomorrow."

Chapter Thirty-Nine

Shan

Shan rested her forehead against the glass window, eyes closed against the endless stream of foliage as they made their way back to the capital, the hours passing away in silence as they left the countryside behind. The roads were empty, the path clear and swift, and Shan watched the sun cross through the sky until they approached the grand city of Dameral, the smell of salt and brine on the air as they turned down the main thoroughfare.

The carriage was silent except for the soft scratch of pen against parchment, the Eternal King seated across from her, writing in the journal spread across his knees, his endlessly clever mind sketching out plan after plan, contingency after contingency.

It had been nothing but that, the two of them working with Mel to test the limits of her inhuman capabilities, the full capability of what Blood Working could do. Mel herself was much more agreeable to work with, now that she was being given human blood to gorge herself on, chasing prisoners across the carefully warded courtyard of the Aberforth estate—her enhanced strength and agility and goddamn flight a sight to behold.

The Eternal King watched her with all the adoration of a proud parent watching his only child take their first steps. He cooed over her viciousness, praised her ferocity, offered her tips and advice on how to hunt more effectively. And when it had come time to head back to Dameral, Mel had submitted to the blood binding without so much as batting an eye, just because he had asked for it.

And now she sat next to Shan, dozing peacefully as the bridge buzzed between them, a low hum in the back of Shan's mind, a precaution done just in case.

Samuel had been right to fear this. What Isaac had made of himself was incredible, but Mel was quickly surpassing him. She cast a lazy glance towards the King's notebook, both fearing and dreading what new laws would be enacted once his secretary parsed that looping, slanted script.

The King put the pen aside, placing a ribbon in the notebook to hold his page. His gaze flicked over to Mel, noting her apparent catnap, before he spoke at last. "I noticed you are no longer wearing your ring, Shan."

Shan was surprised that he hadn't noticed sooner, or if he had, that he hadn't brought it up right away. Still, she didn't respond, letting the magic bud in her fingers as she plucked at the bridge. Mel's rest was not an act, but Shan still sent her tumbling into a deeper slumber. She wouldn't wake until Shan allowed her to.

The King smirked, no doubt sensing the manipulation of magic in the carriage, a quick incline of his head showing that he saw and approved.

"Samuel," Shan said, taking care to keep her voice flat, to hide the pain that hadn't lessened in the days since Samuel had returned to Dameral, the ring that was the sign of her engagement gone with him, "has some doubts after seeing what we are planning."

We, she said. Like she had any real choice in the matter. Like she was little more than a marionette the King controlled, plucking at her strings as she danced to his tune.

"Unfortunate," the King said, with a sigh. "But not unexpected. How are you holding up?"

Out of all the things the King could have asked her—their engagement was the cornerstone of so many of Shan's personal and political goals, the union of the Royal Blood Worker and the Lost Aberforth the beginning of a new age in politics—she hadn't expected this.

This was a kindness, and Shan didn't know what to do with it.

"As you said," she said, reaching into her reticule for the slim, silver case she had become so attached to lately. It didn't take her a moment to pull a cigarette out, a lit match in her other hand as she took a long inhale, the harsh drag of chemicals in her throat tempered by the buzz that immediately hit. "It was not unexpected."

The King held out a hand. "May I?"

Startled by the ask, by the simpleness of sharing a smoke with one so powerful, Shan just held out the case, the lid flipped open to expose cigarettes lined up in a neat row. He took one with almost exaggerated care, plucking it with his claws before he leaned forward.

Pressing the tip of his against the burning end of the cigarette hanging from her lips, he breathed deep as he lit his off hers. The smoke billowed between them, his lips curved into a gentle smile, his eyes closed as he savored the taste. It softened the harshness of his features, as if he had shed some of the mystery he carried—the burden of ruling, of eternity, dropped just for a moment.

This close, she could see the soft brush of hair on his jaw, as if he hadn't bothered to shave before they had set off this morning. His lips were chapped from the cold, red and a little raw, and as he exhaled, she noticed his left eyetooth was just a hair crooked.

A series of small imperfections in an imperfect man.

And who was she, to see such vulnerabilities in her King? What right did she have to know the man behind the crown, especially when he was her greatest enemy? Was supposed to be her greatest enemy, at least. But that was before she had been pulled under his wing, before he had shown her into the deepest secrets that Blood Working had, had helped to cultivate her greatest talents and her cruelest instincts.

It was before Samuel had left her, before she and Isaac had ended things for a second time. Now, the Eternal King was all that she had left, in all his endless, brutal glory.

So, why shouldn't she take what was offered?

He settled back in his seat, the cigarette hanging loose in his fingers. "Do you want him back?"

Shan's voice came out harsh, the smallest fracture in her carefully maintained composure. "You cannot deny that the match is advantageous."

"That's not what I asked, Shan." He said her name like a caress, low and rumbling in the tight space between them.

"No, it's not," Shan muttered, dredging up another half-lie, deflecting from the very real pain by offering a sliver of truth. "But it is what is most important, isn't it?"

"Perhaps," the King said, pressing his fingers to the latch holding the window fast. It opened a sliver, enough for a burst of cold to fill the carriage as he flicked the ash from his cigarette. "Yet, my darling, I asked about *you*."

She didn't understand his blasé response, the way he kept deflecting from the very real political ramifications of it. Because he was right—if she stopped to look at it for even a moment, she would shatter into a million pieces, and she did not know if she had the strength to put herself together again. "What I want doesn't matter."

She had learned that awful truth years ago, the harsh realities of the world whispered into her ear by a father who never knew what love even was. She should have learned then—perhaps then she wouldn't have gotten her heart broken thrice-over.

No, she had to focus on the things she could control, on the power that felt like it was about to slip through her fingers. Despite the title the King had given her and the leverage she had earned on her own, being tossed over by the Lost Aberforth would be a blow to her already fragile reputation. One that she might not be able to recover from.

"That, Shan," the King said, not with judgement but with a barely restrained fury that reminded her achingly of Samuel, "is where you are wrong. Samuel might be my heir, but I have known for a long time that he would never be more than a puppet. But you, my dear, clever girl, have the potential to be so much more.

"If only you would let yourself rise."

"And how," Shan asked, as tears bloomed, falling as soft as the snow in the winter's dying light, "would I do that?"

"Forget Samuel," the King said. "Let him wallow in his own self-inflicted misery. You do not need him. We do not need him."

"I don't—" she started again, but the King silenced her with a touch of his hand on hers, fingers tangling together. Not letting go.

"Give me time to handle things," the King said, and it felt as solemn as a promise. "Samuel will not get away unscathed for his treatment of you, for the way he continues to fail me, over and over again. The Lost Aberforth will seem like a paltry prize next to what I can give you."

The shape of what he was offering, the future he had hinted at, was starting to take shape. And it was grander and even more terrifying than anything she had ever dared dream of. "You cannot mean—"

"Do not," he interrupted, stern and grim, "presume to tell me what I can and cannot do." He pulled her closer, pressing his lips against the soft, delicate skin at the inside of her wrist. The touch was as fleeting as it was intimate, but it left her trembling at all the unspoken potential between them now that Samuel and Isaac had cut her loose. "I know what I want, and it would behoove you to consider my offer. There is no need to be a pawn when you could be a queen."

Shan only nodded, her heart pounding in her chest as the carriage came to a stop and the King let her go.

They must have reached the palace at last.

The footman came around, the door opening to a shock of cold. The King stepped out without another word on the matter, dropping the remains of his cigarette in the snow as he pulled his cloak even tighter around himself.

Shan snapped the bridge between her and Mel, the girl awakening with a start. "Blood and steel, how long was I asleep?"

"For a bit," the King replied, helping her out of the carriage. "Let's get you settled back in, and—"

He turned away to speak to the carriage man, the fading light catching his profile in a soft glow. "Please escort Lady LeClaire home."

Shan inclined her head to both of them, not trusting herself to speak, not as the entire foundation of her world shattered under her feet. Everything she had built felt so precariously balanced, but she could not let this stop her.

No, it was just another step on her path to the top, even if she had to leave behind everyone she loved in the process.

The LeClaire town home felt unusually quiet on her return. The lights were banked low, even for early evening, and the home had a stillness to it that made it feel pristine, unlived in and empty. A shell of what it had been, even at her father's worst.

It was a house, not a home. It had been like this since her brother had moved out. She had been deliberately ignoring that, but after everything she had been through, coming back to this was the worst insult of all.

Her footman had taken her baggage and spirited it up to her room, as precise and polite as always, but there was a new frostiness there, a void that had grown when she wasn't looking. She had sworn that she would run this household on goodwill, that she wouldn't make the same mistakes her father did. Oh, she hadn't become cruel like her father, but she had become distant. Detached. None of the servants had come to her with any whispers lately, no doubt going directly to Bart, because the lady of the house was so busy with her work.

It was never supposed to be like this.

Shan stopped in front of her study, the light from within creeping through the crack between where the door met the wall. Someone was inside, working diligently. Taking over the work that she—the Sparrow—should have been doing.

Anger flushed through her, swirling like a rip tide, and Shan threw the door open, slouching against the door frame as she took in the sight before her.

Bart sat at *her* desk, notes and letters and scraps of parchment spread across it, sorted into piles that Shan knew from experience contained all the secrets of Dameral. He looked so calm and confident there, his shirtsleeves rolled up past his elbows, fountain pen in hand—master of, if not the house, then the network she had left behind. Gathering information and pulling the strings of all the most powerful players. Not a Sparrow but a Hawk, a bird of prey striking at the vulnerable underbelly while she watched on, useless.

"You're back," Bart said, reaching for a glass of amber liquid inches from his hand. "Fruitful trip?"

It wasn't a slight—Shan knew that intellectually. It was just their way, trading information back and forth. But still, with him at the desk and her before him, it felt a little too much like an interrogation.

She swooped forward, snatching the glass out of his hand. It was *her* liquor, after all, taken from *her* liquor cabinet, in *her* study, while he monitored *her* network.

Throwing it back, Shan let the burn work through her. Another vice that felt too good, that she was indulging in perhaps a hair too much, but she slammed the glass back down on the desk with relish. Bart only frowned, a solemn look that was far too humorless on her old friend's face.

But she had already destroyed everything else in her life, so why not this?

"It was quite fruitful," she said, unable to hide the sneer that crept across her expression. "The King showed us why we should fear him, and Samuel, as expected, tucked his tail between his legs and went running."

Bart's frown deepened as he leaned back in her chair, pressing against its tall back as he crossed his leg over his knee. He flicked his gaze from hers to the hand that still clenched the glass, dark eyes going wide as he noticed what was missing.

As all his irritation vanished, replaced by an open, honest sympathy that was worse than any anger he could have summoned.

She was not a thing to be pitied.

"Shan—"

"No," she snarled, flinging the glass against the wall, where it hit the mantle over the fireplace, shattering into pieces as it fell to the floor, the witch light refracting through the shards as red ribbons danced through the room.

A sick memory tore through her—her father hitting the same mantle, his bones snapping under the weight of her magic. The squelch of her knife digging into his neck, cutting to the bone as he bled out before her.

Blood and steel, she should have known it then.

What other path could she have had? She, the one who had murdered her father, who had plotted and schemed and, worse of all, coveted. Her whole life had been temptation after temptation, an endless climb to a summit that she was finally on the precipice of reaching. Oh, she had pretended to do it for love, for justice, for her brother and Bart and every other soul that had been hurt under this damned Eternal King.

But she had lied to herself just as much as she had lied to others. It had only ever been about power. About protecting herself from every hurt her father, her world, her most beloved other parts of her soul, could throw at her.

Greed was her most fatal flaw of all, and it had cost her everything.

"Get out," she said, hollow. Empty. "It's over."

Bart moved to his feet, slowly. Careful. Hands held up in a warning, as if he was afraid she would strike him. "Shan—"

"Take whatever you need," she continued, not giving him a chance to protest. "Take the network, take the notes, take the secrets and plots, take everything that Anton or I have ever given you."

He lurched forward, reaching for her across the expanse of the desk, suddenly so grand that it seemed insurmountable, but Shan stepped back. Dodged the attempt at connection, like she had dodged so many attempts in the past.

At least she could say that she was consistent.

"We are done," she repeated. "There is nothing left for you here."

Bart just stared at her, expression hard. If he felt any pain, he didn't show it, and for that, she was thankful.

There was nothing but sorrow in even addressing it. She inclined her head once—a stiff and formal goodbye—then turned back towards the door, walking out of the room with her head held high.

Bart did not follow her.

She did not expect him to.

Locking herself in her bedroom, she finally allowed herself to cry. To let it all pour out of her, an endless wave of self-pity and loathing. Everything inside her scraped clean and raw, her heart and all the tender parts reduced to a single, aching bruise. Wallowing in the pain until all that was left was an endless numbness.

Only then did she pick herself up, dry her tears. Put away the Sparrow and the woman she had foolishly thought she could be, the happiness that she thought she could claim.

There was a future to be seized, now that there was no one left to hold her back.

Chapter Forty

Samuel

The silence in the room was oppressive, a smothering weight that Samuel choked on. But despite the way he turned the conversation over and over in his head, there was nothing he could find to make it better. Words were empty, especially because it wasn't his role to apologize. Shan had been a right asshole, and as much as he wanted to comfort Bart, there was nothing he could say. It didn't matter that she was self-destructing, it didn't matter that this was a disaster moving in slow motion.

This had been unfathomably cruel, and Samuel did not know if he could ever forgive it.

The man slumped against Anton, who held him tight, like if he eased up even the slightest bit, Bart would fall apart in his arms. Bart hadn't stopped crying since he arrived, not grand, gulping sobs, but a steady stream of silent tears. Not a grand reckoning, but a silent fissure, the bedrock crumbling to dust beneath their feet.

Isaac returned to the room, carrying a tray with a full tea service as well as a bottle of bourbon, both sorely needed. He laid them on the table where they had been finalizing the raid on the Blood Bank, a collection of hand-drawn sketches as they discussed the final details. Rough schematics that Isaac had provided, memories from his time as Royal Blood Worker. A list of the Guard, which Samuel had copied from his own office. Plans of how Anton, Maia, and Alaric would be working the crowds outside as the chaos was sure to spread.

The risk was immense, particularly for Isaac, but it was a solid plan. All they needed to do was enact it.

Samuel stepped forward to help Isaac, adding cream and sugar and a dollop of whisky to each glass. "The others?" he whispered, not to draw the attention of Anton and Bart.

"Gone home to rest before tomorrow," Isaac replied, just as quietly.

Samuel let out a sigh of relief. Alaric and Maia had ducked out of the room as the conversation had turned intensely personal, and Samuel was glad they were kind enough to give them the space they needed to process this.

When the raid was over, when the next part began to roll out, then they would deal with the problem of the Royal Blood Worker. But for tonight, they could mourn.

Isaac passed Bart a teacup, the man accepting it with a terse nod. They stood there, looking at each other, a moment frozen in time, before Bart laughed, soft and helpless. "How did we end up here?"

"I don't truly know," Isaac responded. His smile was brittle, and Samuel stepped to his side, finding his hand and weaving their fingers together—so much easier, without the claws. Without the prickliness of Shan's affection, carefully measured out in public, only freely given in private. Ever mindful of the roles they played and the weight of the eyes that followed them throughout every moment of their lives.

He shouldn't have preferred this, he should have understood the impossible situation of Shan's life, especially after stepping into it himself.

But he was so tired of being understanding.

"Strange bedfellows indeed," Anton added. "The Lost Aberforth and Isaac de la Cruz. I wouldn't have believed it if you told me a year ago. But I guess my sister wrought her own downfall."

"Anton, please," Samuel interrupted, but Isaac stopped him with a squeeze of his hand.

"No, love, he is right." Isaac said it gently, like he was afraid that the slightest injury would send him fracturing into a million pieces, never to be made whole again.

Samuel wasn't sure if Isaac was wrong about that, but he was so tired of being treated like he was fragile. He was stronger than they realized, and holding out hope for Shan did not make him weaker. "Perhaps we—"

"We've tried," Anton cut in, the dismissal flat and final. It was somehow worse coming from Anton, her brother—her twin. The one who had shared a womb with her, had walked in her shadow every step of the way. "I've been trying for far longer than you realize, but Shan ... she has made her choices, and every time she makes the wrong one."

"Not always," Samuel whispered, "she chose me, once."

A brief flicker of hope in a time of fear, when the noose had been closing around their necks. Just as it was now, but ...

"I know," Anton conceded, "and I had hoped that was the beginning of something new, but I've been fooled before. I won't make that mistake again. I—" His voice broke, a crack in his carefully crafted facade, the easy-going rake revealed to be nothing more than a boy. Hurting. Bleeding.

"I *can't* let myself be fooled again," Anton whispered, clenching his fist at his side, wound tight like a wire about to snap.

Bart sat up straighter, pressed a tender kiss to Anton's temple. "You can't convince Shan of anything, Samuel. She's always been this way, so convinced of her talent and her world view that nothing will shake it, not until she breaks herself."

Samuel turned away, hiding the shake in his hands by pressing them hard against the table, pretending to scan their plans for tomorrow's attack one more time. He hated knowing that Bart was right, that they all were right.

But he would hold onto the foolish hope that when Shan did crash and burn, he would be able to reach out and pull her back from the brink. Because she had spent her entire life determined to save others, whether they needed it or not, so perhaps all she needed was for someone to save her. Or maybe he was the biggest fool of all, holding onto a hope that would not dim. Maybe he was the perfect match for Shan in his endless audacity.

Only time would tell, but first, there was work to be done.

And as the others whispered softly behind him, he made a silent vow, that no matter what the morning brought, he would always be there for her.

Because she needed someone to have faith in her, and that much, at least, he could give.

—✠—

The morning dawned bleak and grey, low clouds settling over the capital as the promise of a winter squall loomed. Samuel stared out of the window, looking at the Blood Treasury in the distance, watching the moody sky threaten a mix of snow and rain, a hellish slush that would line the streets slick and icy.

Not a worry to Isaac, who would cut through the skies on wing, his monstrous transformation immune to the extremes of the weather.

Just like Mel was, but that was not something he could think about, not now. That was a complication for later, a worry that was beyond the scope of his role. He had one task and one task alone, and he squared his shoulders and turned away from the city.

The room was basic, bare—another of Anton's little safe houses, this one hardly used—just an empty floor, ready for Samuel to lay a blood ward. A pocket of protection to seal away Isaac's lower half while his upper half wreaked the havoc they needed. Havoc that Samuel was not simply allowing, but actively abetting. He swallowed the guilt and shame down, because he had agreed to do this, knowing full well what he was agreeing to.

Isaac stood across the room, shedding the layers of his clothes, clothes that would not survive the change, folding them and neatly setting them aside. A strange dissonance, the moment of everyday routine before the slaughter. Almost enough to make Samuel forget why they were here.

Isaac stepped forward, naked skin golden and warm in the flickers of witch light around them, his skin flawless and unblemished, coated in a thin layer of dark hair. Everything about Isaac was lean and masculine, from the clench of his stomach to the breadth of his thighs, a pillar of strength forged in fires that would have melted lesser men.

Samuel wanted to fall to his knees, press his mouth to the soft swells of Isaac's breasts, follow the trail of hair with open-mouthed kisses down to the mound between his legs and suck the plump cock into his mouth, worshipping the man until he came on his tongue. But Isaac had him here for a reason.

He needed a Blood Worker—and so a Blood Worker was what he would get. As ill taught and ill prepared as he was.

Samuel grabbed the dagger they had brought for this exact purpose: a simple thing, a thin, sharp blade and a light handle, lacking all the ornamentation or filigree that he was used to, after living among the Blood Workers for so long now. It still sat uneasily in his grip, because no amount of practice would ever make him used to this.

Turning back, he found Isaac sitting in the center of the room, legs crossed and head tipped down. His eyes were closed, his breathing deep, a sort of light meditation as he prepared himself for what was to come. Samuel let him be, moving into place, before he slashed his palm open with the edge of the blade, letting the blood well and pool.

A low growl startled him, nearly causing him to drop the dagger, but it was only Isaac. Watching him with a forbidding glare, the pupils growing to take over the whole of the eye. A snarl caught in his throat as sharp fangs descended, tongue stretching past his lips, not quite inhuman yet, but still scenting the air.

As hunger overtook him, transforming him slowly in fits and starts—but Samuel didn't fear him. He knew he was in no danger from Isaac, even when his hunger drove him to sip from his body, even when the man he loved was subsumed into the beast of legend.

Tipping his hand, he let the collected blood spill, dropping on the floor like paint. Isaac rose to his feet, turning with him, lips pulled back in a half-snarl as Samuel circled around until the lines almost joined. "Now."

Isaac sank his fangs into his own wrist, pulled the flesh free so that his blood welled to the surface—dark, nearly black, thick and viscous as it rose to the surface. Isaac smeared his blood in the waiting gap, closing the circle around himself, mingling their power into the foundation of the ward.

"It's up to you, now," Isaac slurred, the words coming out garbled as his jaw cracked and distended, but Samuel recognized the comfort there, nonetheless.

Closing his eyes, he reached for the magic inside him, still accessible, even as the dark tendrils of his power tried to grow over it, ivy crawling up the walls, roots digging into every crack and crevice they could find. He pulled them aside, a slow and arduous process, as they caught like slime in his hands, but it was enough.

Power rushed through him like a fire, spiraling out from deep within as it raced down each vein and artery, leaving him buzzing like he was made of the pure energy of the sun. It was all-consuming, this magic inside of him, but he didn't let it overwhelm him, like the last time he and Isaac had been together like this, when witch fire burned rampant around him, an attempt to burn away everything Isaac had built.

No, this time Samuel held the control, and he let the magic seep into his palm, poking at the torn flesh as he willed it to heal. The edges of the wound reached for each other, the muscle knitting itself back together before the skin regrew, delicate and unblemished, his hand made whole as if the wound had never been there at all.

The magic still pressed at him, pushing from the inside out, desperate to be used now that it was awakened. He let it rush from him into the line of blood, the catalyst lit as the ward shuddered to life, rising up in a sheet of pure energy from floor to ceiling, wrapping Isaac in a circle of protection that only they could cross.

"Well done," Isaac breathed. "I didn't see it before, but Shan was right. You are so powerful."

Samuel opened his eyes to see the magic he had done, shining between them. It shimmered like the distortion of heat on a sweltering summer day, the stain in the air a sign of his inexperience. But they did not need it to have finesse—they just needed it to work.

And with the warmth running off it in waves of intensity that felt like they would burn the clothes from his body, Samuel knew that he had succeeded at that, at least. "Now what?"

"Now, we begin." Isaac took a deep breath, and then the room was filled with the hideous crunch of bones snapping, Isaac lurching forward to rest his hands on his knees as his spine cracked. The claws on his hands turned sharper, joints popping as they curled in, great things for ripping and tearing—for shredding skin to gain access to the meat below. Gagging, Isaac wrenched his jaw open further, an impossible amount, as that tongue unfurled to hang between his breasts, spit dripping as it twitched forward, searching for his next meal.

Great protrusions moved under the skin of his back, surging forward until the skin tore, dark wings rising as they flapped on the air. A scream of pain tore through him as he leaned back, the skin of his stomach pulling apart, growing thin and translucent, like dough pulled apart and held to the light. The outline of his guts was stark and shocking until the rip pulled far enough for them to spill out, a tangle of blood and tubes, as Isaac's upper half tore from his body, the wings carrying him up to the ceiling.

Samuel hadn't even realized he had fallen to his knees once again, a prayer caught on his lips as he saw, for the first time, the true extent of what Isaac had made of himself.

The manananggal in the flesh.

It was monstrous, yes, but it was also grotesquely beautiful, awe inspiring in a way that felt primal. Isaac had seized control of magic in a way that defied the limits of what both the Eternal King and humanity allowed, becoming the very terror that they needed, taking that sacrifice on.

And Samuel would always love him for it.

Isaac moved through the ward, the magic crackling on his skin as it let him pass, lurching towards the open window at the back of the room. He cast one last look over his shoulder, dipped his head, and flung himself into the sky.

It was begun.

And in the heart of this room, this secret place, Isaac had left his lower half, torn free from his body, protected by a ward that contained all of Samuel's might. The myths said that the manananggal couldn't be killed while his lower half remained safe, and as long as he could return to it and re-form, he would survive. Samuel prayed that it was true, but this much, at least, he could guarantee.

None but him or Isaac would touch his vulnerable remains.

But the day was only getting started, and he had to meet the others for the next phase of the attack. Anton would already be moving through the streets around the Treasury, ready to take advantage of the chaos, and Samuel had to be there as well.

Ensuring that the King and the Guard did not catch him, proving that he wasn't part of this attack.

Chapter Forty-One

Isaac

The cold nip of winter air felt blissfully cool on Isaac's bare skin as he cut through the sky, soaring up to twirl through the clouds. He was so light, having left half of himself behind, his strong wings pulling him higher with each flap, his heart full to burst with the pressure of pure, unfiltered joy.

The city faded fast below him, wisps of clouds wrapping around him like a shroud, leaving drops of condensation on his skin that immediately chilled to ice. But he didn't mind the cold, not with the city spread out before him like a painting, the entire breadth of it visible without needing to so much as turn his head. It looked so small, this capital that he could crush with his bare hands, plucking out buildings from where they were rooted in the streets, the people reduced to little more than ants scurrying around cobblestones.

Dameral was the only home he had ever known, a bitter, cruel world that had no place for a man like him. That made ruinous monsters of them all, even before he had transformed himself into a beast designed to strike fear in the heart of even the bravest Blood Worker, a creature out of myths that they did not even bother to learn.

A myth his father had never even told him, too cognizant of the fact that Isaac was already too different, too other. An entire cultural heritage reduced to scraps that Isaac clung to, irreplaceable heirlooms that existed only in his memory. But he hoped that his father would be proud of what he had become, would understand why Isaac had made these choices.

That the life he and Nanay sacrificed so much for, the future they hoped their son would have, was nothing but a different kind of prison.

That despite the horrors that he had committed and the blood on his hands, he had never felt more himself than in this moment. A manananggal, ready to strike back, returning each cruelty many times over. Not merely justice, but retribution.

He banked, letting the wind pull him towards his destination, gliding towards the Treasury as he left the safe house behind. On foot, this journey would have taken a half-hour, longer by carriage, but on wing it was mere moments till he was circling around the Treasury, casting his senses wide. His nostrils flared as he dipped lower, the faint scent of human musk over the siren call of blood. He could follow the threads of it back to every soul that waited, track the movements of his quarry, each step they took telegraphed by the beat of the hearts in their chests.

The tellers and workers, though, wouldn't be his focus. Despite the way his throat ached for the blood of every living being in that building, his hunger endless and all-consuming, he knew that he wouldn't have the time to slay everyone. But that didn't matter, what mattered were the Guard and the vaults filled with carefully preserved blood. What mattered was cutting the King's supplies out from under him, stopping his plans before they could even get started.

Not giving into a hunger that would never, ever, be sated.

He had dallied long enough—surely everyone else was already in place. Taking to the sky again, he flew up in a grand loop, gaining momentum before he crashed through a high window in the front, glass shattering around him, shards raining onto the marble below.

The glass cut his skin, ribbons of blood dark and thick as sludge burbling to the surface, only for the skin to knit itself shut. It required no effort on Isaac's part, no thought or expenditure of magic, his body brushing off the injuries like they had never even been there, flecks of glass plinking to the floor below.

Screams filled the air as he curved through the great atrium, his innards fluttering behind him. He could hear the way their pulses spiked, the blood pumping through their veins as they saw the monster circle. Unable to control the sudden glee that flew through him, Isaac threw his head back, an ear-piercing screech echoing through the atrium.

The people scattered, tellers ducking under their desks, clients running in all directions as panic erupted. Isaac ignored them, homing in on the first of the Guards, a young white man standing sentry against the ward that led deeper into the Treasury. The man backed up against the wall, all the years of training fading away to terror as Isaac snatched him up, holding him aloft as he tore into the soft skin of the Guard's exposed throat.

Power flooded Isaac as blood filled his mouth, spilled down his gullet as his tongue carved its way into the Guard's neck, curving down into the cavity of his chest as Isaac scraped it clean, muscle and gore sucked up with a sickening slurp.

The limp body fell from his fingers, hitting the floor like a brick. His partner—a young woman whose face was contorted in rage, strands of red hair streaming around her face—closed the distance with the preternatural speed and strength of a Blood Worker, driving a dagger into the space between his shoulders.

It barely even tickled.

The woman let go as she realized how unaffected he was, the anger morphing into pure horror as she staggered back.

Isaac grunted, his body forcing the dagger out, much like the glass, the wound sealing from the inside out as it pushed the metal centimeter by centimeter until it fell, clattering to the marble floor.

He pulled back, entrails fluttering, as he waited for her to move, almost daring her to try again. He was curious to see if her Blood Working would affect him at all, if any of this would even approximate a challenge, or if he would just sweep through, breaking any who dared to stand in his way.

The woman snatched the dagger before darting back, circling around him like she was afraid he would strike. And oh, how he wanted to, but first—

She raised the dagger, a sliver of pink darting out past pale lips, as she lapped the viscous liquid from the edge of the dagger. Her face twisted into a grimace as she spat onto the ground, the taste of his blood transmuted into something else entirely. He could feel her Blood Working reaching out to him, pressing at the edges of his awareness as it tried, so desperately, to latch onto him. The bridge between them was a tenuous thing, little more than mist, and it took absolutely nothing to smash it to smithereens, the magic fizzling out into nothingness.

Isaac couldn't help the smirk that crossed his face, teeth jagged and sharp in his maw, as the Guard stumbled backwards, tripping over the body of her compatriot and sprawling back on the floor. Hands scrambling as she slid backward, unable to catch any purchase on the pristine marble.

Swooping forward, he let his long tongue drag around her throat, licking the sweat from it, tasting the fear pouring off her. It added an unexpected thrill to the hunt, her sudden realization that there was nothing she could do to stop him. That he was far more powerful than what a single Blood Worker could handle.

He dug his claw into the soft hollow at the base of her throat and then dragged it downward, making a smooth cut like a hot knife through butter, the skin separating as he peeled her open. The sounds of her sobs were harsh in his ears, but he simply burrowed his tongue into the crevice, twisting sideways to wrap around the harsh beating of her heart. A gasp caught in her throat as he yanked it out, blood spraying in a beautiful arc as he crushed the organ into a formless pulp.

It fell from his grasp back into the raw cavity of her body, the shock and pain hit as she shook through her death throes. Isaac only took a moment to feast, drawing that macerated organ up through his tongue as he rooted around for all the other soft and tender bits.

Flesh and blood and gore finally sating that bottomless pit of hunger within.

Lifting his head from the ruined remains of the woman in front of him, Isaac eyed the next obstacle. The tellers and patrons of the Treasury had already vanished, either out into the streets of Dameral or deeper into the building, hiding away as if mere walls and wards could stop him.

But he cared not about those fools. Eventually, they would be taken to task for their many crimes and cruelties. His goal was straightforward—he needed to make his way into the vaults below.

He crept forward, his entrails trailing a stream of blood on the floor, eyeing the first in the series of wards that locked away the depths of the Treasury from the main floor, open to the public and the many Blood Workers of Aeravin. He remembered the way from countless trips during his time as Royal Blood Worker, sickened by the truths underpinning the nation he served.

He wanted to destroy it all, collapse the walls to rubble, raze this building till it was nothing more than dust and ashes. He wanted to shred each and every ward, ruin the magic that so many had worked hard to perfect. He wanted to bleed and suffer, earn his success through pain as penance for all the harm he had caused.

Isaac had the power for it, thrumming in his veins, waiting to be unleashed. But he knew there would be more Guards beyond, and it wouldn't take long for the King to muster a response. If he was unlucky, he might even face the King's pet vampire, test his strength against one like him.

He snatched the dead woman's hand, ripping the bracelet from her wrist and winding it through his fingers. Armed with the drops of blood that the ward would recognize, he slipped through the first ward, the magic sizzling across his skin as it split around him.

It was so easy that he almost regretted it.

But he could sense the heartbeats beyond, the bodies moving as Guard gathered. The advantage of surprise would only last so long, so Isaac sped through the halls, gathering momentum as he soared through the narrow corridors, ward after ward peeling away until he emerged in a great open room, the last before the grand entrance to the vaults, where Guards worked the drudgery of a common laborer, hauling carts of blood between the vaults below and to the docking zones, where reinforced carriages would make the deliveries across the city and even to the nation beyond.

It wasn't a glorious position for a Guard of Aeravin, but it was still highly sought after for its relative ease and safety, attracting the least talented and least ambitious members. Fools who wanted to puff out their chests, proud of the station they had earned, heralding themselves as the ones who kept the country safe, but without having to risk even so much as breaking a claw.

And as Isaac took in the weak and frightened fools standing in his way, he realized that it was still true. The best of them had been stationed at the front, where any fools who would have dared to try anything would be stopped.

These buffoons were the cast-offs, children and old men who were far beyond their prime, hopeless against a creature such as him. Even a squadron of them, a full half-dozen, armed with daggers and claws, wouldn't stand a chance.

They stood around the edges of the room, forming a circle around him that would have had him worried, if he didn't smell the piss running down the leg of the young man across from him, the whole room rank with the unpleasant tang of fear.

"Blood and steel," one of them breathed, an older woman with a silver pin in the shape of a rose over her breast, marking her as the senior officer. Her lower lip was bitten raw, the only clear sign of anxiety that leaked through her composure as she flexed her hands at her side, the claws sharp and deadly. "What *is* that?"

"Fuck this," the Guard reeking of urine said, his dagger clattering to the floor as he turned away. "This isn't what I signed up for!"

"Jameson, don't you dare!" the woman snapped, reaching out to grab him around the arm. But he ducked past, more agile than either Isaac or the woman expected, making a mad rush towards the door, ready to abandon his duty and his comrades if he thought it would buy him even the smallest chance of survival.

He could not let that slide.

Isaac's mouth pulled back into a ferocious grin as he dove towards Jameson, driving his fist into and through his chest, the claws punching straight through his sternum and out through the other side with a sickening squelch. The split second between Jameson realizing what had happened and the agony hitting him was a delicious bite of tension between Isaac's fangs, watching the dread cross his expression, his eyes bugging out of his head as he gurgled, the words lost in the spurt of blood that gushed past his lips.

Flying up into the air, Isaac lowered his arm, letting gravity do the work as it pulled Jameson down, slipping past his wrist and the curl of his fist before falling.

The man was dead before he even hit the ground.

"Guards," the woman screamed, a primal roar of rage with just the faintest undercurrent of fear, "kill that monster!"

Twisting in the air, the movement as natural and instinctive as a bird in flight, Isaac plunged back into the thick of it, claws ready to tear and rend.

Chapter Forty-Two

Shan

Shan slid from the carriage into the chaos around the Blood Treasury, the first wave of Guards already spilled onto the scene. They formed an immediate perimeter around the building, herding away the onlookers, their curiosity getting the better of common sense.

Fools, the lot of them. There was a slaughter going on inside that building, and it was only fickle luck that prevented them from being the ones torn apart. Yet they pressed as far as the Guards would allow, craning their necks to look through the grand windows, as if it was some marvelous show, as casual and innocent as the latest opera.

She clenched her jaw, lifting her head as she strode past the perimeter, the color of her robes granting her entry as the Guards immediately stepped aside.

Mel was quick on her heels, her excitement bubbling down the thread of magic that connected them, a barely contained lust curling through Shan that she knew wasn't her own, twisting in her gut and shattering her careful control. Pushing her towards a reckless violence that would be so, so satisfying, even if it wouldn't be helpful.

Shan took a deep breath, ignoring the impulses, the emotions of the young woman bleeding through the magic that connected them. The bridge holding Mel back was a tremulous affair in the back of Shan's mind, not a full restraint on the woman's abilities, but a hook set in place, just in case her eagerness won out over sense. A precaution, because Shan was ever so cautious, laying traps around her, having contingencies in place, never letting herself be caught off guard or go off script.

Yet it still felt like she was being tainted in some way, corrupted by urges that should have repulsed her. But if she was being truly, desperately honest with herself—after all she had been through, she wished she could give in to such a feral joy, even if only for a moment.

But she was not an untamed creature, created for violence and vengeance. No, she was a perfect chameleon, with her many masks and guises, always becoming whoever she needed to be in any given moment, each word calculated and every action deliberate. Perfect, in every single way, since the world would expect no less of her, not if she wanted their respect.

And blood and steel, did she need their respect.

The King turned towards her as she approached, the corner of his mouth turning up in the slightest of smiles as they approached. A flicker of relief before his expression smoothed over, ever the controlled professional. But still, in that spilt second, he had crafted a message just for her, and Shan had been quick enough to receive it.

But this gathering was not for pleasure, and he turned his attention back to the Guard in front of him.

The woman was young, in her early thirties at best, though she wore the long dark uniform of the Guard like she had been born to it. She wore shoulder-length mousy brown hair in a neat bob, her skin the kind of sallow that looked washed out in even the mildest of sunlight, her delicate features making her appear even more youthful than her years. But she stood with her arms crossed behind her back, shoulders strong and head high, looking like a general on the field of battle.

It was only the slight twitch of her eye that gave away the stress she was under, the fractures that were spreading hairline thin as the pressure continued to build. Shan wondered if this would be the thing to crack her, or if she would rise to the occasion like her predecessor had done, so many times over the years.

Because of the golden pin at her breast, the rose of Aeravin gilt in precious metal, this could only be one person. The new Captain of the Guard, who Shan had only ever heard of by reputation. It would be good to have a face to put to the name, even if she knew little else besides that.

The ache she felt over the loss of the Sparrow and the network she'd spent her entire life building was nothing compared to the practicalities she had yet to face. The pain, she knew, would ebb with enough time, but all her successes were built upon the mountain of information she had gathered.

And without that, how would she be best able to manipulate new players?

"Lady LeClaire," the King said, smooth and magnanimous as ever, "this is Miss Strickland."

"My Lady," Strickland said, with a deep bow. "I am sorry we are not meeting upon more fortunate circumstances, but His Majesty has informed me that you will be able to help with this matter." Her eyes flicked towards Mel, the look shrewd and cunning, but Strickland asked no questions.

She knew how the game was played. No matter how useful she proved herself to be, no matter the power that being Captain of the Guard granted her over the rest of Aeravin, at the end of the day, she was nothing compared to her betters. And Shan was, despite all the indignities she had suffered, still counted among them. That was a thrill that ran through her, curling low and warm in her stomach, a sharp bite of pleasure that she could get addicted to.

This is what power was, and she would wrench each and every sliver of it to herself.

"Strickland," Shan said, not returning the bow. She pressed forward with a brisk professionalism, enjoying not having to simper. "Tell me what happened here."

"There has been an attack," the woman replied, "nearly a half-hour past. A ... creature of some kind entered the building through the window, and its first target were the Guards in the lobby."

Shan didn't need to ask about the creature, knowing the truth deep within, but still, a fragile hope flickered in her. A wild and desperate hope. "What sort of creature?"

Strickland grew somehow paler, something Shan didn't expect of a woman with her complexion, tongue darting out to wet dry lips. "The witnesses described it as some sort of monster, with dark wings like a bat. It had claws and fangs that tore through the Guards like they were made of tissue paper."

Strickland faltered, but the King's eyes gleamed with a kind of manic light. The kind that she had seen many times over, the hunger that had nothing to do with appetite. "Tell her the rest."

The Guard stood up even straighter, forcing the words from her lips. "It ... it had no legs, just a weeping mass of innards dripping from the gaping wound where it had been torn from ... itself."

It sounded like madness; it sounded like a nightmare. But as Shan listened, her heart stopped in her chest as something close to fear took her over. As the faint stirrings of a memory tingled in the back of her mind.

Her and her brother, clutching at her mother's skirts as she told them stories of a land they would never have the chance to know. Anton, listening with the delight only a child could have, but Shan had kept one eye on the door, knowing how illicit the information she received was.

"Manananggal," Shan whispered, the word clumsy on her tongue, her mother's language stiff and uncomfortable on her lips. Despite all their researching, every test that she had run, she had never expected this. How long had Isaac known what he was becoming? Why hadn't he shared it with her, the one who could perhaps understand just a bit of what he was going through? That slight hurt the most, another tear in the jagged wound that was her heart.

And despite every bit of rage that ran through her, righteous as it was, she couldn't help the soft sound of pain that caught in her throat. "Oh, Isaac, what have you done?"

"That's the question, isn't it?" the King echoed, seemingly oblivious to the all too real hurt that cut at Shan. His lips curled into a smirk, that fanatical gleam in his eye matching the curiosity that burned within. "And he was kind enough to come to us."

Strickland blanched—clearly, she was calculating the cost. The lives lost; the terror spread. The King, though, didn't seem angered or worried. As much of a disaster as this was, the thrill of learning something new, something terrible, was too great a lure for him.

Mel bucked against the bridge, the excitement souring into impatience as the conversation dragged on. Shan plucked on the threads that bound them, a sharp yank that drew a low hiss out of Mel as Shan reminded her who was in charge.

She would hunt soon enough.

"If that is all?" Shan pressed.

"We have had no contact since," Strickland continued with her report, "and after the first wave of witnesses escaped, no others have emerged. We are forced to conclude that the threat is still ongoing."

"Well, that is something you won't have to worry about much longer," the King interjected, and oh, how Shan wished she felt as confident as he sounded. "We will handle it from here."

Strickland swallowed any complaints or concerns, even though the situation was absurd. The Eternal King could not be contradicted, even if he was walking to his assured death. "As you say, Your Majesty. We will continue to handle things on the perimeter."

"Good." The King graced her with a smile, and Shan saw the ripple of dismay flutter across her expression, the kind of sensible concern that anyone should have after drawing the attention of their monarch.

The same fear that she had, once upon a time.

Shan liked this one. Strickland was smart and obliging, lacking the bluster and pride of Dabney. Perhaps Isaac had done her a favor by murdering him. This woman was a potential ally in the making, if she made it through this unscathed.

"Thank you for your work," Shan said, the sweetness to counteract the King's intensity. "You've done well."

"Lady LeClaire is correct," the King added, tilting his head towards her. An acknowledgment, brief as it was.

It still filled her stomach with butterflies—she had spent so much of her life fighting to be seen, and everyone she had given even a sliver of her heart to had only abandoned her in the end. But she still had this, the esteem of the Eternal King himself, and she would drape herself in that honor, build herself a suit of armor so she would never be hurt again.

The King was already moving towards the entrance, Mel hurrying after him, but Shan paused, laid her hand on Strickland's arm, the sharp tips of her claws against the thin cloth of the Guard's robes more threatening than comforting.

But Strickland still raised her brown eyes up, meeting the Royal Blood Worker's gaze without fear, the little twitch at the corner of her left eye the only sign of her discomfort.

And for that, Shan offered her a kindness. "Whatever happens, do not follow us in. Do not let anyone in, except for the Councillor of Law, should he arrive. We will handle this threat."

"Thank you, my lady," Strickland replied, breathless with relief. "I will send Lord Aberforth upon his arrival."

She said it like a given, and perhaps it was—this was his concern as well, and not just for his position. Isaac had become a problem of their own making, mistake after mistake leading to this moment, and no matter how much she tried to deny it, the blood spilt this day would forever follow her.

Regardless of where they stood with each other, this was something she had to fix, and, with his too bleeding heart and his unshakeable righteousness, she prayed he would stand with her.

He owed her that much, at least.

It was worse, inside, than Shan could have ever imagined. She had seen horror, in her time—wrapped in pageantry on the first day of spring, as the King pressed his mouth to some poor fool's throat. In ruthless efficiency as she stood in the heart of the first Blood Factory, and after as she had spread it to the rest of Dameral. In primal brutality as Mel demonstrated the power she had gained.

But nothing on this scale.

The bodies lay where they had fallen, torn apart in a gruesome display of power. There were gouges in the corpses, made by teeth that Shan was ashamed to say she was intimately familiar with. Isaac had torn through the flesh, the blood arcing from lacerated arteries to spray against the wall where it dripped down the wallpaper.

They moved cautiously through the Treasury, the only sound the soft claps of their steps on the marble and the occasional caught breath, a gasp lodged in the back of a throat before it escaped out into the air. Shan raised her scarf, holding it in front of her nose, the air pungent with gore as she stepped around another set of corpses, watching as the King swiftly dismantled yet another ward—intact and pristine.

Whatever Isaac had become, he had still been aware enough to fish out one of the bracelets that let the Guard pass through the protective wards. Which meant that the transformation hadn't broken him, hadn't rendered him into something terrifying and primal—he knew what he was doing with this massacre.

It should have disgusted her, but something dark and proud curled around her heart. He had finally found his true power, and she would always regret the way their paths had diverged just as he embraced it.

What he could have achieved if he had only trusted her—if they had only been the team they always should have been.

The last ward fizzled out, the magic releasing with a great rush of energy that washed over them, raising all the hairs on Shan's arm. Mel darted through the doorway with a low growl, pulling at the tether like a hound scenting prey.

Shan didn't bother forcing her back—this was precisely what they had brought her for, the only tool in their arsenal that could match

Isaac's threat, and the further they got into the Treasury, the more Shan was sure they would need to unleash her.

The King followed after her, his pace measured and careful. Shan thought the King should be more concerned, given the clear trajectory of Isaac's attack, but the wards below were even more intense than the ones above, and there was no simple trick of the blood bound in jewelry that would work on the advanced wards below.

She prayed it would be enough.

They emerged into final room before the grand lift that descended into the bowels of the Treasury, where the vaults containing all the blood of the Blood Workers were kept. Bodies lay around them, brutalized and ruined, but Shan didn't have it in her to be shocked anymore. She just stepped past them to where the lift had been, glancing down to the shaft to where the grand cage had crashed, the chains and pulleys that held it aloft ripped from their hinges.

Isaac had been quite thorough, and the King only sighed. "The stairs, then. Mel, scout ahead."

Mel's cloak slipped from her shoulders, fluttering to land at Shan's feet, dipping into the pool of blood that leaked from the remains of a young man. His empty eyes stared up at the ceiling, glassy and bloodshot, and Shan was struck by how young he was. Blood and steel, he must have been fresh out of the Academy, but any joy or success his life could have had was ripped away from him, reduced to this empty sack of wasted potential.

Mel stepped forward, pulling at the lacing of her bodice so that her dress loosened, slipping down her shoulders before she pushed it off completely, revealing that she was bare beneath. Smooth, unblemished skin shone pale and perfect under the witch light, and it was so easy to forget what she was.

What the King, and Shan, had made of her.

Mel kicked the dress aside, where it landed over the gory remains of a woman, her torso shredded open and weeping the ruined remains of her intestines. Mel did not notice or did not mind, slipping off her shoes, bare feet on cold marble as she shivered in anticipation. Such concerns were for those who still had a care for their humanity, and Shan could taste the anticipation in the back of her own throat.

The bones cracked under Mel's skin as she shifted, her spine hunching over as the talons sprung forth, wings surging from her shoulders as her shriek echoed to the ceilings above. It was quicker, now. Easier each time Shan saw it, Mel shedding her skin as easily as Shan shifted masks.

There was jealousy burning deep inside, so deep that Shan could almost convince herself that it wasn't real. But as Mel turned, gracing both her handler and her liege with what could only be described as a feral smile, Shan had to admit it.

She was envious of Mel, of the power that they had gifted her and the freedom that she had found.

Mel took one step back, falling over the edge and plunging towards the darkness below. Flying ahead in a way that neither she nor the King could follow, and Shan hoped that whatever Mel found in the vaults was something that the vampire could handle.

Swallowing hard, Shan shifted her attention back to the King. "Stairs, you said?"

"Yes," the King replied, "from before the lift was installed, for when it's in repair."

There was a great groaning from below, the sound of Mel ripping through the sheet metal that was the cage of the elevator. What a sight that must have been, but it was followed up by a great shriek.

Not Mel, the voice deeper, more resonant, the sounds reverberating up the shaft, so loud that Shan had to clap her hands over her ears. Even from this distance, Shan could feel it rumbling through her chest, something in her soul recognizing the sound instantly.

It was Isaac—found at last. Screaming in rage with a rawness that nearly had Shan crashing to her knees.

The King caught her shoulder, looked deep into her eyes—steadying her with a touch. Only to have the ground shake beneath them as power exploded below, a chain reaction as entire vaults detonated with a force that had the very foundations of the building trembling.

"What have you done?" Shan whispered, her mind catching up seconds later as she recognized what was happening. As power roared beneath her, the unmistakable wave of witch fire burning below. He had taken the blood they had stored, the blood they had needed, and turned into fuel for a fire that would burn until there was nothing left.

There was no stopping it, not now that it had begun.

The sheer power required to ignite that much witch fire was staggering, far beyond what she had considered even possible. But Isaac had made himself into something out of myth, and with that power, he ruined everything she had done.

He had ruined Aeravin, and quite possibly her along with it.

Chapter Forty-Three

Samuel

Samuel arrived at the Blood Treasury later than he expected—or perhaps Isaac had made better time than they had projected. Either way, the Blood Treasury was pure chaos, the Guard having already swarmed the perimeter, creating a loose barricade of bodies.

Strickland waved him over as soon as she spotted him, face pale as she struggled to keep control over a rapidly escalating disaster. Samuel almost felt sorry for her, despite the fact that she had been Dabney's right-hand man for years, groomed to take the position after him. Despite the fact that she had been nothing but pleasant and agreeable since her appointment. Despite the fact that this was a crucible that would break anyone, let alone a woman not ten days into her role. Because there was no forgetting what she was—the symbol of the system Samuel had sworn to destroy, the target of this very attack.

But Samuel still had a role to play, so he stepped to her side and donned the mask of Lord Aberforth—cold, cruel, and ever so practical. "What happened here?"

Strickland swallowed hard, and Samuel was once again struck by how young she was, not even a handful of years older than himself. She should have had more time to prepare, to grow, but Samuel had snatched that from her by whispering two words in Isaac's ear, the name of her mentor, and now here she was floundering. It shouldn't have felt good, this small bit of chaos that he had crafted. But it did, a twisted smug sense of satisfaction curling through him as the pieces fell into place.

Perhaps he was more like Shan than he realized, perhaps there was more of the Eternal King in him than he wanted to admit.

"There was an attack," Strickland began, and Samuel only half listened as he studied the building in front of him, the colossal Blood Treasury that he never seen before. Never had reason to see before, just another grand scale institution of Aeravin, a symbol of the casual cruelty and the endless suffering that the Blood Workers placed on their Unblooded brethren. A concrete, physical reminder of their place in the world, little more than providers of blood and labor, the mortar that held this entire godforsaken country together but never recognized for all that they did.

And Samuel was so, so tired of watching the Blood Workers crush the Unblooded under their boot. Of being—however unwillingly—part of that wretched system.

"The Eternal King and the Royal Blood Worker arrived," Strickland continued, snatching Samuel back from his dark thoughts, "with a young woman in tow."

The fear hooked deep in Samuel's gut, a sharp tug that threatened to take his breath away. But they had expected this, had planned for this, even though he still saw Mel in his nightmares, a memory that haunted him whenever he closed his eyes, that young man slaughtered by a creature out of nightmares.

The vampires the rest of the world feared Blood Workers to truly be, their civilized veneers cast aside to reveal the feral, ever-hungering beast at the heart of their society.

"What then?" Samuel asked, but Strickland never got a chance to respond as the very ground upon which they stood shook.

The unexpected tremors took Samuel by surprise, sending him crashing to the cobblestones. But the new vantage point gave him a perfect view of the looming destruction, head tilted back to watch as the entire building shuddered from the ground up, a rolling series of blasts that began underneath the Treasury before the reverberations rumbled upwards.

The windows shook in their frames, the glass panes shuddering as the energy ran up through them, before they shattered outward in a spray of fine shards, raining down onto the cobblestones like a sudden winter squall, tinkling like hail.

A rush of energy followed, invisible but still potent, flowing over them with all the power of rolling thunder, Samuel's skin breaking out in gooseflesh in the wake of it. Before them, great cracks splintered through the walls, growing larger as they reached up and up and up, the whole building shuddered as it threatened to shake apart.

Hells, Isaac had done it. The vaults must have been ignited into witch fire, the entire supply of precious, stolen blood erupting as it burned away.

Strickland forced herself to her feet, pausing only to help Samuel up, before rushing towards the door. She came to a sudden stop in front of the looming doors, a harshly aborted movement, like someone had snatched her by the back of her coat.

Samuel crossed the distance in four large steps, his hand landing on her shoulder and pulling her from whatever internal debate she struggled with. "Strickland?"

Turning wide, panicked eyes on him, Strickland whispered, "She told me not to follow."

"Who?"

"The Royal Blood Worker," she replied. "Lady LeClaire."

Everything slowed to a crawl as his brain processed the words, as he realized that their careful plans had all been shattered. They had expected Mel, they had known that the King would use his greatest weapon. But neither of them had thought that they would put themselves directly into danger. No, that wasn't like them—content to manipulate things from the sidelines while sending others to do their dirty work.

They must not have understood the intention, must not have realized that they were bold enough to destroy it all.

But Shan was in there, and as the building groaned, threatening to come crashing down around them, Samuel found himself moving before he had even come to a conscious decision. Because even now—even after all that had happened, even after walking away from her—he couldn't just let her die, trapped beneath rubble.

Not when there was something he could do about it.

He ran through the open doors, Strickland calling after him, her hand nearly catching on the back of his coat, but he pressed on. The atrium opened high above him, the cracks having spread up the walls and across the ceiling, the grand chandelier wavering in the air. The quake had shaken its moorings loose, and Samuel watched as the chain slipped and snapped, the mass of metal arms and crystal shells falling three stories to crash into the floor.

The shock of the impact nearly sent him sprawling, but Samuel just ducked around it, heading towards the opening in the far wall, following the streaks of red and the broken bodies through the building. His boots slid on patches of wet blood, leaking from corpses so desecrated that they hardly even passed for human anymore, ravaged by a rabid beast. He took care to weave around the shreds of meat and organs ripped from their cavities, the wreckage that had fallen around them—doors knocked from their hinges, sconces tumbled from their mountings in the wall. All around him, the cracks in the walls seemed to grow, the foundations beneath his feet shifting as the floor started to buckle.

It was a winding trail of gore and rubble that should have shocked and disgusted Samuel, but he was too consumed by worry, the panic driving him forward as a strange numbness set in. Later, the disgust would rise, but for the moment he had found a sense of peace and determination he had never known before. There was only the aching wound in his chest screaming for Shan, desperate to find her, because no matter how many times they hurt each other, they would always come back to this. Pulling each other back from the brink of disaster, saving each other again and again, because what was life without her?

They were ruined forever, and if Samuel got her out of this alive, he would find a way to bring her back to his side.

He stumbled through the last doorway to find the Eternal King and Shan huddled together among the destruction, a ward drawn up around them, pale and shimmering. The King had an arm around Shan's shoulder, pulling her close. There was blood on the side of her face, leaking down the curve of her cheek, her dark eyes hazy and unfocused.

The floor around them was littered with rubble and the remains of yet another chandelier, detritus that had hit the top of the ward and slid off, as well as more that balanced, so precariously, above their heads. Enough debris that—without the ward—it would have crushed them completely, buried them alive as the Treasury fell down around them.

That would still crush them, if the King let the ward go for even a second.

Samuel could feel the power of it rolling off the Eternal King, even untrained as he was, as the King fueled the ward with the mess of spilt blood scattered around them. It was nothing like the one he had created back in the safe house, fueled by his own power and blood, instead drawn from the mass of bodies around him. The King looked up at him, brow drawn in intense concentration, sweat beading on his forehead as he held the ward up through sheer force of will. There was no smear of red on his lips, no sign that he had imbibed any of the blood around him, but still, he had called it to them, had painted an unbroken line around them and woven them an impenetrable shield with it.

Just how powerful was this Eternal King? And would Isaac, even as changed as he was, be able to stand a chance?

Samuel clambered over the rubble, wrapped his hands around the chandelier that lay slanted against the ward and ripped it to the side, where it crashed down with the rest of the debris. He cleared what he could, shoved the shattered stones and wooden beams off. It wasn't enough to free them completely, but there was a passageway out now.

That done, Samuel dug the tips of his claws into the palm of his hand, letting his own blood bead to the surface as he pressed against the ward, granting the King enough of his blood to allow him passage. The magic sizzled against his skin, warm and ticklish, but he was able to hear the King's sigh of relief as the ward split open, as he slipped in, ducking down next to Shan.

"Take her, Samuel," the King said, voice gruff with exhaustion. "I'll handle the rest."

Samuel didn't need to be told twice—he pulled Shan into his arms, letting her rest her head against his shoulder as he slid his other arm under her knees. He ignored her mumbled protest, the confusion in her expression as he hoisted her up and carried her back through the ward towards the somewhat stable hallway.

"I've got you, Shan," he whispered, pressing his mouth against the still-bleeding wound. His tongue flicked out, lapping at her cheek, the sudden rush of power filling his mouth as he swallowed it down. It wasn't hard work, mending the bone, sealing the flesh—the power that lived in him rushing forward once again. Shan hissed as it hit her. It wasn't gentle, and it wasn't delicate, but it got the job done.

His beautiful Shan, safe and whole in his arms once again, looking up at him with such unbridled awe that it threatened to steal his breath away.

"You came for me?" Shan whispered, like she couldn't believe he was there. Her hand pressed against the column of his throat, like if she stopped touching him, he would vanish into nothingness. "Still?"

"Always," he swore, solemn as a vow.

"As sweet as this moment is," a low voice drawled, and Samuel's gaze shot back to the King creeping through the ward. As soon as he was free, the King dropped the ward, the magic sizzling out immediately, the wreckage he had protected them from slamming into the ground. The King reached out, bracing himself against the wall with a sigh, head dipped down as he caught his breath. It lasted only a moment before he pushed himself back up, donning that ever serene mask, implacable and unbreakable. But Samuel had still seen through it, a brief chink in the armor where Tristan Aberforth, the ancient and Eternal King, looked so terribly human.

And as he risked that vulnerability to protect Shan, Samuel couldn't help but feel indebted to the man.

"We should move," the King rasped, and Samuel only nodded, already turning back in the direction he had come.

"I can walk," Shan muttered petulantly, and Samuel's lips tugged into a reluctant smile. Oh, his proud, foolish woman, always so confident, never wanting to accept even the slightest bit of help. But it wasn't the time to argue, so he let her down gently, her heels clinking on the marble floor. He placed one hand on the small of her back to steady her as her knees wobbled, but she rejected his attempts to help her. Not unkindly, but firmly.

He hated it and loved it in equal measure—how he wished that she would let herself lean on him, just once. Trust him to take care of her in the same way she worked so hard to protect those she loved. Trade her endless need of control for just a moment of unguarded honesty.

It was the very flaw that had led them here in the first place.

Following at her heels, he allowed himself to be led, because she would accept nothing else. And, deep in his heart, he realized that he had been part of the problem as well, always willing to roll over and show his stomach because she had simply asked him. Letting her claim power over him, without ever stopping to think about limits and boundaries.

Too trusting by far.

The King watched their interactions with knowing eyes, leaving Samuel utterly exposed under that gaze, a thumb pressed into a fresh bruise, and he knew instinctively that somehow, someway, the King knew of the troubles that had recently tore them apart.

The building continued to rumble in the aftershocks, dust floating down from the fissures above. The air was thick with it, grime filling his nose and throat with each breath, choking him as they made their way back to the front entrance. The atrium was somehow even worse than it had been when he had passed through moments before, the flooring cracked wide open in deep rifts, witch fire billowing up in grand rushes of steam and heat, giving the whole room a hazy, shimmering effect that made Samuel's eyes burn.

Below, in the great pits that had once been the vaults of the Blood Treasury, the shrieks rose, inhuman and shrill. It sent gooseflesh prickling across his skin, despite the sweltering warmth that surrounded them, the sounds of a vampire and manananggal at war.

The King, for some unfathomable reason, did not head directly for the door, skirting around to approach the largest fissure, the grand hole that had been created when the chandelier fell, the floor around it cracking under the weight of the impact and the crumbling foundations below.

Shan watched him go, cursing lowly under her breath before making to follow.

"Wait!" Samuel caught her hand, the press of her claws against his skin drawing thin lines of blood. "You don't have to."

She glanced back at him, dark eyes wide, and he could see the way she weighed her options, the quick calculations that endlessly ran through that twisted mind in plain display as her expression shifted.

As she looked at him with such heart-wrenching pity.

She pulled her hand free, rushing after the King, and Samuel let her go—denied, again. Power trumping safety, knowledge trumping good sense, her side chosen as she left him behind.

He almost left them in a burst of resentment, but then the howls returned as two blurry figures whirled through the gap in the floor in a flurry of wings and claws. Deep, dark blood—black and thick like tar—gushed from multiple wounds to spray in wide arcs as they twirled above their heads, a wild tumble.

Samuel was only able to tell them apart by the fluttering of Isaac's entrails, his form so small compared to Mel's. She kicked out at him with her taloned feet, dragging sharp claws into the meat of his stomach, tearing great gashes that should have taken him down. That *would* have taken him down, if he had still been anything resembling human. If his lower half wasn't safely tucked away behind a ward in a room miles away.

Samuel ducked to the side, barely avoiding a great spew of blood, which plopped onto the hot floor where it sizzled. Even with his amateurish levels of Blood Working, he could feel the inherent wrongness of it, slick like oil that sent shivers down his spine as he immediately recoiled.

The King did not have the same repulsion, stepping forward to drag two fingertips through the mess, lifting it up to watch the thick liquid coalesce into a thick globule, clinging to him like half-melted wax.

Mel screeched in impotent fury, the sound ricocheting through the atrium, bouncing off the walls and ringing in Samuel's ears. She slashed again and again at Isaac, but the wounds kept sealing nearly as quickly as they were made, an impossible task that was driving her close to madness as each of her strikes became wilder.

Isaac seized the advantage, slamming one hand into her chest, his claws cutting through the flesh and bone as he drove her all the way up to the ceiling above, wings flapping with great, frantic thrusts as he carried her. Her back crashed against the plaster with a sickening crunch, Isaac ripping his hand free, pulling the very heart from her chest as she gave the most soul-shaking cry. But that wasn't the end of it. Isaac wrapped his maw around the column of her throat, crushing it with the great strength of his jaw as he tore her head straight off.

Unmoored, Mel's body slipped from his grasp, falling towards the ground. It landed not even a foot from Shan, who took one look at the pulverized chest and the torn throat, the shattered edge of Mel's spine reaching out from a collar of shredded meat, before turning to the side and emptying her stomach.

But Samuel turned his gaze back upon Isaac, who hovered above them, great wings beating slow and steady, his torso ending in a long gash, his innards floating below him in a tangle of slick intestines. His jaw was stained red with gore, bits of human flesh caught in sharp fangs, dripping blood. His long tongue unfurling down and hanging between his bare breasts, flicking restlessly—still scenting the air, searching for his next target.

He held Mel's severed head in one hand and her mangled heart in the other, the prizes of his hunt, trophies to be admired.

The King stepped forward, the corner of his mouth stained black, fingers crooked like a claw, and Samuel realized a heartbeat too late what had happened.

"Enough of this foolishness," the King snarled, closing his fist with a grunt. "You have done too much damage."

Isaac clutched at his chest, mouth opening in a silent scream, jaw snapping shut as the sound got caught in his throat. Mel's head dropped like a stone to the ground below, the ruined remains of her heart following after, landing with the soft plop, Isaac's hands spasming as he grasped the empty air, the tendons in his arms standing out in stark relief.

Samuel could feel the bridge reaching between them, a vibrant live wire of magic that thrummed with power as the King attempted to rip Isaac out of the air, bending the manananggal's body to his own will.

It was a brutal thing to watch, the way that Isaac trembled like a hare caught in a snare, his entire body shaking as he tried to fight his way through it. Samuel had seen the same struggle before, when he inflicted his own power upon Isaac, practicing the gift he had never asked for. But this was nothing like the little games they had once played—this was brutal and swift, the King bringing down his full might to destroy his enemy.

"You were a fool to come here," the King continued, sweat beading on his brow, red, still human blood dripping from his nose. But he had the upper hand, grunting as Isaac's chest caved in on itself with a snap, the King reaching through the bond and using the tether he had made to force Isaac's body into submission.

Just like Samuel's power—they really weren't that different in the end.

Samuel shot Shan a desperate look, a plea already dying on his lips as she just shook her head. There was sorrow written clear across her expression, not even bothering to hide the heartbreak and grief, but she had made her choice.

For her power, for her place at the King's side, she was willing to sacrifice Isaac.

But that was something he could never do, so the command fell from his lips, dark and furious, his voice echoing through the atrium as he yelled, "Stop!"

The effect of the single word rippled out, stronger than the tide as every eye jumped to him. Unable to fight the magic that sank into his bones, the King dropped his arm, a puppet under the control of a new master, the bridge immediately snapping and the magic rushing free.

Isaac didn't hesitate, the divots in his body popping out as he healed, banking across their heads as he soared out the window.

Leaving him alone with Shan and the Eternal King in the destroyed remains of the Blood Treasury, witch fire still roaring beneath their feet. The silence was complete—impenetrable—as the King turned his head so slowly, piercing him with a look that scared him down to the very marrow of his bones.

He had seen the King displeased before, had seen him frustrated and disappointed. But he had never seen this kind of fury. Not a wildfire out of control, but something colder, a chill settling over him like he had been plunged into the winter sea.

A dark and frozen depth that threatened to drown him.

Another command was at his lips, but the King was faster, his tongue darting out to lap at his own blood.

The same blood that tied them together across a millennium, an unbroken chain through a family that Samuel wished that he had never been born to, but it was still enough.

He felt the bridge snap to life, pulling at the center of his chest as the King's fury washed over him. He crashed to the floor, jaw snapping shut like his lips had been sewed together, his breath coming out in a huff as he tried to force even a single word out.

But his body wouldn't respond, his control completely sublimated to the King's.

Shan let out a cry—a single sob—before she choked it down.

The King spared her a glance, shockingly tender, and held out his hand. It was a summons, an offering, and Samuel wished with everything in his soul that she would do something—anything—to help him.

To choose *him* instead of her fucking schemes, just once.

But she stepped forward with a timidness he had never seen in her, placing her hand in the King's, and as his goddamn monster of an ancestor leaned down to press his lips to the back of Shan's fingers, Samuel felt his entire heart shatter into pieces.

"I'm sorry, Shan," the King said, and damn him for a fool, if Samuel didn't know any better, he would have thought that the King was sincere. "But we both knew that this was a possibility."

Samuel stared up at him in his forced silence, as if he could force the venom in his gaze to strike the King down where he stood. But he didn't have that power—even with his gift and the legacy he had stepped into, any power he might have had vanished the moment the King decided to rescind it.

And as he flicked his gaze over to Shan, who couldn't even bear to look at him, he hoped she learned the lesson too.

All the power she was so concerned with was nothing but smoke and mirrors, and they would never be more than tools for the King to use and dispose of as he saw fit.

Chapter Forty-Four

Shan

Shan winced as the Eternal King forced Samuel past another ward, the energy sizzling in the air as he tripped and fell. He landed hard on his knees, the bone cracking on the marble floor as he wavered. His hands were bound behind his back, caught in manacles she had taken from one of the many Guards around the Blood Treasury, his own cravat ripped from around his neck and turned into a makeshift gag.

Not that it was needed, really. The King kept the bridge burning between them, Shan could feel in the air, the same method of control they had used on Mel.

Oh, Mel. She may have been a monster, but Shan had felt a twisted kind of responsibility for her, feeling the moment Isaac ripped the girl's heart out of her chest like it was her own body being violated. Shan had been with Mel every step of this corrupted path, had released her into a battle she could not win, against a creature she did not even understand.

A manananggal. How long had he known? How long had Samuel known? A secret they had kept from her, and worse, she couldn't even blame them.

Shan stepped forward, helping Samuel to his feet, her touch gentle but her face carefully expressionless. She could do nothing for him now—if even Isaac, a manananggal empowered by the blood of so many victims, couldn't hope to break the King's control, what hope did either of them have?

None at all.

Even she, the Royal Blood Worker, the second most powerful person in this entire nation, couldn't do anything but play it smart. She hoped that Samuel understood. If he was to make it out of this alive, it would be through luck and cunning. A plan started to form, thoughts coming together in a nebulous cloud. She still needed more information, and she prayed that Samuel would give her the time to gain it.

They emerged back into the once-Blood Factory, the laboratory where they had worked together, slow crafting the most exquisite of beasts. She caught the moment the realization hit Samuel, his fear taking on a panicked edge, and—*oh*.

The King wouldn't do that to him, would he? Even with the hunger that consumed Mel, that drove her, the risk with Samuel was too high. He would be just as likely to bite the hand that fed him. No, this was something else, and that uncertainty scared her more than anything.

"Set him up on the table," the King ordered, before stepping away.

Samuel craned his neck, trying to follow the King's footsteps, but Shan didn't give him the chance. She just pushed him forward with a firm hand on the small of his back, guiding him towards the center of the room where the sole remaining table stood. He let her guide him onto the table, let her wrap the leather restraints tight on his wrists and ankles, meek and submissive. She met his gaze at last, her mouth working but no words coming out, whatever comfort she had nearly given caught on the tip of her tongue.

Still, he reached out as best he could, fingers straining, till her hand found his, fingers intertwined as he held on for dear life. He couldn't speak, not with his mouth still gagged, but he held her gaze, trying so hard to impart the message that she could not miss.

That he would forgive her, no matter what happened.

She blinked away the tears before they could fall and give her away.

After all she had done to him ... she did not deserve Samuel, the goodness and love in him too much to bear.

Apprehension strung taut, weaving around both of them as the King returned to their side. The King studied him, eyes narrowed, before reaching out and working the makeshift gag loose with a surprisingly gentle touch. The cloth came loose with a squelch, a dribble of spit connecting the wadded-up cravat to his lip. Samuel gasped through the sudden freedom and rasped out, "I'm surprised that you would trust me enough for this."

"Oh Samuel," the King said, every bit of the kindness he had shown them melting away. No, that cold, immaculate mask he wore was back, every emotion tucked away—or perhaps the humanity was the mask, and this was the truth of the Eternal King. Perhaps she had been as much of a fool as anyone, believing in those flickers of kindness and empathy.

Did it really matter, in the end?

"Do you really think I fear anything you could do?" the King continued, drawing the tip of his claw down the column of Samuel's throat. "You caught me off guard, I'll admit that, but ..." A glint of power thrummed between them, hanging in the air as hot as a burning coal. "I won't make that mistake again."

Samuel wasn't cowed, and oh, Shan was so proud of him. He wasn't giving up, matching the King blow for blow despite the futility of it all. "Then what is the point of this?"

The King didn't answer, not directly, wrapping his entire hand around Samuel's throat, pressing down to cut off his voice. It was a possessive touch, and the glint in the King's eye—chilling and cold—was hungry. He met Shan's eyes over their prisoner, and Shan realized with a sickening lurch what was about to happen. It wasn't Samuel who was about to be transformed.

No, this was something altogether worse.

"You disappoint me, Samuel," the King continued, with a sigh, unable to resist the opportunity to dig into the wound. The cruelty was directed at Samuel, but Shan felt it as keenly as if it were her throat that was crushed, her failures being dragged to the surface. "You threw it all away, and for what?"

He jabbed the claw into the soft, tender hollow of Samuel's throat, drawing a gasp from the man as the sharp metal split the flesh, grating against the bone. "You could have had the whole world at your fingertips, but you were too much of a coward to seize it."

Samuel ground his teeth through the shock of pain. "I'm braver than you could ever realize."

"Idealistic to the end," the King sneered, lifting his hand so the blood dripped from the claw, a fleck of red under the burn of witch light. "It's not bravery to throw your life away. Our dear Shan learned this lesson, tempered herself into something stronger."

The King smiled at her, like they were sharing in some great conspiracy, and Shan forced herself to match his glee, even if she felt nothing but terror and heartbreak.

"And to think, she could have been your bride." The King pressed metal against his own lip, licking the stain away until it shone clean. "And you, fool that you are, lost her."

"Indeed," Shan agreed, lying like she had never lied in her life, infusing the smirk she wore with all the disdain and disappointment she felt—not at Samuel, but at herself. With Samuel lying on the table before their King, a specimen to be taken apart, she finally saw the depths that she had fallen too.

In trying to protect Samuel, in trying to protect *herself*, she had become the very thing she had sworn to fight against, and the King looked at her with something akin to affection.

"No matter." The King picked up a gleaming dagger, the light glinting off its polished shine. "You were not enough for her, but I will be."

Samuel sucked in a harsh, sudden breath, but Shan barely heard it, too focused on the King's words. On the way everything that had happened between them over the past few months suddenly reframed themselves.

The King pressed the sharp edge of the blade against Samuel's pulse, almost daring his heir to speak.

He didn't.

"It's better this way," the King said, the dagger carving a thin line into Samuel's flesh, but his attention was on Shan, his mouth curved like he was presenting her with the most thoughtful gift. "With you, she would have been a magnificent rose, blooming only for a season, but I will make her more than you ever could." He bore down, the blood welling and weeping across Samuel's throat, and still, his gaze was on her. "A Queen worthy of Aeravin."

"Your Majesty—" Shan breathed, just as Samuel started to struggle against his bonds, thrashing on the table like a man possessed.

"You will destroy her!" Samuel bellowed, but it didn't move the King, only her.

But she couldn't show it, not with the King watching her, testing her mettle, ensuring that she could live up to every misplaced hope he set on her shoulders.

"You don't get to tell me that," she said, looking down at Samuel like he was the mud beneath her boot. It hurt her to watch his expression fall, but she hoped she could explain it to him, one day. "I will not be destroyed."

The King just smiled, speaking lowly, deadly as a promise. "I will remake her."

She wanted to scream, to cry, to tell them that this was never what she wanted, even as the lure of the truly endless power and potential the King offered sang like a siren in her head. But as the King slammed Samuel's head back against the hard metal, she knew that no matter what the King offered her, she would never take his hand again.

Oh, what a fool she was, to have finally found the line she wouldn't cross when there was nothing she could do to stop the tragedy she'd set in motion.

"I will remake myself as well," the King continued, "becoming something so powerful that none will dare stand against us. Not an innocent fool like you, not a desperate aberration like de la Cruz."

He moved the dagger, a sudden slice freeing Samuel's hand, the restraint cut through entirely. "These rebels will stand no chance, not against me, not against the future Queen, not against the vampires I will make. All your foolish plans will fold like the house of cards they are."

The blade dug into his wrist, and Shan couldn't stop the sympathetic wince as Samuel howled in agony. His scream echoed in the tight space, a sound of raw torment that would never be heard, trapped as he was beneath so many layers of stone and rock.

"And I will do it by taking what should have been mine in the first place." The King sank to his knees, but it wasn't reverence that he offered. His fingers held Samuel in place as he clamped his mouth over the wound, sucking straight from the artery, the erratic beat of Samuel's heart driving the blood straight into the King's willing throat.

Shan gasped, reaching out to steady herself on the table as the power erupted around them, the bridge the King snapped to life burning with such power that she swore it would incinerate her along with everything else.

Lifting his head, the King didn't bother to hide the manic gleam in his eyes, and Shan realized that this, at last, was the true face of the King. Not a carefully polished politician or a trusting mentor or a heartbroken man who had seen so many of the people he had cared for diminish and die around him. No, he was a pit of endless hunger that would never be filled, no matter how much he consumed. The Eternal King would crack the very foundation of the world under his heel, if he could.

And he would take her with him, immolating any part of her that was still good and kind in the process.

"It is done," the King said, lapping once more at the torn flesh before pulling back.

Shan stepped forward, her body moving on its own as her mind struggled to catch up, holding out a clean cloth.

"Thank you, Shan." The King took it, wiping his face clean as she struggled to calm her expression, to tuck away the shock and the fear.

The King didn't comment on it, if he had noticed it all, too focused on his new toy. "That is all for now."

"Your Majesty," Shan began, still reeling from all these revelations. He was to make himself a vampire, had taken on the Aberforth Gift, and had declared her a Queen in the making. "Are you sure—"

He cut her off with an indulgent smile, not a hint of anger and resentment to be found. "I appreciate that, but I have things handled here. There is no need for you to witness the interrogation. That said, I do have need of my Royal Blood Worker."

Shan swallowed hard. Of course that was what came next, using his newly acquired power to drag as much information out of Samuel as possible.

A flicker of fear burned in her core—fear for Isaac, for her brother—but she squashed it down. They were both smart. The moment the King had captured Samuel, she knew they would be moving all their operations, just like they had when it had been her.

"Go summon the Royal Council," the King instructed, pulling out his pocket watch to check the time. "Have them assemble in four hours in my study. That should be enough time to get things in order."

"And the reason?" she pressed, as if she could change his mind. As if she could find an excuse to stay by Samuel's side, through it all. "For the gathering?"

His smile slipped into that all-too familiar smirk. "We don't want to ruin all the fun, now do we? Don't worry about that. As the Royal Blood Worker, you act with my full authority. They will come."

It had been a futile attempt, but she had to try, even if she knew that it only could have ended this way.

"As you say, Your Majesty." Shan dipped into a low curtsy, before sparing Samuel one last, lingering glance. Praying that he would understand that she hadn't given up on him. "Until later."

The words were directed at the King, but they were for Samuel. All she had was her own cunning to find her way out of this mess. But for the love he had shown her, for the way that he had saved her again and again, the way that he had forgiven her when she had never deserved it, she would save him.

Even if it damned her in the process.

The King caught her hand before she could leave, pressing his newly cleaned mouth to the back of her hand. "I know you have many questions, my darling. But once this matter is settled, I swear to you, I will answer them."

She merely nodded. "I understand, but for now, I have work to do."

"Ever diligent," the King said, brushing her hair back from her face. "I do adore that about you."

Shan forced herself to blush, just a smidge. "I have to summon the Council."

He let her go, and Shan held back the sigh of relief. She did have to summon the Council, but first, she needed to find a bird.

Chapter Forty-Five

Shan

Shan dismissed the serving girls with a wave of her hand, taking a step back to study the set-up. A perfectly arranged tea service was spread across the King's desk, the space cleared for the occasion. Elegant bone china stood on matching saucers, exquisitely rendered rose buds nestled in a bed of ivy. Two full tea kettles brewed the King's favorite blend, featuring the same hand-painted motif. A three-tiered cake stand held a collection of small pastries and biscuits, each individual treat carrying the delicate work of the King's personal pâtissier.

Really, given the timeframe she had to accomplish this get-together and the time it took to find a bird, it really was a little triumph. The summoning had been sent, the gathering arranged just so, and Shan still had several minutes to spare.

She should have been proud of her work, but now that she had a moment to gather her thoughts, the only emotion that ran through her was a dull sense of disquiet, muted by her own shame that she dared not look at head-on.

Snatching her reticule, she pulled out a cigarette and lit it, inhaling deep off the nicotine as the buzz hit her, soothing her frayed nerves. The window latch was freezing under her touch, but she opened it to the frigid air, letting the blast of flurries dance around her. It should have hurt, the bite of winter on her face, but she was numb to it all.

The early sunset cast the capital below in a cloak of shadows, dusk blurring all the details into obscurity, the sudden winter squall blocking out even the brightest of witch light, the lanterns that lit the grand boulevards snuffed out.

Strange to think that it was only this morning that she was summoned to the Blood Treasury, that she had seen Isaac in all his glory, that Mel had met her grisly end. Only hours ago that Samuel had made his move against the King, not that she could blame him.

She had done foolish things for love as well, but none quite as foolish as this. For now, somewhere below her feet, the Eternal King had Samuel in his grasp, doing heavens knew what to him. She had seen the depths to which the Eternal King could fall, had stood by his side as he had dragged her under.

No. That wasn't right—he hadn't forced her. He had held out his hand, a simple offering, and she followed him into the darkness. If it was the price of power, of knowledge, of every ill-gotten thing she ever hoped for, she would let herself be ruined.

She hadn't expected it to be the ruin of Samuel as well. He had been hers to protect, hers to have and hers to hold. And yet, he had slipped through anyway.

The wall in the back of the room creaked, the telltale sound of the King's private passageway sliding open. Bracing herself, Shan turned to watch, the bookshelf rotating on its pedestal with a great groan.

Samuel staggered out first, the Eternal King shoving him forward. His white shirt was stained with blood and sweat, his hair a long and matted tangle down his back. He bore thin, scabbed lines across his throat, a bruised mass centered over the tender hollow—the wounds only slightly healed, closed just enough so that he wouldn't continue to bleed out, but not enough to be fully gone.

Raising his arm, Samuel braced himself on the edge of the bookshelf, and Shan traced her gaze over the horrid mess of meat that was the inside of his right wrist—the skin scarred and raised, deliberately mis-healed, and Shan swore she could still see the imprint of where the King's blunt teeth had been.

It was a petty kind of suffering that the King had left him in, a cruelty that he enacted just because he could. It was lesson and punishment all in one, and Shan inhaled deeply off her cigarette to hide the tremor in her breath.

Following Samuel out, the King looked as pristine as ever, his skin shining with vitality. He looked so vibrant and powerful, emerald eyes glinting and mouth pulled into a smirk that sent shivers down her spine, no matter how much she tried to suppress it. There was something magnetic and magnificent about him, daring her to lean in.

"Samuel," he intoned, and something slick and dark slid into the air, wrapping around the shaken man like shackles. "Take a seat and remain silent."

Samuel snapped upright, like someone had seized him by the back of the shirt and yanked him into place. He moved towards the first chair he could reach as if puppeteered, his movements stiff and ungainly, before collapsing into the sturdy chair. He ducked his head low, breath shaky, not bothering to hide the tears that streaked down his face.

The Aberforth Gift, finally fully taken from him, but given to the Eternal King, a new terror unlocked.

The King turned to her with a gracious smile—a too gracious smile. There was something shifting between them, something that she couldn't quite put her finger on, but it scared her to her core. "My darling, you've done a lovely job. Are the others coming?"

A knock resounded on the door, as if on cue, before a Guard swung it open. "The Royal Council of Aeravin," the Guard announced, before they all filed in, one after the other.

The suspicion in their eyes turning to outright fear as they saw Samuel slumped in his chair, brutally beaten and broken.

"Your Majesty," Lady Belrose said, dropping into a deep curtsy before the desk. The others followed suit, Lady Dunn and Lady Morse flanking her to each side, while Lord Rayne simply inclined his head, his shaking hands gripping his cane as he struggled to remain steady on his feet.

"Please, friends," the King said, even crossing the study to place a steadying hand on Rayne's shoulder as he helped him to a seat. "Do not stand on formality, have a seat."

The unease grew stronger, the Councillors sharing furtive glances with each other as the King continued his little kindnesses, going so far as to pour a cup of fresh, fragrant tea for Lord Rayne. The door to the room shut with a low *thunk*, and Shan had the absurd thought that they weren't given the grace of privacy but trapped. Alone like victims tossed in with a madman who was simply playing with his food.

Shan had learned her lessons well, from studying at her father's knee to branching out on her own, building her own web of power. The key to success was in learning the particular patterns and habits of her targets, of knowing how to respond and demur and fawn—but this attentiveness was not like the Eternal King. Not with his Councillors, not with the Lords and Ladies of Aeravin. No, this was a ploy of some kind, unsettling them so they could not find their footing. But for what purpose, Shan wasn't sure.

Stubbing her cigarette out, she tossed the remains out the window before sealing it shut—the last opening to the world outside. The King would want her by his side, and she had done so well capitulating to his demands already, so she couldn't stop now. No, her deception had only begun, and she would not give the King even a second to doubt her loyalty.

Taking her place by his side, she carefully poured out tea for the rest of the Councillors, handing them each a cup of the steaming rosehip blend. Her hands didn't shake in the slightest, not as she carefully cut the cake on the highest tier of the stand, offering equal slices of white sponge and delicate buttercream.

The Councillors all took it with a grateful incline of the head, though she could tell none of them were hungry, simply toying with their forks after taking the requisite bite.

She didn't offer any to Samuel, who still sat quietly off to the side, an exile among his own peers.

The whole thing was a farce, and the battered remains of Shan's heart railed against it. But the King only sent her one of those little sly smiles, there and gone again, making her feel like she was some grand co-conspirator.

And maybe she was, by the simple virtue of not fighting back. When had she become so afraid, so quick to fall in line? So desperate to cling to the scraps of power she had collected like broken seashells, fragments of their once glory, a pale imitation of what they had once been.

"Your Majesty," Lady Belrose began, ever the brave one. "Not that we need an excuse to enjoy the fruits of the royal kitchens, but is there a particular reason you have called us here?"

"Of course, of course," the King said, clapping his hands together. "I assume you've heard tell of what happened at the Blood Treasury this morning?"

He was still so cheerful, even when discussing the veritable disaster. Shan chanced a sidelong glance over at Samuel, his hands gripping the armrests, fingers curled like claws, blunt fingertips digging into the armrest. Energy thrummed through him, a low vibration that suggested that he was crawling out of his skin—but he was still unable to speak, the command the King had bound him with holding him tighter than any chains or manacles could.

"I had heard, Your Majesty," Belrose began, only for Morse to cut her off.

"The witch fire is still burning," Morse said, expression drawn tight in a troubled frown, "and as such it is impossible to get an exact calculation of the full damage. But it is unlikely that any of our stock remains."

Inclining his head, the King beamed at her, perching on the edge of his desk. "Thank you, Penelope. Exact as always. That constant attention to detail and unwavering dedication to order is precisely why I picked you to be the Councillor of the Military. I know I can count on you for what is coming."

Morse didn't flush, didn't stammer any soft words to demur. But her unease deepened, the King's continued cheer at the discussion souring even Shan's stomach.

"It was quite a morning, and we saw the full extent of de la Cruz's madness." Something shifted in the way he held himself—the smile remained, but a subtle tension appeared in the stiff way he held his shoulders, the feathering of a muscle in his jaw. "And we lost a brave new soldier in the process."

Shan tracked the flicker of unease that went around the Council. So, they had heard of the vampire, then. Even if none of them had been quite bold enough to bring it up. Amelia cast a glance her way, and Shan could only lift a shoulder in a brief shrug. She had no more control here than the rest of them.

"I cannot lie," the King continued, with a little more decorum, a hint of solemnity creeping in. "This is going to be a tough blow to recover from, as I am sure is their aim. But Aeravin is a strong nation, and we won't let a few fools with their ideas of rebellion undo a millennium of work."

Lord Rayne cleared his throat with a rough, phlegmy grunt. "Forgive an old man his fears, Your Majesty, but what is the course of action?"

"There is nothing to forgive, Matthias," the King said with a sigh. "You've served me well for so long, and I regret that the twilight of your reign couldn't come in a more peaceful time. But I will need you, all of you, if we are going to handle the threat at our doorstep."

That got Lady Belrose's attention. She set the cup to the side, squared her shoulders and tipped her chin up. Ever ready to seize on an opportunity.

How Shan once admired her, the power she wielded as one of the Royal Council, the spot she held leading the House of Lords, the counsel she gave to the Eternal King himself. The effortless way she glided through Aeravinian society, perfect in every moment, the world bending around her, following her in her wake like the tide followed the moon.

"We are ready, Your Majesty," Belrose swore, re-dedicating her fealty to her liege. "Just give us your command."

Shan sucked in a harsh breath as the King smirked—the trap had been set, and eager to please, eager to steal yet another scrap of power, Belrose had rushed in head first, pulling the others after her. Eager to avoid another embarrassment like last time, when he had stormed into the House of Lords and upended the entire balance of power that this nation ran on.

And to avoid that, Belrose handed herself over wholly to the King's ambitions, and Shan knew with a sickening lurch of her stomach that whatever schemes the King had would be vicious.

But Belrose had already committed, and one could never simply break a promise to royalty.

"I knew I could count on your loyalty, Jenna," the King said, her name a caress on his tongue. The familiarity a gift, offered so freely, that lured them in. "And I will need your help, all of the Royal Council's help, for this is a time of great risk.

"First, I have decided to make the suspension of the House of Lords permanent."

The silence was so complete that Shan could have heard a pin drop, the Royal Council absorbing the information. Dunn turned her head towards Shan, a foxhound on the hunt, sensing the new opportunities even as one door closed. Belrose made no reaction at all, only sat there with her hands trembling in her lap. Rayne, for his part, looked only more exhausted, the weight of his years an ineffable yoke around his neck.

Lady Morse, however, was eager, leaning forward to rest her elbows on her knees as she remained lost in thought.

"It was a grand idea," the King explained with just the right amount of ruefulness, "and it worked well for a long time, but in the coming months we will need the ability to move swiftly, making sweeping changes without waiting for the approval of popular votes."

"What sort of changes?" Dunn asked, betraying not a sliver of emotion. She was waiting for the right cue before committing herself one way or the other, and Shan felt a sudden surge of disgust.

She never should have recommended Amelia, she had only created a new, cunning enemy to outsmart.

"I have been too lax." Ducking his head, the King looked shamed, as if waiting for the harsh judgement that none of them would ever be foolish enough to admit. "Too caught up in my own studies and pursuits that I forgot my first and most solemn duty to the nation I founded and the citizens I rule."

He pushed away from the desk, crossing over to the mantle and the roaring fire within. He kept his back to the Council, his face shrouded in shadow, though every word he said was clear. "I was the one who chose to elevate de la Cruz, I was the one who decided that the Unblooded, numerous as they are, were below our attention."

Shan could feel the sway, the way the King pulled the others along, a more masterful performance than she had seen on any stage. Because, if she knew him even a little less, if she had just a little less cunning, she would have believed him too.

Especially when he turned back to look at Samuel at last, a glare of such hate and disappointment that it hit Shan like a punch to the gut. "I was the one who elevated a gutter rat to a near prince, but an esteemed lineage and careful guidance couldn't lift him beyond the muck he was born to."

Oh, there was some truth to this after all. Yes, Shan could see the thin seams at the edges, but there was real emotion behind it all. The King may have been nigh immortal, may have been the most powerful and shrewd being Shan had ever met, but somewhere beneath all the years and mysteries he shrouded himself in, there was still a heart that beat human and real.

And somehow, that made it all the worse.

"If I may, what did Lord Aberforth do?" Belrose asked, with an eagerness that surprised Shan. It wasn't concern, not really, but curiosity. Shan had known that he wasn't popular with the rest of the Councillors, had dismissed it as of little importance in comparison to the goals they pursued. But to see it so starkly, the open contempt for Samuel as they all ignored his plight in favor of their own lesser sufferings.

It broke what little resolve she had as a sickening wave of shame cut through her, every mistake she had made on this long, twisted path crystallizing in perfect clarity.

She had been the one to allow this—every bit of it was her fault. It had been her who dragged Samuel into the wolves' den, who led him to the King's embrace. Her foolishness that missed her brother's budding revolution, Isaac's endless pain and the blood he had shed in retribution. It had been her who attached herself to the King in the aftermath, who had stepped into the role of Royal Blood Worker with a fervor that wasn't strictly necessary.

At any point along the way she could have changed course, could have made the right decision, for once in her goddamn life. But she had chosen power, again and again, even when she should have known better.

The entirety of not only her life, but her world, was falling apart, and it was her own damned fault.

"It is because of Samuel that de la Cruz escaped," the King snarled.

Shan saw the way that Samuel flinched, each word cutting like a blade. The King wasn't done, grabbing him by his hair and yanking his head up so that he was forced to look upon everyone there. Tears budded, drawing more attention to the sunken bruises under his bloodshot eyes, and still, Samuel did not say anything—*could* not say anything.

Couldn't fight for himself because the King had commanded him to silence, turning the very magic that Samuel had spent his whole life fearing into the means of his own destruction. Perhaps the others saw it as strength, or as misplaced pride, but Shan knew the truth behind all the lies.

Practical but cruel, the Eternal King that Shan had come to know so well, ensuring that Samuel would feel every second of his punishment.

"But, as annoying as that was, it proved to be a boon in the end. It took little work to make this canary sing." He shoved Samuel forward so that he toppled out of his chair, landing on his hands and knees with a thud. "Because he was able to reveal to me the truth I had suspected all along—de la Cruz has joined with these fool rebels, and by taking out one we will destroy the other."

The King lifted his face, his green eyes glinting with something like sympathy, and Shan schooled her expression to one of mild confusion even as horror ran down her spine like ice. There was only one reason he would look at her like that—Samuel must have been forced to reveal Anton's part in all this. And because she had been playing her part all too well, he must believe her to be innocent of her brother's crimes.

Terror and elation ran through her at the same time, two interwoven currents running in opposite directions, nearly enough to overwhelm her, but there was still a chance for her to salvage this. For now, she put that aside, burying that seed of hope so deep that it wouldn't dare show in her expressions or mannerisms.

"For his part in this," the King continued, shifting his back to Shan as he stared down his Council, "Samuel Aberforth has been stripped of his title, his lands, and his fortune. He is henceforth cast out of Aeravinian society, and as his final punishment, his Blood Working has been taken from him."

Belrose inclined her head. "The wicked should be punished, and Your Majesty is fair as ever."

She couldn't see the King's expression, if he was pleased by this blatant groveling or if he found it just as sniveling and disgusting as she did. Regardless, the work was done, Samuel's fate sealed.

"Lady LeClaire," the King said, summoning her forward.

Shan stepped up, placing her hand in his offered grip. He leaned down, brushing his lips against her knuckles. "Handle Aberforth for me, will you? I have much to discuss with the Council, and it's not for the ears of dogs like him."

He didn't give her a chance to flinch, but also didn't make a command of it. No, this was a request. A test. And she had to manage the next few steps very carefully.

"How would you like me to dispose of him, my lord?"

"I don't care." The King traced her cheek with his claw, too gentle to be a threat, too pointed to be innocent. "He has hurt you too, my dear, and so I leave it in your hands. Do with him whatever you desire."

"Aren't you concerned?" she breathed, and the King shook his head.

"No. He's no threat to us now, I've seen to that personally. Kill him, drop him in the ocean, keep him as a pet." His mouth pulled into that too-cruel smirk, the kind he so rarely showed in front of others. "Hell, let him wander the streets of the capital, a warning to those who will dare stand against us."

He really believed that. She could see the disdain and dismissal in his eyes. Now that he had stripped Samuel of his magic and his title, he truly believed that the man proved to be no threat.

She had been so wrong. She would never be the one to dethrone this King of Vampires. It would be his own disdain for the Unblooded that would destroy him, in the end.

She just had to make sure that they had a chance—and by whatever fractured remains of her soul remained, she would see it through. She had already set it in motion.

"As you say," Shan said, dropping into a curtsy. "Well, I have never been one to waste an opportunity."

"That's my girl," he breathed, a whisper shared just between them, and Shan knew she had passed this test.

Now all she had to do was ensure that Samuel made it out of this alive. Even if he never forgave her for her part in it.

Grabbing him by the back of his shirt, Shan dragged him to his feet and towards the door. "Let's go, Aberforth. We have much to prepare you for."

Chapter Forty-Six

Isaac

The room was completely bare, Isaac noted dispassionately. No chairs to sit on, no table to gather around, just the undressed windows on the far wall and the winter's night dim outside. It felt fitting, as empty as he was inside, a pit that grew as the hours went on, knowing that Samuel had sacrificed himself so that he had the chance to escape.

He shouldn't have taken it; he shouldn't have left Samuel behind. He knew the King's cruelties, and there wasn't anything he could do to save the man he loved.

"Why are we here?" Isaac asked, impatience growing. "We should be doing something—"

"Bart said this was important," Anton interrupted him, not harshly. Kindly, gently, like he was afraid Isaac was about to shatter.

He was wrong. Isaac wouldn't shatter. He was as strong as ever; he had proven that this very morning as he ripped that vampire's head clean from her shoulders. All he needed was a target, a direction, something or someone to kill. Not this interminable *waiting*.

The door opened, Bart slipping through with a cloaked figure behind him, the dark velvet shielding their visitor from view. Isaac didn't need his enhanced senses to pierce her disguise, didn't need to listen for the beat of a heart all too familiar, didn't need to scent the faint traces of perfume that she had not been able to scrub clean. He could have claimed it was his manananggal nature that told him the visitor was Shan before she even removed her hood, but the truth was altogether worse.

He knew her as well as he knew himself, and she would never be able to hide from him.

But she wasn't hiding—she had reached out to *them*, had come to them. Here she stood with shoulders drawn in, her head hung low, twisting her bare hands in front of her, no claws to be seen. Just her slight form, looking suddenly so small, not a Lady at all.

Where was her pride and surety? The very things that had pulled them apart, gone. She just watched the three of them, a unified force standing against her, and Isaac saw the exact moment her heart broke.

"Why are you here, Shan?" Anton asked, direct and blunt as a club.

Shan didn't hide the wince, her dark eyes flicking to her brother, and Isaac swore he saw the shine of tears in her eyes. *That's* what felt off. This wasn't Lady Shan LeClaire, Royal Blood Worker. This wasn't the industrious and clever Sparrow. This was the truth behind all the masks, the scared and lonely woman who had nothing left to lose.

Once, he would have been moved. Once, he would have given anything to see her this open and honest with him. But now, he wasn't sure he could stand to be in the same room as her.

"I know I owe you, *all* of you, an apology," Shan began, "but I'm not here for me. I'm here for Samuel."

Samuel, the one he had left behind. The one she had doomed. The one they needed to save. He shared a quick glance with Anton, who clenched his jaw but nodded. None of them liked this, but they would use it.

They would use whatever they had.

"Fine," Isaac said, "talk."

Shan blinked away the sorrow, her voice coming out strong and steady. "The King has taken the Aberforth Gift from Samuel, along with his Blood Working. You saw the vampire he created—" her eyes focused right on his, and Isaac could taste the pungent wave of fear that came from her "—and in addition to creating an army of vampires to fight you, he will be one himself."

Isaac closed his eyes as he processed it, ignoring the way that Anton pressed his sister for details. This was worse than he feared, the step he had been so sure the King wouldn't take. His entire empire of blood had been built on carefully calculated decisions and the utmost control, so Isaac figured the King would never let himself become a slave to the hunger that haunted his every breath.

He had, once again, been wrong.

"And in the morning," Shan said, drawing his attention back to the very real problems in front of them, "Samuel will be executed. *I* will have to execute Samuel. Unless you step in."

"Anton—" Isaac was already turning to the man for permission, but he just held up his hand.

"We will, Isaac," Anton said. "Don't you worry about that. But first, what else do you know about these vampires? What is the King planning?"

"I don't know any more," Shan said. "But as soon as I do, I will let you know."

Silence fell, so complete that Isaac could hear his own heartbeat. But it was Bart who stepped forward, who spoke, who threw acid in Shan's face. There was hurt between them, too much for Isaac to fully understand, even if he did empathize, even if he had known his own kind of suffering under Shan's cruel mercies.

"Oh, will you, Sparrow?" The old title was a weapon, one that struck true. "Funny, how just two days ago you were ready to wash your hands of everything we built."

"I was unkind," she admitted, and the laugh that came out of Bart's throat was so strangled it hurt.

"Unkind," he repeated, just this side of hysterical. "Shan, I don't know if you've ever been kind a day in your life, and I am done pretending we ever had anything even close to a friendship. Did you ever care for anyone but yourself?"

"I did," she gasped, as the tears started to fall in earnest, her masks stripped away and leaving her bare. "I *do*."

Bart rolled his eyes, but Isaac knew the truth. She had cared, she had cared so damn much but had no healthy way to show it. So, she did this because she thought it was love. Because she wanted to protect all those around them, and never once stopped to ask what they wanted. What they needed. It was twisted and hurtful, but it was honest—and that was the worst truth of all.

"You do care about us," he said, stepping forward as she tilted her face up to his. He caught the wetness with his thumb, and she grabbed onto his wrist like he was the only thing keeping her from collapsing. "But you care about control more."

"I know," she breathed. "I am trying to change, and that is why... why I am doing this." Letting go of Isaac, she squared her shoulders and turned to Bart, her first friend.

Her only friend.

"Let me prove to you," she said, presenting it like it was an offer. A deal, not a demand, trading herself for a chance to re-earn their trust. And through it all, she wouldn't beg, because she knew she was useful. It was all she had left to deal in, having wasted the affection of those she once called close.

It was, as always, a masterful thing to watch.

"This is why I am here," she explained, this time to Bart and Anton. "I am not the Sparrow anymore, but if you'll let me, I'll be your bird. The one we never could place, the one at the King's side."

Anton's voice cracked, the anger slipping away to reveal the truth beneath it. Fear, stark and unalloyed. "You don't want out?"

Shan shrugged, like it was nothing, like it wasn't even a consideration. "I do want out, but that's not the best use of me. For the King, he..."

"He what, Shan?" Isaac asked, that fear spreading to him, sour and inescapable. "Has he threatened you?"

"No, worse." She clenched her jaw, forced the words out. "He wants me as his Queen."

Something inside Isaac snapped, a near feral craving that shattered his control. The mere thought of it, the King's hands on her, his mouth on her lips, his body against hers—

He could not let that happen. He did not consider himself a possessive man, not really, but this was something he could not allow. "He will not have you."

"He will not," Shan agreed, this time reaching out for him, taking his hand and putting it over her heart, letting him feel the steady way it beat. True and constant for him, a promise that she did not even have to put into words. "Not here. Not in any way that truly matters."

Chancing a glance over her shoulder, she said, "Bart, Anton, can you give us a moment?"

Bart started to protest, but Anton reached out, clasping him around the shoulder. "It's all right, Isaac can take care of himself, and we'll be right outside."

It was a warning, pointless as it was. If Shan wanted to leave, there was nothing either of them could do to stop her. The only one who could stand up to her was Isaac, and he was not afraid of the woman in front of him. She had lost her control over him long ago, just as he had lost his control over her.

Here they stood, perhaps for the first time, as equals—and it felt like everything hinged on what came next.

"I'll be fine," Isaac confirmed. "She's right. We need to talk."

"Fine. You have five minutes, then we need to figure out how we're saving Samuel. Use it wisely." Bart charged out of the room, Anton following behind after tossing them a jaunty salute, and they stood in silence until the door clicked shut behind them.

Five minutes. Not enough time to undo what felt like a lifetime of hurts, but it was a start, and Isaac would not waste it. He reached out, planning to grab a hold of Shan and hold her close, but she sidestepped, danced right out of his reach with a wistful smile.

"I haven't earned that, yet." She leaned back against the wall, the only relief in this plain, empty room. But the distance seemed to give her strength, and he recognized what this was. He didn't need to go to her, she needed to come to him. She had already started, she was here after all, but she still needed to take that final step.

If he could convince her.

"It's not about earning," he said, surprising himself with just how much he meant it. "I think that's been our problem all along. Keeping score, trading favors, calling in debts. That's not how this is supposed to work."

It was what they were taught, the fickle and ever-changing lives of Blood Workers, alliances broken and reforged with each passing dawn. Trust no one, not even your family, not even those you loved the most, *especially* not those you loved the most. They had the most opportunity and reason to hurt you.

"How is it supposed to work, then?" Shan asked.

"We need to trust each other," he said, even knowing that he was the one who had cut that first wound. "We need to be ... honest."

"That easy?" she huffed, and he could hear the waver in her voice. She was close to breaking—and he could push her completely over the edge or snatch her back from the brink.

He couldn't let her fall. "So let me start. I am sorry for cutting you out, all those years ago. For leaving you to the wolves, for not trusting you when I first started this mad plan. For not thinking about what the King would do to you should I fail, for not understanding even when I—of all people—know just how impossible being Royal Blood Worker is."

It was strange, now that it was out in the open. He had expected this to hurt more, to be like ripping out thorns that had embedded themselves in his heart, scabbed over by scar tissue as they continued to prick. But this was as easy as breathing, and all he felt was relief.

"I was wrong," he admitted, "and I hurt you. For that I am sorry, and I will spend the rest of my life making it up to you, if you will have me."

Swallowing hard, Shan replied, "Thank you. I ... needed to hear that. But you are not the only one who needs to apologize." She tilted her chin up, the words falling from her lips like a waterfall that had finally burst through its dam. "I hurt you as well. You're right, I never considered what you wanted, I only wanted what I thought was best. I was—I *am*—so afraid of not being in control that I draped myself in every cruelty I could as protection. And in that, I have hurt you."

Her voice fell to a whisper. "I have hurt so many people . . . I don't deserve this."

"No," Isaac agreed, "but you can still earn it, if you want to."

"I can?" she asked, so small, and he never wanted to hear her so unsure of herself again.

"You can," he repeated, knowing that he would repeat it as many times as it took, until she understood that she could always come back. All she needed to do was believe in herself. He held out his hand.

And she took it.

Pulling her in, he wrapped his arms around her, holding her tight as she collapsed into sobs against his chest, all the fear and pain rolling out of her in a wave that was tinged with the bittersweet burn of long-awaited forgiveness.

"I thought I lost you," Shan choked out, her words muffled, but he heard them clear as day. "I thought I lost Samuel as well but he . . . he—"

"He what, darling?"

"He saved my life today," she whispered, "right before he saved yours. He's always doing that, even though we don't deserve it."

He tipped her chin up, pressed his mouth to her forehead. "Ah, but we do."

"But what if," she asked, and here it was, the biggest fear of all. "What if I don't? What if I fall again?"

"Then," Isaac said, "we will be there to catch you, Shan. You don't need to be alone in this. You have your brother, Bart. Myself. And—" he dropped his hands to hers, squeezed them tight "—Samuel, once we save him."

The balance that they needed, the goodness they could still reach for. The missing part of this relationship that they hadn't even realized they were lacking for so long. That, now that they had it, they would never let go of.

"You're right," she agreed, and she pressed herself up on her tiptoes, catching him in a kiss. It wasn't hungry, like so many of the ones they had shared in the past year—it was gentle, it was an apology and promise all wrapped up in one, their rough edges finally fitting together like two halves of the same broken whole, and Isaac wished they could linger in this moment for the rest of their lives.

"Ahem," Anton coughed, and they pulled apart from each other. "We told you that you only had five minutes, but if you'd like some more—"

"Oh, shut it," Shan said, crossing the room to give her brother a playful shove before turning to Bart. "I'm sorry, truly."

"I know, Shan," Bart said, crossing his arms over his chest. Still closed off, but not quite shutting her down. "And we've got a lot to talk about, but we don't have time right now. Not if we're going to save Samuel."

Shan nodded, wiping away the last of her tears. "Of course. Samuel is to be executed tomorrow morning, and you—" she crooked her finger at Isaac "—need to rescue him."

"Easy," he began, but she wasn't done.

"That's not all, if I am going to stay at the King's side," Shan said, giving her brother a stern look before he could object, "and I am. So you need to make this look real."

"Real?"

Her smile was so sad. "Real. I'll have to fight you, and you're going to have to defeat me. Don't pull your punches, love."

Isaac wavered, thrown by the calm certainty with which she asked him to hurt her, just because it was necessary.

"Afterwards, we will need to be careful," she continued, her confidence returning, and he realized just how thoroughly she had thought this through. "No in-person meetings, dead drops only. Whatever your plans are, wherever you muster, I cannot have that information. I will not be the one who leads the King to you."

"You'll have no backup," Anton said, his tone uncommonly serious. "No way out should things go sideways."

Shan just shrugged. "I know, but this is the point of it. This isn't about me, anymore." She smiled at her brother, so openly proud. "I will never be able to fix Aeravin, but you can. It doesn't need a Sparrow, or a Royal Blood Worker, it needs you and your rebellion."

She turned to Bart, offering her words like a gift, the first brick with which they could rebuild what she had torn asunder. "It needs a Hawk, someone with the talons to see this through."

Finally, she turned to Isaac, and there was such love and trust in her eyes that she might as well have stolen the breath straight from his lungs. "It needs you, Isaac. A manananggal who will bring the King to his knees.

"So let me be the bird, because this is what I've been training for my whole damned life." She tilted her head up, so brilliantly radiant, so sure of herself even as she put herself into the lion's den. "Let me fly."

"All right, darling," Isaac agreed, letting her go, even though it felt like he had just gotten her back, this love of theirs having crawled its way back from the dead yet again. But he had to let her go free, trusting that she would come back to him.

And trust he would. "Now, let's save Samuel."

Chapter Forty-Seven

Samuel

The central square of Dameral glittered all around Samuel, the shards of early morning sunlight reflecting off the pristine snow an assault to his already overloaded senses. The ride over in the carriage had been terrible, Samuel feeling each and every bump in the cobblestones, the sounds of common life in the streets like a dagger to the brain, digging into all the soft and bruised parts of his mind.

A foul morning on top of a foul night, shoved into a spare bedroom in the King's grand palace, a luxurious cell that was, despite all its fineries and comforts, still a cell. Tired and hurting, Samuel had been stuck stewing in his own suffering, impotent in his uselessness. In one of his better moments, he had even torn his own flesh with his blunt nails, tearing apart the ill-healed wounds chasing the Blood Working he had never wanted.

But there was no power left in him, just the slick taste of salt on his tongue.

Just this vast, empty crevice in his chest where his power—his *magic*—used to live. His body trembled, aching like his bones had been scrubbed clean with steel wool, his head stuffed with cotton as his skull throbbed. It lingered in him, ebbing and flowing, but the momentary relief wasn't enough to counteract the depths of the suffering as the pain always returned.

And now he stood, swaying, on display before what felt like the entire world. But it was only a squadron of Guards, pulled from their patrols to form a protective barrier around the central square, a quickly and shoddily erected fence pressing up against a crowd of eager and confused citizens.

Blood Workers, most of them, with their glinting claws and thick coats. But further out, past the leeches that sucked them dry, was an entire flock of Unblooded, huddled together in the frigid winter morning. From this distance, Samuel couldn't make out their faces or expressions, but there was something comforting about it. Even if they never knew how he had fought for them, never understood the full role that he played in this, if Samuel was going bleed this day, he would do it for those he had been trying so hard to save.

A hand landed hard between his shoulder blades, shoving him forward, the kiss of steel claws a threat against the thin layer of his shirt. He was underdressed for the season, a deliberate choice, he was sure, his torn shirt and thin trousers yet another insult to add to the many, many injuries. Perhaps it was to make him suffer a little more, perhaps it was meant to make a spectacle of just how far he had fallen.

It didn't matter in the end.

Samuel didn't turn his face back towards the Guard, not caring which soul was spurring him on to the conclusion of this grand farce. Not when there was someone else there, waiting for him on the small ramshackle stage that they had managed to erect, a mere shadow of the normal pomp and circumstance when the King came out to parade his annual sacrifice before the masses.

The King didn't even bother to attend this morning, having delegated this task to the only one he could—Lady Shan LeClaire, the Royal Blood Worker.

She stood facing him, her back to the crowd as the breeze caught her hair, the chill bringing a fetching flush to her cheek. A thick cloak wrapped around her shoulders, the same deep red as her robes of office, spilling down her body like a slick of wet blood, clinging to the curves that he had memorized with his hands and his lips.

Flurries swirled around her, soft and ethereal, painting her as pretty and picturesque as a work of art.

Her expression was serene, no trace of hurt or sorrow in her features, except for the brief shine in her eyes. Tears? Or just the natural response to the wintry chill around them?

Samuel would never know, but fool that he was, he took that brief flicker of hope and held it close. If he did not make it through this, he would die clinging to the love that had saved him and destroyed him in equal measure.

Shan turned as he came up to her side, leaving him to stare at the elegant line of her profile as she took a deep breath, summoning the attention of all watching to her.

"Greetings, my fellow citizens," she called, her voice as clear as a bell, ringing across the square. She could have been a diva on the stage, a debutante seducing the ball, a Queen before a throne. She was so achingly beautiful, and Samuel thanked the King for giving him this last gift.

"I am sorry for the sudden notice," Shan continued, not so much as glancing his way. "And for the uncooperative weather, but I am sure many of you have heard of the tragic events yesterday at the Blood Treasury."

Murmurs broke out, trickles of worry rippling back through the crowd, shifting to anger. But Shan just held up one hand, and the whispering stopped.

"I know there are questions about what this means for us," Shan continued, and how easy it would have been for her to break here. To beg and plead for understanding. But she stood tall and strong, just as unflinching as ever. "How it will affect all the aspects of our lives, from the Academy all the way down to our daily requisitions. The Eternal King and I are working on a new program, and I beg your indulgence in this matter. New guidance will be forthcoming. But today, we are here for justice.

"It is with a heavy heart that I stand before you today," she said, at last casting him a glance, only sidelong. Yearning and shame, loss and anger, flickering across her expression as her mask broke, if only for a moment.

If he had known her a little less, he might have believed it. But all this was carefully calculated, and Samuel could feel the energy swell, not the brush of Blood Working or his own lost Gift, but something simpler than that. A woman plucking on the strings of her audience, whipping them up slowly, building their fury and frenzy. Conducting this orchestra like a master, layering tense strings of wrath, harsh and shrill and grating, over the steady percussion of fear.

Letting them eat out of the palm of her hand.

If things were different, Samuel would have been so proud of her. If he was being honest, he was still so proud of her, even though it was his own fate that hung in the balance. She had grown so much in the past year, finally allowed to step out of the shadows, tossing aside the rules that had ruled her entire life. And in doing so, she had become glorious.

Why had she settled for being the King's lackey, when she could break the world under her boot, if she only dared to?

But he didn't have the chance to dwell on that, to chase his flight of fancy down paths of what could have been. Not with the eyes of what felt like half the capital on him, not with the icy grip of winter biting into bare skin.

Not as he focused back on the words that Shan was saying.

"—and for his part in the attack on the Blood Treasury, for his part in the destabilization of everything we hold dear, for committing high treason against the crown, Samuel Aberforth..." her voice cracked, not losing any volume of clarity, but shaking nonetheless "... has been stripped of his position as the Councillor of Law. He has been stripped of his title and fortune. He will be executed in a way that is befitting his crimes, and you, my fellow citizens, shall bear witness to it."

A pair of Guards stepped up behind him, their actions coordinated as they both struck him in the back of the knee with heavy batons, the sudden crack of pain enough to send him tumbling down. They grabbed his arms, hoisting him to his knees, arms pulled back and head tilted towards the sky. There was no fighting their grip, not as their claws curled around his forearms, ready to slip into his flesh and tear it asunder.

There was no escaping, not as Shan pulled her cloak to the side, retrieving a gleaming dagger from the sheath at her hip. She wore no claws, her fingers bare—an intimacy that shouldn't have moved him. But there was something calming about it, knowing that she would touch his skin with hers, one last time, unencumbered by metal.

"I am glad," he said, even as the Guard yanked on his hair, baring his throat to the crowd. "That it is you and not him."

Some real emotion broke through the performance, the dagger jerking in her hand, her eyes dark and unfathomable. She swallowed once, her mouth forming the shape of his name, when a chilling shriek echoed through the square.

Spinning away, Shan turned to the east, raising her arm to shield against the light of the sun, as Isaac crested over rooftops, his entrails fluttering behind him. He looked both glorious and terrifying, backlit by the sun, his vicious maw stretched into a gaping chasm of fangs, his long tongue flicking in the air, scenting his targets.

A fierce joy sang through Samuel as understanding hit—Isaac was here, risking himself again to save him.

Pulling his wings in tight, Isaac cut through the air, diving directly down towards the stage, building momentum until he banked suddenly, snatching Shan around the waist as he lifted her up into the sky, the dagger flying from her grip to clatter in front of Samuel.

Despite the way that his heart threatened to beat out of his chest—he couldn't even make sense of them, tangled together as they were, twisting through the sky—Samuel took advantage of the chaos, struggling against the stunned Guards. They didn't fight him, shoving him back into the wooden planks as they hurried to the edge of the platform, the useless prisoner no longer worth their time as they focused on saving the Royal Blood Worker.

Not that they could do much, armed with claws and blades and

Blood Working that needed a bridge to work, if they could even manage to affect a manananggal, something that the Eternal King himself had struggled with.

Screams broke out as the crowd panicked, those closest to the stage pushing and elbowing their way towards the side streets around the square. But their stampede was stopped as the Unblooded pushed back—going against common sense as they pressed tighter around the Blood Workers, a throng turning into a noose to keep them trapped.

Pushing himself back up to his feet, Samuel watched the sway of the crowd, the cacophony around him taking the low throb of pain in the back of his head and ratcheting up to a roar. Staggering, Samuel wrapped his arms around himself, forcing past the sudden agony to focus on the events spilling out around him, on the way the movement was coordinated in such a way that felt intentional. Anxiety curled in his stomach as he scanned the crowd, spotting a familiar tall figure off to the west—Alaric rallying those around him. On the other side of the square, he spotted Maia's braids as her hood was knocked down, a fierce smile on her face as she goaded those around her.

This was more than just Isaac, this was a planned coup, an organized attempt to seed chaos—this was the rebellion come to save *him*. And though he did not understand how this had come to pass, the work that it must have taken to arrange this in such a short time, Samuel knew that this was his only chance.

But as the crowd surged forward, knocking the barricades down to the cobblestones, the Guards broke free from their stupor, rushing to hold the masses back. It freed Samuel from their attention, yes, but as the panic skirted desperately close to something more dangerous, it left him with little options to escape.

Glancing again towards the sky, he looked up just in time to see Isaac shake Shan loose, her unclawed hands slipping along his bare flesh.

As she fluttered, free-falling, in the air, her cloak billowing around her, before she fell a good fifteen feet to land on the platform in front of him with a bone-shattering crack.

Samuel lurched forward towards her, even though he should have been rushing in the opposite direction. Even though he shouldn't be risking himself in this manner, knowing that this entire operation was a chance for him to escape. But he'd never been able to resist her gravitational pull, chasing her across the heavens until he burned out completely.

He skidded to his knees, afraid to touch her, knowing that the injuries from the fall went deeper than what he could see on the surface. Moving her was probably a bad idea, as he did not know what additional damage he could do the undoubtedly broken bones and worse within. Blood Working would have helped, but the King had stolen that from him, leaving him completely and utterly useless.

Samuel fisted his hands at his sides, trying not to cry. Despite everything, the mistakes she had made over and over, the knife she had held in her hand not moments before, ready to drink his blood, he could not stand to watch her dying.

How could Isaac have done this?

She lay where she had landed, back against shattered wooden planks, her breath a rasping rattle in her chest. A dribble of blood leaked from the corner of her mouth, but her eyes were open, flickering back and forth until they landed on him.

Shan spluttered, a low, gasping sound, as she turned her head, the sound of bone scraping on bone sending shivers down his spine. "Samuel," she wheezed, anger glinting into those dark eyes, her mouth pulled into that familiar thin line, "why aren't you running?"

"I—" he started, even though he didn't have an answer. There was nothing he could do to help her, and yet, he lingered. "Shan ... I—"

"Flee!" she spat, a globule of blood splashing onto the ground between them. "Before it's too late."

Samuel rocked back on his heels, confusion washing over him, but before he could even make a conscious decision, a pair of strong arms wrapped around him, yanking him off his feet and into the sky.

The sudden rush of the movement was disorienting, the low pain that he had pushed away overtaking him. Bile forced its way up his throat, but he choked it down, twisting in the manananggal's grip to wrap his arms around Isaac's neck.

He buried his face in the tender space between Isaac's throat and shoulder, clinging tightly as tears welled and fell. A clawed hand placed itself on his lower back, holding him with such gentleness, Isaac's other arm pressing Samuel flush against him.

It would take nothing for Isaac to tear him open, but Samuel knew that he wouldn't. It was insanity, a trust that went beyond all logic and sense, but Samuel recognized the care and tenderness that Isaac granted him, finding safety in the monster's embrace.

"I have you," Isaac purred in his ear. "But hold on tight."

With a great flap of his wings, Isaac rose high into the morning light, cutting across the grand spread of the capital. Isaac swerved, catching the flow of a breeze off the sea, carrying Samuel off away to where the King couldn't touch him.

But Samuel didn't watch it, pressed against Isaac's body, eyes closed as quiet sobs moved through him.

Chapter Forty-Eight

Shan

Shan lay on the settee in the Eternal King's office, her hand hanging off the side, fingers twitching even though the injuries had been long healed. It was just an echo in her mind, she knew that, a bit of trauma that lingered even hours later, but she swore she could still feel the crunch of her spine, the shattered bones that had splintered inside her skin, the way her blood spilled and pooled around her organs.

It could have killed her—it would have killed her, if she hadn't been surrounded by Blood Workers, the Guard swarming her as soon as Samuel had been carried off. None of them were Healers, of course, but they had enough basic training to stabilize her. To ensure she lived long enough to be taken to one who could help.

To the Eternal King, who had taken one look at her before tearing his own flesh with his teeth, pressing his bleeding wrist to her mouth so that she could lap him up. He had pulled her into his lap, head dipped low to brush his mouth against hers, laving against the dried blood on her lips, his tongue soft and warm as the bridge sizzled to life between them.

Then, the magic had begun, tearing her through as he wrenched her body back into place. As he made her whole and strong once more.

She had only realized it after, once the pain and delirium had dulled, that his teeth had glittered in the light before he tore his skin open, that they had been just a hair too sharp and long to be natural.

That he too was changing, the slow and inexorable shift to vampire already begun.

He had wrapped her in a blanket afterwards, placed her on the settee by the roaring fire. He entreated her to rest, brushing her hair away from her face, murmured sweet words that were so at odds with the persona he showed the rest of the world. But he was right—the body might have been fixed, the Blood Working swift and efficient, but the mental and emotional scars remained.

Every time Shan closed her eyes, she still saw it—Isaac's face as he relaxed his grip, following her plan, committing to letting her drop. The pain and sorrow in his eyes, his expression so still clear to her, despite the monstrous fangs and the teeth like daggers. The way he had reached for her, regrets unspooling between them, but there had been no other option.

It had been the only way to end it—Isaac had to hurt her to make it believable, to make it so the King wouldn't doubt her loyalty. If she was going to be of any use to them going forward, she had to play her part perfectly.

And what was a little pain in the light of that?

Shan pushed herself to her feet, glancing towards the clock ticking away above the mantle. It had been hours since she had seen anyone, trapped alone in one of the many unused spaces that the King had claimed for himself. She was at the Parliament House, but this office was his, an empty but precise shrine to their liege who spent so little time among those tasked with ruling the nation.

She did not know why the King was here, why she had been brought here to recover, but whatever was happening, it could not be good news.

The blanket slipped from her shoulders, and she glanced down at the underthings she still wore. The healers had removed her dress and her corset, leaving her in a state that she should have been embarrassed by. But she was too tired to care. Shame and regret would come soon enough, but for now, she needed a plan. And first among that was some proper clothes.

Grabbing the cloak that she had worn this morning, still streaked through with her blood, she tossed it around her shoulders and approached the door. It wasn't locked, and Shan knew that she wasn't a prisoner here. Still, it felt dangerous to try to slip out from under the King's care.

The Guards outside turned towards the door as it opened. A pair of them, both older than her by at least a decade, strong men with thick arms, harsh claws on their fingers and blades at their waists. The best that the King had to offer, left to protect her as she recovered.

Shan knew she should be touched, but that creeping fear returned, the sense that there was something she was missing. A piece of the plot slipping through her fingers.

"Good afternoon," the one on the left said, "my lady. Are you well? Shall I send for some refreshments?"

Her throat was terribly dry, and her stomach ached with emptiness that came from a day without food. Blood and steel, she hadn't even had breakfast this morning, too nervous to eat anything before the morning's events.

"Yes, that would be much appreciated," Shan said, glancing down demurely. She pulled her cloak tighter around her shoulders, making herself small and unthreatening. "And I do not know if this is within your capabilities, but a fresh set of clothes would be much appreciated."

The Guard sputtered, a flush creeping up his cheeks, but the other man simply cleared his throat. "Of course, my lady. We will also inform His Majesty that you are up and about. He has been quite worried about you."

"That is kind of him," Shan replied. "Thank you both." They bowed before her, a mechanical bit of respect thrown her way, but she slipped back into the office.

Now, there was little to do but wait.

It didn't take long for the Guard to summon what they

promised—opening the door not ten minutes later, holding a tray with a steaming pot of tea and a plate of warm, buttery scones. It wasn't a proper meal, but it was enough to quell the ache within and steady her nerves. A serving girl arrived not long after, her cheeks still flushed and ruddy from the cold, suggesting that she had come from elsewhere. Perhaps the palace or one of the many boutiques in Dameral?

Regardless, she carried with her a garment bag nearly as tall as she was and a box of toiletries. Depositing the box on the desk, she hung the garment bag on the back of the door, unzipping it to reveal a deep red dress, just a few shades lighter than the color of her robes of state. Despite its clearly fine make and the luscious fall of silk that made up the skirts, it was clearly off the rack, designed so that it could be laced up the back, allowing it to be tightened to fit snug against the corset of whomever bought it.

Shan couldn't remember the last time she wore an outfit that wasn't expressly tailored to her. But as needs must.

The maid was excellent, helping Shan first into the corset that came along with the dress, then the gown itself. It was a little loose on her, but the maid tightened the laces, pinning the excess material with pins cleverly hidden in the fall of the silk. It would be a pain to get out of later, but that was something Shan could handle with her own girls back home. For what it was, the maid tucked her and made her look not only presentable, but wondrous.

Makeup and hair came next, and Shan perched on a stool, accepting the work done to her. The maid tutted to herself, one eye on the clock as she braided Shan's hair into an elaborate crown around her head, a quick and easy way to hide the uneven waves that they didn't have the time to properly tame. A dash of kohl around the eyes, vibrant red paint on her lips, and the maid was holding her by the chin, turning to study her face in the light.

It was more than Shan had anticipated when she had asked for a change of clothes. She had merely wished to leave the Parliament House with dignity, but this was more than that. The King needed her primped and perfect for something, but she hadn't the foggiest idea what.

"It will have to do," the maid muttered, stepping back with a decisive nod. "I apologize for the hasty work, but you are needed soon."

Shan melted, just a little, laying her hand on the woman's wrist before she pulled away. "You did a marvelous job," Shan said, with sincerity.

The maid blinked, then dropped into a sudden curtsy, thrown by just the small drop of kindness. "Thank you, my lady. But the King has requested your presence with the rest of the House of Lords at the top of the hour."

Shan glanced at the clock—she had a little under ten minutes. "I see. Well, I shall sing your praises to the King, Miss ..."

"Miss Jane," the woman said, with another curtsy. "You are too kind."

She really wasn't, but Shan didn't have the time or inclination to correct that assumption. Not when she had so little time.

Shan saw herself out of the office, striding towards the grand chamber where the House of Lords met to debate legislation and policy. The Guards peeled off from their posts, falling into place behind her. An honor guard that she did not ask for. But they stalked behind her, silent guardians following her through the halls as she moved ever closer to her goal.

She could feel him as she drew close, the Eternal King, the power radiating off him in waves. It was an unsubtle display of power, one meant to intimidate, but she held her head high as she stepped through the doors to the chambers and stared down into the pit below. The benches were filled with her compatriots, a good two-thirds of the spots filled, enough to reach a majority vote, should it be needed.

Though Shan didn't think that would be the case, not after the announcement he had made to the Royal Council the day before. Not after how he had thrown aside all structures and rules the last time he had been here. But it was different. Then she was but one of the many left in the dark. A pawn in a carefully planned game of chess.

But that wasn't her fate now—now the King had summoned her specifically, had arranged whatever this was for her benefit. Had once again seen her clothed and prepared, ready to be presented as the Royal Blood Worker ascendant.

The King caught sight of her, his gaze tipping up to her as a lazy smile crossed his face. Unlike her, he wasn't dressed to perfection, hadn't styled himself to perfection. He stood before his subjects in a distressingly vulnerable state, his fine suit rumpled and stained, dark patches of blood showing at the cuffs of his sleeves, splattered across the open neck of his shirt, his cravat long gone.

With a jolt, Shan realized that was *her* blood on him, left over from when he had healed her. A mark that she had left on him, unwittingly or not, that he had not bothered to remove.

But for all his casualness, for the unhidden circles under his eyes, the stress that lined his face, the King still radiated power and authority. The rush of magic was even more intolerable now that she was in the room with it. She couldn't see it, precisely, none of them could, but the air around the King seemed to crackle with energy, filling the room from floor to ceiling, catching in the back of her throat like syrup, sickly sweet and cloying.

This version of the King might be a little less polished than the terrifying and distant liege they had grown used to over the past few centuries, but he was just as powerful as he had ever been, only now—

It was as if he no longer cared about appearances or rules or dignity, as if he was tired of holding himself back.

Shan glanced around the room, taking in the expressions of the rest of the Lords and Ladies, from carefully blank to trepidatious to outright fearful. Most refused to meet her eyes, but Amelia did, offering a soft and reassuring smile. It took her by surprise—the look wasn't calculation, but relief that she had survived this terrible morning, that she was still here, standing strong.

If Shan didn't know any better, she would have thought that Amelia was looking at her like a friend would.

None of the others, though, seemed to care a whit that she'd survived. There was only the all-consuming presence of the King standing below. And none of them knew the truth that she did, the monster that the King had finally allowed himself to reach for, the vampire that was being born right in front of their eyes.

The King was more dangerous than ever, but Shan tucked that knowledge and fear deep away where it couldn't touch her. She'd mourn the world she helped destroy later, she'd scheme her way out before the trap grew too tight around her throat, but for now, she stood tall and proud, untouchable and powerful.

And when the Eternal King held out his hand, summoning her to his side with a curl of his fingertips, Shan descended the staircase with poise and grace, every eye on her.

"These past few months," the King continued, carrying on with the speech he had been giving before Shan's arrival, "has been one challenge after another." His voice was low but clear, washing over her like the cold fall of rain, raising gooseflesh along her skin. "We have found traitors in our midst, have discovered rot in even the oldest of bloodlines. The very mechanisms of our society have been torn from their foundations as the Unblooded we have so graciously accepted into our lands bite the hand that feeds them.

"But it has not been without gain," the King said, turning his gaze upon her as she came before him, sinking into a deep curtsy. He caught her chin, the tips of his claws a keen prick as he guided her up.

It felt like the sting of a hook, lodging itself somewhere in her chest, piercing her through the heart before ripping her from the depths. She could no more fight him than she could stop the journey of the sun across the sky, and so she let him steer her. Put her hand in his as she came to his side, tipping her chin up to look at those gathered around her.

At the faces of all who had viewed her as lesser for so many years, dismissed her for the failures of her father and the stain of her mother's foreignness.

As terrible as it was, she couldn't help the thrill that came from being chosen, the glee that bubbled in her chest, a laugh that she swallowed down, because after all the judgement and shame, she was the one to land on his arm.

She would get them all back for their cruelties—she swore it to herself, but first she had to play the part the King expected of her. The role of a lifetime, the final mask she had to don, and oh, she would lie her twisted little heart out.

The King was still looking at her, like she was something precious, a jewel in his crown, a blade to be wielded. "We have lost much this year," he said, his voice carrying to the entire chamber, but his words were just for her, "and yet, we found the most brilliant mind that Aeravin has seen in an age. Lady LeClaire has proven herself as a most capable Royal Blood Worker, an unmatched scholar, and will help lead us into a new age. If, that is, she will have me."

Silence fell, so thick that Shan felt like she would choke on it, the rapid beat of her heart roaring in her ears as the King sank to one knee. So, this is how it was to be done. The elaborate show he had made of this was for a purpose, designed to elevate her even further. And there was *one* place for her left to ascend to, a position that had not been filled since the founding of their nation.

The fulfillment of a promise made over Samuel's broken, bleeding body—but she wasn't doing this for him or for herself. Wherever he was in the moment, wherever Isaac had squirreled Samuel away, she hoped he would appreciate this, the moment she stepped into the belly of the beast.

The King produced a ring, a heavy and gaudy thing, the thick band of gold inlaid with more diamonds than she could count, glittering before her eyes. It must have been worth a fortune, but Shan ached for the one she had returned to Samuel.

The simple band of silver and single ruby, a lone drop of blood.

But she couldn't think of him now, not him or the other man she loved. The King was still waiting, and Shan knew there was only one answer that he would accept.

"I do," she breathed, and he slid the ring onto her finger. It fit perfectly, though the weight of it felt like shackle, binding her to the man she feared the most.

And as the crowd burst into applause, he pulled her close, wrapping one arm around his shoulders as he dipped her low, the claws on his other hand gently tracing where her jaw met her throat. He was smoldering with power, with vitality, with life—and as much as she feared what was coming, a rotten, insidious part of her did not want to resist it. He looked at her like she was the most cherished prize, like they were made for each other, like they were the only ones who could match each other's ambitions.

He dipped his head to hers, capturing her mouth with a kiss that felt bruising, pressing his way past her lips like he was trying to wipe away the traces of those who had come before, rewriting her entire history so that it could only have ever led to this.

To him.

"My daring, darling girl," he whispered into her ear as she trembled, "we are going to change everything."

Chapter Forty-Nine

Samuel

Samuel stared out the window, eyes half closed at the pounding in his head, watching the flurries continue to fall, a near endless snowfall that had continued to paint Dameral in the days after the attack on the Blood Treasury. The roofs of the capital were covered in a thin, plush layer of white, a stark contrast to the dark slush that lined the cobblestones below.

From his vantage point above, it almost looked lovely, but Samuel had lived in those streets, had made his way across the slick patches of black ice and the muck that dripped from the awnings. The noble Lords and Ladies, the Blood Workers of means and influence, they could tuck away in their homes, cozied up in front of the fire with a mug of warm drinking chocolate in their hands, but everyone else?

They had to trudge through the filth and the slush, unable to ignore their responsibilities and their lives, their fortunes hanging by a thread.

It was strange that Samuel missed those times, when he would hug his ratty coat tighter to him, but after nearly two days of recuperation in one of Alaric's private suites, he would have given near anything to go back to the way things had been.

But he couldn't—he was stuck here, waiting for hells knew what, trapped in his own gilded cage. Oh, it was all for his own good, for the lingering migraine that refused to abate and the aches that echoed through his entire body, but it chafed at him to know that while Isaac and Anton and the others were all out there, working to turn their rebellion into outright revolution, he was stuck here.

Resting in comfort.

It was lovely little room, a small but lavish bedroom complete with finely made furniture and its own washroom. A grand wardrobe was filled with comfortable and well-made clothes, including the velvet robe that Samuel wrapped himself in. The far wall had a bookshelf filled with books, adventure novels and romances, historical treatises and even a few beginner's tomes on Blood Working.

Samuel had ignored the books, having spent most of his time lying in the bed. It was as plush and soft as the one in his own home, and Samuel sank into the mattress, wrapped in blankets to block out the chill that the empty fireplace let seep into the room. But the nest he had built for himself wasn't enough to ease the relentless throbbing in his skull, even the sweet relief of sleep escaping him as he curled up on his side, caught in an unending pool of pain.

The silence was the only relief, as Samuel had been left alone for the most part. There was the sweet-natured healer who had tended to him on the first day, an older woman who treated him with all the kindness of a mother, but sadly was unable to do anything. The Blood Working slipped off him, running off him like water, repelled by something twisted and ruined within him.

Whatever the King had done to him had left him broken in ways that they did not even understand yet.

After that, it had only been Isaac, stopping by in regular intervals, always bringing with him simple soups, brushing Samuel's hair from his face and trying to coax him to eat. Like he did now, sitting next to him on the chair, a half-full bowl in hand, the spoon held up in offering.

The meal should have been appetizing, a rich soup of chicken and herbs, thickened with rice and flavored with spices. Before this, he would have loved it, but now he could barely bring himself to eat at all. The nausea was too much, bile twisting in his gut as the too rich food assaulted his palate, the pungent aroma of lemon and ginger overwhelming, the little bit he managed sitting like a heavy stone in his stomach.

He leaned away, pressing his forehead against the cool glass as his eyes slid closed. The chill was soothing, and Samuel wanted nothing more than to melt into it. "Enough, please."

"Well, it was more than last time." Isaac sighed, but he did place the bowl to the side, the spoon clattering just loud enough to send spikes of pain stabbing into the tender points in the back of Samuel's head. "Let's get you back to bed."

Samuel groaned his acquiescence, and Isaac wrapped his arm around his lower back, easing him off the seat. It wasn't quite a full carry, but still Isaac took on most of Samuel's weight, lifting him like he was nothing as he tottered his way back to the bed.

Had Isaac always been this strong? Was it a side effect of him becoming a manananggal? Had he bit his own cheek, using Blood Working to enhance his strength? If he had, Samuel couldn't sense it. There could be magic fluttering all around him, slipping into his veins, sinking into his bones, and he still wouldn't know, would never know it again.

He had thought himself Unblooded for so long, had not realized that the dark power deep within had been Blood Working. Though he had precious little time with it, unfiltered and unrestrained, it had still been a part of him for his whole life, lingering at the edges of his consciousness, there even when he had not noticed it.

But now there was nothing, just silence as Samuel moved through the world, like cotton stuffed in his ears, deadening his senses. Oh, he could feel Isaac's touch, the warmth of his body pressed against his. Could smell the soft, pine scent of soap on his skin, the lingering smell of cigarette smoke on his clothes. But there was still a distance between them, a preternatural awareness that he knew he would never feel again ripped away.

He had been a fool to think that Isaac had truly stripped him of his power all those months ago. He thought he had known what emptiness was, but it had only been a gap into which his natural Blood Working had flowed. It was temporary, small, and nothing compared to the truth.

He would be empty forever, and the only thing left in him was pain.

Isaac helped him back to the bed, eased the soft robe off his shoulders. Samuel only wore a thin pair of sleeping trousers underneath it, but Isaac didn't look on him with heat or lust—just tenderness, freely and openly given.

"Lie down, darling," Isaac whispered, brushing a tender kiss against Samuel's temple. "I'll be right back."

Samuel heard him puttering about, hanging the robe back in the wardrobe, putting the half-finished meal out in the hallway for the servant to collect, the soft rustle of something that he couldn't quite place. Samuel just breathed in, slow and deep, and out again, waiting for the world to stop tilting.

The bed dipped as Isaac slid in behind him, his weight and his warmth a comfort that felt too good to be real. As Isaac snuggled up against his back, arm draped over his middle, Samuel realized Isaac had shed his shirt and binder. Nestling in as if to sleep.

"Isaac," Samuel breathed, even as he softened against him. It was comforting, being held like this, Isaac wrapping around him like a satisfying weight pressing against his aching bones. "Don't you have things to do?"

"Not tonight," Isaac replied, his lips warm against the tender point behind his ear. "So let me take care of you."

Samuel shook his head, only to immediately regret the action, the sudden spike of pain ricocheting through his head like marbles shaken in a glass jar. Clattering and sharp, spinning in endless coils, round and round again.

Isaac noticed immediately, his hand coming to up to massage at the achingly tender spot where Samuel's neck met his skull. The discomfort surged as Isaac's thumb dug in, pressing on the inflamed skin, but it quickly ebbed into an almost pleasant throb.

It became just nearly tolerable.

Samuel melted into it, boneless as a cat in front of a fire, as Isaac continued to tend to him. Strong hands roamed his shoulders and neck, easing the tension away. But Samuel feared the moment Isaac stopped and the pain returned.

"Will it ever go away?" Samuel breathed. The words came out with a whimper, his tears dropping to the pillowcase in fat drops, but Samuel didn't have the energy to feel shame.

Isaac hesitated, then, "Celeste said the migraine has to run its course. But it will pass." He said it with such conviction, such hope, that Samuel didn't fight it, even though they both knew it wasn't so simple.

The unknown probability that hovered between them, the warning the Blood Healer had given. That migraines were a terrible affliction, that it could become a chronic condition, that this could become the rest of Samuel's life, days split between unending suffering and the life that he wanted so desperately to live.

And there was so much work to do.

"I'm sorry," he mumbled, words catching in his throat. "You don't have time for this. *I* don't have time for this." He trembled, but Isaac didn't censure him for it, didn't try to shush away his fears or pretend that things were better than they were. And as coddled as he was, Samuel appreciated that—the past two days he had been treated with all the care of a young child, unable to face the dark realities that waited just outside the window.

And he was so tired of being patronized.

Somewhere out there, Bart had taken over the remains of Shan's network. Somewhere out there, Anton was working with Alaric and Maia to solidify their next steps. Somewhere out there, Shan was ...

He didn't even know, and that hurt the most. Not knowing what had happened to her after Isaac had whisked him away to safety. Not knowing if she had even survived the fall.

The fall that Isaac had told him Shan had requested, that he had no choice but to let happen. He didn't fully understand it, truthfully, despite the way that Isaac had explained it to him while his head was still swimming with adrenaline and agony. The way that Shan had risked herself, setting herself up to be their bird in the place. The way she had given them enough information to be able to save Samuel, arranging all the pieces just so and casting herself in the role of the villain.

How Isaac had to make it look real.

Isaac had made it look too real, in Samuel's opinion. He could still see her, when he closed his eyes, as sleep eluded him. Lying there on the ground, shattered and broken, left to die.

Rolling over to face Isaac, Samuel swallowed the groan that followed, ignored the flare that ran through him. "Please, Isaac. Just tell me what you know."

Isaac hesitated, teeth catching on his lip. There was so much worry in his eyes, concern that wasn't entirely misplaced, but Samuel was sick of being handled with kid gloves. "Please," he repeated. "If you know anything about Shan, I need to know."

"Shan lived," Isaac breathed, and Samuel felt a weight lift off his shoulders, only for the fear to slam its way back on the next exhale. "But..."

"But what?"

Isaac ran his hand across his face, looking so desperately lost that Samuel almost regretted pushing. "But things have changed in the court of Aeravin. The King ... he's making plans to fight us. The House of Lords has been dissolved, completely and formally. Lady Morse is taking over the Guard, your former position being folded into hers. There will be a new elite squadron of Guards formed, made entirely of vampires. And that is not the worst of it."

Samuel swallowed hard, his mind already swimming with all the implications. "How could it get worse?"

"Easily," Isaac ground out, expression flickering with something so dark and furious that even Samuel couldn't bear to look at it. "Because in addition to all this, the Eternal Bastard has decided to take Shan as his bride, giving Aeravin its first queen since the founding of the nation."

Despite the firm mattress and the soft touch of Isaac against his skin, Samuel felt like he was drowning, falling into the depths of some dark emotion that he dared not name. A glimmer of something so loathsome and horrid, but burning true and fierce.

Perhaps the darkness in him hadn't been his magic, after all.

"He what?" Samuel gasped, and Isaac glanced away.

This was it, then, what Isaac hadn't wanted to tell him. Though whether that was kindness or calculation was anyone's guess, but Samuel had enough of this with Shan. "How dare you hide this from me."

"It's not like that," Isaac said, clutching Samuel's trembling hands. "I was going to tell you, but Celeste advised that we keep your stress in check, as much we could."

The anger dimmed, just a little. "That's not your decision to make," Samuel said, driving the point home. "I cannot ... I cannot keep living like this."

Something in Isaac's expression settled, understanding dawning. "I understand," he said, pressing his lips to the mangled scar over Samuel's wrist, ill healed from the King's vicious bite. "And I will not do it again. But there is little we can do in the moment."

"But Shan—"

"Knows what she is doing," Isaac interrupted. "She made her choice. The King, for whatever godforsaken reason, trusts her, and you know it's too valuable to pass this up. With her at his side ... "

"She could die," Samuel whispered, the words barely audible, as if the mere fact of speaking it out into the world would make it come true, an ill-focused wish.

"She could," Isaac agreed, "but so could we. You have already been wounded by this, as have I. Neither of us are the men we were when this started, but we cannot back out now."

The tears returned, not of pain, but of despair. The sheer frustration of coming so close to success but losing something precious in the process. "I cannot lose her."

"We won't," Isaac said, with such certainty that Samuel felt a fool for doubting. "She trusts us enough to put herself in this danger, so we owe her the same trust in return. She will survive this, and then when it is done, be returned to us."

His lips pulled back into a snarl, his teeth sharp and glinting in the low light. He looked more than the man, not quite the beast—caught somewhere in between, beautiful and terrifying in equal measure. "After everything else this world has taken from me, it's the very least we deserve."

It was heartbreaking, but Samuel knew the universe wasn't that kind. If they wanted a future where they had a chance at happiness, they would have to fight for it. And to get it, Samuel wouldn't let Isaac fall to darkness alone. He was already ruined, so why hold himself back anymore?

Isaac and Shan had already done so much for him, and it was time to return the favor. There was no more room for incremental change, for lesser evils, for hoping to scrape out a future that would be only just a little better.

No, if the King wanted war, then let there be war.

"All right," Samuel breathed. "Let's bring Aeravin to its knees."

He leaned in, pressed his mouth to Isaac's. Ran his tongue across those too-sharp teeth, ignoring the painful prick as the warmth flowed between them.

Sealing his promise with blood.

The story continues in Prince of Ash, *coming in 2026!*

Acknowledgments

Writing a sequel is difficult—writing a sequel in 2024 was damn near impossible. Between the endless onslaught of terrible news across the globe, I struggled to believe that there was a place for my stories in this world. It would have been so easy to give into despair. But I didn't, because of all of you.

To my agent, Jennifer Azantian. Thank you for your continued support and expertise, for being there to talk me through the most difficult days and strategize how to move forward in uncertain times. Your wisdom is grounding and guidance invaluable.

To my editor, Nadia Saward. Thank you for working with me to find the heart of my story, to dig past the surface to find the truths beneath. Working with you has made *Lord of Ruin* so much better, and I cannot wait to see what we do next. To my US editor, Tiana Coven, your support and enthusiasm for these books is so uplifting, and I'm so lucky to be working with you! To the Entire Orbit Team, including Aimee Kitson, Nazia Khatun, Anna Jackson, Joanna Kramer, Serena Savini, Jess Dryburgh, Lauren Panepinto, Stephanie Hess, Alex Lencicki, Natassja Haught, Kayleigh Webb, Ellen Wright, Bryn McDonald, Rachel Goldstein, Angela Man and Tim Holman. And of course, to Felix Abel Klaer for the beautiful art and to Ella Garrett for creating another gorgeous cover. Isaac is everything I could have hoped for.

I would also like to send a special shout-out to the critique partners that made *Lord of Ruin* the book that it is—Ladz, Kalyn, and Laura.

Your comments on the early drafts were so insightful and lifesaving. This one is for all of you!

To my friends, old and new. To my Guillotine Court, thank you for always being there when I needed you. To the ones who have been with me from the beginning—your endless support is what has kept me going, even through the most difficult days. To the Auden Appreciation Society—Saint, Laura, and Maddie, it is a genuine joy to have a space for the high highs and the low lows. To new friends: Sophia, Ava, mars, Ally, Clare. I am so glad to have you all in my corner.

To you, dear reader. Your support and welcoming of this dark, twisted love story have been nothing short of remarkable. I knew I was taking a gamble putting out a story of messy queers, filled with the uncomfortable reality of being diaspora and how difficult it is to be othered, but each and every kind word I've received has given me the strength to keep going. So, thank you from the bottom of my heart.

Finally, to Eric, my beloved husband. It has been a year of ups and downs, but thank you for reminding me that love is real, and that it is powerful. These stories would not exist without you.

About the Author

K. M. Enright is the *Sunday Times* bestselling author of *Mistress of Lies*. Find out more about his writing at kmenright.com or follow him on social media at @KM_Enright.

Find out more about K. M. Enright and other Orbit authors by registering for the free monthly newsletter at orbit-books.co.uk.